The Shadow Universe I
The Ways of Darkness

William G. Davis, Jr.

Published by
William G. Davis, Jr.

ISBN: 978-1-959880-01-1
Library of Congress Control Number: 2022921152

First Edition: January 2023

Acknowledgments

Special thanks to Pastor E. C. Fulcher, Jr. for his support. To Ursula Crouse, Linda Shoaf, and Alyx Bliesener for feedback on continuity, spelling, and grammar corrections. Finally, to Sergeant 1st class Marc Schenker, his valuable help explains certain unclassified army procedures and jargon specifics.

The cover design is courtesy of www.Pixabay.com.

Chapter 1

Earth
The Regime - Washington, D.C. - Capitol Building
May 6, 2452

General Hank Saunders watched the ushers escort representatives from the Texas Labor Union to their assigned seats through the one-way glass of the auditorium's secret doors. They were here to secretly petition the Regime for help in seceding from the United States of America. This meeting was the first step in adding another state to the Regime's alliance. It was tricky because Texas must secede and ask for a confederation.

The Regime's guests sat, so Saunders opened the door and walked straight to his assigned seat in the front row. He could feel all the eyes in the auditorium turn toward him and hear their whispers. Beneath the surface of the business-like veneer gathering, there was always the fear that if things did not go right, it would either plunge the two countries into war or, worse, mire the state of Texas into the horrors of a second civil war, but why him? Although he was a garrison commander, not a combat one, his orders were to attend this meeting. Even generals had to jump, especially if the order came from Jay Porter himself.

Before his thoughts could take him further down that line, General Saunders heard the private door open at the back of the stage. He watched as Jay Porter, Supreme Commander of the Regime, walked from his private entrance to the podium. *He always looks more prominent in real life.* Seeing Supreme Commander Porter on a vid-screen or an over-life-sized news board was an everyday event. Porter looked about six feet, two inches tall in real life. His tailored suit hid his thin frame, and his short, thick black hair, brushed back, seemed too perfect to Saunders. The General read that he was in his mid-thirties but looked to be in his mid-twenties. *Genetic engineering?*

The Supreme Commander did not look at the crowd; he did not have to because they came to see and hear him. When a state left the old union, the Regime's responsibility was to follow all procedures to the letter. Millions of lives depended on it. By the time he reached the dais, the audience had become silent, breathless with anticipation. Porter let them hang for a few more moments before beginning to speak.

"Ladies and gentlemen," he began, "I'll get straight to the point. Texas business owners have petitioned the Regime to help them secede from the United States."

A smattering of applause interrupted Porter, so he waited for it to settle down before continuing.

"Change is inevitable. As we all know, most governments do not end with a big explosion from war and violence. Instead, political corruption, like cancer, spreads to the leaders in every position of authority so they do not take advantage of their society's enormous potential for growth, condemning their citizens to a lifetime of poverty. I take no pleasure seeing the U.S. of A succumb to this dreaded disease.

"Civil wars and riots have continued almost non-stop for hundreds of years. Gangs have forced law-abiding citizens to create walled cities for protection while mobs of dissidents continue to ravage the old towns and surrounding suburbs. Due to these horrific changes, many global experts have considered the U.S. functionally dead. For those reasons and many more, you have petitioned to join us.

"Although the Regime is far from perfect, we have enjoyed the same high standard of living the citizens of the United States had many years ago. I've always considered us a child of the land of liberty. The ideas of freedom and prosperity we hold are similar. It should not be a surprise to learn that our founder started our government within that great country. With that said, our conditions are non-negotiable. When you entered this building, my staff gave everyone an electronic notepad. Within it is a contract, having all the details. Remember, we are not offering a utopia. More importantly, if granted, your request will have consequences, so consider it carefully."

He paused to emphasize the weight of his following words, "Be assured that if your leaders discover your intentions, they will arrest you for treason."

After another brief pause, he smiled and continued, "Now, in our experience, for this endeavor to go smoothly, you will need the support of at least eighty-five percent of your state's population. If you do not obtain that amount, we will not move forward. Thank you."

Without waiting for a reaction, Supreme Commander Porter left the stage. Again, there was a smattering of applause. Saunders stood and watched the representatives form into small groups around their Regime assistants; no one made a sudden break for the door. *It's a good sign that they all show sincere interest.* The General made his way back to the Local Transportation Station. He punched in his home address and waited until a portal opened to a similar destination; the vortex stabilized, and he walked through the event horizon. It transported him to his home garrison, Fort McNair, where he tapped the release button, and the portal closed behind him. His assistant, Lieutenant Colonel Jones, had been waiting for him with an electronic notepad.

"Good afternoon, general. Here's a list of the meetings you have left for today," Lieutenant Colonel Jones disclosed, extending the notepad toward his boss.

"Thanks, but I'm going to have lunch first," the General pushed it back to him. "I'll meet you in my office at 1300 hours."

"Yes, Sir!" Lieutenant Colonel Jones answered, slipping the notepad under his arm.

He stood to attention as the General walked past him. Saunders went straight to the cafeteria, bought his lunch, and sat. All morning, he craved two hot dogs with mustard and sauerkraut. The General inhaled deeply, savoring the cooked cabbage's heady aroma, and grabbed the closest bun, but before taking his first bite, Michael and Alex walked over and stood beside his table. They were his two top civilian research scientists. Saunders liked them. Michael reminded him of his son or what he thought his son might have been like had he lived.

"Do you mind if we sit?" Alex asked.

"No, go right ahead," mumbled the General, eating.

Saunders noticed that Michael did not look like his usual upbeat self. His black hair was unkempt, as if having missed a trip or two to the barber, but it was still within civilians' regulations.

Saunders decided not to comment on it because there was something more profound. The General sensed an uncharacteristic sadness about Michael. The glint was missing from his eyes, and he was losing weight.

Saunders wrote it off as Michael's broken love affair from an earlier security report. *It's time this young man got over that.* The General finished his hot dog and casually watched the two young men. Michael was a few inches shorter than Alex, who stood about five feet, ten inches tall and always seemed in good spirits. Alex's security reports revealed that ladies found him attractive. He was the opposite of Michael. Alex's classic good looks and wavy blond hair set off his blue eyes, often bringing flirtatious glances. Their dossiers also included that they had been friends from childhood and hung out together during their free time.

Michael was the talk of the senior staff and management of the Regime because he was a genius at genetic manipulation. He revolutionized modern warfare with his subcutaneous body armor, a small device attached to the adrenal gland that, when activated, turns the first four layers of human skin into an impenetrable body shield. The effect only lasts for about thirty minutes. Also, the agent could call upon the unique ability three times after a brief rest between uses but must return to have the device refilled. Although the only downside was that it needed a massive caloric intake to replenish the body's energy; secret tests conducted in the field have proven their effectiveness. *No wonder Jay Porter wants daily updates on him.*

Michael and Alex knew better than to start a conversation with the General during lunch, so they waited in silence out of respect. Meanwhile, Alex bounced with anticipation, but Michael sat as still as a statue, keeping his hands folded in front of him on the table. They remained silent until the General popped the last of his hot dog into his mouth and reached for his coffee.

"Have you heard anything about my contract?" Alex blurted before the General could swallow.

"No, not yet," Saunders answered, taking a few sips from his cup. "I told you it would take three weeks to hear from them, but sometimes these things take longer."

"He's worried because there's been a rumor about cuts again," Michael added.

"It's true, we've had to slash some programs, but I can't see them touching our portal outreach mission. Without your research, we wouldn't be as close to reaching Mars via portal technology. You improved the capacitor, bringing us one step closer to exploring and colonizing other planets without traveling by spaceship. They won't ignore advancements like that," assured the General.

"He's right," Michael chimed in.

"I hope so, Sir. I have an innovative design for a capacitor that will have twice the power as the last one. We'll land on Mars before you know it."

Saunders did his best to console him, "I appreciate your enthusiasm, but be patient. The committee meets again tomorrow; I'm sure you'll hear from them soon."

"Thank you, Sir. I do feel better," Alex replied. He faced Michael for a moment, returned his gaze to the General, and continued, "I need you to do me a big favor."

Saunders' coffee cup froze halfway to his lips, "You do realize that generals are not in the habit of doing favors."

"I hope you will make an exception in this case," Alex smiled wryly.

"What exactly do you want me to do?" the General questioned cautiously.

"Order Michael to join me tonight. I am heading off base. Every time I ask he gives me the same excuse."

The General smiled; Michael protested, "You know I am working on ten priority experiments!"

"Yep. That's the excuse. Look, you haven't been out in months. It's time you give yourself a break. It's only a couple of hours," Alex insisted.

"I am working on an experiment that will revolutionize our tracking technology, but I must continually monitor it," defended Michael.

"He's lying, right?" Alex asked the General.

"No, he's telling the truth, but Alex is right. You need to get out of here, Mike. Everyone needs a change of scenery, occasionally. Get one of your assistants to watch over it until you return. If anything happens while you're gone, he or she will notify you."

"Please don't make me go; I'm so close to a breakthrough," Michael begged.

"It can wait a few hours. I'm making it an order. I want you off this base for at least three hours tonight. Relax. Let your hair down. Get a haircut. Alex, you make sure he has a good time."

"Yes, Sir," Alex smiled in victory.

Michael was unhappy because the General was right; he had put a lot of time into his work and could not fool anyone, "Where are we going?"

"To Union Station. Julie will be there," Alex offered.

"It would be nice to see your sister again. It's been ages," reflected Michael.

"Good, it's settled," affirmed Alex.

Saunders raised an eyebrow with sincerity, "Alex, just make sure he's not injured or too drunk to show up for work tomorrow."

Alex smiled playfully, "Come on, General. It's me!"

"That's why I'm warning you. I'm holding you personally responsible if anything happens to Michael," Saunders warned. "I'll clear you for the Local Transportation Station at 1800 hours. Now, be off, both of you!"

Michael and Alex stood and left the General to his thoughts. *Texas.*

Chapter 2

Akil
Argi City
The 22,270[th] Terrestrial Rotation of the Second Summer

As Zorion slept, he had the same dream, which repeated every sleep cycle since the last yellow harvest. He took the private walkway to his office and noticed the sentries were missing. The lights flickered and went out; they did not alarm him. In the darkness, he waits for her, just like the other times. He raised his hand to cover his eyes, expecting her arrival.

Brilliant light shined before him. He tried to look at his mysterious visitor through a crack between his fingers, but the brilliance prevented him. Her glow dimmed, so he lowered his hand and smiled. *I have missed you,* he said to her. She opened her arms without a reply, inviting him to come closer. They firmly embraced each other.

He wrapped his arms around her small, muscular frame, and she entwined hers around his neck. Unable to resist, he gazed into her beautiful blue eyes. They remind him of the videos that showed the oceans that once covered his planet. As before, he found it easy to become lost in them. He moved his lips to her ears and whispered, *"Please, tell me your name."* Still, she did not reply.

The smell of her light-yellow hair was intoxicating. Zorion let go, pulled back, and saw her smiling at him, but without warning, she pulled him toward her, and they embraced in an enthusiastic kiss. His desire for her becomes more intense with every dream, and he desperately hopes she feels the same for him. For a moment, they paused to admire each other.

"When I am here with you in my dreams, I am happier. I never want to wake up," Zorion told her. With her right hand, she gently caressed his face. Every time she looks at him, he feels her gazing at his true self, making him feel naked. Soft music begins to play. *No, not yet*! Her image faded.

His hands reached out to her and passed through her translucent body. As her image faded, he felt despair. *Please, do not leave!* He yelled, and in an instant, she disappeared. He woke, sitting up with his arms extended, just as they were in his dream, but at least this time, he did not yell out to her.

"Alarm off," he whispered.

The music stopped, so he slid out of bed and looked at Thea. His departure caused her to stir, but she did not wake up. The last time she found out he dreamed of someone else, it led to an argument. Although disagreements were part of any relationship, he was unsure if they were *together* anymore. Over the last few hundred Terrestrial Rotations, he noticed she had become increasingly distant. He tried to discuss his concern, but she dismissed it, telling him he imagined it.

He went to the adjacent room to dress. Standing at arm's length, he combed shoulder-length black hair in front of the full-body mirror in his dressing room. The action sent tingles across his scalp and a wave of chills down his spine. Later, he increased the light's brightness and moved closer to the mirror to examine his face. A new wrinkle appeared that was not there a couple of Terrestrial Rotations ago.

What is this? More gray hairs! He reached for the touch-up comb but stopped in mid-motion. *No. Leave the gray. It is a sign of wisdom. My image is everything. No, the perception of that image is everything. Still, not too bad for someone who has been around forty yellow harvests.* He dressed in black trousers, a white shirt, and a red overcoat, replete with the required decorations. *Where the shadow and the Akilian meet.*

Firmly and unyieldingly, he gazed at the reflection in the mirror and assumed the mask that the others saw and feared. *The sovereign of the city. How long? Eighteen, nineteen yellow harvests of peril and solitude. In this coat, I am a fortress without sympathy, remorseless. However, do I command, or am I just a puppet to some mysterious thing, some hidden lord and master that controls me against my natural longing? Is Zorion, Zorion? Or am I someone else? Whenever I put this coat on, I wonder: am I the one who lifts this arm and wipes my brow? Or does some invisible power invade my body and take over my brain? Who or what rules here?*

Stepping away from the mirror, he walked over to his weapons drawer, where he found an assortment of blades at his disposal. *I would prefer not to wear one, but if I left unarmed, Broll would never let me hear the end of it.* He contemplated, reached down, and picked up his *Gaddar*. He knew Broll, his 'Chief Administrator of Security,' would approve. The blade was precisely the length of his forearm. It was double-edged. The lower part was sharp enough to cut anyone in half, and the upper edge was equally honed but only extended four finger-widths back from the point. The rest had soft metal, designed to snag an opponent's blade. The handle formed to his hand, making the weapon a lethal extension of his arm.

He buckled the Gaddar in place and walked back to the mirror; feeling confident that his carefully crafted image was perfect, he returned to the bedroom. Out of habit, he leaned over to kiss Thea, but before his lips touched her cheek, he stopped and backed up to study her. The covers were off to the side, exposing her naked body, surrounded by the sweep of her long brown hair as if she were lying on a pure bed of brown moss. Although Zorion considered Thea beautiful, he noticed flaws in her character soon after the light-yellow-haired female's dreams started. During that time, more defects in her personality appeared.

One glaring example he recently discovered was his favorite hologram recording showing them at a celebration during the third yellow harvest of his reign. He would meet with the city's Moss Farmers every three-hundred seventy Terrestrial Rotations to celebrate the event. It was the second yellow harvest since he and Thea had joined houses. The recording played in a loop every few heartbeats. She was taller than most females yet still half a forearm shorter than him.

Thea stood beside him, looking off in the distance with a scowl. Her expression made it clear she did not want to be there nor took pleasure in Zorion's presence. It bothered him because he remembered the recording much differently. His version had him seeing her stand on her toes to kiss him as a memento of the event, but as he watched it again for the tenth time, what his mind remembered did not happen. He wondered if she had misplaced the original; she insisted there were no other recordings. *How did I remember it differently?* It made him question his sanity.

His timekeeper vibrated, reminding him it was time to go to work. He left, pondering if the responsibilities of his position as a sovereign had caused her to resent him. This sacrifice, from his birth, had been part of his training. Nothing changed since he reached the age of maturity and ascended to the sovereign's seat. Zorion had always wanted to rule but did not expect it until his fiftieth or sixtieth yellow harvest.

He and his counterparts had lost two generations of parents simultaneously. Their deaths caused a big stir throughout the five cities. The authorities investigated Zorion and his peers for thirty Terrestrial Rotations but found no evidence of any crime. The scandal turned most Akilians against them, and the Information League did not broadcast their coronation. Many yellow harvests passed before their citizens showed any signs of trust. Even now, surveys showed that most Akilians had little to no confidence in them; only the younger generation favored them.

He checked his locator bracelet, and a small digital map appeared on the wrist screen, displaying the exact position of each guard. They patrolled every access point, ensuring anyone who entered had the authority to be there. It made him feel safe, knowing that nobody and nothing would get past them. They were each hand-picked by him, and he trusted them completely.

Zorion opened the front door and headed toward the Capitol, the city government's central hub. There was no need for sentries to escort him to his office because the Executive Citadel, which occupied the entire top level of the city, was only for him, his family, and any guests. However, Broll and a few guards always remained close. The doors opened to the administrative section, so he approached the legislative hall and stopped at a fork in the avenue. The private entrance to his office was to the left. The walkway that led to the main entrance was to the right. It had been a while since he walked through the front door. Although it was not an obligation, the ritual kept him centered, reminding him of what everyone else saw if they approached the seat of his power.

With a look, Broll knew his intention. The guards hustled over to catch up with him before entering the public domain. By the time Zorion reached the bottom of the stairway, Broll and his team had arrived. Each curved row of steps emitted a soft but visible light. Water cascaded down hand-made streams that poured into several small pools along the way.

Zorion took a deep breath and began to climb, with Broll and his team close by him. The light from the steps illuminated him, casting strange shadows on the ceiling. He made it to the top level without meeting a single Argian, but it was still early. Most government workers were leaving their residences and would not arrive for a few hundred heartbeats.

He pushed open the tall, thick glass doors that led to the circular lobby. Inside, he could see the polished dark green gemstone floor shining brilliantly in the bright light emitted by the glow-orbs in the dome above. The sound of moving water filled the chamber. Urki, the sovereign who refurbished the Capitol, put a massive fountain in the lobby's center and placed a statue of his likeness, holding a sword that reached the top of the dome ceiling.

Hand-carved streams led the water from the central fountain to the ones near the steps outside. Zorion never liked the thick clear plates that covered them; granted, it allowed visitors to walk safely over the hand-made streams, but the glass needed cleaning four times in one work cycle. Looking at the statue, he thought, *you were wasteful, Urki. You chose elegance over practicality*. He approached his office and saw the clerical staff members, who had arrived earlier, get out of their seats and approach him.

"A pleasant work cycle to you, Sir. It is a pleasure to see you again," greeted a young worker, with her palm forward in the standard Akilian salutation.

"A pleasant work cycle to you too. Thank you for all your hard work. If there is anything I can do, please let my assistant know. Have a wonderful work cycle," Zorion replied.

His voice echoed throughout the lobby, calling the attention of even more employees and visitors. Seeing him, they rushed over to greet him. Fifty salutations later, he finally made it to his office. He walked by Shilda, his diminutive assistant, without saying a word. She knew from earlier experience to give him a few hundred heartbeats to settle in, especially if he came through the main entrance. Inside, he sat in his chair, hoping his greeting ritual would help his popularity. If word spread that he showed concern for his employees, his citizens might be more inclined to trust him.

As the Information Terminal started, his thoughts returned to the yellow-haired female from his dreams. A smile softened his features as he thought of meeting her for real. *Zorion, stop fantasizing*, he scolded himself. *It is a luxury you cannot afford.* He shook himself out of his reverie, noticed that the executive office's outer door was open, and heard Shilda answering calls and taking messages. Her work cycle started a couple of thousand heartbeats before his arrival. He had not looked directly at her but noticed in his peripheral vision that she sat on several ancient historical books to make working at her desk more comfortable. On many occasions, he offered to get a new office chair, which could accommodate her petite frame; she always refused.

Hearing Shilda hard at work made him reach for the intercom, but he stopped halfway. About a hundred Terrestrial Rotations ago, he asked her to obtain the images of all eligible females who fit the description of the one in his dream. He told Shilda it was a personal request, and even though he did not tell her, she knew not to share it with anyone. By now, he was sure she had forgotten about it. The Information Terminal beeped, and he decided to take a few heartbeats for himself.

He selected the last image viewed on his monitor. The top right corner of the screen told him how far he was into the file. He was looking at image number 60,485. *Only 1,464,915 left.* Although the feeling of hopelessness grabbed him, he tried to shrug it off, but the possibilities continued to assault his mind. *She may have already joined houses with someone else by the time I find her.* Even so, he was not one to easily give up on a task, especially something so personal. *How am I ever going to find you?* He searched through another thousand images and stopped. Frustrated, he closed the database and signaled his assistant to start another work cycle without finding her.

"Yes, Sir," Shilda rushed from her desk to the doorway.

She stood in the center of the frame, waiting for his permission to enter.

"What is on the agenda for this work cycle?" he inquired.

"You have several early meetings. The first is with Noka; there is a problem with Argi Electric; he is waiting in the outer office. Next, you have a meeting with Yanamai, and then you have…."

He cut her off, "Send in Noka. I want to get that one over with now."

"Right away, Sir," she replied and disappeared from his sight.

He heard another door open and her voice calling for Noka in the adjacent room, who jumped off the couch and briskly walked toward Zorion's office.

"Thank you for seeing me," Noka cautiously waited at the doorway.

Zorion motioned for him to sit. As Noka approached, Zorion studied him carefully. It was a trick he learned from his sovereign before his untimely death. *You can tell a lot about a subject by how he moves toward you. Is he confident, scared, or unsure of himself? That way, you are prepared to answer before he even opens his mouth.* Noka was wealthy and young but had a homely look about him. Zorion thought him too young to hold his position at Argi Electric. *I am just more comfortable dealing with Argians my age.* Noka walked like someone on a mission.

"What is wrong now?" Zorion inquired.

"Well, Sir. Elzer has withdrawn his share of electricity for the Science Division, claiming that more funds are needed to build additional energy consoles on the surface before his city can continue contributing. He says that the amount of electricity Vlor Electric produces is not enough to support his city and the Science Division."

Zorion contacted his assistant and growled over the office communicator, "Shilda, get Elzer on the video com!"

Shilda hastily contacted Elzer's assistant and, within moments, had him on Zorion's video com.

"What is it, Zorion?" Elzer asked tiredly.

His lean face filled the screen from top to bottom, leaving wide gaps on each side. The background showed that he was not at his office.

"Noka tells me you refuse to supply your share of electricity to the Science Division."

Zorion was trying to keep calm but felt the veins in his forehead pulsing. He and Elzer had a history of confrontations.

"I am not refusing. I simply cannot afford to spare any electricity. The citizens of Vlor, my citizens, need the power to function."

"What happened to the Sovereign Cubes the consortium gave forty-five Terrestrial Rotations ago?"

"I spent those on debts the city accumulated over the last two hundred fifty Terrestrial Revolutions."

"Those Sovereign Cubes were designated for energy consoles!" Zorion yelled.

"Do not raise your voice to me! I am not your underling! I am your equal!" Elzer responded smugly.

"Some of those Sovereign Cubes came from Argi, so I have the right to raise my voice! The moment your family took control, your city needed financial help. I have always suspected that many of your city's Sovereign Cubes have ended up in your family's coffer!"

"Careful, Zorion. Do not make accusations that you cannot prove."

"Somehow, I will find a way, Elzer, and I am sure our counterparts share my feelings on this matter. I will call an emergency meeting, and we will see what they say about what you have done with the Sovereign Cubes we entrusted to you."

"I will see you at the meeting," Elzer disconnected the communication before Zorion could respond.

Unable to control his rage, Zorion slammed his fist on the desk. The force of his blow shook it and the floor beneath it. A hologram of him and Thea fell off the counter and broke. Had this been the first time Zorion's temper flared up, Noka would have jumped out of his chair, but he had seen it before.

"Forgive me, Noka," Zorion grumbled, struggling to reclaim his calm.

"No need to apologize, Sir. I completely understand," Noka respectfully responded, doing his best to hide his nervousness. "What should I do in the meantime?"

"See if any other cities can spare more power and do what you can to increase our share."

"We must transfer electricity from other grids, which will cause certain areas of the city to be without power."

"So come up with a plan to rotate the grids, but make sure the businesses do not lose power during the work cycle."

"I will have my team figure something out right away."

"Good. I will deal with Elzer. You may leave unless there is something else?"

"No other business for this work cycle, Sir, and I understand your dilemma. I have heard rumors of Elzer's accounting practices from multiple sources. You have your job cut out for you." Noka stood, approached Zorion, and extended his hand palm forward, "Thank you for your time."

Zorion calculated the cost of the gesture and extended his own, "I will let you know if I hear something. Meanwhile, find out the cost of building extra energy consoles for our city. I will start putting as many Sovereign Cubes aside as I can. We will use them for their construction and installation."

"Of course, I will have the estimate to you in three or four Terrestrial Rotations," Noka turned and walked away.

Zorion smiled. *Young but efficient.* A few moments later, Zorion buzzed Shilda again.

"Yes, Sir," she rushed to his office door again.

"I want to speak with Olan during this work cycle."

"I believe you have some time after Yanamai's visit, so I will have him waiting for you."

"Thank you." He sighed, feeling the weight of politics. "Shilda, I am going to the tower for a few hundred heartbeats. When Yanamai arrives, tell her I will be back shortly."

"Yes, Sir," Shilda answered.

Sensing his mood, she turned and shut the door behind her. Zorion picked up the broken hologram and put it back on his desk. The recording was still playing beneath a cracked pane. The video recalled the same scene as the one he watched earlier. *How could I have missed this?* Turning, he stepped inside his private elevator and selected the icon to take him to the top. He ascended toward the planet's surface and felt the elevator re-orient to follow the Celestial Revolution. *Has it been that long since I took this trip?*

He opened the closet at the back of the elevator and removed protective gear. Before reaching the top, the thermal jumpsuit, helmet, and safety goggles were on his person, ready to protect him from the sun's harmful rays, so he moved to the elevator door and turned his back on it. Using calming techniques, he took several deep breaths to relieve his stress. Again, Elzer put himself before the safety of everyone else on Akil. One way or another, he would find a way to hold him accountable for his actions.

In the meantime, he needed to stay diligent. He needed that extra energy. THEY needed that additional energy, even if his citizens did not trust him. The daunting task of looking for a new planet had him on edge, and now Elzer's failure to aid in that expensive endeavor pointed to something else that must be happening beneath the surface. *What could be more important than our survival?* A few hundred heartbeats later, the elevator doors opened. The red light from their dying sun enveloped him. He flipped the protective visor into place with his right hand, turned around, and stepped out of the elevator.

His first stop was the observation deck to the viewing station, where he could look out over a planet that was nothing more than an ice ball in space. From one horizon to the other, drifts of snow greeted him. From his birth, he never saw it any other way. No living Akilian had. *Once upon a time, we thrived under all that.* Zorion shook his head. *If it had not been for the museums, they would have lost the planet's entire culture. It had only taken a few generations for the surface to freeze.*

Zorion wondered what it must have been like living through the Great Change. Everything was ordinary on one Terrestrial Rotation, but the following Revolution, their sun exploded and started emitting higher radiation levels that slowly killed all plant and animal life, except for the multi-colored mosses and the Akilians themselves. The increased radiation caused a temperature drop, so the Akilians moved their cities underground to be closer to their geothermal energy source. During the Great Change, Akil's population suffered a massive loss, and over time, other transformations took place.

Among them was the females' gestation period, which decreased to ninety Terrestrial Rotations, give or take a few. Akilian scientists accredited it to the moss, which they had adapted for food and clothing. The surviving cities grew underground as their population rebounded from near extinction levels. Construction workers carved out more territory from the planet's living rock with the population increase.

As a child, Zorion spent thousands of heartbeats in the museums, where he played among the large dioramas. It showed what life had been like on the surface of Akil before the freeze. The realistic replicas of the long-extinct animals inspired him to talk and play with them. They were very lifelike to his young mind, so he thought they would come alive but never did. Their scientists had tried cloning and other genetic experiments to bring them back from extinction, yet all their efforts failed because no animal could ingest the moss.

Looking almost directly above him, he could see Akil's two moons. Each was close to half of Akil's size. They appeared as gigantic orbs in the sky, even though they were far away. According to the historical records, the southern moon used to have a blue hue around it, and the northern one had a yellow halo. Their tones turned green when they lined up; the Akilians commemorated the event by creating the Green Festival. He longed to see the cosmic occurrence, but generations ago, their sun exploded, and the solar winds stripped the moons of the thin atmosphere that created their hues. Now, they were nothing more than a couple of dull red orbs in the sky. Beneath the frozen crust, Akilians still celebrated the Alignment Festival. Planet-wide, everyone dressed in green and colored their faces. He almost smiled, remembering Thea coming home with her face painted green. She had seduced him before the sleep cycle by pretending to be an alien. He frowned. *Did that even happen?*

A few hundred heartbeats later, he turned north to face the Akilian Crisis, which was their sun. As a child, his parents insisted that he attend classes with the other children, something future sovereigns rarely did. *You will rule them on one Terrestrial Revolution, so you should know how they think and feel.* He learned about Akil's horizontal axis at school, which meant the planet rotated eastward. The entire northern hemisphere faced the sun during the second summer season, yet it was not hot enough to melt all the snow. He stood on the equator, but only a crescent part of the star was visible over the horizon. It would not rise and fall until the equator faced it again in the following summer season. Akil's Celestial Revolution was exceptionally long. Even if he lived to his expected age, it would not be enough to see the following summer.

Thinking about Akil's two summers, he snickered at the irony. The Akilians celebrated sixty-two yellow harvests during each summer and winter period. The sixty-first harvest happened only five Terrestrial Rotations ago, which meant the second winter would be upon them soon. Staring at the sun, he could see fountains of plasma shooting aimlessly out from its surface through the filtered viewing portal. As the Terrestrial Revolution continued, other spouts of plasma would rise in the northeastern sky. Those currently visible would set on the northwestern horizon, but the crescent view would not change until the following summer. He wondered how much longer Akil had before the sun's gravity diminished, causing it to explode. *Will we even see another yellow harvest?*

Near the tower, Mount Gaurette loomed on the western horizon. Mounds of snow were extremely high in some places, and it would take excavating machines to move through them. On the northern side of the old city to his right, he saw the pyramid's summit that Gau, an Akilian god, was rumored to have built. Even though many Akilians worshipped him, Zorion did not believe in Gau. He had no use for his mythology because it was dark and evil. Whoever constructed the monument wasted resources because it did nothing to help the citizens of Akil. It was merely a pile of carved, rectangle stones. Zorion believed that Gau, if he existed, was just an egotistical sovereign who wanted his descendants to remember him. Looking below, closer to the tower, he squinted to see the abandoned buildings his ancestors occupied long ago. Some ruins were visible above the snow, especially in wind-swept westward areas.

On the western horizon, just above Mount Gaurette, he saw 'The River of Fire,' a long plume of orange-red plasma stretched out from the sun's surface trillions of paces into space to a nearby younger, more massive star. Due to Akil's Revolution, he could see the stream moving directly above him at mid-work cycle, where the moons were now. He slightly adjusted the protective visor and saw deeply into the swirling eddies of the long plasma arm where Akil's sister planet, Yovis 5, once orbited. Once upon a time, Yovis 5 had been a bright blue light in their heavens and spaceships traveled between the two worlds.

Yovis 5's orbit had been higher in the cosmic plane and nearly an entire season ahead of Akil in its Celestial Revolution. It had been one of several uninhabitable, barren planets without an atmosphere at the edge of their solar system. When their sun began morphing into a red giant and turning Akil into an ice ball, that same process transformed Yovis 5 into a habitable world. Zorion felt that it was as if some higher power played the children's *Hop the Wiffle* game with them; as one planet died, another was born to take its place. Once their technology reached space travel capability, Akil sent over its best scientists to terraform the land. They set up a life-sustaining atmosphere, so the principal cities could begin colonizing Yovis 5, and from the rock, sister cities appeared.

The population shifted from the dying planet to the new and precisely sixty yellow harvests ago, 'The River of Fire' burst its banks and sent its incinerating arm across space into the path of Yovis 5. Two Terrestrial Rotations later, the planet's orbit plunged it into the midst of its all-consuming fire. Millions died. Only a handful of Yovisians escaped. *Two Terrestrial Revolutions were all they had.*

Zorion tried to imagine the horror and the panic of those last moments, knowing that soon, Akil could face an even shorter deadline. *When the sun explodes, it will only take five hundred sixty heartbeats for the shockwave to reach us and tear us apart. Will we find a new home? Or will we be a fleeting memory in the cosmos? After we are gone, who will remember us?* He felt emotional, staring at the *River of Fire* because it had widened. This fiery stream continued to drain their sun of its life-sustaining plasma. With every passing heartbeat, their sun becomes lighter until there will not be enough mass to contain the star's natural explosions, which will destroy everything in its path. He took a deep breath, wondering if it would be his last.

With his gaze firmly fastened on the snowy village beneath, he walked the circular viewing balcony until reaching the tower's south side, but there was not much to see. Only the very tops of the tallest buildings were visible. *Sadly, this is the warmest time of the Celestial Revolution.* During the colder months, snow blanketed the entire area altogether. Even Mount Gaurette appeared to be a hill rather than a looming mountain.

Continuing forward, he saw the frozen casements of the palace his ancestors built many Celestial Revolutions ago. They barely broke the icy surface. He often wondered what it would be like living in that palace now. Yanamai, his Chief Administrator of the Science Division, told him that everything should be exactly as his ancestors left it all those generations ago before they led their citizens underground. *A city on top of another, the old, on the frozen surface, and the new, thousands of paces beneath.* The palace was the second largest building in the ancient city; the pyramid was the largest. Once upon a time, it had been a symbol of his city's wealth and power. Now, it was merely a sad, hollow testimony of what his civilization had once been.

Before moving forward, he took a moment to look at the memorial, honoring the scientist who taught the civilians how to build the machinery needed to tunnel beneath the ground. Although the identity of this Akilian faded in the annals of history, the knowledge he or she passed on also helped to create a foundation for them to build a portal machine. It took many Celestial Revolutions for the scientists to make such a device, but they finally completed the first model sixty-five yellow harvests ago, allowing them to begin their systematic search for a new world. Even so, with the sun in its current condition, the possibility that he would be Argi's last sovereign loomed over him like a dark shadow.

Lastly, he walked to the east side of the observation deck to examine the city's energy consoles. Many boards stretched away from the observation tower toward the north's wind-swept horizon, most of them now inoperable. If they failed, it was too costly to remove them, so they put new ones beside them. Daily maintenance kept them from disappearing under the frosty tundra. Currently, a pilot was running a hovercraft over section 4C. The vehicle released a steady stream of a hot chemical compound. When the clear liquid made contact, the ice and snow dissolved, allowing the panels to work correctly.   The dull, repetitive actions of the hovercraft were mesmerizing. Its pilot rocked the craft from side to side, directing the hot chemical to flow across the face of the energy panel with pinpoint precision. The operator edged his way across one board until it was completely free from all obstruction. It was a slow, tedious process but an essential job. Watching it, Zorion started to fall asleep.

Chapter 3

Akil
Argi City
The 22,270[th] Terrestrial Rotation of the Second Summer

Yanamai's timekeeper chimed as she finished typing her thoughts into her Information Terminal. Now it was time to get ready for her meeting with Zorion. Her home and office were directly below the Executive Citadel Level, and it was her responsibility to provide him with frequent updates. There were three elevators close by, all within easy walking distance, but Yanamai was not in a rush because nothing was new to report. Although she did not have far to travel, sometimes the journey was an imposition, especially with her work schedule.

She walked to her bathroom to freshen up before her meeting. Due to a noble, who excessively pursued her, Yanamai requested to live in her office. Zorion agreed but insisted on installing a bedroom and bath with a connecting door. Knowing that the aristocrat obsessing over her could not access her level gave her peace of mind. It had been a long time since she thought about her stalker because, after her promotion, her prior responsibilities as a scientist continued.

Yanamai had to oversee the whole division's budget, regulations, policies, and procedures. It kept her busy beyond the normal work cycle. Her primary goal was to find a habitable planet, and she was aware of her work habits, even if others were not. Her bedroom was only a few paces away. She had fallen asleep on the sofa again, waiting for the latest reports on the cluster of star systems with planets they discovered in sector 2-0, but none proved to be habitable.

There were millions of sections within the galaxy, and it took many yellow harvests to explore each one, which is why they were only this far in their search. Before taking the news to Zorion, Yanamai wanted to make herself presentable. Once in the bathroom, Yanamai disrobed and untied her hair. It fell to the floor. Like every other Akilian female, her hair stayed uncut from birth because tradition dictated that all female body parts were Gau's gift.

Due to his popularity, the custom became law over time, forbidding them to cut it. With a practiced sweep of her right arm, she gathered her hair in two separate folds along her forearm and climbed into the tub. She arranged her hair beneath her head like a soft pillow, laid back, and reached for the water controls. The round tub was about one and a half forearms deep, and the water jets set above her in the outline of her favorite flower, now long extinct.

She liked to look at all the swirls and loops of the petals and wondered what it must have been like sitting beneath a grove of these delicate buds as they opened to release their fragrance. She allowed her imagination to displace all the data looking for space in her mind and turned on the water. It flowed from above like a small waterfall, soaking her whole body and massaging her tired muscles. Yanamai allowed the eddying current to take her hair and stretch it to its full length as the tub filled. A few moments later, she sat and reached for the special cleaning combs. It took a few hundred heartbeats for her to clean her body, wash her hair, and arrange it for the drying process.

Yanamai stepped out of the tub and walked into the drying booth. With a slight smile, touching the corner of her lips, she closed her eyes, turned on the heat, and stood still. Warm air flowed through the booth. In just a few hundred heartbeats, her skin was dry, and her hair was dancing around her as if it were alive. This warm air massage was her favorite part of the Terrestrial Rotation. It was a much-needed break from the demands of her job.

She stayed in the drying booth longer than necessary, but no one was around to chide her for wasting electricity. Later, she wore a clean, government-issued uniform and arranged her hair into a bun. Several yellow harvests ago, she was still in school, and her teacher said that several deaths sparked Zorion to pass a law demanding all females to restrain their hair outside of their private homes. Of course, it was for their safety, but Yanamai scoffed at the idea. *A couple of females die doing something stupid, and the rest suffer because of them.*

Her uniform consisted of a gray pantsuit, black shoes, and a yellow shirt with three red stripes depicting her status. To quickly figure out the hierarchy, others in her field wore different colored shirts depending upon their rank, but they all wore the same color suit. The distinctive clothing made her feel self-conscious outside the lab, where she seldom ventured.

Tadra, her assistant, wore a blue shirt, and Garbi, Yanamai's sister, wore a white shirt. Yanamai recalled the little brain teaser she learned as a rank white shirt all those many Terrestrial Rotations ago, *"when in dread, turn to red."* Everyone knew that things could go very wrong quickly with their equipment, and without the proper maintenance, capacitors had a reputation for exploding. Moreover, knowing whose orders to follow and when would save time and lives.

Before leaving to meet with Zorion, Yanamai put Tadra in charge, "Do not contact me unless something is on fire."

"What if…" Tadra tried to ask, but Yanamai interrupted her.

"Just do not contact me," she replied with a polite smile and left.

Outside, the second level was already busy with the hustle and bustle of Argians going about their ordinary activities, and they were all dressed in the same style of government-issued outfits. Zain, a guard Zorion assigned to protect her, escorted her to the elevators. A few workers crossed her path along the way, wearing the Clerical or Maintenance division's uniform. She approached the elevator and passed another young worker. She could tell by his look that he was interested in establishing a relationship. Yanamai considered his appearance average, and as they passed each other, she smelled his pheromones and realized he was not for her.

This heightened sense was something all Akilian females shared from birth. As a child, she learned that the unique ability, amid others, appeared in their ancestors shortly after eating the moss. This genetic mutation somehow bypassed Akilian males, leaving them with an ordinary sense of smell. Over time, various rituals arose surrounding the new gift the females had. Some were harmless, but others demanded the ultimate price. Proper etiquette required truth, not deception, so Yanamai fixed her eyes straight forward and kept walking, clearly disinterested.

*****

Crossing in front of the elevator, a young maintenance worker noticed a gorgeous science yellow shirt with red stripes walking toward him. As they crossed paths, he glanced at her to see if she was interested. She kept her eyes fixed forward and did not slow down to talk with him, so he realized that there would be no connection between them. He stopped and leaned against the safety rail to look out over the city. Several classes of hover vehicles and buses sped back and forth, heading to their respective destinations. Letting his mind wander for just a moment, he pondered whether his future companion was riding in one of them.

Having reached the age of maturity thirty Terrestrial Rotations ago, his parents began to pressure him to find a partner. Joining houses was a serious business, and neither side could not take the endeavor lightly. Uniting with the wrong Akilian often caused financial disaster for everyone involved, among many other issues. Still, society expected young adults to look for a significant other, which did not help that venture. Everyone knew where they stood on the social ladder, and his status as a maintenance worker was close to the bottom, so it did not surprise him that the beautiful scientist ignored him. Although it was disappointing, it did not deter him. He had to find someone soon, or his family would step in and hold a gathering for him. Unable to find a partner on your own was a fate worse than death because it was humiliating.

Just as he was about to leave, the ceiling caught his attention. Thousands of panels stretched across the dome to display a live broadcast of their sun. The image showed the top crescent of the red orb hovering over the northern horizon. The large fountains of plasma rising forth from the surface were a constant reminder that time was running out. *Another work cycle begins, but there is still no news of a planet to call home.* A horn from one of the vehicles going by brought him out of his brooding. Compressed air from the brakes loudly whistled as it tried to stop. Drivers barely avoiding an accident, gave each other insulting hand gestures, and drove off.

Returning his attention to his job, he looked at the work order and the pass that would allow him to enter the city's amphitheater. The Information League would broadcast the upcoming event. Otsoa, Zorion's heir, would reach the age of maturity during the following Terrestrial Revolution. Since nobles did not mingle with average citizens, their parents held a celebration, including the pageant. Everyone was welcome, from elites to the poorest of the poor. Only during this event could a female at the bottom of the social ladder elevate herself to the top within one Terrestrial Rotation.

Whoa! There will be more eligible females in one place during the pageant than I would ever get a chance to see in a lifetime of traveling around Argi fixing things. It is the opportunity I hoped would present itself. I will find a way to get into this celebration. I could "almost" fix something that would break down during the ceremony, which would force me to go back and do it again. Go back to all those eligible females, all in one place, all looking for a significant other. The corner of his lips turned upward. *I wonder what I can break.* With new enthusiasm, he rushed off to secure his role in the celebration.

Chapter 4

Earth
The Regime - Washington, D.C. - Fort McNair
May 6, 2452

Michael dressed and headed to the Local Transportation Station, where Alex waited for him, pacing.

"It took you long enough," quipped Alex.

"I'm only fifteen minutes late," defended Michael.

"Fine, but you must stay fifteen minutes later to make up for the lost time."

"Whatever. Just open the portal so we can go."

Alex slid his Transportation Card into the slot, typed in the address, and a portal opened before them. They could see the Union Station's landing bay at the Main Hall entrance on the other side and stepped through the event horizon. Their landing triggered the vortex to close behind them automatically. Michael remembered reading that at one time, the Union Station served as a central train station, but following the invention of portal machines, the Regime converted it into a vortex transportation hub. It had been the busiest rail facility and shopping destination; today, they used the trains as traveling restaurants rather than transit, reminding everyone of the benefits portal transportation provided.

The government had renovated Union Station many times over the years; it was home to the east coast's largest shopping mall and included a train museum with rides. Millions of people visit yearly. Michael tried to remember how long it had been since his last visit. *Oh, that's right. I was shopping with Chu Lian.* Union Station had everything from grocery stores, clothing, restaurants, gaming, and anything else the imagination could conceive. As they made their way to the restaurant, Michael noticed large monitors displaying advertisements for the businesses.

The store's mega speaker system played classical music. Although not a fan of the genre, Michael found it oddly soothing. They took an escalator to the second floor and walked until reaching the restaurant. To Michael's surprise, Julie waited for them at the entrance. She had not changed much since he last saw her. Julie was still five feet, one inch tall with blonde hair set in a ponytail, blue eyes, and a gymnast's body. She smiled pleasantly and briskly walked to greet them. First, she hugged Alex and then Michael.

"I'm so glad you came," she smiled, genuinely happy to see him.

"If General Saunders hadn't ordered him, he wouldn't have come," Alex declared accusingly.

"I'm just glad you came," she remarked, smiling sweetly at him.

"I'm glad to see you, too," Michael chimed in. "It's been way too long."

"Did you get a table?" Alex asked.

"Yes, follow me," Julie replied.

Alex saw a young woman seated in the booth as they approached their seats; he discreetly took Julie's arm, and pulled her to the side.

"What are you doing?" he demanded.

"I told Rachael about Michael. She was willing to meet him," she stated.

"Damn it, Julie! I wish you would have told me; I invited someone too!"

"What do we do?"

"I'll tell her something came up at work. I'm sure she can reschedule," Alex remarked.

"I think Rachael and Michael will hit it off tonight, so don't set up another date yet."

"We'll see," Alex whispered to himself and dialed the number to his friend.

Julie arrived at their seat and found Michael sheepishly standing near the table. Since Michael was too shy to initiate a conversation, Julie introduced them.

"Rachael, this is Michael; he's the one I told you about," encouraged Julie.

"Hi, it's a pleasure to meet you," Michael smiled and shook her hand.

"Michael, why don't you sit over there," Julie pointed to the seat across from Rachael.

"Sure, Julie, whatever you say," he responded, sitting.

Julie sat beside Rachael, "Michael, Rachael is on the Regime's National Swimming team. She's poised to be in the upcoming Olympics."

"That's very impressive, Rachael. I understand the training is intense," Michael noted.

"It is. I'm swimming twice a day now and eating five thousand calories to keep my energy up," explained Rachael.

"Wow! That is insane," exclaimed Michael.

"Aren't you going to introduce me?" Alex queried, sitting beside Michael and interrupting their conversation.

"Yes, forgive me. This neanderthal sitting alongside Michael is my brother, Alex, *whom I've warned you about*," Julie emphasized the words.

"Neanderthal?" Alex frowned and covered his chest with his hand, pretending to have hurt feelings.

Rachael smiled at him, which only aggravated Julie.

"Rachael will be in the upcoming Olympics. She's on the women's swimming team," Michael shared.

"I thought you looked familiar. Michael, don't you recognize her?" Alex questioned.

"No, I'm sorry," Michael commented.

"This is Rachael Hughes. She's won - like - three gold medals already," Alex boasted.

Rachael blushed.

"I'm sorry. I don't watch sports or much of anything these days. I always seem to be working," Michael frowned sheepishly.

"I remember cheering for you during each event! You were awesome!" Alex exclaimed.

"Thank you. It helps to know the people back home are rooting for me," Rachael smiled.

Alex's phone vibrated, so he stood, "I'm sorry. I need to take this. I'll be right back."

With Alex out of the way, Julie tried to focus Rachael's attention on Michael.

"Why don't you tell us what you've been working on lately?"

"I'm sorry. I can't. It's classified," Michael apologized.

Rachael nodded but was not impressed.

"Is there anything you can tell us?" Julie queried, hopefully.

"I'm sorry. Everything I do is classified," Michael shrugged his shoulders.

"I thought you were a botanist?" Rachael inquired.

"I am."

"People who study plants create all sorts of things we can use," Julie interrupted.

"Like what?" Rachael questioned.

"I don't know; help me out here, Michael," Julie pleaded for his help with her eyes.

"Pharmaceutical companies make many medicines from plants," Michael offered.

"You see, he makes medicines."

"What medicines have you made?" Rachael wondered.

"Oh, I haven't made any medicines. I was trying to help Julie out," he smiled, holding back a laugh.

Julie rolled her eyes, about to give up.

Alex returned, "Hey, Rachael, we can go to my lab if you're interested. I have some cool photos of Mars taken through the portals we've opened."

"It sounds like fun," Rachael smiled.

"I thought you hadn't reached it yet?" Julie interjected.

"We're close enough to take stunning pictures but not as beautiful as you," Alex faced Rachael and smiled.

There was a thump underneath the table.

"Ouch! What was that for?" Alex blurted.

"Sorry. My foot slipped," Julie growled through gritted teeth.

Ignoring her, Alex continued to flirt and talk to Rachael. Before long, she was laughing, flirting, and smiling at him too. Michael tried to take mental notes of what Alex said and did, but it was impossible to figure out precisely what made him so appealing. Michael could only conclude that it was due to his good looks, charm, and charisma, things he lacked. Alex could talk about shoveling dirt using those three gifts, and they would be impressed. They finished their desserts, which Michael did not bother ordering, and Alex and Rachael left together.

As they walked away, holding hands, Julie swore under her breath, "Damn him. He did this on purpose."

"Oh, was Rachael meant for me?" Michael pretended not to know.

"Stop it, Michael. I'm already mad at Alex. Don't you start," she warned.

"I'm sorry, Julie. I couldn't resist teasing you. You are, after all, the worst matchmaker I've ever known," Michael chuckled softly.

Julie looked at him, angry at first, and then busted out with laughter, "I know. I don't understand. I showed her your picture and background. She seemed genuinely interested."

"She's an Olympic swimmer, Julie! I'm just a nobody," Michael joked.

"Stop it. You are somebody. You just need to realize it."

"If you meant for us to connect, why did you invite Alex? You know he has a certain *je ne sais quoi* when it comes to women."

Julie knew the reason Alex lured Rachael away. He wanted Michael to meet his mystery woman. Alex was egotistical, but to steal Rachael the way he did was low, even for him.

"I knew you wouldn't meet with her if I called, so I had to ask him to trick you into showing up."

"I appreciate your enthusiasm for my love life, but please, don't try to set me up again. I'm still struggling."

"I can't help myself. I want you to be happy," Julie responded emotionally.

"We know why you're doing this."

"That has nothing to do with it."

"Really?"

"Fine. I still feel horrible about what happened between us. I shouldn't have deceived you. I swear it was unintentional."

"You didn't trick me. You acted like a friend; you were and still are my friend. It's my fault; I misinterpreted kindness for affection. Of all people, you should know that I don't have a clue about women. I'm socially inept."

"Fine, I promise, no more blind dates."

"Thanks."

"How are you holding up?"

"I have good days and bad days."

"Chu Lian really hurt you."

"I had planned to ask her to marry me. I thought she wanted the same thing. After she left, my entire world fell apart."

"That's the reason you need someone else in your life. Trust me; you will find the right one, and she'll make you forget all about Chu Lian."

Michael kissed her cheek, "Thank you for being my friend."
He left and returned to work.
"Take care."

Chapter 5

Akil
Argi City
The 22,270[th] Terrestrial Rotation of the Second Summer

Before accessing the Executive Citadel Level, Yanamai had to walk through a security post. Several massive, intimidating sentries, wearing black overcoats, searched her pockets and inspected the data device she used to present the information to Zorion. The process was tedious and demeaning, but she understood the necessity. To speed things up, she stopped taking her bag with her. With it, her time at the station was even longer because Security authenticated each item before allowing it through.

The guards examined her pockets and outer clothing contents and led Yanamai into a small booth, where they temporarily restrained her until a Screener confirmed her identity. It took her less than a heartbeat to ensure that Yanamai was indeed Yanamai, and they released her. She opened the door to Zorion's office; Shilda was on the communicator and waved for her to take a seat.

Shilda disconnected, "He went to the tower. He said he would be back shortly." Before she stopped speaking, the intercom on her desk lit up. "Yes, Sir?"

"If Yanamai is there, please send her in," Zorion instructed.

"Hmm, that was fast," Shilda whispered to herself.

Yanamai waited at the doorway.

"Please, come in and have a seat," Zorion gestured.

Shilda closed the door behind her. Instantly, Yanamai sensed something was wrong. Behind his desk, Zorion sat as she remembered him, with piercing blue eyes, long black hair, and a square jaw. It looked like Zorion and sounded like him, yet she could still feel something was off until realizing the sweet smell of purple moss was missing. Since it is his favorite food, the pleasant aroma often lingered around him like a beacon, but he seemed three-dimensional rather than four without it. *Could he be testing me? Could I be talking to an experimental hologram?*

"What progress have you made so far?" Zorion asked.

Yanamai stuttered, trying to regain her focus, "Uh…Uh…Yes, there it is. Over the last seven work cycles, we have explored thirty thousand planets in sector 2-0. They were all uninhabitable."

She opened her Data Device and let the information transfer to Zorion's Information Terminal.

"Yanamai, how many planets have you explored since you started?"

"Since I have been the Chief Administrator of the Science Division? About half a million, Sir."

"Have you selected every one of these planets in sequence?"

"Yes, it was agreed by all the leading scientists that it was the most efficient way to search."

"What if you jumped ahead to another sector?" He paused to look at his hand, studying it for several heartbeats, "How about sector 1-5-6-9-2-4-1?"

"Sir, I realize it takes a long time, but please understand. There are more than two billion stars in this galaxy. What makes a planet habitable is much more complicated than its location from the host star so that water can be liquid on its surface. Numerous geophysical and geodynamical aspects can be close yet not sufficient for life; it is not something at which we should guess."

"I understand your objections, but I insist you search that sector at once."

Yanamai's face flushed because her job was hard enough. She did not need or appreciate anyone, even Zorion, interfering in that process. It was reckless to gamble on which sector may or may not have life. Nevertheless, he was sovereign and the one in charge of the city. She pushed down her anger deep inside with significant effort, hoping it would not show.

Yanamai pretended to smile, "I will begin the process immediately."

She thought the meeting was over and stood, "Will there be anything else?"

"There is one more thing," he hesitated.

"What is it?" she sat again.

"I do not mean to pry into your personal life, but I wondered if you were planning to attend Otsoa's celebration during the following Terrestrial Rotation?"

"No. My work keeps me busy, and now, with your new orders, it will take my team half a work cycle to recalculate our landing."

"I realize your job is important; still, I want you to be there."

"Why? What purpose does it serve?"

"Otsoa does not want to begin the next chapter of his life without apologizing to you first."

"I do not need an apology from him."

"I know you do not, but *he* needs to say it."

"I do not understand. You are the one who insisted on placing a restraining order on him, and now you want me to be in the same room?"

"I understand your concern, and I know that what I am asking is unexpected. What if I assign four guards to watch over you during your visit with him? Would that help ease your fear?"

Yanamai hesitated to reply. She hated being in the same city as Otsoa, let alone facing him again.

Seeing her delay, Zorion added, "I know Otsoa has said inappropriate things to you, but he is still my heir. I still care for him, and I believe that if he apologizes to you, it will help him move forward with the peace of mind of trying to make things right, so I would consider it a personal favor."

"Very well, I will meet with him. Just know that if he says or does anything to harm me, I will press charges, even if it hurts you politically. I do not want to do it, but you leave me no choice."

"I agree. Thank you, Yanamai."

"Will there be anything else?" she anxiously wanted to leave.

"No, I think you have done enough for one work cycle. In fact, you may take the rest of it off. I insist."

Yanamai stood, bewildered by their conversation. There were many things off about this meeting. The absence of purple moss in the air, him changing their sector, and finally, asking her to speak with Otsoa. It was like talking to a different Akilian. As Yanamai left mumbling to herself, Shilda closed the door to his office, and Zorion left through his private entrance to the walkway. Moments later, the elevator doors to the tower opened, and Zorion stepped out. He felt refreshed after visiting the surface.

He sat in his chair and hit the intercom button, "Shilda, you may send in Yanamai."

"She just left, Sir."

Zorion frowned, "Is everything all right?"

"Yes, Sir."

"Did she reschedule her briefing?"

"Sir?"

"What is so difficult to understand? Did she reschedule her briefing?"

"You just spoke to her."

Zorion checked his Information Terminal and found her report, so he turned on the hologram of him and Thea. *Am I losing my mind? Did I somehow forget my meeting with Yanamai?* He started to panic. If his mind continued to play tricks on him, he would have to resign. He paced until seeing that the door to his private entrance was ajar, and he knew someone else had been there.

"Shilda, have Yanamai return at once. I have more to say to her."

"Yes, Sir. Right away."

Zorion waited until she stood in the doorway. He waved her inside, and Shilda shut the door. Yanamai cautiously entered and sat. This time, she smelled the purple moss.

"Shilda tells me we just had our meeting. Is that correct?"

"Yes," Yanamai responded, thinking it was a trick question.

"You must not repeat what I am about to say to anyone, understand?"

"Yes, Sir."

"You did not meet with me. I was in the tower until a few heartbeats ago.

"Now that makes sense."

"What do you mean?"

"Whoever sat in your seat looked exactly like you, but there was one thing missing, the smell of purple moss."

"Did he have any noticeable scent at all?"

"No, he did not."

"He must have bought the new drug from the Shadow Economy. It suppresses the pheromones for a brief time."

"That would explain his three-dimensional appearance."

"This Akilian also must have been someone my size. We can mimic another's appearance but cannot increase or decrease our body mass."

"I agree. Someone smaller would look like a miniature version of you. I would have known right away."

"Although I record every conversation in this room, I want you to recite your discussion."

"The imposter ordered me to change the sector for our upcoming search."

"What sector did he give you?"

"1-5-6-9-2-4-1."

"Is that on the other side of the galaxy?"

"Yes, and it will take enormous power to open a portal there."

"What else did he say?"

"He wants me to attend Otsoa's celebration and speak with him privately. He claimed Otsoa wants to apologize to me."

"The impersonator was Otsoa."

"How can you be sure?"

"It should be obvious. Otsoa is still obsessed with you and is close to my body mass. I hope you did not agree to go."

"Yes, I did. He promised to have four guards escort me there and watch over the meeting. I felt pressured to go, especially because he insisted you considered it a personal favor."

"You cannot go to the celebration. Otsoa has gone to the extreme to get you there, so he must have something nefarious planned."

"Thank you. I did not feel comfortable going."

"Please, accept my apology on my family's behalf. Had you attended his celebration, there is no telling what he might have done to you."

"Should I continue with sector 2-1?"

Zorion rubbed his chin in thought, "No, search the sector he gave."

"But why?"

"Otsoa does not know anything about the cosmos. It would surprise me if he knew your team divided the galaxy into sectors. That means he is working with someone else, maybe more than one."

"That would explain why he studied his hand before giving it to me. He must have written on his palm. I do not understand why they want us to look there?"

"I am not sure; by manipulating Otsoa, their plan must be to use my office to make changes. I want them to continue believing he was successful while I have someone investigate it and hopefully find these Akilians."

"Then, I must meet with Otsoa."

"Absolutely not."

"Sir, if you want them to think that Otsoa was successful, I must go, or they will become suspicious. Maybe his accomplices will show up."

"I will send an agent to take your place."

"It will not work. I knew something was wrong when Otsoa impersonated you. Without having experienced that kind of deception, he fooled me. Otsoa will know if someone takes my place."

"I cannot and will not ask you to do this."

"You are not asking me; I am volunteering. No, I insist. We have traitors in our city, and we must find them. It is my Argian duty to help."

"If anything were to happen to you, Yanamai, I would never forgive myself."

"I feel the same toward you, Sir. Still, they are trying to interfere with our search for a new planet; it could mean these spies are working to destroy us."

"Very well. Just know that I will be close, and you will have four guards with you. Here, I want you to take this," Zorion stood, removed his Gaddar, and handed it to her. "It is smaller than a sword, but it will protect you. I will ensure that the guards remove all Otsoa's weapons before he sees you. Still, if he tries anything, remove his head."

Yanamai took it from him, "Thank you, Sir. I will wear it."

"Until it is time, stay in your office."

"I will."

"Very well, go; I am sure you have much to do."

Zorion's face turned into a scowl as Yanamai walked away. He found it hard to believe that his miserable excuse for an heir was the final product of his many yellow harvests of guidance. It was as if his words did not affect him. Otsoa was impulsive, untrustworthy, self-indulgent, careless, and even heartless. Now he was convinced, more than ever, that Otsoa would not rule in his place. He would create the necessary documents later to ensure it, but he had to speak with his Chief Administrator of Intelligence for now.

"Shilda, is Olan here yet?" Zorion spoke into the intercom.

"Yes, Sir."

"Send him in."

Olan stepped to the doorway, dressed as an Argian business owner, and waited for Zorion's permission to enter. The consent was not forthcoming, so Olan took a long look at his sovereign. It was clear that Zorion was thinking intensely on a matter. He was running his left hand absently through his hair, and his eyes stayed fixed on his Information Terminal. It did not matter to Olan. He would wait until Zorion signaled for him to enter or not. Preoccupied with his work, Zorion waved him inside without looking up.

"Close the door behind you," Zorion paused until no one could hear them, "I need information."

"I have data files full of information, Sir. Tell me what you want to know, and I will get it."

"Early this Terrestrial Revolution, Elzer and I argued. He is not sending us any power. The other rulers, including myself, have given him millions of Sovereign Cubes so that his city could construct new energy consoles to aid in our search for a planet. However, earlier this work cycle, I found out that he did not use the Sovereign Cubes as we intended. Instead, he used them for something else. I want to know where those funds went."

A chill of excitement ran down Olan's spine. He lived to spy. It was the sole reason he worked so hard to become the Chief Administrator of Argi's Intelligence, "This is a delicate operation. First, I will need to recruit someone from within his city."

"Do not bother me with the details. Just get it done," Zorion responded curtly.

"I only meant to make you aware of the risk. If Elzer's Intelligence agency catches our informant, Elzer may find out you are involved. Even without proof, he may still suspect you because of your conversation this work cycle."

I hate politics. "I understand the risk. Just make sure your source does not know whom he or she is working for."

"It will be done."

"I also have another matter."

"Whatever you need, Sir."

"I want you to put an agent on Otsoa. I have reason to believe he is collaborating with traitors. If your spy discovers something, record it and report back to me. Do not engage until we can identify this criminal, and Olan, I expect discretion."

"I will oversee it myself, Sir!"

"Good. Dismissed."

Olan returned to his apartment. In his secure room, he accessed his Information Terminal. A list of potential informants appeared on his monitor. Everyone had a weakness; he just needed to figure it out. Once he found it, they would have to give him the information he wanted. During his search, he found one individual that caught his attention; he had the right job, the right level of clearance, and a family.

Olan knew that exploiting someone with a family made his job less complicated, so he arranged transport to Vlor city. Olan often traveled under a business owner's credentials to keep his identity dependable. His real name and status were only known to Zorion, Broll, and Dolas, Olan's second-in-command. Everyone, including Shilda, believed he was an essential intra-city commodities broker who often traveled to Akil's municipalities.

He changed into a new suit and headed directly to the small restaurant for lunch. His alter ego stayed highly visible to keep his disguise intact. He believed that hiding in plain sight was his best defense. The waitress took him to his usual table in the corner, where he sat with his back against the wall. He could see everyone who entered and left the establishment from this position. A hooded female entered and walked directly to his table as he ate.

He recognized her before she was halfway across the room, "Nayrah, my love, I was not expecting to see you. I left you a message that I would be out of town."

Nayrah kept her face hidden beneath the long hood; her tones were soft so that no one could overhear their conversation, "I got your message. That is why I am here. I want you to cancel the trip."

"I am sorry, but I cannot."

To emphasize her desire for him to stay, she pulled back her hood, slightly exposing her face to him. It was a move he had rarely seen her perform in public. With just a glimpse behind the black hooded curtain, he could see her shoulder-length, dark-black hair. Unlike other females, who kept theirs in a bun, obeying the law, she allowed her hair to hang free, which is a sign of her rebellious character. His eyes moved to hers, and she had the deepest blue irises he had ever seen. Her face was oval, her nose small and perfect, and her lips were full and inviting. Whenever he was around her, she had his full attention.

"Please, Olan," she begged. "I have not seen you in a long time. At least delay it one Terrestrial Rotation. I promise to make it advantageous," the right side of her lip curled upward, creating a devious grin.

Olan smiled in return, knowing her meaning, "Very tempting, my love, but business is business."

Nayrah pouted playfully, keeping her voice to a whisper, "You do not love me anymore."

He gently took her hand, saying, "I do love you, Nayrah, but Argians count on me, so I must go."

"Just delay it one Terrestrial Revolution."

She squeezed his hand, and he felt a warm sensation move through his body. It was a feeling he often had during their encounters. That pleasure made it impossible for him to resist her.

"Very well. I will delay my departure."

"Thank you, my love; I knew you still loved me."

He shoved the last morsel of moss into his mouth with his free hand, swallowed, and left a few Sovereign Cubes on the table. They stood simultaneously and, without another word, left separately. Later, they met in an elevator. It headed down to the lowest level where Nayrah's apartment resided. Olan tried to keep his composure, but the warm feeling grew hot.

Without warning, he backed her against the doors, pulled her hood off, grabbed the back of her hair, and kissed her passionately. They stayed in an embrace until the elevator doors opened, and in the heat of the moment, Olan pushed forward and guided her home. Nayrah walked nimbly backward the entire way without tripping.

Inside, they raced to remove their clothes, and for a few thousand heartbeats, they made love.

Spent and lying on the bed, Nayrah cuddled up beside Olan and drew little figures softly on the skin of his abdomen. Nayrah smiled playfully, watching the bumps rise on his flesh.

"Now remember, you promised to delay your trip."

"I always keep my promises, my love," Olan replied, running his fingers through her hair.

Nayrah smiled, knowing she could still control him.

Chapter 6

Earth
The Regime - Washington, D.C. - Capitol Building
May 7, 2452

Supreme Commander Porter sat at his desk, drinking his morning coffee while reading a compendium of the day's news on the holo-screen, and with no one to bother him, it became his favorite time of day. There were no meetings scheduled and no one to interrupt him, not that the security androids would allow anyone to enter until he activated the access protocol. Locked in his private office, insulated from everyone and everything, he was in a world unto himself. The alarm on his watch beeped. He turned it off. There was no need to look at the time because he knew that it was precisely 9:25 AM. *Time to go to the vault.*

Instinctively, his right hand moved under the desk and hit the hidden button, summoning his private elevator. The camouflaged panels in the wall behind him slid aside as the elevator doors opened. He took a final sip of his coffee and placed the cup on the desk before walking into the mirrored chamber. The rules said that he should take nothing with him except the key. The elevator had sensors. Any other foreign object would keep it from working.

Porter selected the only button available and pressed it. The elevator doors closed, and he descended to a location deep within the Earth. He looked at his reflection in the surrounding mirrors on the way down. It was his style to comb his dark hair back. The gel ensured there was not one hair out of place. In his reflection, he saw his immaculately pressed, gray faux-flannel suit. His hand moved to his tie, but he stopped, seeing no reason to adjust it. The spray tanning kept his skin the perfect shade of bronze without the harmful side effects.

A few minutes later, the elevator stopped. Porter was deep in the ground, below the level that any surveillance could reach. He stepped out as the doors opened and walked down the long, empty, brightly lit corridor to the vault door. There were no identifying marks on it. The metal gleamed with pristine clarity in artificial lighting. It was the one duty he never liked performing. A single panel jutted out from the wall. He placed his hand on it and felt the laser's heat, scanning his palm. The vault door opened. Jay smiled, rubbing his hand. The laser always burned away a layer of skin to ensure against counterfeits.

Entering, he mused about the other man. Only two people on Earth had access to this vault; Jay and his replacement. If anything were to happen to him, someone he did not know was ready to take his place at a moment's notice, just as he replaced his predecessor. It did not bother him because his instructor taught him to follow the rules, and he had to follow them to the letter. If he did not, the council would remove him. *The secrets here are too sensitive to share with anyone. Once they no longer need you, there's no point keeping you around.*

Inside, many folders sat neatly in hundreds of filing cabinets set in several aisles in a vast room. There were no electronic devices down here. The information inside was much too valuable to keep on a server, where it was vulnerable to hackers, or a "magnetic" accident could destroy it. The cabinets themselves were fireproof; the Regime's Founder dated each one by year.

He stopped at the fifth filing cabinet on the left, reaching the middle aisle, with 2452 embossed at the top. He removed the key from his pocket and opened it. Turning, he looked to the right and saw the cabinets labeled 2453, 2454, and 2455 and wondered what was in them, but that was as far as it went. He opened the drawer, removed the file dated May 7, 2452, closed the drawer, locked the cabinet, and left the vault.

The great door swung closed behind him. It would be 24 hours until he could return; those were the rules. He retraced his steps to the elevator and rode back to his office in silence, his mind empty of all thought. The file stayed at his side, unopened. He placed the document in the center of his desk and sat. Yesterday's folder instructed him to open this one precisely at 10 AM. Although the instruction was unusual, it did not come as a surprise. To begin with, the whole idea of the filing system downstairs was abnormal. It took him months to feel remotely comfortable using the information within them.

His watch beeped again, precisely at 10 AM. His index finger slid across the surface until it reached the tab where he opened the folder and read the instructions carefully. As a personal rule, he always read the directions at least twice, ensuring an exact outcome. When dealing with information this important, he vowed to leave nothing to chance. He memorized the letter's orders and pressed the button on his desk that "officially" began his day. With the access protocols enabled, he activated the intercom to his assistant.

"Ms. Bradshaw, please contact Jared and ask him to come to my office."

"Right away, Sir," she answered. "He's already logged into the building. I'll send a messenger droid to track him down. Oh, and I have a Mr. Tim Martin on hold on a secured line, number three. He's very insistent on speaking with you this morning."

"I'll take it." Porter smiled. *Perfect timing.* "Personal secured line number three." He waited for the beep, "Hello, Tim. How are you this fine morning?"

"I'm very well, Supreme Commander," Tim replied.

"How may I help you?

"I have some good news for you."

"I always enjoy good news."

"After the meeting yesterday, each of us read the agreement. We discussed it this morning and voted. I'm pleased to tell you that we have agreed to the terms. We want to move on to the next step."

"That is good news. I'm sending someone to assist you," Porter paused to look at the file. "His name is Jared. He will have a chip with his identity as a Texas businessman with credentials to negotiate trade agreements between certain Texas and Regime business interests. He will be posing as one of yours."

"Understood."

Porter continued to read from the file, "Just before the border crossing at the Sabine River, there is an abandoned gas station on your side. Have someone meet him there at noon."

"I'll be there personally."

"What will you be driving?" Porter asked.

"I'll be in a red SUV. I'll send the details electronically."

"Jared will arrive driving a motorcycle. He'll pull up behind you and flash his lights twice, then twice again. It should keep cameras from placing you two together so close to the border, compromising Jared's cover. I also suggest you drive your vehicles to the hotel."

"Agreed. I'll be there at noon."

"How will you get past the gangs and dissidents?" Porter inquired.

"They usually stick to the main roads, so I've mapped out an alternate route. We'll be taking many backstreets."

"It's a good idea, but Jared will handle it if you run into trouble."

"That's good to know. Thank you."

Porter disconnected and stared at the file because Jared would not have been his first choice for this mission. There are three bionic-enhanced agents, Jared, Oliver, and Vincent. Of the three, he would have preferred Vincent, who was the most cerebral. The last thing he wanted was another Florida incident. It weighed heavily on his mind.

A generation ago, his predecessor bungled, bringing Florida into the Regime. During negotiations, the Regime offered fully paid relocation and compensation to anyone unwilling to live under the new government. They rejected it and formed a resistance. Things turned bloody fast, and many died during the revolution. Porter touched the file gently as if it were an ancient document.

How could my predecessor have screwed up so badly? He would have his files and his orders to follow. Did the Founder want the Florida incident to happen? Granted, because of it, the Regime instituted the 85% rule, but at what cost? His predecessor shredded the orders. It was another rule, one they all had to follow. Still, the question lingered, *did he do what the file instructed? Or did he veer away from its direction? If so, did future documents say this would happen?* Porter started to feel dizzy thinking about it.

*****

The messenger droid found Jared in the gym, squatting a few hundred pounds that rested on his shoulders. An android walked up to him and presented a brief three-dimensional hologram as he pushed the weight upward. The message was from Ms. Bradshaw, informing him to report to the Supreme Commander's office. He acknowledged the summons and got ready. Within twenty minutes, he was in Porter's waiting room.

"The Supreme Commander said to show you right in," Ms. Bradshaw commented.

With a nod, he kept walking but felt a chill seeing the Security Androids. Their life-like appearance always bothered him. Behind the façade of a human face were wires and chips. He would replace them all with real humans if it were up to him. As he stepped inside, Jared's eyes took everything in; nothing had changed since the last time he was here.

Supreme Commander Porter's office was Spartan in its simplicity. Jared saw men, who wielded far less power, occupy incredibly ostentatious spaces; Porter was different. His office only had two large windows looking out at the eastern and western parts of the city. The rest of the room consisted of two wainscoted walls and a mahogany desk with a leather inlay top. It was the most extravagant item in the room, but that was all.

He stood a few feet in front of Supreme Commander Porter's desk. His hands crossed behind his back near his lower spine as he waited for Porter to acknowledge him. Jared stared over his head and noticed a slight discrepancy in the wall directly behind his chair. *Private elevator.* Jared smiled. *All great men have secrets. Discover one, and the rest will fall like dominos.*

Supreme Commander Porter did not stop typing when Jared walked in. He wanted to finish his thought. Afterward, he closed the applications and looked up. Although not his first choice, Porter did appreciate the man's talents. Jared was versatile, athletic, and looked good in a suit. As with all his agents, he knew how to kill in many ways. More importantly, he knew how to make those deaths resemble accidents if necessary. Porter wondered what lay ahead for Jared on this mission.

"Details of your assignment are in this file. Memorize it and give it back to me," Supreme Commander Porter handed him a tablet computer. "You will go to Texas as a citizen. While you're there, if their spies try to hack our servers, there is a backup identity for you. It's all there in the file."

Jared navigated through the tablet pages using his index finger, committing to memory as much as possible. His training improved his ability to memorize information, but he did not have a photographic memory and would forget some details. That was always a risk. A few minutes later, he handed the tablet back to Porter. The two men looked at each other with total understanding. Jared nodded, turned, and left without saying a word.

Chapter 7

Akil
Vlor City
The 22,271st Terrestrial Rotation of the Second Summer

Grox woke securely strapped to a chair in the middle of a small room. The viciously thin restraints bit into his wrists and ankles. He squirmed and twisted, trying to free himself until the cords made his flesh bleed. The chair was on rollers, yet that did not help him because someone secured his ankles to the front legs a couple of finger-widths off the ground. He saw eight metal spheres evenly fastened to the wall in a circle, and a large metal arm hung from the ceiling. He craned his neck from side to side to see what was behind him. As far as he could tell, the room was empty. Three of the walls were black and solid-looking. The room seemed very strange to him.

The wall behind him had a floor-to-ceiling, door-like one-way mirror. He wondered who was watching on the other side. The last thing he remembered was standing on the avenue on the three-hundredth level, waiting for the extortioner in the black cloak to arrive. He risked everything to get the unknown thug the information to save his family, but the other was late. Grox waited a long time and worried that the other would not show.

There were plenty of Vlorians around; he still did not feel safe. Someone bumped into him as he searched the area, and suddenly, everything went black. Grox licked his lips. They were dry and cracked. Dehydration was a sign that he had been unconscious for a long time. *But how long?* His mind was still foggy, making it hard for him to focus. He blinked his eyes, trying to regain clarity, and the door opened.

Grox snapped his head around, "Elzer! Oh, it is you!"

Elzer did not say anything. Instead, he circled Grox twice before stopping to face his captive.

"Please, you must help me," Grox begged.

Elzer removed a small Data Device from his coat pocket, activated the video, and spun it around so that Grox could see. The screen displayed the time, Terrestrial Revolution number, and list of

Sovereign Cube transactions he copied from within the government's database. Grox began to shake nervously.

"Who are you working for?" Elzer asked.

"No one."

"If you do not tell me what I want to know, there *will* be severe consequences."

"I cannot tell you what I do not know."

Unable to look Elzer in the eyes, Grox hung his head in despair. He was not lying. The Akilian who threatened him never gave his name, nor did he see his face. The only thing he remembered was the raspy voice that threatened the lives of his family. At first, he did not believe him until seeing a video of them tied up, just as he was now, convinced him it was not a prank. Their lives were in danger, forcing him to cooperate.

Elzer remained quiet, so Grox spoke, "I am not working for anyone. I promise."

Elzer nodded, "You are brave, Grox, but no one will ever know because I deal with traitors differently from the other sovereigns."

Fear grabbed Grox, who tried to keep it from showing; it felt like his effort had failed. Elzer moved behind him and grabbed the back of his chair. He heard a loud humming, like the sound of electricity running through wires, and the floor shook. The spheres attached to the wall began to glow red, and the metal arm moved. In the end, a laser beam shot out several times in the center of the spheres.

The floor vibrated increasingly violently until a swirling vortex opened within the circle of spheres. On the other side of the event horizon, the scene was horrific. Plasma was falling from the sky, setting the landscape on fire. Akilian-style homes burned as flames lashed out at everything. Citizens were running aimlessly in every direction to find shelter. Some saw the event horizon and jumped with outstretched hands, but it opened too high for them to reach. As others ran, plasma fell on them, disintegrating their bodies instantly. Many were running with burned skin or open wounds, with no one to help them.

"Do you know this place?" questioned Elzer.

Although Grox's eyes fixed on the terrible sight, he heard Elzer's words and shook his head.

"Perhaps I should have said, do you know *when* this place is?" Elzer smiled wickedly.

Baffled by his question, curiosity replaced fear; Grox looked at Elzer and inquired, "What do you mean, when?"

"You are looking at Yovis 5, a quarter of a Terrestrial Rotation before the River of Fire destroyed it."

Turning back to the event horizon, Grox struggled to decide if Elzer was telling the truth, "That is not possible. The River of Fire destroyed Yovis 5 more than sixty yellow harvests ago."

"Oh, it is possible. Anything is possible if you have enough Sovereign Cubes. For this reason, your employer wanted you to gather all that information because I used the funds the other sovereigns gave me to build my own Time Portal Transmitter."

"Are you trying to tell me you built a time machine?" Grox laughed incredulously.

"I think the evidence speaks for itself."

"For what purpose?"

"Power, Grox. Currently, Zorion oversees the science division responsible for finding a new planet. Once he discovers a new world, I will send the coordinates back to myself, build a city there before anyone is the wiser, and rule the new world as the Supreme Sovereign; only those willing to accept my authority will leave this dying ice ball."

"Has your plan worked?" quizzed Grox.

"What do you mean?"

"I mean, your future self should have sent you the coordinates by now, right?"

Elzer frowned, considering his logic, and after careful deliberation, he realized Grox was correct. Although the machine had been operational for just a few Terrestrial Rotations, he should have received a message from himself by now. *What went wrong? Did the sun destroy Akil before we found a new planet?* It was the only logical answer. Angered to know his plan failed, he punched Grox in the mouth.

"Ouch! Why did you do that?"

"Because you have not told me what I want to know. Who hired you to betray me?"

"I did not betray you, Elzer," Grox lied.

Even though he could never name him, if Grox told Elzer the truth that someone was threatening his family, the extortioner would kill them.

"You disappoint me, Grox. I had hoped you would be more cooperative. Now, it is time to die."

"What? Why?"

"A chain is only as strong as its weakest link, so I must remove you, Grox, to make the chain strong again," Elzer pushed the chair forward.

"Please, do not do this!"

"Give me a name; give me something I can use!"

Images of his family held captive flashed in his mind's eyes. Having no choice, Grox had to resist giving any information for their sake. His only hope was that the extortioner would release them because Grox knew Elzer would kill him.

Angered by his circumstances, Grox spat, "I curse you, Elzer! May Gau's judgment fall upon you like the plasma falling from the sky on Yovis 5!"

Elzer laughed, pushing Grox through the event horizon. As the vortex swallowed him, Grox traveled back in time. The sensation of falling made his stomach lurch inside until he hit the ground and toppled over. Elzer watched from his side of the event horizon. Still tied to the chair, Grox rested on his side, struggling against the restraints.

Someone jumped over him, screaming; it was an eerie wail, a high-pitched keen. Others around him were shouting and howling. There was no order as Yovisians were running every which way. Some were on fire. Some had gaping holes in their bodies where the plasma hit them. Smoke filled Grox's lungs, causing him to cough violently. As he struggled against his bonds, trying to free himself, plasma rained down, burning him alive. There was no time to scream. In an instant, he became vapor.

Elzer shook his head with displeasure. *It was too quick, but now the chain is secure again.* Elzer turned and gave the signal for his controllers to close the Time Portal Transmitter. As the machine started to wind down, a large plasma mass hit the event horizon, causing the vortex to explode. The force of the blast hurled Elzer through the one-way mirror, knocking him out.

Later, Elzer woke with members of his staff fussing around him. They were doing something to his arm, or rather, they were doing something to the stub of his arm where his wrist and hand should have been. He tried to sit up, but someone forced him back down, and he felt a mind-numbing pain shooting up his damaged arm and into his shoulder.

Through gritted teeth, he demanded, "The transmitter?"

Disoriented, he found it hard to form the words.

"Destroyed," a voice responded.

Elzer groaned, unable to decide what hurt the most, the pain in his arm or the loss of the Transmitter.

Chapter 8

Earth
The Regime - Washington, D.C. - Fort McNair
May 7, 2452

Having received his new mission, Jared headed straight to Fort McNair to prepare. Over a year ago, Supreme Commander Porter handed him a small palm computer. "Here is your passport to almost anywhere in the world," he had said. Jared never questioned it but occasionally did wonder how Porter collected all the top-secret information given to him. *Can anyone be this good at obtaining so much classified intelligence?*

Although the passport would get him into most countries, it would not help him where he was going. His first task was to create a preplanned means of leaving in a tricky situation for himself, the Texas business owners, and their families. He configured a plan in case something went wrong because they would all have to leave in a hurry. Blending into an extensively watched society was never easy, but there were ways to trick the system.

In Texas, miniature computer chips stored everyone's identity. The government surgically implanted them under the skin near the left shoulder blade at birth. The one he planned to use on the mission had specific features to protect him, so he went to the medical department, where the physician on duty inserted one under his skin, near his left shoulder blade. The process only took a few minutes, so he gathered his things and took them to the Interstate Transportation Station.

The Portal Technician opened the vortex, and Jared stepped through to the Regime satellite base near the border, where he went straight to the garage. Different assignments called for various modes of transportation. The Regime satellite base garage housed an assortment of vehicles. His orders were to travel by motorcycle on this mission, which became the standard transportation mode. He inspected several models and chose a six-cylinder. *You never know when you'll have to run.* Jared checked the tank. It was full.

On the Regime side of the border, they rarely used vehicles that burned fossil fuels. Portal technology and electric-powered hovercraft were the basis of the Regime infrastructure, making paved roads unnecessary. Being near the border meant that the route to Texas had to have blacktop roads connecting the facility to the nearest checkpoint. *What did Jay say in one of his speeches?* Ah, yes: *if you can't keep up with technology, you fall behind.*

The Regime was willing to build Transportation Stations in the western states, but negotiations broke down because the U.S. demanded the schematics. Since the Regime guarded its technology carefully, they could not broker a deal. Jared threw his leg over the saddle, turned the key, and the six-cylinder engine sprang to life. He waited for the engine to warm up and sped away toward Texas. Once free of any restrictions, he hit the throttle.

The front wheel momentarily left the ground as the bike accelerated. Without a windshield, warm air swirled around him. The thermostat on the motorcycle read seventy-three degrees Fahrenheit. Jared smiled. It was a pleasant feeling. An hour later, the Texas mainframe began uploading the signature from the chip in his back. By the time he reached the Logansport checkpoint and the bridge across the Sabine River, the server had absorbed his cover.

Jared approached the Regime sentries that guarded the Louisiana side of the bridge and slowed but did not stop. The scanners sent red light beams across the bar code on his jacket. The green light lit, and he continued to move forward. A drop-arm barred his way on the Texas side of the bridge, so he stopped, and a thin, heavily armored, older man with white hair stepped out of the guardhouse. In his right hand, the man carried a wand to read the computer chip under the skin on his back.

Turning to face him, Jared saw a 9-mm holstered to his waist. He waved a wand over Jared's shoulder, which beeped. They waited for the computer to respond, and Jared started to worry that there might be a problem. If the green light did not show soon, he would have to leave in a hurry. Jared put the bike in first gear, but the light changed from red to green as he was about to hit the throttle and turn around.

"Do you have anything to declare?" the guard inquired.

"Only that they wasted a week of my life."

The guard chuckled, "Welcome home, kid. Drive safe."

Jared gave him a friendly nod and felt relieved, speeding away. Now he knew for sure that the chip in his back worked. It transmitted all kinds of information; some were correct, and some were not. He drove another fifteen minutes and arrived at the rendezvous point. On the side of the road, near an abandoned gas station, he saw the red SUV. He pulled up behind it and flashed his lights twice and then twice again.

Jared could only see the man's eyes in the rear-view mirror. The SUV's engine started and moved forward. The bike's GPS told him they were heading toward Nacogdoches. Initially, gangs and dissidents destroyed the cities and moved to the burbs, but they met resistance. Over time, the citizens abandoned the suburbs, built walls around the municipalities, and rebuilt businesses and homes, leaving the outlaws behind. The barriers protected the cities, and the military moved in with the farmers to defend their food from criminals. It was a never-ending battle between them.

The roads broke down; weeds and grass eroded the pathway. The red SUV took several side streets through deserted neighborhoods, making it a slow journey. Almost every home had visible damage, overgrown lawns, trash, and debris. Even though the houses were dilapidated, he knew that criminals occupied some. They had to be careful. At least it was daylight. The residents were known to be more active at night, so he hoped they were still sleeping.

The driver in the red SUV let off his brakes at the stop sign, so he moved forward. Jared stopped, looked both ways, and followed him. Before he got too far, a vehicle pulled up behind him, raced around, and stopped in his path. Four men jumped out of their car; Jared recognized their tattoos. They were part of the *Diablo* gang. *Damn, I guess there are a few still roaming the streets in the morning.*

In response, Jared shut off the motorcycle and got off. High adrenaline levels automatically triggered his subcutaneous body armor. He could feel the outer layers of his skin tightening into an impenetrable barrier; it was the latest advancement to come out of the Regime research and development. Jared heard that his older brother, Michael, had something to do with it. Jared smiled. None of the men approaching him noticed anything different. Two men had retrieved knives from their belts along the way: the other two held guns.

"What's so funny, cuz?" one of the men asked.

"Nothing," Jared replied.

"My boy here, Miguel; he likes your bike. Why don't you give it to him?"

"I'm using it right now," Jared answered.

"I don't think you need it," Miguel quipped, sitting on the bike. "Give me the keys."

"I suggest you get back in your car and keep moving," Jared warned.

The four men laughed, "If you don't give us those keys, I'll shoot you and take them out of your pocket."

One of the men pointed his gun at Jared. The barrel was only inches away from his forehead. Jared brought his right arm upward in a circular motion, catching the other's arm and pushing it to the side. The gun fired, but the bullet ricocheted off Jared's temple. The slug passed through Miguel's hand and landed in the bike's gas tank. Jared pulled his attacker toward him and hit the underside of his nose with the palm of his hand. The force broke his nose, sending the nasal bone into his brain, killing him.

As his body fell to the ground, the other two men attacked Jared with knives. They sliced and stabbed at him, but they did not draw blood. Using his arms, Jared blocked each attack and countered with his fists. His unyielding body armor enhanced each punch, which wore them out; he twisted the knife from one, grabbed the blade with his bare hand, and used it to slice the man's throat. Jared lunged forward as the other attacker came at him, shoving the knife into his chest. By now, Miguel was off the bike and standing behind Jared. Before he could turn around, Miguel started firing his weapon. The bullets ricocheted off Jared's skin.

"What the hell are you?" Miguel questioned.

"Someone you don't want to mess with," Jared responded.

The red SUV appeared. The driver had circled the block, aimed the bumper at Miguel, and hit him. Miguel flew several feet, landed, rolled to a stop, and did not move.

"Hurry! Get on your bike, and let's get going!" exclaimed the driver.

"I can't. There's a bullet in the tank," Jared nodded toward it.

"Ok, get in before he wakes up!"

"Just let me get my things out of the saddlebags."

Jared sat in the front seat of the red SUV, and the driver sped off.

Seeing his shirt ripped in several places, the driver panicked, "Do you need me to take you to a hospital?"

"No. I'm fine. Just get us out of here."

Once the attackers were no longer in sight, the driver extended his hand, "I'm Tim Martin."

Jared returned his greeting, "Jared Sharp."

His last name was a cover.

"I can send a tow truck to get your motorcycle," Tim offered.

"No. It's not worth risking anyone's life over it," he insisted.

Feeling ravenously hungry, Jared ate one of several high-calorie protein bars; it was the downside of the subcutaneous body armor. As he hastily ate them, Tim looked at him in disbelief.

"I missed breakfast," mumbled Jared between bites.

"That guy must have terrible aim. I heard the shots going around the block. I thought for sure you were dead."

"Yeah, it's a good thing for me that these guys can't shoot."

"The moment we pass the checkpoint, we'll be safe behind the wall. There's no law out here anymore. It's kill or be killed."

"I've noticed."

As they approached the checkpoint, they found a barbed-wire fence, ten feet tall, as far as the eye could see in each direction.

"This is the border between the suburbs and the city," Tim slowed down for the sentry.

A small military force patrolled the city's side of the border. Tim showed the guard his credentials, and the sentry let them through without question. Even from miles away, they could see the city's skyline. An hour later, they were in the shadows of the tall buildings.

"I'm impressed. It used to be a small town," Jared noted.

"Everyone from the nearby suburbs lives here, so we had to build up to make room."

The twenty-story hotel, where they would meet, was the centerpiece of a gated compound that included an 18-hole golf course and European-style fountains. Attractive women, in their swimsuits, walked between the old-style European statues and the day spa. Jared found the surroundings pleasing. It was the perfect cover.

Tim's group rented a large meeting room and passed the assembly off as a marketing development session. The announcement board listed Jared as the guest speaker. Tim parked the car in the garage, took Jared to the front desk, and checked him into his room. Tim signed the book, and Jared smiled. *Tonight, a five-star hotel. Tomorrow, someplace so seedy that I would be better off sleeping outside.* Once in his room, he showered and changed into a black suit, white shirt, and a yellow and light green striped tie. He looked at himself in the mirror. *My image is everything.* Afterward, he met Tim in the restaurant on the first floor.

"Are you still hungry?"

"I could eat a horse," Jared answered.

Tim signaled to the hostess, who showed them to a table near the window, where they had an excellent view of the spa and the lovely women, who were sunning themselves by its edge.

Jared viewed the menu and spoke softly, "I want to check out the conference room before the meeting. The government has them bugged somehow, so I want to find it and set up a counter imaging device."

"A counter imaging device?" Tim inquired.

"Have you ever watched an old, dubbed movie?"

"Not recently."

"It works on the same principle," Jared explained. "During our meeting, we will be saying one thing, but whoever is watching will be hearing different words coming out of our mouths. To them, this will be a marketing meeting in which I will try to sell you and the other business owners on a joint advertising venture, so everything will look like it's on the up and up."

"Do you know where the bug is?"

"Not yet."

The waitress came by, and Jared ordered a steak dinner with all the trimmings.

Tim looked at him in disbelief, "Where do you put it all?"

"I have a good metabolism."

They finished lunch, so Tim took Jared to the meeting room. Jared walked around, moved a chair or two as if setting up for the presentation and kept an eye on his watch. He would appear as an anxious public speaker to any observer, but the clock served a second function. It gave him the location of any hidden electronic bugs.

It did not take him long to find it in the large chandelier that filled about half the ceiling. It was a gorgeous crystal and brass antique, casting a soft light over the whole area. It hung in the center of the room like the clapper of a great bell. The dome-shaped room directed all sounds back toward the chandelier. *Ingenious. There are no safe spaces in this whole room. They can hear every conversation from each nook.*

Jared took the counter imaging device out of his jacket pocket and placed it directly under the chandelier in the table's center. It was about the size of an average billfold. He hid it under the flower arrangement.

Before turning it on, he faced Tim, "This is the prize. The folks at this table will get twenty free minutes of airtime."

He flipped the small switch on the side of the device.

"Airtime?" Tim frowned.

"That was for the benefit of anyone already listening," Jared explained.

It was time for the meeting. Tim escorted Jared to the stage. They sat near the podium and waited for the others to arrive and take their places. Twenty minutes later, the business owners filled the room.

Tim began the meeting, "Friends, today is a new beginning for the citizens of Texas. Only together can we make the needed changes. As you know, the vote to continue seceding from the old union passed unanimously. This vote set things in motion, and now, here to help us continue that momentum, is Jared Sharp of the Regime."

Everyone stood and clapped as Jared went to the podium.

Jared motioned for everyone to sit a few seconds later, "What Tim said is true, but you will need to stick together. The mission we have before us is treasonous. Until we finish, be careful about allowing anyone new into the group. Always be suspicious. You never know if a friend might be a spy. This undertaking will not be easy, but you will have the full support of the Regime if we meet the eighty-five percent threshold.

"If we cannot reach our goal for some reason, the Regime will grant citizenship to anyone who wishes to leave, so from now on, I'll be your spokesman. Most of their attention will be on me and not on you or your families. Tomorrow, I'll meet with Congressman Ron Kelly and ask him to introduce a bill that would allow Texas to divide into five separate states.

"Once this bill passes, and we are sure it will, the Federal Government will challenge it in the courts, taking it to the Supreme Court. We believe the Federal Government will not allow this to happen because it would give Texas eight more seats in the Senate. If the Supreme Court denies the petition, it will nullify and void the agreement that originally brought Texas into the union several centuries ago. Texas would be on legal grounds to legitimately secede," Jared paused as they began to chatter among themselves.

"Why not just put a bill in to secede?" a man yelled.

"Petitioning the government to divide into different states hides our true objective. Your President will see it as a grab for power rather than secession and turn the request down, hoping to resolve our request with bribes or political favors. After the courts reject Texas' petition, the state can legally secede and join the Regime," answered Jared.

"What if he approves it?" another man shouted.

"We'll deal with that situation if it arises; we must stay focused on the main objective for now."

The crowd began to mumble among themselves but quieted down, so Jared resumed, "Once Ron introduces the bill, I'll meet with as many House members as possible to let them know, without divulging any names, that the business owners are in full support of Texas's division. Also, I'll place advertisements in every media format to get public support. In a few days, it'll be on everyone's topic of conversation."

Jared stopped to let another man ask a question.

"What if support doesn't grow for the bill?"

"It will. The points of the ads are twofold. First, they'll say that Texans will be better off if we divide the state. There will be more jobs, more money, and less crime. Secondly, denying our request to divide creates an environment for disappointment, making the people more amenable to a secession message. I'll keep Tim informed of the bill's progress, and he, in turn, will ensure to keep each of you up to date as well.

"One last thing, I suggest you have an emergency travel bag packed. You might need to evacuate in a hurry. Before you leave, aides will distribute a small communicator to each of you in case of an emergency. If you feel that your life is in danger, use it, and we'll help. Thank you, gentlemen," Jared finished his speech.

Before anyone could get up, he motioned for them to stop, "I have one more favor to ask of you. Once I leave this platform, I will walk down to the center table and retrieve a little device that has kept us all safe during this meeting. When I hold it up, applaud."

Chapter 9

Akil
Argi City
The 22,271st Terrestrial Rotation of the Second Summer

Olan followed Otsoa to the elevator and watched him step aboard, it descended, and Olan saw the numbers decrease on the level indicator. The lights burnt out, leaving Olan to figure out which level Otsoa would exit. He plugged into the shaft's board to track him using a hand-held Information Terminal. Before seeing any data, he felt a sharp pain in his lower back, and everything went black.

Otsoa took the elevator down to the lowest level. The doors opened, and cold, damp air encompassed his body, chilling him and making him shiver as he walked out. Most of the lights on this level were either dim or broken. The damp twilight surrounded him. He hated coming down here because it was too quiet for his taste. The only noise he could hear was the faint sound of dripping water.

This level was vacant, except for one Argian who lived here. The darkness gave him an eerie feeling. There were moments in the perpetual twilight it seemed as if he were the only one left alive on the planet. The feeling of loneliness was oppressive. Shaking off the melancholy mood, he moved toward his destination. Plodding along the edge of the avenue, he instinctively put his hand out for the guide rail, which was not there. He forgot they did not install them on the lowest level because there was no ledge to fall off.

He stepped off the boulevard onto the land and looked up. The smell of moss filled the air. It grew wild on the damp soil beneath his feet. Out of thousands of fountains above, excess water leaked and created a thick mist. The haze hung in the air around him, creating a rolling fog that made it impossible to see the next level. Beyond the mist, the entire city of Argi opened in layers, tiers, and causeways. Millions of Argians moved, loved, and lived, and all were invisible to him from where he stood. The cloud absorbed the sounds above, keeping the lowest level in perpetual silence.

He heard the footsteps of bare feet and unsheathed his sword. *Is this a test? Or is there someone out there ready to kill me?* Otsoa trembled, waiting for the attack; it did not come, so he returned to the avenue and ran. His boots hit the solid surface and echoed down the street, making him even more apprehensive. *I am making myself a target!* He ran a few hundred paces and reached his destination, but he stopped to look around before approaching the door, ensuring no one followed him. For a few heartbeats, he held his breath, listening for the sound of bare feet on concrete.

Satisfied that no one followed him, he walked to the apartment door and knocked. Nayrah, his tutor, opened the door for him to enter. Once inside, he bowed to her and stepped aside as she closed and locked the door. As he watched her, a childhood memory came to mind. Thea delivered him to a sentry he never saw again and handed him sealed orders. The guard opened them, read them, and nodded to Thea. Otsoa remembered her taking him by the shoulders and telling him about the personal training his new instructor would give him, teaching that she did not want Zorion to discover.

He did not understand why at first. Zorion taught him how to fight and how to rule the city. What more was there to learn? However, he found out that Zorion's ways were not Nayrah's. Forced to keep his new instructor a secret, Otsoa began learning the art of deception and lies on an unimaginable level. On one fateful Terrestrial Revolution, he tried his newly developed talents on her; she discovered his duplicity.

An invisible set of hands lifted his body and thrust him against the wall; it was a painful lesson that had made an indelible impression upon him. Nayrah held him, suspended with his feet dangling in the air, and revealed her Skean identity. At first, he did not believe her because Zorion said they were a myth, but the invisible force holding him against the wall convinced him. Although that was long ago, he remembered it as if it had just happened.

"Someone followed you," she looked at him indifferently.

Otsoa spun around and drew his sword.

"Not here, you idiot! On the upper level, before you had entered the elevator!"

"Oh, I am sorry. I heard footsteps on the walkway," Otsoa replied, embarrassed.

"Those were mine. I just returned from the upper level, where I prevented your pursuer from following you here."

"Who was it? Tell me, and I will remove his head."

"I took care of it, but you must be more careful in the future. Remember the lessons I taught concerning pursuers."

"Yes, Nayrah. I will wear disguises and change my appearance several times before committing to this level."

"Speaking of appearances, did you complete the task I gave you?"

"Yes. Yanamai did not know it was me," Otsoa smiled proudly.

Nayrah's expression did not change. She looked forbidding. Her straight, dark black hair framed her pale oval face, making her look alien, and her piercing blue eyes had power behind them. Otsoa was twice her size but often lacked the strength to look directly at them, so he faced the floor. Whenever they met, she always wore the same thing; a black, hooded cloak draped over a black shirt and pants, which only added to her dark aura. Even more puzzling was that she had a strangely seductive air about her. The thought made him shudder.

"I do not trust you, so repeat to me what you told her," Nayrah demanded.

Otsoa looked at his hand, "I told her to search in sector 1-5-6-9-2-4-1."

Nayrah's eyebrows furrowed, processing his response. "What did you say?"

"1-5-6-9-2-4-1."

"You fool! I said 1-5-8-9-3-9-1!"

"No…no…it cannot be. I wrote it down on my hand. See," Otsoa held his palm out to show her.

Nayrah glared at the smudged numbers. Not only did Otsoa have poor handwriting; he wrote them on the creases of his palm, which changed three of the digits. She felt rage building within her but smiled to hide it, took his hand, and crushed it using her power. Otsoa screamed in pain and fell to his knees. Nayrah let go and paced, leaving him holding his shattered hand and weeping.

"Now, I must find another way to get them to search in that sector. I cannot believe you messed this up!"

"Please forgive me, Nayrah," he wept softly.

Seeing him humbled touched something deep inside her; she felt pity and did not understand why. He messed things up so horribly that he deserved severe punishment. The only way she could fix it was to drug Yanamai and force her to remember the numbers correctly. Even with her abilities, getting to her home would be a challenge. Having decided to remedy the situation herself, she felt her anger dissipate and experienced an uncharacteristic emotion in its place, compassion.

"Never mind. I will deal with it another way. Now give me the pheromone suppressant," she demanded with her hand out.

Otsoa used his other hand to retrieve it and gave it back to her. She was about to dismiss him but stopped.

"I just realized something. It is the first time someone has followed you, and right after you tried to complete the task I gave you. It can only mean one thing."

"What is that?" Otsoa inquired nervously.

"Zorion knows it was you. You failed to give Yanamai the correct sector, and you did something else to alert him of your presence."

"I left before he arrived, just you like said."

"No, you did something wrong. Tell me. Remember, half-truths and lies will only increase the pain level of your punishment."

Otsoa lowered his head and told her about his conversation with Yanamai.

"You idiot! Zorion would never ask her to speak with you! Also, he would never ask her to do it as a personal favor!"

"I just want to apologize to her before I go on with my life."

"I have told you, repeatedly, to forget about Yanamai. I have seen your future with her, and it ends badly for you."

"Please, I must speak with her one more time before I accept another."

"Perhaps I am wasting my time with you," she tapped her chin with her index finger, contemplating.

The unknown scared him. *What happens to me if I can no longer be a benefit to her?*

He answered nervously, "No, Nayrah, you are not."

"I have told you before you will never join houses with Yanamai. She is not for you."

"Then, who?"

"That is none of your concern!"

"I must know."

Nayrah walked over, grabbed the hair on the back of his head, yanked hard downward, and glared into his eyes, "I see many futures, Otsoa. One of them is where you continue to pursue her. Gau will cut you asunder if you follow that path, and I cannot stop him, so you better grasp the importance of what I am telling you. Leave Yanamai alone!"

"I wish I could stop, I want to stop, but I cannot; I love her."

Her patience with him had run dry, so Nayrah made a clenching motion with her hand, and Otsoa felt all the air leave his lungs. It felt like a big band wrapped around him as he suffocated, squeezing so tightly that his abdomen could not move.

"You will join houses with whomever I tell you. Love has nothing to do with your future," she spat through gritted teeth.

He started to turn blue, so she released him. Otsoa gasped loudly and breathed deeply for several heartbeats.

Once his breathing returned to normal, he lowered his head in defeat, "With whom do you want me to join houses?"

Nayrah knelt and, with a gentle smile, Otsoa rarely saw on her, lifted him back to his feet. Otsoa, still trembling, sat in a chair. Nayrah stood behind him and brought his head to her bosom to comfort him, as a mother would her child.

"I understand the pain of wanting something or someone you cannot have, but you must be strong," she paused to move in front of him, looked directly into his eyes, and continued, "If you pursue Yanamai, you will die. I do not want that to happen."

"Please, take my desire for her away from me," he pleaded.

"That is something I cannot do. Skeans are not permitted to love, so we know little about it," lamented Nayrah, fighting back tears.

"I am doomed because I cannot help how I feel about her."

"Listen to me!" she exclaimed. "I have chosen someone for you. She is even more beautiful than Yanamai. Give her a chance to win your heart, and in time, you will love her more than Yanamai. Choose that path, and you will live to rule Akil. Stray from it, even a little, and you will die a horrible death."

"Tell me what to do."

The corners of her lips curled into a smile, but only for a moment, "At your celebration, you will have ten eligible females to choose from."

"Ten?" Otsoa looked bewildered.

"Of course. Why do you doubt yourself?"

"It is a very high number."

"You are a noble and the future sovereign of Argi. Those of my gender crave power as much as yours, so pay attention. Among them, there will be one that stands out. Her name is Durnah. She is the most beautiful Argian in the city, and I picked her just for you. Her skin is light brown and without blemishes. Her hair is pure white. It is softer than the finest moss-cloth made, and…," she paused to look at him. Her smile widened, "Her eyes are maroon. The combination is rare among Akilians."

Otsoa forced a smile, "I will choose her and hope that I will grow to love her in time."

He stood and walked to the door, unwilling to give her another reason to injure him.

"Otsoa."

Otsoa stopped and, without turning around, responded, "Yes."

"I will be watching."

Otsoa did not turn to look back at her; he did not have to because her words hung like the dark, looming fog outside, "I understand."

Outside, he was happy to be absent from her presence. Nayrah headed for her kitchen but stopped because the video com beeped, and with a slight motion of her hand, it came on.

"Hello, sister," Kemena began.

"What is it? I am busy," Nayrah answered.

"Have you meditated on future events recently?"

"Why? Is there something wrong?"

"Domeka contacted me earlier this Terrestrial Rotation and said that while in a trance, something odd happened. Her visions of one single event changed repeatedly."

"Impossible."

"Perhaps you will have success where others have failed."

Nayrah closed her eyes and used the Night Lord's power to bring up a vision of the future. At first, she saw the expected, what they had been working toward for many yellow harvests, and just as Kemena said, it suddenly changed from one outcome to another. Multiple fates of a single event rolled through her mind's eye, but what frightened her the most was the one where she and the other Skeans were no longer alive, and another different destiny appeared where she saw the destruction of Akil.

Lastly, another fate passed before her, and she saw someone, with eyes as black as the universe itself, standing before her, holding Gau's sword. That vision made her tremble, but none of the images stayed in her mind long enough to understand what caused the change or how she could control it. Frustrated, she turned her attention back to Kemena on the video com.

"What is causing this?" Nayrah queried.

"It can only mean one thing."

"A Saiph? Are you sure?"

"Has anything changed in your city that could cause this kind of interference?"

Nayrah shook her head, "Nothing comes to mind."

"I will speak with Gecheana and ask for guidance."

"Let me know how she wants to proceed."

Kemena nodded and disconnected.

"Do you think a Saiph is on Akil, Nayrah?"

Turning, Nayrah saw a younger version of herself standing in the kitchen. It was her daughter, Jadell. Nayrah had trained Jadell to eavesdrop on conversations but warned her not to use that talent against her. *I wonder what other abilities she has used against me without my knowledge.*

"It seems so," Nayrah answered.

"I will kill this Saiph when we find him or her!" Jadell exclaimed.

Nayrah bit back a chuckle, "Do not be too eager to face one, Jadell, especially alone. From the stories Gecheana has told me, they are very formidable."

"Certainly, there are enough Skeans on Akil to destroy one Saiph."

Nayrah could hear the contempt in her voice, "Having never faced one, I could not say. All I know is that we must prepare ourselves and be diligent. Only together do we have a chance to defeat one."

Chapter 10

Earth
The Regime - Washington, D.C. - Fort McNair
May 7, 2452

Michael pushed back from his computer console and banged his fists on his thighs in frustration. "I'm not going to let some damn microscopic bit of organic technology beat me!" Thankfully, there was no one around to hear his tantrum. He looked at the clock, it was a few minutes past 6 PM, and everyone else in the lab had left for home an hour ago. Michael stayed behind to work on a project as a personal favor for Supreme Commander Porter.

It was one thing to have the General hanging over his shoulder, waiting for results. It was quite another to have the Supreme Commander of the Regime doing it. A team discovered the micro-organisms on Mars during the last shuttle mission. At first, they seemed like the average, run-of-the-mill bacteria until he found that the organisms had a strange way of communicating. No matter how he divided them up and hid them around the building, they always found their counterparts.

Supreme Commander Porter wanted Michael to discover their connection. He almost figured it out before noon, but the test results came back negative just now.

"Miserable little sons-of-bitches," Michael mumbled under his breath.

In frustration, he hit the escape button, and a photo of him and Chu Lian appeared on his screen. All his anger with the micro-organisms evaporated in the painful memory of their relationship. He stared at the photo and remembered the exact moment Alex snapped the picture.

"Come on, Mike. It'll be the first photo of you without your glasses," Alex teased.

"It still feels strange not having to keep pushing the frames back up my nose," Michael remarked.

"You look so much more handsomer," Chu Lian tripped over her English.

"I could never have done it without your support," Michael offered.

"Yep. I will call this one 'Mike comes out of his shell,'" Alex joked, triggering the camera.

I didn't even know I was in a shell until she came into my life. Look at my hair. Was it her idea or mine to change styles?

Michael stood, stretched, and walked around the lab to clear his head. It did not work. Thoughts of Chu Lian always pushed everything else out of his mind. Looking back at the photo, he wondered if it was before or after dinner. She had prepared a traditional Chinese meal for him. He remembered how beautiful she looked that evening. She wore a Chinese dress that clung to her figure, and her straight, long black hair hung to the middle of her back. The outfit was red silk, not the faux silk that became all the rage, but the real thing. Also, the red was so deep that the color alone mesmerized him.

"You look enchanting tonight," he remembered saying, walking into her apartment.

"Thank you. You look handsome yourself," Chu Lian smiled.

"Yeah, right, I always look handsome in my lab coat and work clothes. I wish you would have given me time to change. I want to look my best for you."

"I wanted you to come over as soon as possible. I missed you."

"Really?" he asked, genuinely perplexed. "We were together just last night."

"Do you question my affection for you?"

"No, I'm just surprised, that's all."

And he was. No one ever paid this much attention to him, except his younger brother, but it wasn't the same, not even close.

"Didn't you miss me at all today?" she inquired.

"Of course, I did. Hey, something smells good," he tried desperately to change the subject.

"That is our dinner," she noted, briskly walking into the kitchen. "Please, have a seat at the table. I'll be right in."

He sat, remembering how the assorted flowers at the center of the table scented the room with their fragrance, and together with the candles, they created an atmosphere that made him nervous and excited. A few moments later, she returned with a teapot, poured some into a small cup, and set it before him. He remembered taking a sip and could almost sense the flavor still on his tongue. "Delicious." In his mind's eye, he could see her smile.

"I've prepared Kung Pao chicken, noodles, and an assortment of other dishes. I hope you'll enjoy it."

"I'm sure I will."

She brought several bowls filled with various foods and put a small sample of each onto his plate, "Please, eat."

Michael sat back in his chair several helpings later and grabbed his belly, "I can't eat another bite."

She smiled, "I'm glad you're pleased with the meal."

"Are you kidding? It was the best I've ever had."

"If you have finished eating, let's go into the living room and have a drink."

He waited on the couch as she went to the kitchen to retrieve a liquor bottle. She returned to the living room, and he watched her intently. She was so beautiful that it was hard not to stare; she sat across from him and poured them a drink.

"You look ravishing." *Could I have said anything more stupid?*

"Thank you. A girl can't hear those words enough."

Her smile, the way she played with her hair, and the sensual curve of her hips against the silk dress haunted him.

He remembered gushing, "I thought that maybe we could take some time off and go somewhere together."

"Where would you like to go?"

His words came out so fast; they almost ran together, "Everywhere, anywhere, as long as we're together, it doesn't matter to me. You are the most beautiful woman in the world, and I want to be by your side forever."

Her response confused him because she twitched. At that moment, he thought his presumption had just blown it. He remembered thinking that he should have kept his mouth shut because everything was going great. Frustrated, he reached over for the drink she poured for him. Unable to look at her and contemplate his stupidity, he closed his eyes and started to toss back the liquor, but the glass never reached his lips because she slapped it out of his hand.

"Why did you do that?"

"Did you mean what you said?"

"Yes, I did."

"Tell me exactly how you feel about me."

As the blood rushed to his face, he felt hot, "The last few months have been incredible. I've never been this happy before. When we're together, I feel alive; I feel whole. I think of you at work. I think of you at home. I think of you all the time, so I guess what I'm trying to say is, I love you."

Fear made his heart race, and he could hear the blood pumping through his eardrums. Never had he been that scared. She was his first real relationship, and he was sure his confession ruined any chance of it moving forward, but to his surprise, she pulled him close and kissed him. The move caught him off guard.

He stared at her eyes on the computer screen, continuing to think of her. The high-definition image gave them a life-like, three-dimensional quality, making the memory seem recent. It was like being in the room with her at that very moment. He could feel her hand guiding him to her breast, and her soft lips pressed firmly against his. She tasted sweet and minty. Soon, they were in the throes of passion. Later, they lay alongside each other in a warm embrace, panting from their physical expressions. He took a deep breath, remembering his content feelings for her.

The computer beeped, and her image faded from the screen as the latest figures from his running experiment replaced the photo with their cold calculations. With a loud sigh, he scanned through the results. There was nothing new, so Michael programmed the next experiment stage and returned to his apartment.

Feeling restless, he changed into his workout clothes and walked to the sparring room. The area was empty, except for a series of androids sitting rigidly against the wall. He set his bag down in a corner, took off his warm-up jacket, and removed a training sword off the rack. It was a light, sharp-pointed dueling sword-like weapon, about three feet long, stiff, and not whippy. He warmed up by executing a couple of practice lunges to stretch out his muscles and approached the application interface.

He punched in his code, "Computer, start android six-three-seven-five, level one fencing."

The human-like machines stood six feet tall, but only one moved and walked to the floor's center. It bowed to him. Michael looked at its face and could tell that it was a newer model because the rubber skin looked more realistic than in the earlier version. Out of habit, Michael bowed to his opponent. Before beginning, he checked his sword to ensure it was functioning correctly. If it contacted the skin or synthetic latex in the android's case, the blades gave the opponent a small electrical shock. Of course, the android would not feel any pain, and at level 1, Michael would only feel a little jolt from the touch.

Although tempted to apply a higher setting and thereby get a more substantial shock, in the end, common sense won out, and he decided against it. *What's the use of torturing myself? I'm not good at this, not like my brother. Damn, he could do anything after setting his mind toward something. At least everyone is eating, so they won't see me make a fool of myself.* Satisfied that his sword was in working order, he put himself in the '*en garde*' position, "Begin."

The android came alive. Its eyes brightened at the command. It even seemed to smirk as if it enjoyed fighting, causing Michael to swear at the programmers. *They made this version too damn human.* The android came at Michael with a slow basic attack. Michael moved to defend but found himself off balance. *Parry, parry, cut, thrust.* He concentrated on his footwork and remembered watching his brother work out.

For the first three years of training, the instructor did not allow him to touch a weapon until he had good footwork. Michael changed his center of balance and launched three quick attacks. The android blocked each one. *Damn, I used to be better than this. I used to survive level two, and here I am, beaten on level one.* Michael did not want to think about the nineteen other difficulty levels, but he did. The momentary loss of concentration cost him. The android countered Michael's thrust and attacked his defense, scoring a point on his left shoulder.

"Ouch!" Michael yelled.

"Sorry, Sir. Your guard was down," the android noted.

Its mouth moved as it talked, which was an upgrade from the earlier version.

"I know; it was my fault."

"Indeed, it was, Sir."

Michael incredulously frowned, "I guess they programmed you with a smart mouth too."

"My software has twenty distinctive sword fighting techniques and ten unique styles of martial arts skills, but none of them refer to the smart-mouth artistry. Is that something I should ask my programmer to update in my system for our next encounter?"

Its response made him smile, "No, it was just a figure of speech."

"I see, Sir."

"Begin!" Michael shouted and attacked at once.

The android software enabled it to be ready for attacks that start if an opponent gave a surprise command. The android parried Michael's strike with little effort and responded in kind. Within a couple of minutes, the android scored on Michael again.

"I can't believe this! I used to score a lot more on level one!" Michael yelled in frustration.

The android froze for just a moment, its eyes staring blankly ahead as if it had lost power, and it came to life again, "This is true, Sir, but it has been six months, twelve days, three hours, fifteen minutes, and twenty-nine seconds since your last practice. My programming tells me that humans tend to lose speed and strength if they do not exercise regularly."

Irritated, Michael hung his head in shame; it was hard to believe that the android was correct and had him down to the second. Since Chu Lian left him, he neglected everything and everyone, including himself. For the following hour, Michael sparred. It was a never-ending session of humiliation. Exhausted, he decided to end the match. The android printed out his score on the monitor, which Michael erased before anyone saw it.

"I recommend another session tomorrow, Sir," the android advised, returning to his seat.

Michael shook his head, remembering the score. The android tallied forty hits to Michael's five. *I just gave the most pathetic display on record. I should come back tomorrow, or I'll never get past level one.* He returned to his apartment to shower and change. Before finishing, he heard someone knocking and went to answer it with a towel wrapped around him.

"Good! You're almost ready," Alex smiled expectedly.

"Right, I'm almost ready for bed," Michael frowned, looking at Alex quizzically.

"Bed? It's only eight o'clock!"

"I have a lot of work to do tomorrow."

"I was hoping you would come with us tonight, but if you're too tired."

"Us?"

"Yeah, me and Rachael."

"I appreciate it, Alex; I'm not interested in being a third wheel."

"We've invited a friend," Alex tempted.

"Oh great, another blind date. I'm sure you'll have both women in your arms by the end of the evening. Meanwhile, I get to pay the bill. No, thanks."

"Look, buddy, I'm sorry about that. We just clicked. Come on. Let me make it up to you. I promise this woman has no interest in me."

"What's wrong with her?"

"Nothing, she's from the immigration district," Alex explained.

"Look, I'm done with blind dates."

"How about this? I'll talk to Rachael, and you get ready. I'll have her tell Mai it's not a date; we'll consider it a casual get-together."

"Again, I don't feel like it."

"No," Alex spoke defiantly.

"What do you mean, no?"

"I mean, no. You will change and leave with me once you're ready," Alex urged.

Michael raised his eyebrow.

"I mean it, Mike. You're coming with me. I must insist."

"You're acting strange tonight."

"I've talked to Mai. She's pretty and nice, and I think you two will hit it off. I want you to be happy."

Since Alex would not take no for an answer, Michael sighed loudly, "Fine, just give me a few minutes to get ready."

"Great! You won't regret it!"

"I already do."

Michael and Alex went downstairs to the Interstate Transportation Station. Alex typed in the address, and they walked through the event horizon. Alex rented a Hover Taxi just outside the terminal to take them to Rachael's home. She lived in an old-fashioned, bungalow-style house, surrounded by various brightly colored flowers, bushes, and trees. Alex knocked. A few seconds later, Rachael answered. Michael tried not to stare; it was difficult. His eyes inconspicuously ogled at her tight-fitting, purple dress that ended about mid-thigh. It was short-sleeved and off the shoulders. Michael turned away as Rachael gave Alex a quick kiss on the lips.

"Any problem finding my place?" Rachael asked.

"No problem at all. Did Mai arrive yet?" Alex inquired.

"Yep, here she is now."

Hearing that his blind date was approaching, Michael cringed but turned to look. Standing in the doorway was a stunning woman with straight dark hair below her shoulders. In contrast to Rachael, Mai wore low-rise jeans and a shirt with one button between her breasts, exposing her navel and most of her upper chest; he also noticed that she looked like Chu Lian. *Did Alex find her doppelganger on purpose?*

"You must be Michael," she smiled and walked toward him with her hand extended.

Michael returned her greeting, "It's a pleasure to meet you."

"Where are you taking us tonight?" quizzed Rachael.

"Have you heard of the Rave Club?" Alex responded.

"I thought we would have dinner somewhere within the Inner Circle District," Michael suggested.

"We can always stop by on the way home. I think music and dancing are more fun. Don't you?" Alex faced Rachael.

"It's fine by me," Rachael agreed.

"I heard there's a waiting list to get in there," Mai warned.

"I know one of the bouncers. He'll get us in," Alex assured them.

Michael looked at Alex quizzically, "Who?"

"It's no one you know. Now, shall we?" Alex extended his elbow for Rachael to take.

Not willing to spoil everyone else's evening, Michael went along with Alex's plan. The taxi returned them to the Interstate Transportation Station. They took the standard route to the nightclub, but a line extended down the walkway and around the building. Alex walked up to the security guard and gave his name. He scanned the list on his tablet and let them in. Alex extended his hand, and the guard shook it; Michael noticed a Regime Talon in his grasp.

"Where did you meet this guy?" Michael questioned.

"Where do you think? Here, of course. They're very appreciative if you tip them."

Inside, the music was deafening. It was so loud that Michael could feel the bass drum pounding against his chest. As the group walked toward the bar, everyone looked for a place to sit, but no seats were available. However, there were shelves fastened against one of the walls. People who could not find seats stood near them, using the ledge to hold their beverages. Seeing an open spot, Alex asked the girls to claim their place while they got their first round of drinks.

Alex and Michael approached their spots; Alex carried two beer bottles, and Michael had two mixed drinks with little umbrellas at the top. Alex rolled his eyes, but Michael insisted it was what Mai ordered. Alex and Rachael took a few sips of their drink and headed out to the dance floor, leaving Michael uncomfortably alone with Mai. Although it felt awkward, Michael summoned the courage to start a conversation.

The music was booming, so he shouted near her ear, "How long have you been in the immigration district?"

"A couple of months."

"You don't have an accent, so you must be from one of the western states."

"Yes, California."

"Why did you leave?"

"It's a long story."

"Oh, that's all right. You don't have to tell me."

"I don't mind; I just don't want to bore you."

"I would like to know."

"Sure, but remember, you asked. My dad worked for a company in China. They opened a satellite business in the U.S. and sent him there to work; he brought my mother and me. I was only two years old at the time. Everything was wonderful until I turned sixteen; they died in a car accident."

"I'm sorry. That must have been horrible to deal with."

"Yes, it was. I ended up in foster care, and it should not be a surprise that no one wanted to adopt a sixteen-year-old girl. Most couples want babies. A few years later, I left and worked different jobs here and there, whatever I could find, but employment is scarce, and I found myself living on the street."

"Wow! You've had a hard life."

"Things *were* bad until I met Erica. She identified herself as a Regime scout."

"I've heard about that program. Scouts look for people throughout the world who are seeking a new beginning. It's perilous. I've heard that if caught, the country they are in will charge them with espionage."

"I wouldn't be surprised, but I'm glad she found me. She completed a background check and invited me to live in the Regime. Now that I'm here, things are starting to look good for a change."

"I'm very happy for you," Michael smiled.

The loud thumping noise stopped, and a slow song began to play. Mai smiled, took his hand, and led him onto the dance floor.

"I have to warn you. I'm not a good dancer," informed Michael.

"You'll do fine," she guided his hands to her lower back.

The move reminded him of Chu Lian. She put her arms on his shoulders and looked up at him with a smile. Michael politely smiled in return. A few moments later, he found the situation too intimate and decided to look over her shoulder at the crowd.

"Alex told me about your break-up," Mai probed.

"How *much* did he tell you?" Michael inquired.

"That you're taking it pretty hard. He says you're still in love with her."

"I thought she was *the* one."

"I get it. It's never easy getting over your first love."

"Is it that obvious?"

"Hey, everyone has been where you are. What you're going through is normal."

"Thanks, I needed to hear that."

"Alex tells me I look a little bit like her. Is that true?"

"You look a lot like her. I hope that wasn't too weird."

Mai chuckled softly, "No, not at all. I brought it up. As I said, Alex told me about your situation."

"Why on Earth did you agree to go out on a date with me? It's obvious that I'm damaged goods."

"Oh, you're not damaged. You're just hurting. Besides, Rachael showed me a picture of you. I thought you were cute, and even though you're still having difficulties letting go of her, I believe if the right person comes along, you might be able to forget her."

"Ah, so I'm a project," Michael smiled knowingly.

Mai chuckled again, "You're reading too much into it."

He briefly allowed himself to indulge in the fantasy of being with Mai. There were subtle differences between her and Chu Lian; there were also enough similarities that Mai could be her sister. He was unsure if it was good or bad because it would be easy to confuse them. He allowed her to pull him close. Their bodies pressed together and swayed to the music. The smell of her hair, the warmth of her body, and her skin were familiar; it felt too good to be true. The song ended, so he looked at her again, but her smile faded into a frown.

"What's wrong?"

"Someone I know just saw me and is coming over. Please, Michael, go back to our spot. I'll be there shortly."

Michael turned and saw a huge man approaching.

"Hurry, Michael, before he gets here."

"That's all right. I won't leave you."

Mai sighed, knowing what was about to happen.

"Mai Li. Is that you?" the man shouted, with a thick southern accent. He stopped a few feet from her, "Yep, that *is* you! I didn't know you made it to the Regime!"

"Hello, Max. I didn't realize you made it here either," Mai cringed.

"Awe, is that any way to greet a friend?" smirked Max.

"We were never friends," she insisted. "Now, if you don't mind, I would appreciate it if you would leave us alone."

"Us?" he looked down at Michael. "He can wait. You have a debt to settle with me first."

"I'll get security," Michael started to leave.

Max grabbed him with thick, beefy hands, "You ain't goin' nowhere; Mai and I go way back."

Michael struggled against his grip, but Max was too big and strong for him to outmaneuver.

"Let go of him, Max!" Mai yelled.

"Hey, there's no need to get upset. All I want is a refund," he paused, faced Michael, and continued, "You see, me and Mai here had a business arrangement. I gave her money for a certain service, which was interrupted by the pole-ice." He paused to face Mai and continued, "Now, I don't blame you for the raid, darlin', but I do believe I'm entitled to a full refund."

"If you want money, I'll get you your money; just let him go!" Mai screamed.

Max looked at her expectedly and put his other hand out, "Where is it?"

"I don't have that much on me. Just meet me here tomorrow, and I'll bring it."

Max laughed, "Oh, no. I'm sorry, darlin'. I don't trust ya."

"Max, if you don't let him go, I will call the police myself."

Outsized and outmatched, Michael remembered something his brother, Jared, told him. With all his might, he kicked Max squarely on the shin. Max grunted in pain but did not release Michael from his grip. Instead, Max threw Michael toward the bar like a rag doll. Michael hit the counter and then the floor. Max walked over, picked Michael up, and set him on his feet.

Dazed, Michael did not see the punch coming. Max struck him on the top left corner of his left eye, and the force of the blow bounced Michael against the table. Alex appeared and delivered a high soccer-style kick right in the middle of Max's back. Max buckled to the floor. Alex helped Michael up, and the two started for the exit.

Rachael met them on the way and got on Michael's right side to help him walk. Max struggled to his feet, turned, and shouted obscenities at Michael and a few threats. Before he could do anything else, Mai returned with Security. She pointed at Max, and they tackled him to the floor. Michael, Alex, and their dates left before the police arrived.

Alex stopped to look at Michael's injuries outside, "You should see a doctor. You're bleeding. You need to put accelerant on it," Alex warned.

Michael shook his head and slurred, "Just get me back to the Research Lab."

"Oh, Michael. I'm very sorry," Mai apologized.

Michael nodded but did not say anything.

"Please, let me explain," Mai begged.

"Don't," Michael interrupted her.

They made their way in silence to the Interstate Transportation Station. Alex tried again to talk Michael into seeing a doctor or even a medical droid, but he refused. Alex dialed the Research Lab's address, and Michael walked to the other side without any help; he did not bother to wait for Alex. Instead, he closed the portal behind him, cutting off Alex as he apologized to their dates. Standing alone in the Interstate Transportation Station, Michael left the terminal before Alex could redial the address and limped back to his apartment. *No more blind dates.*

Chapter 11

Akil
Argi City
The 22,271st Terrestrial Rotation of the Second Summer

Yanamai finished triple-checking the last of the calculations needed to start their search of sector 1-5-6-9-2-4-1. Satisfied with her computation, she told Tadra to begin. The goal was to extend a robotic arm through the event horizon into the region's center. They fastened a pod consisting of a high-definition camera and long-range sensors at the end of it. They programmed it to take detailed, high-definition images and record a battery of tests that would help them detect any planet that could support their life form. Tadra ran a final diagnostic on their instruments to ensure everything was working correctly. The launch was ready, so she signaled Yanamai.

"Clear the room," Yanamai ordered. Everyone left, so she closed the door, sealed the chamber, and turned to Tadra, "Engage the shield."

Chills ran down her spine as she heard the electromagnetic field activate around the launch room, creating an invisible shield. Opening a portal in space was incredibly dangerous. Currently, they were pumping all the air out of the room, so Yanamai could open a vortex, allowing Tadra to send the long mechanical arm out into space. The computer accumulated information as the machine pointed the camera lens in every direction. It even moved underneath and behind the event horizon. It allowed her to document everything at a 360-degree angle from the destination point.

The process took one-third of a work cycle to complete, and she always worried about the shield failing while the portal was still open. Even though they sealed the door to the launch room, accidents had happened where the atmosphere vented out into space. Redundant safety measures protected the lab technicians at the time, but what *terrified* her was stardust.

She knew if space debris, whether large or small, moving at about the speed of light passed through the event horizon, it would slam into her lab, causing catastrophic damage. Anyone in the vicinity would be in danger. If the debris was large enough, it could even destroy their portal machine, leaving them stranded on Akil to die. Finally, the shield was in place, and all the air was out of the room. Now it was time for Yanamai to open a vortex. She had been charging capacitors for several Terrestrial Rotations, but since the destination was on the other side of the galaxy, her team used four backups to reach the landing site.

Yanamai initiated the portal. Power flowed through cables to the metal spheres, causing the floor to vibrate. The vortex opened with a clap of thunder. The monitor showed the event horizon as it formed. *If we return to this area, I must find a way to reduce that noise.* The camera's eye and sensors on the pod pointed toward the opened portal into unexplored space.

The sheer, raw beauty of the universe fascinated her. Yanamai could see countless stars forming an almost unbroken line across the horizon of her vision. *Incredible.* Satisfied they were not in any immediate danger, she executed the exploratory application that directed the mechanical arm. The pod moved into position, and the camera and sensors sent back information.

"Keep an eye on the shield power; if it tips over the line, we must shut it down before it collapses," Yanamai warned.

Moving to another console, she started the analysis application. It was another one of her creations, which electronically distributed the information from the probe to two hundred scientists. Garbi, her sister, was one of them. For a moment, she thought about Garbi. Yanamai envied her because she would receive part of this data before anyone else on Akil, including her.

Everything was running as expected, so Yanamai faced Tadra, "Let me know when the exploratory application finishes."

Tadra nodded.

Yanamai left the room to complete her other duties as Chief Administrator, and a third of a work cycle later, Tadra knocked on her office door.

"Come in," Yanamai responded, not even looking up to see who it was.

"My team retrieved the pod and closed the portal," Tadra paused, "Mission accomplished."

"Good," Yanamai nodded.

"Now, it is time to get ready for Otsoa's celebration," Tadra cautiously prodded.

Yanamai sighed, "Yes, I am painfully aware, but thank you for reminding me."

"I do not understand why you are going. You have made every effort to avoid him, and now that he is of age, you are attending his celebration?"

"I have my reasons. I am sorry, but I cannot discuss them with you."

"Hey, it is your neck."

"Do not worry; nothing will happen to me. Just keep an eye on things around here until I return, and contact me if you need advice."

"All right, I hope you know what you are doing."

"Me too," Yanamai whispered to herself.

Yanamai shut down her Information Terminal and went into the adjoining room to get ready. She changed out of her work clothes, locked the door to her office, and met the four guards on the avenue. They dressed in regular clothing so as not to draw attention to her.

Zain moved beside her, "Zorion explained everything, so do not worry; we will not allow Otsoa to harm you."

Yanamai smiled politely, "Thank you, Zain. I feel better knowing you are with me."

Zain led her to the elevators, where lines started queuing up. Hundreds of Argians were laughing and talking about the upcoming festival. Yanamai was in no mood to subject herself to their giddiness. The auditorium was five levels below. The doors opened, so Yanamai and her guards merged with the hustle and bustle of a large, festive crowd. The carriage filled quickly, and the doors closed. It did not take long to reach level seven.

As they exited, thousands more were moving toward the auditorium. One of the many shuttles that circled the boulevard stopped right in front of the elevator exit. As Argians started to board, Zain and his team saved two rows of seats for them. Zain held Yanamai's hand to help her step onto the car. His crew sat behind them, carefully watching the crowd to ensure no one came near her.

Everyone sat, and the shuttle started moving again, leaving several angry Akilians behind to wait for the next shuttle. Yanamai could see hundreds making their way toward the auditorium to her right. Some sat on benches waiting for shuttles with vacant cars, and others decided to walk. Along the way, she saw jugglers, musicians, and vendors selling sweet purple moss. Decorators hung multi-colored lights everywhere, creating a festive atmosphere.

Usually, Yanamai enjoyed taking the shuttles because it gave her a chance to be around her fellow Argians. It also reminded her of why she worked so hard, but this celebration was much different. Farther to her left, she saw even more spectators making their way toward the auditorium, taking their time and window shopping at some of the stores. Even with so many distractions, she could not push aside her reason for being there. The thought of facing Otsoa made her fidget in her seat.

Hoping to comfort her, Zain spoke soothingly, "Relax, Yanamai. It will be over soon."

The shuttle stopped. Yanamai and Zain disembarked in front of the auditorium, where the crowd was even more intimidating. She had never seen so many in one place before. The noise was overwhelming because everyone talked loudly, even though they were standing beside each other. Looking around, Yanamai noticed the young maintenance worker who had walked past her earlier on the avenue. He was repairing a piece of equipment near the main entrance. Nearby, she saw a few eligible females pointing and looking his way. *Good for you.*

In the noble's room, Otsoa paced restlessly behind a two-way mirror perched on the second level within the arena; the room looked out over the main entrance. He was waiting for Yanamai to arrive. Furthermore, he was nervous, extremely nervous. More than two yellow harvests ago, he waited for Nayrah to return to her apartment. She left the door unlocked, and he innocently stepped inside. It was the first time he had been there alone.

As he waited, curiosity got the better of him, and knowing that there would be a painful price to pay if she caught him, he still explored her home until finding a book of potions lying open on a table in a back room. He assumed it was ancient because the binding was old and worn. Also, they did not make books anymore because all the trees had died. At first, it made no impression on him, but as he read some of the formulas and their effects, it occurred to him that Nayrah might have something that would cause memory loss.

He searched for a few hundred heartbeats and found the formula. The instructions gave amounts based on how much memory loss the user wanted for the target. Since Yanamai could not remember several yellow harvests of their time together, he imagined Nayrah must have given her the maximum dosage. Now, all he needed was the antidote.

He found it on the next page but feared Nayrah would return soon, so he took pictures of it with his Data Tablet, returned it to its original open page, and diligently obtained all the ingredients, which were not easy to acquire. Also, he had to keep his quest secret from Nayrah because she would certainly punish him for trespassing.

The instructions said to spray a mist toward the subject's face. Otsoa planned to fill an atomizer with the potion, bring it to the ceremony and, while apologizing, discreetly remove it from a secret pocket in his dress cape and spray it at her. Once Yanamai inhaled the mist, her memories would return, and she would enter the pageant. At that point, not even Nayrah could stop him from legally joining houses with her.

He based the entire plan on the hope that Nayrah had given Yanamai the memory loss drug. If he were wrong, things would only get worse between them. Nervous, his heart pounded fiercely. The wait was excruciating. He saw Yanamai through the glass as she entered the auditorium with four guards. He felt ill, realizing they were not the ones he chose. *Damn you, Zorion!*

They escorted Yanamai to the noble's room, where Otsoa waited, smiling pleasantly. Zain pushed him against the wall, frisked him for weapons, and nodded his approval. Yanamai moved forward, and so did the other guards. She stopped within arm's reach of Otsoa; Zain stood to her left, only one pace away. The others spread out around Otsoa but a little farther back.

"Thank you for coming," Otsoa smiled.

Yanamai slapped him across the cheek, making a loud clap. Zain and the others chuckled.

"That is for making me a prisoner in my own home!" she spat.

Otsoa held his cheek and lowered his head in shame. He was unsure which hurt the most, her slap or knowing the effects his persistence had on her emotions between them; he stood to his full height and faced her.

"I am sorry for all the emotional stress I have caused you. Please know that I pursued you from a place of love. I never intended to inflict pain or discomfort. It hurts me to know you have suffered because of me. I wish you happiness; it is all I have ever wanted."

"Is there anything else?"

"Can I have one last hug?"

"No!" Yanamai, Zain, and the other guards responded simultaneously.

"Very well, may Gau's blessing be upon you, always," Otsoa smiled and bowed.

Yanamai started to leave as Otsoa discreetly reached into the secret pocket of his dress cape to retrieve the atomizer. Zain started to leave keeping an eye on Otsoa but did not notice his hand disappear into his cape.

"Oh, wait! There is one more thing," Otsoa entreated.

Yanamai stopped and turned to face him, "What it is now, Otsoa?"

He was several paces away but had designed the sprayer to reach a long distance. Before anyone knew what was in his hand, Otsoa released the drug toward Yanamai's face. The mist made her cough violently and choke. Zain lunged at Otsoa and tackled him to the ground. The others held him as Zain twisted the aerosol out of his grasp, breaking the same hand Nayrah did earlier in the Terrestrial Rotation. Zain repeatedly punched Otsoa's face until he fell unconscious and returned to Yanamai's side. Hearing the commotion, Zorion and Thea arrived a few moments later. Seeing Yanamai in distress bothered Zorion more than knowing Zain beat Otsoa unconscious.

Yanamai grabbed her throat and gasped for air. Unable to breathe, she collapsed to the ground. Her head hit the concrete; it did not knock her out. Instead, she convulsed as her body fought to rid itself of the toxins in her bloodstream. The veins in her neck, forehead, and extremities swelled and turned dark purple. The blood vessels in her eyes burst, making red spots in the sclera. She remembered seeing Zorion running to her side before everything went black.

Zorion knelt and lifted her head to his shoulder, speaking to her tremblingly, "You will be all right, Yanamai."

Thea tended to Otsoa. Zain had broken his nose and blackened both eyes. She placed her hand on the bridge of his snout and set it straight again, making a loud, crunching sound.

The pain woke Otsoa, "Ouch!"

He tried to stand as one of the guards pressed his shoulder to prevent him. Otsoa watched in horror as Yanamai lay lifeless in Zorion's arms. *What have I done?* Thea studied Otsoa's expressions and, knowing how to read him, believed he did not try to kill Yanamai, which meant he had an alternative motive. She did not know what Otsoa did, but it had to do with somehow getting Yanamai back into his life, assuming she was ever in it. He failed miserably. Yanamai gasped, took a deep breath, her eyes opened, and she looked up at Zorion quizzically.

"Yanamai. Yanamai. Do you remember?" Otsoa yelled.

A guard swung at him, but Thea grabbed his arm in mid-swing and stopped him from connecting to Otsoa's face. Her strength surprised him.

"Leave him alone. She is still alive," Thea growled.

Zain kneeled beside Zorion and showed him the atomizer, "He sprayed her with what he believed was a memory restoration drug."

"Analyze it. I want to know what he used," Zorion ordered.

Yanamai composed herself, and Zorion and Zain helped her stand.

"How do you feel?" Zorion queried.

"Better, thank you."

"Yanamai, do you remember us now?" Otsoa yelled.

Yanamai frowned, shook her head, and threatened, "Do not ever come near me again!"

She turned and left with Zain. The other guards stayed behind to ensure Otsoa did not follow her.

"Throw him in prison!" Zorion yelled.

Thea stood between Otsoa and the guards, "You will not touch him!"

"Stand down, Thea. You cannot save him from punishment this time."

"I will discipline him. You cannot confine him without canceling his celebration, and the Information League will make inquiries. If they find out you put our lead scientist in danger, the one you have touted as our best hope to survive, they will turn on you. If you think their approval is low now, wait until they learn of your incompetence.”

Although he would never admit it, Thea was right.

“You three,” he pointed to the guards. “You will watch him! If he puts one foot on the second level, remove his head at once!”

Thea smiled smugly at Zorion.

“You may have won the battle, Thea, but you have not won the war,” Zorion whispered, walking past her to return to the dais. “If he is not ready in seven hundred heartbeats, I will tell everyone he is ill.”

Thea made the guards retreat to the other side of the room to speak privately with Otsoa. She helped him stand. “Foolish Argian!” she spat as he stood. “What were you thinking?”

“I had one last chance to bring her back to me, and I failed.”

“I have told you to stay away from her.”

“Yes, you and Nayrah told me.”

“I told you to obey her in everything! None of this would have happened if you had listened to her instruction!”

“When it comes to Yanamai, I cannot help myself.”

“Let us go to the celebration. Once you find someone to replace her, you will feel better, forget about Yanamai, and move on with your life.”

“I wish it were that simple.”

Nayrah retrieved a cream and applied it to his eyes, “It will hide the bruising until it heals. Now come,” she firmly pulled him forward.

Otsoa could not resist her strength. He stumbled at first and walked to the dais with her by his side. Thea escorted Otsoa to the custom-made celebrant’s chair, which faced the crowd. Zorion moved to the podium and signaled to the assembly that the event was about to begin. As Zorion performed the opening protocols, Otsoa’s thoughts drifted to Nayrah. His failure to create the proper memory restoration formula had to be the result of her interference. *I am always watching you.* He shivered at the thought until Zorion’s voice brought him out of his brooding.

“First, I would like to thank everyone for attending. I am happy to see my fellow Argians gathered. This celebration is to acknowledge that Otsoa is coming of age. Now, if everyone is ready, let the pageant begin.”

There was a smattering of applause as eligible females entered the auditorium. Zorion took his seat and noticed Yetta, Otsoa's twin sister, sitting beside his youngest heir, Va'ron, on the dais. He briefly thought it was Yanamai sitting alongside Yetta but realized Garbi, her sister, sat there. They were not twins, even though Garbi's appearance was an exact match for Yanamai. Zorion often wondered if she used her shapeshifting ability to mimic her. Still, seeing them sitting together reminded Zorion of how much time had passed since they were infants.

He returned his attention to the celebration. Initially, the pageant stayed just that, but it developed into something more elaborate over time. Hoping to catch the attention of the guest of honor, some began dancing to stand out from the rest. The formal, elegant music created a soothing atmosphere. The contenders gracefully spun with their arms and hands moving in synchronization. Some twirled light fabric tied to sticks as they advanced around the arena rhythmically.

The festivity brought back memories of his celebration. He had chosen someone familiar, and they started their life journey together, but it ended because she died only a few Terrestrial Rotations later. Thinking of her brought a wave of grief. Secretly, he still had the hologram taken of them at that moment. It had been ages since he looked at it, mainly because it made him feel incredibly sad.

The pageant continued for what seemed like an eternity. Each celebration brought more participants than the last. Some only take part for a few moments of fame, while others are serious about their intent to the celebrator. Otsoa left his seat to discuss his choice with Zorion and Thea once it was over; it was just a formality. In most cases, the parents did not recommend their preference unless asked.

On the dais, Thea embraced him, "I am proud of you, Otsoa. You have attracted a great many beautiful females. Any of which could give you plenty of heirs and help you forget Yanamai."

Otsoa remained silent. *How could I ever forget Yanamai?*

Thea took Otsoa by the arm, and they walked over to the podium where Zorion waited.

Knowing the earlier events and seeing the look on Otsoa's face, Zorion wished to have canceled the ceremony. *I am sure nothing good will come of this.*

"Tell me which one you will choose?" Thea whispered, walking beside him.

He did not respond.

"I like the one with white hair and maroon eyes," she hinted.

Stopping, he turned to face her, "Have you been talking to Nayrah?"

"No. Why?"

"She recommended her too."

"We must have the same taste," she smiled.

On the podium, Thea and Otsoa stopped near Zorion, who turned to face them, "Whom did you choose?"

"How many are there?" Otsoa asked.

"Ten," Thea replied.

"Must I decide now?" Otsoa inquired.

"It is the custom. Everyone here expects you to leave with someone," Zorion answered.

"I feel like a roll of moss that a merchant sells for a few Sovereign Cubes," Otsoa whined, fidgeting.

"No one is selling you. You are the one with the power here. The choice is yours to make," Zorion rolled his eyes, wishing Otsoa would decide so he could return to work.

Otsoa raised an eyebrow. *I have all the power.* The thought almost made him laugh. *No, Nayrah has all the power.* She is the one who foretold the exact number of participants. *If you can see the future, you can manipulate it.* He understood that all too well. Nayrah had controlled him from his youth, and there seemed to be no way of escape.

Otsoa surveyed the candidates, huddled together and standing on the painted image of Gau's watchful eye until seeing Durnah. He would never admit to Nayrah that he found Durnah attractive, but she was not Yanamai; she was not what *he* wanted. As anxiety levels grew, he found it hard to breathe. From the beginning, Nayrah told him what to do, where to go, and now, with whom to join houses. If he chose Durnah, Nayrah's control over him would be complete. *How can I escape Nayrah's invisible grip?* He had an idea.

Zorion stood patiently at first, but the silence became uncomfortable.

"Otsoa," Zorion whispered, smiling nervously at the crowd. "I need a name."

"I cannot decide," Otsoa blurted his response directly into the voice magnifier for everyone to hear, including Nayrah, wherever she was. In the silence, his voice echoed throughout the stadium. Several spectators gasped, and everyone began to murmur.

"He is only joking," Zorion remarked, hoping to correct Otsoa's mistake. "He will choose someone, I promise. Just give us a moment."

He turned off the voice magnifier and whispered angrily into Otsoa's ear, "What in the universe are you doing?"

"I am not doing anything. I cannot decide; how can I?" Otsoa turned the voice amplifier back on and continued, "I want the all-seeing eye of Gau to make my choice. Let Gau be the judge. Let Gau decide my fate."

There were more gasps this time. Moreover, many jeered and heckled him. The crowd's noise rose, making it impossible to hear unless someone shouted.

Zorion pulled Otsoa away from the voice amplifier and yelled, "Remember something, Otsoa, if they revolt and remove me as sovereign, *you* are the first one I kill."

"I am not doing this to hurt you." *Still, the side benefit is an unexpected bonus.*

Zorion regretted not throwing him in prison because he could have avoided this catastrophe; now he had to figure out how to fix it. Stepping to the right side of the dais, Zorion called for one of his advisors to find a solution. They discussed common law at length, leaving Zorion with only one choice.

He returned to the podium and quieted the angry mob, "Friends. Friends. Please, let me speak." Their voices diminished, and he continued, "Otsoa's decision is a surprise, and even though I requested he choose someone, he still insists on deferring his fate to Gau," he paused because some yelled out obscenities. "I understand your anger. I am angry too. I do not wish to see any bloodshed, but I am pleased to announce that my advisor has given us a choice. Any participant, now standing within the watchful eye of Gau, who wishes to leave, may do so now."

As the crowd mumbled, Zorion felt someone grab his arm; it was Otsoa.

"What are you doing?" Otsoa exclaimed.

"I am trying to save lives!" snapped Zorion.

"I will be disgraced if that happens!"

"Good! You are a pitiful excuse for an Akilian. What you are doing is unforgivable, and unless you reverse your decision, it will follow you for the rest of your life."

"I will not yield!" defied Otsoa.

Three left the image of Gau's eye at once, and a few more departed until there were only four. Zorion waited patiently, hoping the last few would leave; they did not, so he stepped down from the dais and approached them. No one in the crowd could hear him speak without a voice amplifier.

Standing in their midst, he spoke softly, "Please, I can tell you that Otsoa is not worth the risk. He is selfish, untrustworthy, disloyal, and even hateful. These are not the qualities of someone with whom you should join houses. I would have canceled the celebration, but tradition dictates I must host it. Otherwise, we would not be here with this dilemma."

Two females faced the floor, embarrassed to stay; they did not leave, and the other two defiantly remained.

Hoping to change their minds, he added, "I will remind you that the judgment of Gau is to the death, so I beg you to reconsider. Otsoa is a miserable excuse for an Akilian and not worth your time, let alone your life, so leave the eye now."

Despite his warning, they all agreed that Gau's judgment would decide their fate. He tried to dissuade them for hundreds of heartbeats but returned to the dais, unsuccessful.

He spoke into the voice amplifier with a heavy heart, saying, "I have just confirmed that the final four have all agreed to let Gau decide their fate. The competition will begin tomorrow, during the last quarter of the Terrestrial Revolution."

He abruptly turned away from the voice transmitter and returned to his office without saying a word to anyone else. Otsoa found himself standing alone on the dais. As everyone started to leave, he saw many admonishing looks; there were some, more than he thought possible, who smiled approvingly at him. Before leaving, Otsoa looked at the four standing on top of Gau's watchful eye. Seeing Durnah among them did not surprise him. *I must see Yanamai again.*

*****

Yanamai and Zain left the noble's room and rushed to the walkway. Zain used his identification badge to secure an emergency ride home and drove the hovercar swiftly through traffic until they arrived. Zain opened the door and walked her to the office.

Before she entered, he said, "You have experienced severe trauma; you should rest."

"Thank you for protecting me."

"No. I failed because I did not think to inspect his cape. If you wish to replace me, I will understand."

"It is not your fault. Otsoa is sly. I am sure he has planned this event for a long time. No matter how much of him you searched, you would have never found it."

"I do not deserve your compassion; thank you."

Yanamai smiled and kissed him on the cheek. He knew it was only a friendly gesture, but still, it made him feel good. He turned and fastened his eyes to the walkway's open areas and paid close attention to the shadows.

Yanamai told Tadra everything and sent her home to her family. Yanamai returned to her office chair, switched on her Information Terminal, and immersed herself in the data from the probe, hoping to forget Otsoa. A few thousand heartbeats later, her computer chimed, alerting her that a video communication was waiting.

Yanamai could not believe her eyes, "How dare you contact me after what you did!"

"You have every right to be angry; I only want to apologize for what happened. It was not my intention to harm you in any way. That has never been my goal."

Yanamai smiled pleasantly at him, "I know you want me to love you."

"Yes, Yanamai. It is the only thing I want!" Otsoa exclaimed, thinking the potion had finally taken effect.

"Very well, but you must do what I tell you."

"Anything, just name it!"

"Go to the walkway, step up onto the railing, and jump."

"I will fall to my death."

94

"That is what it will take for me to love you, Otsoa. Goodbye," she started to disconnect their signal.

"Wait! Wait! Please, look at this before you go!" he sent a file.

"What is this?"

"It is a page out of a book of potions. This concoction was supposed to restore your lost memories of what happened between us."

"Are you saying that you believe someone magically wiped away my memory from hundreds of Terrestrial Rotations ago?"

"I know it sounds crazy."

"That is because you are insane and should be locked away."

"Yanamai, I did not imagine our time together, and I did not envision the ingredients for the cure; you are looking at a picture of the actual ancient book, which is rare!"

"Are you serious? You show me potions from an ancient Skean book, trying to convince me that I somehow lost my memories. What kind of fool do you think I am?"

"Skeans are real."

"If so, tell me why it did not work?"

"I must have done something wrong."

"Goodbye, Otsoa. If you contact me again, I will press charges, and everyone will know that you have been excessively pursuing me."

"What I have told you is the truth."

Yanamai disconnected their communication and returned to work.

Chapter 12

Earth
The Regime - Washington, D.C. - Fort McNair
May 8, 2452

Michael's alarm woke him out of drug-induced sleep. Last night's misguided adventure forced him to take three sleeping pills to get some rest. He felt tired but still got out of bed. Every muscle in his body ached. His throat was dry, so he went to the bathroom for some water, looked at his reflection in the mirror, and lowered his head. *Damn. No way am I going to explain this one away.*

His reflection revealed a classic black eye with puffiness. It radiated from the bridge of his nose to his ear. Moreover, the colors - the colors were almost fascinating. He never saw a sunset with such a vivid range of blues and purples, with just a touch of yellow where Max's fist split his right eyebrow in half. *Alex was right; I should have put accelerant on it. I will make an appointment with a medical droid today.*

He touched his cheek with his right index finger to evaluate its sensitivity and regretted it. A further examination showed bruises on his chest, arms, and legs. *Man, he really did a number on me.* He changed clothes and went to the kitchen to get some ice out of the freezer. Using a ready-made ice pack, he held it against his face. The cold felt soothing. A few minutes later, he threw the ice pack back in the freezer, made an appointment with a medical droid to meet him at his office, and left for work.

His apartment was only a short walk from the facility where he worked. Inside, he took the elevator to the twelfth floor. It stopped on the tenth, the door opened, and Alex boarded. He took a long look at Michael.

"You don't look too bad."

"Oh, shut up!" Michael growled.

"Stop whining and rub some accelerant on the injuries. The bruising and swelling will go away in a couple of days."

"I have a medical droid on the way to my office."

The elevator opened, and Michael stepped out.

"Hey Mike, before you leave, I want you to know that I'm sorry about last night."

"It wasn't your fault. I should have just stayed home."

"No, you should have gone to the hospital with Mai. She would have taken good care of you."

"It wasn't the proudest moment of my life, Alex. It's not something I want to share with a stranger."

"You should talk to her. She felt bad about what happened and wants to talk to you."

"It's not entirely her fault. I was just in the wrong place at the wrong time."

"I got her number for you. I think you should call her. Go out on a private date, just you and her. Work things out between you."

"No, thanks."

"Why not? She likes you, and she's interested!"

"Alex, I was completely humiliated last night! I can't face her again."

"I'm telling you; she *really* likes you. What happened last night didn't change that."

"Look, Alex. Max said some things last night that were troubling."

"Like what?"

"Did you know Mai used to be a prostitute?"

"Did Max say that?"

"It was certainly implied. Mai owes him money because there was a police raid. She offered to pay him back the following day; he didn't want to wait, so I look like this."

"Hey, she's had a rough childhood, and jobs aren't as plentiful as here. Sometimes you do what you must to survive; you shouldn't hold it against her."

"I'm not judging her, but you should have told me before agreeing to a date; it doesn't matter because I'm not going out with her again."

"I sent her contact number to your phone."

"Are you deaf? I just said I would not go out with her again!"

"I think you're making a big mistake by not calling her."

"Sure, Alex. Whatever you say."

"I'll see you at lunch?"

"Yep, see you then."

Inside his office, Michael sat and exhaled loudly. As he turned on his computer, someone knocked. It was a medical droid. Following a thorough examination, it applied accelerant to his injuries. Michael knew from experience that it would take a few hours before the pain subsided and about a day for the black eye and swelling to disappear completely.

The droid finished and left, leaving Michael alone with his thoughts. Looking at his phone, Michael found Alex's text with Mai's number. Although he desperately wanted a companion, Mai set off too many red flags. The fact that she looked like Chu Lian and Max's appearance last night revealed a sordid past, made the situation difficult for Michael to accept. Alex's unusual behavior, urging him to see her again, also bothered him. His finger hovered over the 'delete' icon as he carefully considered his action.

There were times when the loneliness was hard to bear. Removing her number would ensure no contact with her, even if he regretted his decision. He decided and pressed the 'delete' button, checked his email, reviewed all his receipts, and frowned because Chu Lian still had not replied to any of his messages.

With a few keystrokes, he accessed one of the Regime's orbiting satellites over China. Within minutes, the whole country was on his monitor, but he considered the consequences of his actions before going further. If his superiors discovered that he used the satellite for personal reasons, he could get into big trouble. *It's been a year since I've seen or heard from her; I need to find her.*

He adjusted the lens's zoom and direction and used the mouse to magnify her last known address found on the beach in Hong Kong. She had shown him a hologram of her last night before coming to the Regime, and he saw the house number within the three-dimensional image and committed it to memory. Earlier tries only showed an empty home. It was his eighth attempt using the Regime satellite to find her.

Its position in the sky allowed him to see her backyard, which faced the ocean. On his monitor, he saw waves crashing on the sandy beach, several yards from her home. The image was brilliant; it felt like he was there. The only things missing were the sound of seagulls squawking and feeling the ocean breeze on his face. For several minutes, he waited, watching for any sign of her. Before disconnecting, he saw a car pull into the driveway and stopped.

The sun was setting, leaving enough light to see, so whoever entered the home did not bother turning on the lights. *Come on, come on. Step outside so I can see you!* The occupant did walk outside onto the wooden patio and looked out over the ocean. *Yes!* The only problem was that he could not see the person's face, but the body shape and the long black hair gave him hope that it might be her. With a few more clicks of the mouse, the lens zoomed in closer until the subject's upper body filled the screen.

He briefly froze. It was Chu Lian, and she looked sad. As the satellite's orbit went lower in China's sky, its position gave him a complete frontal view of Chu Lian. It was as if he was standing right in front of her. The image detail allowed him to see tears in her eyes. *Why are you crying?* Whatever problem she was facing, he wanted to help her.

He entertained the thought that she might be thinking of him because he believed she loved him once, mainly because their last goodbye was tearful. Knowing where she lived, he planned to vacation in China to visit her. This time, he would not give up so easily. He touched the screen, remembering how her soft skin felt against his, and before too long, he was crying. He longed for her touch, hearing her laugh, smelling her hair, and holding her in his arms.

She wiped tears from her eyes, and her expression changed from sadness to anger, and without warning, Michael saw her slam the wooden rail with her hand. Her mouth moved, but he could not hear what she said without a microphone on the premises and wished for the ability to read lips. She spun around with determination and went inside. There was a knock at his door. He jumped from his seat, knocking over a can that held microchips, so he put the can upright, swore under his breath, and disconnected from the satellite, "Come in."

He panicked, and his palms began to sweat. *Please don't let it be the General. Please don't let it be the General!* The door opened, and he heard the soft sound of servos moving. *An android!*

"Good day, Sir," the android spoke politely. "General Saunders was unable to reach you on your com. He asks that you meet him in his office at once."

Damn!

Chapter 13

Akil
Mount Gaurette
The 22,272[nd] Terrestrial Rotation of the Second Summer

Gecheana stood inside Mount Gaurette to meditate. Many Celestial Revolutions ago, an unnamed High Priest built the first temple of Gau at its base. Hundreds of marble pillars kept the mountain from caving. Unlit torches hung on the walls, leaving the sanctuary in complete darkness. Gecheana could see without the lamp's help and preferred the dark over the light as a Skean.

She climbed the monument (a miniature replica of the pyramid Gau built across from Mount Gaurette) within the temple at its center. Reaching the summit, she admired the two sarcophagi that held Gau and Izar. She used the Night Lord's power, and the lid rose, exposing Gau's corpse. Lying on his chest was the sword the Night Lord had given him, made from a dense alloy of the Shadow Universe.

High Priest Shun told her that no one other than Gau or a direct descendant of his could ignite it, so Gecheana had to try it for herself. However, she failed and left it with him until needed. Every so often, she made the frosty trek to the surface to ensure no one had disturbed it. To her knowledge, other than High Priest Shun, Gecheana was the only Akilian who knew of its existence.

She replaced the lid and returned to the pyramid's base, where she studied the monument, which brought back memories of that fateful Terrestrial Rotation sixty yellow harvests ago and the events that led to it. Gecheana was not always a Skean. Initially, she had begun training to become a Saiph, but Strell, her former instructor, unwittingly led her down the path of darkness.

As a young Argian, Gecheana was a beautiful socialite and had just celebrated her eighteenth yellow harvest, so her family began to apply the expected pressure to join houses with another aristocrat. As a result, Gecheana often found herself on her peers' guest lists, who held many ceremonies. That is when Strell entered her life. They first met on the walkway as she headed toward a close friend's coming-of-age celebration. Thinking he wanted her to notice him, she breathed in deeply and evaluated him, as is their custom.

Finding him desirable, she smiled and allowed him to speak. He said that her aura had a blue haze, which meant she could become a Saiph, but he did not tell her that it meant she could also become a Skean. Being young, she thought he was trying to impress her, mainly because Saiphs and Skeans were fables.

She asked him to join houses; he declined, having already committed to another named Ma'rah. Gecheana was heartbroken, but Strell insisted she had enormous potential and pleaded with her to join them; Strell was part of a secret order of Saiphs. He told her they safeguarded their existence, keeping a watchful eye to ensure Skeans did not rise again.

She believed that if he instructed her, there might be time to convince him to change his mind about Ma'rah, so she went through the trial and began her training. Working every Terrestrial Revolution together brought them close as she had hoped. Expecting Strell to change his mind about their relationship, Gecheana refused to attend any of her family's ceremonies to find her a partner to join houses, so they banished her. Gecheana did not care. She wanted Strell and was willing to do anything and give up anything to get him.

To her delight, Strell postponed his ceremony with Ma'rah. It gave Gecheana hope that he would accept her. During practice, Gecheana bested him. She remembered how he smiled proudly at her. He had told her she would become great, and by the following yellow harvest, her fighting skills would be unmatched. Excited by his praise, she hugged him, and he unexpectedly kissed her. They fell into an embrace and began an affair that lasted until the yellow harvest.

After the celebration, Strell had asked another Saiph to take over her training. Gecheana tried to speak with him, hoping to find out why he would not talk to her, but he refused to meet with her. His constant evasion made her furious, so she demanded to see him at his home. Being there alone, Ma'rah answered, and Gecheana told her of their relationship. During her visit, Gecheana learned that Strell and Ma'rah had joined houses more than a yellow harvest ago. Ma'rah wept from hearing the news of their romance, and Gecheana left incensed at his betrayal.

Later that Terrestrial Rotation, Strell confronted Gecheana at her home. She had never seen him angry before, and he directed all his rage toward her. Gecheana begged him to leave Ma'rah, telling him everything she gave up just for the chance they would join houses. He refused and threatened to harm her if she ever spoke to Ma'rah again. They argued for thousands of heartbeats. Strell never wanted to see her again. He started to leave, but Gecheana grabbed his leg, using her weight to keep him from going. She wept on his thigh, pleading with him to stay.

Strell hit her with his backhand, supported by the High Lord's power, and it sent her across the room, knocking her unconscious. She woke in pain, looked in the mirror, and saw bruises on her face, so now, with every Terrestrial Revolution that came, hate replaced the love she once had for him until her heart turned black. That is when the shadows began speaking to her. Blinded by her disdain for Strell, Gecheana followed the voice to the city's lowest level, where she found a hologram and turned it on.

A Skean named Tivi appeared and offered to teach Gecheana *the ways of darkness*. Seeing a path to avenging herself from Strell's betrayal, Gecheana accepted Tivi's offer and trained at the city's lowest level, but on one fateful Terrestrial Rotation, Tivi told Gecheana she had to make a choice. She had to reject the High Lord and accept the Night Lord, or her Skean training would end.

Knowing the cost of her decision, Gecheana took the sleep cycle to think it over. She ascended to the higher levels where Strell lived, moved in the shadows as Tivi taught her, and spotted Strell and Ma'rah together on the walkway holding hands. Knowing Ma'rah had forgiven his transgression (and seeing Strell happy) filled Gecheana with savage fury. Upon returning to the lowest level, Gecheana activated the hologram.

Tivi guided her through the process, and Gecheana arose a Skean before the work cycle began. Now that Gecheana had changed sides, Tivi gave her a plan to bring back the Skeans and destroy the Saiphs. Following her instructions, Gecheana returned to the level where Strell lived and waited in the shadows until the work cycle started. The moment Strell left, Gecheana visited her.

Having changed her likeness to one of Ma'rah's neighbors, Gecheana knocked on her door with arms full of moss, which hid her pheromones and identity but doubled as a gift. Inside, Gecheana questioned her like a nosey neighbor to discover why she forgave Strell and discovered that Ma'rah was pregnant and did not want to become a single parent. Gecheana left, smiling. She knew how Strell would suffer after finding Ma'rah's lifeless body lying on the kitchen floor.

Hiding in the shadows outside his apartment, she watched him return home. He opened the door and called out for Ma'rah. Gecheana saw a crack in the entrance and moved out of the shadows long enough to see and listen until it happened. Gecheana watched as Strell shrieked, weeping loudly, holding Ma'rah's lifeless body in his arms. The image gave Gecheana great satisfaction, but she was just getting started.

Gecheana planned to use every skill Tivi taught her to destroy the Saiphs. She chose to put drugs on their food to make them weak, removed their heads as they dozed off to sleep, and used the Night Lord's power to toss their bodies over the rail. Their corpses landed at the bottom of the city. She laughed at how easy it was for her to slip them the tainted meals. Having bought a cart, she sold the moss every work cycle. The Saiphs walked up to her and paid Sovereign Cubes for the drugged snacks.

She destroyed the Saiphs and made a profit doing it. Over the following several Terrestrial Rotations, Gecheana slew each Saiph within the secret order, leaving only Strell alive. Like the others, she drugged his moss to make him half-witted, but not enough to make him sleep. Strell ate it and sat at the table, sobbing over the loss of Ma'rah. Gecheana changed her likeness to Ma'rah's during that sleep cycle and entered Strell's home.

With the drug still in his system, Strell thought it was Ma'rah, so Gecheana led him to the bedroom and seduced him. Later, she rested in his arms and checked herself to see if her feelings for him had changed. They had not, so she straddled herself over him and smiled sweetly. Strell told her that he loved and missed her.

"I know you do," Gecheana spoke with Ma'rah's voice and reached out with her hand, allowing the dark power to flow through her.

A Skean sword appeared in her hand. Strell's eyes widened in fear.

His last words were, "Ma'rah, please!"

Gecheana tossed his corpse over the railing with the others, giving her great gratification. Now that the last of the Saiphs was dead, she began recruiting eligible young females with a blue-hazed aura. She put them through the trial and taught them the ways of darkness as

Tivi taught her. Later, Gecheana took Strell's sword apart and fused half of his white blade with her crimson edge.

In her mind's eye, she saw the outcome before it happened. Using the Night Lord's power, she heated them until they softened and merged. White and black electricity arched up and down the sword as she forced the opposing metals to join. She finished and had a unique blade; one side was white, and the other crimson, a combination of Skean and Saiph. Both would consider her creation an abomination. Even Tivi rebuked her for making it, but Gecheana wanted a constant reminder of what made her a Skean, love.

Tivi continued to train her, and before the yellow harvest arrived, she had told her how to increase her power a hundredfold. It would help her finish what Gau had started, which was not easy. Gecheana met with High Priest Shun, who ran Gau's temple. He and his acolytes dug a path to the pyramid on Akil's surface under the snow. She had many obstacles to face. First, it was not the right time of the season. The pyramid would not face the star directly, making it more difficult to destroy. Second, on Akil's surface, the weather did not support life. The air was freezing, and the constant high winds made it even colder. Third, the air was so thin that several acolytes suffocated, digging a path under the snow.

Although the odds were against her, Gecheana was determined to succeed because the reward outweighed the risk. At the height of her power, she wrapped heavy coats over her entire body, covered her face, and climbed the pyramid alone. Using the Night Lord's power, she created a sphere-shaped shield around herself, which helped her reach the summit alive. The orb allowed her to breathe, but it could not protect her from the piercing cold. Every muscle in her body froze.

Standing on the pyramid's summit, she felt the shadow universe beneath, urging her to lash out at the dying reddish sun. Gecheana extended her arms upward; the pyramid magnified the Night Lord's power, and it went forth to deplete the sun of its plasma. Due to the monument's position, it took longer than if it had pointed directly at the star. Gecheana continued beyond what her body could tolerate and blacked out before completing her goal.

She woke several Terrestrial Rotations later in High Priest Shun's temple, where he told her they retrieved her body and brought her back. Many acolytes died in the process, but Gecheana was indifferent to his loss. Her main concern was the sun. Returning to the surface, she saw firsthand what her failure had done to the star. She lost consciousness and did not contain the explosions while depleting the sun's plasma. Now, fountains sprang upward, reaching heights beyond the planets' orbit.

A nearby star's gravity caught one of the fountains and turned it into a stream of plasma, dragging it toward it, creating the River of Fire. Two Terrestrial Rotations later, Yovis 5 entered it and vanished into the plasma stream. Of course, it was never Gecheana's intention to cause that disaster, but it did not bother her that so many died because of her action. What did concern her was that she made things worse for herself.

Due to her failure, she significantly decreased the amount of time they had left before the sun would finally explode. Since that Terrestrial Revolution, she has been plotting to get off Akil and onto a safe, habitable world. That is the reason she came to meditate. There were five cities underground, and in each one, she had placed a female Skean. Due to their position in society, each had offspring. Gecheana allowed a few to become Skeans and ensured her control by placing a veil over their minds, but their numbers were starting to grow, which was dangerous. The more Skeans occupied Akil, the more risk she faced that one would turn on her because the veil would only hold for so long.

They secretly worked to find a habitable world for Gecheana to rule, but if Zorion's team found one before she did, it would take longer for her to overthrow the government. Since she was in the twilight of her life span, time was running out for her, and now, the machine she had worked so long to build exploded, yet there was something even more sinister at work. Recently, she discovered that something or someone compromised her ability to see the future. The only being that could do this was a Saiph, but there were no Saiphs on Akil. *Where are you?* Having called a meeting with the other Skeans, she was determined to discover the source of this obstacle and remove it without mercy.

Chapter 14

Akil
Argi
The 22,272[nd] Terrestrial Rotation of the Second Summer

Nayrah stepped off the hover bus and walked toward the Argi Intercity Transportation Station. Disguised as a beautiful, eligible socialite, many business owners held open doors or gave up their seats, hoping that she would show them interest. Although she considered them beneath her, their attention to her alter ego made her journey to Krek entertaining. For her, it was the only way to travel. Gecheana had imperiously ordered a meeting of the five Skeans. Nayrah did not like the summons or its manner, but Gecheana was Gecheana, and she could not deny her command.

Gecheana insisted that they should meet in Krek. Nayrah did not like returning to her birth city. There were too many painful memories for her there. She looked at the map on the wall, with its *'you are here'* red dot showing her location. *Of course, I am here, you idiot. Where else would I be?* The map was an interactive panel outlining the five cities as they were under the surface. Together, their shape reminded her of an extinct flower with white petals and a yellow center.

The main arena was at the heart of the map, which sat directly beneath Mount Gaurette, hundreds of paces from Akil's surface. Engineers built the underground amphitheater to resemble the flower's small yellow disk, which connected each metropolis at its end. The oval cities looked like petals. Evenly spaced, they circled the main arena.

There were two Intercity Transportation Stations. Transport One, where she was now, moved in the direction of the planet's revolution. Several levels below, Transport Two moved counter-rotational. Each tunnel made a complete circle around the yellow center on the map as it passed through every municipality's oval tip. There were five intercity trains, and each left its perspective stations simultaneously. Conductors at each station coordinated the departures.

A long time ago, Nayrah used her alter ego to seduce one. Under her influence, he showed her how the system worked. Each complex had two lights on the panel, one orange and the other blue. Every municipality had a conductor responsible for all departures. If they approved it to leave, the signal for that city changed from orange to blue, but only if all the lights were blue did the trains leave.

Nayrah reached up and pushed the teal Krek oval. A digital sign above the map flashed the estimated time of her train's arrival at her station and in Krek. She checked the schedule and looked at her timekeeper. *It should be here any moment now.* Closing her eyes, she allowed the Night Lord's power to flow through her. With her senses heightened, she could feel the train as it approached. It was a few thousand paces away.

The trains' design gave them silent motion. They used electromagnets for hovering and forced air for propulsion. The conductor told her that engineers installed specially designed air ducts every fifty paces to keep the train's motion smooth and effortless. Nevertheless, her keen senses made her feel a slight vibration in the thick, flat metal tracks the train used to hover over. *It will be here any heartbeat now.*

To stay sharp, she tested her abilities often and in many ways. Seeing the train's lights, she pulled the traveling hood over her head to keep the impending wind from messing up her hair. Using her powers, she waited until the last heartbeat before turning her face away, avoiding the rushing wind as it swirled through the crowd. Hidden by the shadow of her hood, her eyes watched anonymously as the gale tousled expensive hairdressings, leaving them in various stages of disarray. She snickered.

The train slowed down and came to a complete stop. The doors on the departure side of the carriage opened, and hundreds of commuters disembarked. Once the ticketing agents verified the remaining passengers, the entrance doors opened on Nayrah's side of the station, and everyone boarded to secure a seat.

The stations often sold more tickets than the trains had seats, leaving some to stand for the journey. The crowd surged past Nayrah, but she did not mind. Inside, there was a whole compartment waiting just for her. As she stooped down to retrieve her bag, a young, anxious business owner ran up and lifted it for her.

"May I?" he hinted pleasantly.

Nayrah smiled flirtatiously, "Of course."

They reached the train, and the business owner allowed the conductor to scan his data device, which displayed a standard pass.

The conductor examined Nayrah's ticket, "Ah, you have a whole compartment all to yourself."

In her peripheral vision, she saw her new chaperon smile. She almost laughed, knowing what he was thinking. Once onboard, she led the business owner to her compartment. Standing in the doorway, Nayrah pointed to the window seat.

"Set the bag down there."

He brushed himself off, "Are you expecting friends to join you?"

"No."

He looked at the empty benches, "Perhaps I could join you."

It was the moment Nayrah expected, "No, thank you. I prefer to be alone."

The look on his face was priceless. Outwardly, Nayrah expressed indifference, but she was bubbling with laughter inwardly.

She stepped aside and pointed to the door, "If you do not mind, I would like you to leave now."

Perplexed, he left, scratching his head and wondering how he could have misunderstood the visual cues. Before leaving, he turned, still in disbelief. Nayrah slid the door closed between them. Amused at his confusion, she smiled until the train left a few hundred heartbeats later. She always dedicated her free time to meditation. With her eyes closed, she thought back to her first lesson as a child. Gecheana said that the Saiph and Skeans were mortal enemies. *Darkness and light cannot dwell together, and just a tiny light can drive the shadows away.*

Gecheana taught that the obligation of a Skean was to destroy all Saiphs, but Nayrah had never met one and did not understand the conflict. Gecheana had revealed vague circumstances about murdering her former instructor. *What was his name? Ah, yes. Strell.* He died before Nayrah was born, allowing her to grow in a Saiph-free Akil. To ensure no Saiph would rise again on Akil, Gecheana took firm measures.

It was a delicate and cruel tactic that worked for many yellow harvests. Gecheana taught them to keep track of all newborns, and during the sleep cycle, they sneaked into the home and looked at their aura. If they saw a blue haze, it meant the child had the potential to become a Saiph or Skean. Neither were welcome. Once they discovered one, Gecheana sneaked into the home and put a few drops of her potion into the water. The poison accumulated in the mother's milk, killing the child as it fed.

The last one with a blue haze died more than several yellow harvests ago, making Nayrah think the High Lord had given up on Akil, but her last video conference with Gecheana made her question that theory. Their discussion concerning the possibility of a Saiph arriving on Akil upset Gecheana. Nayrah knew her little tells even better than her own. A flinch here, a crack in her voice there, told her everything she needed to know about Gecheana's state of mind. *If she is this afraid of the Saiph, we must be in grave danger.* It all centered around their collective inability to see a set future. That was a definite warning that one was nearby. *But where?*

The train came to a stop, bringing Nayrah out of her contemplation. Looking out her window, she saw Vlor's Intercity Transportation Station; Krek was the next stop. She took a deep breath and returned to her meditation. This time she focused on the veil, through which her mind's eye could not penetrate. The curtain had been there since childhood. It kept answers from her that she knew would make her more powerful than even Gecheana. *If I only knew how to get past it.*

She told Gecheana many times; her only response was to keep practicing, which never seemed to work. Each time she thought the veil was about to fall away, allowing her to see past it, there appeared to be some invisible hand that prevented her from going further. The situation frustrated her. Not figuring out this mystery made her feel weak, and this was not the time to doubt her abilities with a Saiph approaching.

This time, she tried a different approach. If some invisible hand prevented her from moving the veil, she would try to cut it off at the wrist. Her mind traveled to that remote part, wherein lay the source of her Skean power. The veil was still there; only this time, the unknown hand withdrew itself as if it knew that she was looking for it.

As time passed, her anger and frustration grew, but she could not find it; the train came to a stop, snapping her out of meditation. She stood, stretched out her arm, and summoned the bag to jump into her hand. With a wave of her finger, the door opened with force. Again, anger ruled her emotions, causing her to ignore Gecheana's warning not to use her powers indiscriminately. *Remember, secrecy is our most potent weapon. If someone catches you using the Night Lord's power in public, you will endanger us all.*

Feeling the dark energy surging through her, Nayrah thought, *To Abadose with secrecy, I do not care if everyone knows who I am. Who will stop me?* She stepped off the train and followed the exit to the elevators. Each city had thousands of levels, so engineers installed three tubes of lifts every seven hundred paces. The first was for local travelers; it stopped within fifty levels. The second stopped on every fiftieth tier. The third was an express elevator that stopped every hundredth deck.

Since her destination was at the bottom, she took the hundred-tier express and used the Night Lord's power to summon the elevator many paces away. Before she reached it, the elevator arrived. Inside, she selected the lowest level. The elevator's timer held the door open for a few heartbeats to ensure all potential riders could get on, but since patience was not one of her virtues, she motioned with her hand, and the doors closed.

She saw a couple running toward her, asking to hold the door open. *Not a chance.* Another motion of her finger and the pair fell to the ground, dropping their luggage. Before the elevator started to move, she could hear them cursing at her. Their calamity brought a chuckle as she turned to look out the glass wall. The elevator moved slowly and then sped up, causing her stomach to lurch. The elevator's Tier Indicator numbers rapidly decreased as she plunged into Krek's dark underbelly.

Outside and below the circular glass barrier, she saw darkness approaching. The fog only reached a hundred decks above ground on many Terrestrial Rotations, but now, it was different. The car plunged into the mist at the three-hundredth level, where moisture condensed on the glass, and hundreds of drops of water moved upward as air blew them off the smooth surface. The tiny beads mesmerized her as the elevator slowed to a stop.

The doors opened, surprising her. *Gecheana would be disappointed with me; I should not have allowed anything to distract me.* Outside, she took a deep breath as the cold, moist air washed over her body. She exhaled, walking toward Gecheana's home, and changed her appearance to that of her Skean identity; it was something else that troubled her.

Nayrah had many alter egos, but all the female Skeans shared their identity. This deception, Gecheana told her, was to hide their numbers. Even though the logic was sound, Nayrah would have preferred some differences between them. At twenty paces away from the door, she sensed that all her Skean colleagues were there. Inside, she found them at the kitchen table. Remnants of purple moss on their napkins told her they had finished their dessert.

Nayrah quietly sighed to herself. No matter what, she was always the last to arrive. Of course, no one said anything. They did not have to; she could feel their sanctimonious stares. *I do not understand; I should have been the first to arrive because I left more than four thousand heartbeats earlier this time.*

"Get something to eat," Gecheana offered.

"No, thank you. I am not hungry."

"Very well, take your seat. We have much to discuss."

There it is - that hint of disappointment in her tone. Nothing has changed. As Gecheana sat, Nayrah surveyed the surface before her. Domeka, Gecheana's favorite, sat to her right. She was the oldest, and Gecheana never hid her preference above the rest. Domeka's twin sister, Udara, sat to Gecheana's left; Tesol and Kemena, the second set of twins, sat on each side.

Nayrah sat on the opposite side of the table from Gecheana, as was her assigned seat. *I certainly feel contrary to her most of the time.* Looking at her Skean companions, she often wondered what happened to hers. Gecheana never talked about it; Nayrah believed she died during the trial. There were only five cities, so there was no need for a sixth Skean sister. The thought triggered a painful memory of her own. Gecheana forbade her to put Otsoa through the trial but allowed his female twin to take it.

Nayrah fought back tears, remembering their walk to the Chamber of Life and Death. Even though the child failed, Nayrah defended her. Gecheana warned that she would betray the Skeans, so Nayrah had no choice. Either she ended her life, or Gecheana would. It was the most painful thing she ever had to do. Nayrah took a deep breath and pushed the thought away because that memory always moistened her eyes, a visible sign of emotion. Gecheana did not allow them to love anything or anyone, including their offspring, and would invoke a harsh punishment if the sentiment caught her attention.

"I called this meeting because we must discuss the issue of the pending Saiph," she paused to look at each of them. "You are all aware of their threat to us, so I expect an honest response to my questions."

They all nodded in agreement.

"Since I am sure there were no Saiphs spawned here on Akil, he or she must be coming from another world. It is the only logical explanation," Gecheana paused again to look at Nayrah. "Were you able to persuade Yanamai to begin searching in sector 1-5-6-9-2-4-1?"

Knowing that Gecheana never tolerated failure, Nayrah felt nervous about answering. She could have corrected Otsoa's mistake with more time, but it was a luxury she did not have.

Nayrah gulped, "There has been a small snag."

Although her response was calm and relaxed, a storm of fear raged inside.

"I see. What is this snag?" Gecheana inquired.

Even without using the Night Lord's powers, Nayrah knew that within, Gecheana kept her rage boiling behind a mask of calm.

"In a vision, I saw an opportunity. Zorion was in the tower, so I sent Otsoa to impersonate him since his office was empty. Yanamai arrived to give a report, and he ordered her to search within sector 1-5-8-9-3-9-1, but do not worry; I have a plan to fix his mistake," Nayrah babbled, rushing her words.

"You cannot fix this mistake! Otsoa gave her the incorrect sector, which means she will undoubtedly find a planet with a Saiph living on it, which means you have brought the cursed light upon us!" Gecheana spat venomously.

"It is only off by three numbers. I can persuade her to change them, it is not that difficult, and once I finish, the Saiph will never arrive," Nayrah insisted.

"You fool! You do not understand how the process of time works! Had you corrected it in the future, we would have never sensed the Saiph's imminent arrival; it means you cannot fix it! Yanamai will find the planet before you reach her!"

Udara cautiously spoke, "We still have the Time Portal Transmitter."

"No, we do not have it anymore," Gecheana grumbled.

"What happened?" Nayrah inquired.

"What do you think happened?" Gecheana quipped.

"I have no idea," Nayrah frowned.

"Olan happened. You were supposed to keep him from going to Vlor!" Gecheana yelled.

"I did prevent him from leaving! At least, I thought I did," Nayrah responded nervously.

Unable to hold her rage, Gecheana lashed out. Using her power, she wrapped an invisible cord around Nayrah's neck. It tightened, preventing her from breathing.

"I should kill you now and let your daughter rule Argi city," Gecheana growled.

Struggling for air, Nayrah used the Night Lord's power to wedge an opening to breathe and managed a small gap from Gecheana's grip, allowing her to swallow some air. Unsatisfied and still angry, Gecheana guided the invisible cable further down her torso. It constricted as it wrapped around her, making it impossible for Nayrah to breathe. She looked to the others for help; no one moved.

"I…. I do not know what went wrong," stuttered Nayrah.

"Because you are an imbecile! Everything was in place. Once Yanamai found a habitable planet in the original sector, we would have Elzer send the coordinates back in time to himself. It would have allowed us to build one large city to support every Akilian. Elzer would have been Sovereign of that metropolis; thus, he would have been the ruler of every Akilian until I was ready to take his place. Now, due to your incompetence, we may die at the hands of a Saiph or by the sun's plasma stream!"

As Nayrah's face turned dark blue, Gecheana reflected on her use of the veil. Before he died, High Priest Shun had told her that Skeans often worked alone due to the Night Lord himself. He pushed every Skean to fulfill his will, even if they had to kill each other. High Priest Shun informed her that the only way for multiple Skeans to work together is to keep a veil over the subordinates. It allowed her to control them; the downside was that it made them weak and apt to make mistakes, much like Nayrah did. Now, she must create a new plan, but there were only a few options with time running out.

Domeka cautiously interrupted, "We could use this to our advantage."

Gecheana released Nayrah from her grip. Nayrah fell to the floor, loudly gasping for air.

"How?" Gecheana faced Domeka frowning.

"There is already tension between Zorion and Elzer, so all Kemena needs to do is convince Elzer to kill him. Once Zorion is out of the way, Otsoa will be sovereign, and we could have him change the sector so that Yanamai will look in the area you originally intended," Domeka explained.

"You realize that Elzer will not become Sovereign of the new planet if your plan works. Instead, Otsoa will have access to the portal, which means he will take his place," Kemena argued.

"Elzer forfeited his position for his role in destroying the transmitter. At least we will stop the Saiph from coming here and finding a stable home. Plus, it will give us time to design a new scheme," Domeka countered.

"She is right," Gecheana agreed. "Elzer is no longer a choice for us. There is not enough time to build another Transmitter. Now that he has destroyed it, we understand why we never received a message from our future selves. Domeka's idea will work if we all succeed. Even with the Saiph's pending arrival, we can use Otsoa to find the other world and escape to it. Our chance is slim, but it is the only one we have, thanks to Nayrah."

"We must do it quickly," Domeka warned. "Yanamai has already probed the sector."

"Agreed," Gecheana moved toward her cupboard, where she removed a vial and set it before Kemena on the table. "Give this to Elzer. Have him select someone to eliminate Zorion. The potion will enable him to imitate a guard named Molo, which will allow him to get close to Zorion."

Kemena put the potion in her pocket.

Nayrah finally regained her strength and stood, "Zorion is my responsibility! If you want him dead, I will do it!"

"You dare make territorial demands after two colossal failures!" Gecheana shouted.

Her voice pushed Nayrah backward and into her chair, nearly knocking her to the floor.

"Do not speak again unless spoken to!" Gecheana spat. Gecheana turned her attention to her others, "Perhaps we could salvage the situation." She stared blankly in thought and continued, "Just in case this plan fails, we need a backup. Domeka, Udara, and Tesol, I want you to start making Skean swords."

"How many?" they asked in unison.

"Twenty from each of you. I know it will take some time, but I plan to put together a militia to help defend against the Saiph if we have a confrontation," Gecheana answered.

"We will begin right away," they responded in unison.

"The meeting is over," Gecheana waved for Domeka to speak with her in the corner.

"Go see High Priest Elazar; tell him I will need volunteers from his congregation, one volunteer for each sword we build. It would be best if they were single in case they die in battle."

"I will leave right away," Domeka nodded.

As the five Skeans stood to leave, Nayrah sensed their anger toward her. They each had extra work to do, and it was all her fault. It seemed like her mistakes were piling up, and she did not know how to stop them. She noticed that Tesol gave a signal to speak privately on her way out, so she walked to a nearby court with a fountain and waited.

Moments later, Tesol arrived, "Gecheana knows that Otsoa has declined to choose Durnah and has put his fate in Gau's hands."

"All of Akil knows it. She did not hesitate to list all my other failures, so why did she not say anything about it during the meeting?" Nayrah questioned.

"She is waiting to see the outcome."

"And if I fail?"

"She will give Argi to Jadell and make you her subordinate."

"She cannot do that!"

"These are her cities, not ours. We are only stewards, so you better not fail to turn this situation around."

Tesol turned and left, leaving Nayrah alone with her thoughts. Nayrah felt the weight of her mistakes, everything from the approaching Saiph to the destruction of the transmitter. Now, if Otsoa did not join houses with Durnah, she could not bear the thought. Part of her problem was Otsoa's insatiable obsession with Yanamai, which puzzled her. Over the last several yellow harvests, he insisted there was a relationship between them. This hallucination was complete; he even produced dates and times.

She investigated by reviewing the school grounds and avenues video; there was no evidence of his claim. Also, she checked his pheromones without his knowledge to see if someone had drugged him and found no evidence. She wondered if Gecheana or one of her sisters used their powers to imprint his mind with these thoughts, but he remembered too many details. Moreover, it would be counterproductive on Gecheana's part to make her job more challenging.

It left her with no answer. Otsoa had stopped talking about her over the last few yellow harvests. Nayrah thought he had finally moved on, but his coming-of-age ceremony triggered a relapse. She was sure that he believed they were in love, so he acted on that belief, making him difficult to control.

She became frustrated during her search for a solution and stormed toward the elevator. As each step brought her closer, her anger became hotter toward Otsoa. *He blatantly disobeyed me!* His mistake caused a cascade effect, and now a Saiph was coming to their planet, putting them all in danger. His public disregard for her direct order was unforgivable, even if he hallucinated.

The answer came to her, and she smiled wickedly. *I will deal with you later.* She summoned the elevator using the Night Lord's power, and her thoughts drifted away from Otsoa toward Olan. The anger faded, turning into sadness. *I care too much for him.* If Gecheana discovered Nayrah's affair with Argi's Chief Administrator of Intelligence, she would kill her with no regrets or hesitation. *Love is forbidden!*

Nayrah had tried not to love Olan, but her feelings for him were beyond her control. She had to figure out what her next move would be with him. The elevator arrived, and she entered. As it began to ascend, she removed her cloak, looked at her reflection from the elevator doors, and changed her likeness to her alter ego, Thea. The image was harrowing. Unfamiliar eyes stared back at her. Over time, Gecheana chipped away at the Thea identity until there was only Nayrah left.

Before she faced the trial on her fifth yellow harvest, Nayrah remembered having a vision. Looking back, it may have been a warning. In it, she met someone and fell in love; they had children she was proud to raise, but Gecheana took that away and forced her to couple with Zorion, whom she loathed. She would never admit to Gecheana that part of her cared for her children, even though Gecheana told her before they were born that they were merely pawns, Gecheana's pawns.

Gecheana controlled every aspect of Nayrah's life from her earliest memories and now, even her offspring. Nayrah was not even sure Gecheana was her biological parent; she just assumed, they all assumed. As a result, Nayrah often struggled against her instinct to protect Otsoa, despite all the disciplinary actions against him.

With all the chaos surrounding her, it had not escaped Nayrah that Gecheana was forcing Otsoa to be with someone he did not love. If Gecheana had not forced her to be with Zorion, she would have joined houses with Olan instead. Nayrah's problem was not knowing her house. Was she part of Gecheana's house or someone else's? She scolded herself for not using all her powers to persuade Olan to obey her. Instead, she gently nudged him at the proper time, hoping that her feminine charms would do the rest.

Now she realized, a bit late, that his loyalty to Zorion was too strong for such tender tactics. She admired him for it in some small way but could not make that mistake again. Knowing he broke his promise to her hurt deeply and convinced Nayrah that Olan did not love her as much as she thought. It almost brought a tear to her eye. As the elevator began to slow down, she exhaled loudly and changed her appearance to that of the beautiful, eligible elite; the elevator doors opened, and she continued her trip home.

Chapter 15

Alex left Michael at the Research Lab and returned to the Mars Outreach Facility. The Regime built the installation underground because they used dangerously high power to create a stable portal to Mars. The Regime had to make sure its citizens were safe in case something went wrong. Over the last few weeks, he and his team ran multiple simulations to get closer to the red planet. Now that they had the correct calculations, he headed for the testing room, called the Interplanetary Transportation Station.

His long-legged, auburn hair assistant, Stacy, waited near the entrance and handed him a tablet with the checklist. His team spent the last week getting everything ready. The goal was to open a portal on the surface of Mars. To date, they achieved two-thirds of the distance needed to reach the red planet, but the heavenly bodies were in constant motion, causing the gap between the two worlds to change perpetually, making the task even more difficult.

They had to traverse sixty-eight million miles to reach Mars' surface at Earth's current position. If they were successful, today would be monumental. They created chamber walls, where they would open the portal, with transparent aluminum. It was strong enough to withstand almost anything. Alex checked the pressure valve of the test room; it read zero. His team had already evacuated the air. He performed a last-minute system check on the probe and inspected the seals to ensure they were secure.

During one of their preliminary tests, a seal broke before they came this close to Mars. At the time, they used thick tempered glass for walls. It prevented air from escaping the room and protected them from space debris. However, one time, the vortex opened in space in the middle of a passing meteor shower, and the rocks pummeled the glass, which held until one of the seals came loose. Pressurized air pushed the cracked walls out into space, catching Alex and his team off guard. As the rushing wind pushed them toward the event horizon,

Alex grabbed a rail and hit the emergency shut down, just in time. Had he lost his grip, they would be floating corpses in space.

Now, a computer watches the air pressure. The application will automatically close the portal if it senses any drastic changes in air pressure. Alex already reviewed it yesterday but looked over the emergency protocol again to ensure he and his team accounted for all possibilities. They had charged the capacitors for several days, and Alex hoped his latest adjustments would add another twenty million miles to land him on Mars.

While the capacitors charged, they triple-checked their figures for accuracy. If their calculations were correct, the vortex would open on the Valles Marineris system of canyons near the equator. Alex checked the room temperature; it was a brisk 32 degrees Fahrenheit, ensuring everything was ready.

"Stacy, engage the transmitter," Alex instructed.

She typed in the commands, and within a few seconds, Alex heard the transmitter's familiar hum as vast amounts of electricity rushed into its coils. The room shook, reminding Alex of a 4.5 category earthquake. He watched the temperature gauge climb from 32 degrees to 125 degrees.

"All parameters normal," Stacy reported.

Alex built a new transmitter for this experiment with a design from ancient technology: The Tesla Coil. He always thought it ironic that people centuries ago had the key to portal technology at their fingertips but did not realize the potential. Sadly, even the inventor never realized the full scope of his creation, so Alex went back to the basics for this project.

During their first attempt, the transistors melted from the heat. The explosion was catastrophic, destroying most of the facility; they had escaped just in time. Alex realized that modern alloys were atomically too unstable to handle the kind of energy that spatial warping entailed, so moving forward, they constructed the transmitter with twenty-inch-thick carbon steel bars encased in copper and cooled with liquid nitrogen to keep the whole thing from melting. Also, Alex changed the transmitter's shape, making it conical to focus the directional beam and theoretically sustain the vortex at interplanetary distances; the antenna glowed from the heat as the electricity ran through the cables.

"Increase the flow of liquid nitrogen," Alex ordered.

Stacy adjusted the instruments, and the glow subsided. Everyone put on their safety goggles, and Alex nodded to Stacy, who engaged the Tesla Coil. Inside the depressurized test room, the target wall began to phase. In a flash of blinding light, the event horizon appeared, and after the light show was over, everyone removed their protective eye gear. Mars' atmosphere rushed into the test room, blowing red dust inside.

They saw the surface of Mars, and in the distance, colonial buildings, housing thousands of people who moved there from earlier rocket missions, covered the landscape. If Alex got approval for his new transmitter, the Regime could deliver supplies more often and at a cheaper cost.

"Send in the probe. We need measurements to ensure the vortex is stable at the other end," Alex directed.

An eight-wheeled, one-ton vehicle moved forward and landed on Mars.

Stacy faced Alex, "Sir, the event horizon is breaking down again."

"More power to the transmitter!" Alex yelled.

"We're at maximum now, but the portal has nearly depleted the capacitors," a lab tech responded.

Alex cursed under his breath. It was always an issue of not having enough power. No longer hungry, she put the uneaten portions of food away, returned to her office, sat at her desk, and reviewed the data stream from when Garbi interrupted her. Somehow, his calculations were wrong, again. As the event horizon flashed, phasing in and out, the view of Mars' surface began to flicker.

Without enough power, the vortex collapsed with a roaring sound. It was like an old gas-engine backfiring; only this misfire produced so much force it blew several seals. Red dust squirted through the broken seams. Alex ducked, but his lab coat received a good dusting. *Damn it*, he thought, brushing his coat clean. Stacy started to giggle.

"What's so funny?" Alex asked.

"Remember the adage, "If you can't go to Mars, you might as well make Mars come to you?"

"Well?"

"It looks like you just did," Stacy smiled.

Alex looked at the dust on his coat and smiled too.

"I see your point," he paused. "All right, Stacy. Send the results to my office computer so I can review them later," turning, he faced the rest of his team. "For now, get this mess cleaned up. We were so close that we've got Martian grit to sweep up. I want to be ready for a second go the moment we can get this place re-sealed and our power back online. I want that probe back in this lab before the end of the week."

He turned and headed toward the door; before disappearing, he stopped and turned around, "By the way, good job, everyone."

Chapter 16

Akil

Argi City

The 22,272nd Terrestrial Rotation of the Second Summer

It was early in the work cycle, and Yanamai reviewed the data sent by her technical staff. There was so much information to go through, and she had to meticulously review every critical piece of information. Time passed. Her administrative assistant brought in her mid-work cycle moss, but she left it untouched on the table because there was too much work on her desk. Everyone's life depended on her, and she continually felt the weight of that responsibility.

The mounting pressure drove her to work without sleep. Her staff shuffled as they left, which caught her attention. It was time for the second part of Otsoa's celebration. His decision to allow Gau to decide his fate did not surprise her and vindicated her feeling of dread whenever he was near. Now, because of some savage ritual created by a deity that does not exist, three young females would die, fighting to join houses with a noble who did not deserve them.

Are they fighting for power, prestige, Sovereign Cubes, or love? Only they knew the answer. In any case, Yanamai did not believe any of those answers were worth dying for, even love. *If I could have talked to them, I am sure I could have changed their minds.* From her youth, she allowed science and logic to guide her. Of course, emotions played a role, only after making rational decisions. Only then would she feel comfortable allowing herself to care for someone else. Garbi knocked, tearing her away from the thought.

"Yes, what is it?"

"I am sorry to bother you, but you should see this," Garbi advised, walking toward her and setting a memory stick on her desk.

"I appreciate your enthusiasm, Garbi, but you should submit it through the proper channels. Just because we are sisters does not mean you can bypass protocol."

As Yanamai looked at her, she thought it was like seeing a three-dimensional hologram of herself. Every detail was the same, yet that had not always been true. She remembered that Garbi's hair was dark at an early age, not yellow like hers. Although, over time, Garbi's appearance changed as if it occurred naturally, still Yanamai had doubts. Now, it was almost impossible to tell them apart. It made her wonder if Garbi used her shapeshifting ability to mimic her. *But why?*

They used to get along famously and, for a time, were inseparable. Thinking back, Yanamai remembered as their relationship started to change. Being very adept at learning, she entered the workforce earlier than most. By her fifteenth yellow harvest, she had already moved up the chain of command in the Science Division. Before realizing it, she became consumed by her responsibilities, leaving no time to spend with Garbi, the rest of her family, or anyone else. Everyone seemed to understand, but Garbi often complained about her absence.

"We missed you at our last family dinner," Garbi spoke indifferently.

Although there was no emotion in her voice, Yanamai could sense a hint of pain and realized what she had missed.

Her eyes widened, "Your 'Coming of Age' celebration!"

"Ah, she remembered a little too late."

"Oh, Garbi. I am deeply sorry. I cannot believe I forgot."

"Do not worry. The rest of our family was there."

"You should have reminded me."

"I did. I told you early that work cycle."

"I feel terrible. Please forgive me."

"There is nothing to forgive. I did not expect you to come."

Standing, Yanamai walked around her desk to embrace her; Garbi pulled away, "What are you doing?"

"I am trying to give my younger sister a hug."

"Save it for our parents the next time you see them. I do not want your affection."

"Do not be this way."

"It is the way you want our relationship to be."

"That is not true. I want us to be close."

"As a scientist, I have learned how to discover the truth about many things. For example, if you wanted us to be closer, you would try, so I can only draw one conclusion since you have not bothered. You care more about this job than you do anything or anyone else."

"This is not just a job, Garbi! It directly affects whether we survive! I am sorry you feel neglected, but if we do not find a planet soon, none of us will be alive to even worry about being ignored!" Yanamai exclaimed.

Garbi looked at her timekeeper with detachment, "I will be late for the celebration if I do not leave now. You can look at the information I found or ignore it. I do not care either way."

She stopped at the door and turned around on her way out, "So that you know. I requested a transfer. Do not worry; I put it through the proper channels."

"Why are you leaving my department?"

"Because you have not promoted me since I have been here. Everyone else has moved up except me." "

"I did not want to appear as if I favored you above everyone else."

"I never asked for preferential treatment, but everyone thinks I am not doing my job because of you!"

"You are right. That is my mistake. I will give you the promotion now."

"I do not want it from you. I will work my way up the ranks in another department. Just sign my request to transfer."

"If that is what you want."

"It is. Goodbye, Yanamai."

Yanamai closed her door and set her back against it. Garbi's transfer request hit her harder than she would like to admit. Garbi's presence in her department had always given her comfort. It was like having family around all the time, even if she did not see her for several work cycles. The fact that she was there was enough, but Garbi made it clear that she took her for granted.

She made a mistake by not promoting her sooner and could fix it if Garbi would let her. Garbi's lack of empathy angered her because it showed an inability to understand her job and its pressure. Still, Yanamai did not like arguing with her. Upon returning to her desk, she stared at her computer. The stress of her job and relationship with Garbi surfaced, and tears streamed down her cheeks.

Chapter 17

Akil

Vlor City

The 22,272nd Terrestrial Rotation of the Second Summer

Looking at his Locator Bracelet, Elzer confirmed that everyone on his security team was in place. He had instructed Lenck, his Chief Administrator of Security, to ensure that everyone was on high alert. Having destroyed the Time Portal Transmitter, Elzer knew his life was in danger and cautiously walked to his private elevator to summon it. The doors opened to reveal Kemena standing in the center of the lift. Fearing for his life, Elzer unsheathed his sword and drew it back, ready to strike.

"How did you get up here?" he demanded.

Kemena smiled, "How I got here is not important. What you should remember is that I got past your security."

She stepped out of the elevator toward him, "Such a task is easy for a Skean. Now put your weapon down."

She did not yell, but there was mystic power behind her voice, making Elzer question his resolve.

"No, I-I-I do not trust you," he stuttered.

Her smile widened. Elzer's attempt to be strong amused her. She waved her right hand, yanked his sword from his grip, and tossed it several paces down the avenue, far out of his reach.

Elzer panicked and yelled into his bracelet, "Lenck, you better get up here now!"

Again, she beckoned, and his bracelet flew off his wrist toward her. She caught it and crushed it in her grasp. Metal pieces jangled as they hit the concrete floor as she continued her slow, steady pace toward him.

"You destroyed my Time Portal Transmitter, Elzer."

"It was an accident."

"It was stupidity! You had no right to use the device without my expressed permission."

"I rule this city, not you!" Elzer shouted defiantly.

Again, she waved her hand. Elzer's feet flew from beneath him. He landed with a thud on the solid surface.

"I rule this city!" she yelled.

Elzer was quiet.

"Say it, or I will kill you right now."

With a curled lip, Elzer mumbled, "You rule this city."

"Now get up!" she demanded.

Elzer got to his feet.

"Although you deserve to die for your transgression, I will give you a chance to redeem yourself."

Elzer did not believe in second chances and was sure Kemena did not either. He thought that she would make him pay for the destruction of the transmitter because it is what he would do. This visit was their third encounter. The first time they met, she presented him with the schematics for building the transmitter and gave him a plan to fund it. Everything had been a success.

She also revealed her Skean identity. Having heard rumors of their cult, he ordered Gau's priests to educate him on the sect. They told him the Skeans were secretive, only exposing themselves when necessary. Moreover, they were powerful, but they had a weakness, Saiphs. The last known Saiph died sixty yellow harvests ago. Unable to match Kemena's strength, he had to obey her demands.

Kemena appeared to him the second time he finished construction on the transmitter and told him of her plan, but Elzer had to wait until Zorion's team found a habitable planet. Once Elzer knew the coordinates, he would use the Time Portal Transmitter to send them to himself in the past. It would give him plenty of time to build a city there before Zorion's team found it, and then he would notify the sovereigns of his findings.

Everyone would have to accept him as the 'Supreme Sovereign' of the Akilians if they wanted to leave their dying planet. He dreamed of that moment thousands of times, but that fantasy died after the transmitter exploded. It explained why he did not send the coordinates to his past self. It was his fault, and Kemena came to make him pay for it.

"What will you have me do?"

"Kill Zorion."

"What?"

"Are you deaf? I said kill Zorion!"

"I can assure you; I have no love for him, but if I kill him and someone discovers it was I, the other sovereigns will execute me."

"If you refuse my order, I will kill you now."

Elzer shook his head and backed up. Kemena moved forward, matching his steps until he reached a wall. They stopped simultaneously; she removed her hood, intently glaring at him, revealing her piercing blue eyes. He felt a warm sensation move through his body, calming him. He believed she was using her power to subdue him. Fear faded, replaced with relaxation. Gazing into her eyes, he found himself drawn to her.

"You will do as I say, Elzer," she spoke with that mystic power behind her voice.

Elzer nodded, "I will kill Zorion."

Satisfied, she reached for her pocket but stopped, seeing him wearing a glove. Gently, she took his wrist and raised it.

"Did you get hurt in the explosion?"

"Yes," he nodded.

She gently moved her hand over his and noticed a few digits were missing.

"They could not find them in time. There was too much debris," he explained.

"If you would like, I could use my power to bring them back."

Elzer nodded. Another wave of warmth moved through him. It was pleasurable; his knees nearly buckled, so he placed his free hand against the wall for support. His fingers reappeared inside the glove; he moved them and smiled.

"Remember, Elzer. What I give, I can also take away."

"I understand."

"Good," she replied, retrieving the bottle from her pocket. "Here. It will help with your mission."

"What is it?"

"It is a potion that contains a synthetic of Molo's pheromones."

"Molo?"

"He is one of Zorion's bodyguards. Use it to infiltrate his security team and kill him at the right moment."

"I will put my best Vlorian on it," he took the mixture from her hand and placed it in his pocket.

"Do not fail me again, Elzer, or the next time you see me will be the last."

Turning, Kemena put on her hood and walked back to the elevator. Reaching the inside, she gradually spun around. As the doors closed, she smiled at him, and the elevator descended. As the distance between them increased, his feeling from her presence faded, but the memory stayed. He leaned back against the wall and breathed deeply, trying to regain his composure until hearing footsteps running toward him. It was Lenck and the security team. Elzer folded his arms and waited for them to arrive.

"Are you all right?" Lenck asked, breathing heavily from running.

"Just fine," Elzer stepped away from the wall.

Elzer drew abreast of Lenck, closed his newly healed hand into a fist, and smashed it into Lenck's face. Lenck spun around and slammed into the wall before bouncing off and collapsing to the floor. As Lenck struggled to his knees, Elzer knelt beside him, grabbed a handful of his hair, and twisted his head around to face him.

"Lenck," Elzer whispered, "we must have a serious talk about my security."

Chapter 18

Akil

Argi City

The 22,272[nd] Terrestrial Rotation of the Second Summer

Yanamai composed herself but still felt hungry. Reaching inside the coolant box, she removed the moss-filled bowl her assistant had delivered earlier and put it on a hot plate. Once it was ready, she set it on her small table with a tall glass of water in the small dining area near her office and took a hard look at her life. The number of family events and essential gatherings that she had missed due to work was beginning to accumulate.

She never imagined being alone in her old age, but her talk with Garbi made it seem likely. Unless she adjusted her work schedule, eating, sleeping, and living alone would become a permanent way of life. Due to her job, she had bypassed her coming of age celebration. Although her family understood, they were not happy. By now, everyone her age had joined houses and had as many as four offspring.

Her teachers and school officials noticed that she could absorb and understand copious amounts of information, so they placed her into advanced physics and application coding courses. She learned her skills quickly and, within a brief time, was at the head of her class. The better she did, the more they gave her until work consumed all her time. She had done so well that the former Chief Administrator of the Science Division brought her name to Zorion, who kept a close eye on her. As she moved through the ranks, he set up frequent visits between them in his office, but he unexpectedly gave her the Chief Administrator position on one work cycle. Zorion made it clear that he trusted in her ability to save them.

From that time until now, she carried that burden alone. Garbi did not know about this responsibility and Yanamai did not feel comfortable repeating her private conversation with Zorion. She wished there was time to do other things, yet if a distraction caused her to miss something, all Akilian blood would be on her hands. She loved Zorion like a parent but resented him sometimes for putting this burden on her. *He* took her life, and there was nothing she could do about it. The most frustrating part, so far, is that she had not found a suitable planet.

She took a deep, cleansing breath and let her thoughts dwell on the hope that kept her going; the belief that she would find a new world for the Akilians. She often wondered what wonderful foods they might discover in this new place. She read in school that their ancestors had hundreds if not thousands of different herbs and imagined how they smelled and tasted. Without anything to compare, everything ended up smelling and tasting like moss.

Several moss species survived the great freeze, and, depending on their color, they prepared them in specific ways to bring out their flavors. The blue and green mosses were best heated. The red, orange, and brown mosses tasted best boiled. They ate fresh purple moss for dessert because of its sweet flavor. The only moss that was inedible was the yellow moss, which was poisonous. They cultivated it to make clothing and other necessities.

Yanamai stared at the empty seats around her table, chewing the warm, green moss. *Is this my future? Do I, or do we, even have a future?* No longer hungry, she put the uneaten portions of food away, returned to her office, sat at her desk, and reviewed the data stream from before Garbi interrupted her. The cold, unfeeling statistics helped push away her melancholy, at least at first.

She analyzed the data from the stopping point but still had difficulty concentrating. Images of Garbi kept flashing in her mind's eye, and in frustration, she pushed back from her desk and accidentally found the memory stick Garbi left behind. Although she tried to ignore it, the annoying little thing caught her eye, so she grabbed it and fed it into her analyzer.

The probe took thousands of images with complementary sensor readings. Garbi's part had a modest hundred or so. At least Garbi had the foresight to place the data at the front so that Yanamai would see it first. That information had the high-resolution image of a blue, brown, and white planet and the sensor readings. Yanamai studied the photos and magnified one to its highest setting.

After comparing what she read to Garbi's notes, it made her gasp. *No, it cannot be!* She opened the file having the sensor results and confirmed Garbi's findings. The planet was emitting vortex signatures. Some were powerful enough to reach a nearby planet. The discovery sent chills of excitement through her. Zorion needed to know this right away, so she sent an electronic work order to the night shift to open another portal closer to the planet and obtain more detailed information. A few moments later, she jumped out of her chair and ran straight to the arena.

Chapter 19

Leaving his office, Michael sidestepped the android that had delivered the message, berating himself inwardly for not taking his communicator off call forward. The General's office was on the first level, close to the Interstate Transportation Station, so he ran down the hall and pushed the button for the elevator. As he waited, his imagination began to run wild. *Shit! They must have tracked my link to the satellite. I must brainstorm a good excuse if the General calls me on it.*

As the elevator ascended, he paced within its walls. *The General's been a good friend, but he'll have to fire me for using the spy equipment for personal use. I'll bet they've recorded everything.* Unable to explain his actions, he lowered his head into his hands. *Damn, damn, DAMN!* The elevator stopped; he took a deep breath, stepped out, and casually walked to the General's administrative assistant. He noticed several people waiting ahead of him, and they all stared at him quizzically, even the General's assistant. *Everyone knows what I've done. I'm in big trouble.*

"You can go right in," she paused, "The General wants to see you right away."

Michael smiled politely, "Thank you."

Outwardly, he presented a calm demeanor but inwardly felt a raging storm of fear. Inside, the General sat behind his desk, talking to someone via video com.

"Yes, Sir. He's here now," the General motioned for Michael to come around the desk.

Sir? Michael thought. *Whomever he's talking with outranks him. Oh, man, this isn't good for me.* Calmly, Michael rounded the desk. The General looked in his direction for the first time since he came into the room.

Simultaneously, two voices exclaimed, "Damn!"

"What in the hell happened to you?" the General asked, sitting up in surprise.

Confused, Michael looked from the startled General to the equally startled face of Supreme Commander Porter on the monitor. *Oh, what a dolt I am. My black eye, that's why everyone was staring at me.*

"It's a long story," Michael's cheeks turned red.

"I certainly hope the other fellow looks worse than you do," joshed Supreme Commander Porter.

"I'm afraid I got the worst of it," Michael frowned.

"General, you had better get that young man some good old-fashioned combat training," Supreme Commander Porter added.

A huge grin spread across the General's face, "I'll take care of it as soon as this meeting is over."

"Supreme Commander Porter, how may I help you, Sir?" Michael inquired nervously.

"I have a situation that needs your attention. I'm conducting an interrogation, and there seems to be a malfunction with one of your inventions. I believe you call it the Mind Reader," Supreme Commander Porter commented.

The machine was Michael's first notable creation that labeled him a "boy genius." He built it at just seventeen years old.

"The correct name for it is the Neuro-Electric Impulse Interpreter," Michael paused, "The Mind Reader is a shop nickname that one of my friends gave it."

It occurred to him that thoughts and memories were nothing more than electronic impulses, which the brain stored on living tissue, just like computers stored information in matter memory gel. It was a simple scan-and-retrieve function that he solved by making an electronic copy of the brain's data.

"If you don't mind, I like the term Mind Reader. It makes it easier to remember," Supreme Commander Porter noted.

"Of course, Sir; Mind Reader, it is," Michael nervously agreed, "So, what seems to be the problem?"

"I can't discuss specifics over the video com, so I need you at Precinct 5A as soon as possible. I've sent an assistant to fill you in on all the details. He'll be waiting for you at the coordinates I've already given to the General. He'll also have the electronic file for you. Take care of the situation, and I want constant updates," Supreme Commander Porter ordered.

"Yes, Sir," Michael answered, but Supreme Commander Porter disconnected the line before he finished speaking.

"You have your orders. Here's the address. You better get going," advised the General. "Oh, and Michael…"

"Yes, sir?"

"When you get back, throw a raw beef steak on that eye."

"I've already had a Medical Droid put accelerant on it."

"You do what you think is best, but I've always liked the old remedies."

Michael nodded, ran to the Interstate Transportation Station, and punched in the address. Within seconds, a portal opened, so he stepped through and landed at the Precinct. He saw a young man on the platform, wearing an expensive suit, standing nearby.

He extended his hand, walking toward him, "Good day Mr. Stewart."

The young man distractedly studied Michael's injured eye.

"Hello," Michael responded, shaking his hand.

"If you'll come with me, I'll explain on the way."

Michael walked beside him.

"First, my name is Stan Hill. I'll be your assistant for this project. If you need *anything*, you're to tell me, and I will have it delivered to you at once."

"What's going on?"

"It seems that State Comptroller," he paused and looked down at his datapad, "Mr. James Bradley was arrested for fraud yesterday, but since there wasn't enough physical evidence to convict him, the court subjected him to an MR."

"You mean the Mind Reader."

"Correct. We followed all the standard procedures; my team reviewed the scanned memories, and there was no sign that Mr. Bradley had committed the crime. To make matters worse, it showed that he was nowhere near where we believe he perpetrated the offense. The problem is that there's an eyewitness placing him at the scene."

"Can you trust this witness?"

"Yes, beyond any doubt. Now, you can see my dilemma."

"Is the machine malfunctioning?"

"We've run a full diagnostic. It's in perfect working order."

Just as Stan finished his sentence, they entered the MR Information Processing Room.

"Let me look at the video and sound you retrieved," Michael suggested.

Stan motioned to the technician, who brought the video and audio up on a large screen monitor.

"What's the date of this memory?" questioned Michael.

"December 15 of last year," the technician replied.

Michael studied the video. Although he invented the machine, it never felt comfortable seeing memories through someone else's eyes. Since the recording encompassed the entire day, Michael asked to fast-forward it to find the day in question. The 15th was on a Saturday. Mr. Bradley claimed that he spent the day fishing off a pier on Crystal Lake. The video supported his claim, but Michael noticed something and scratched his head.

"What's wrong?" Stan queried.

"I'm not sure; something's not right." Michael paused, turned, and continued, "Play the fishing sequence again, from the beginning. I want to see the whole drive out to the lake."

Again, everyone watched the trip in real-time as Mr. Bradley left his house and drove out to the lake in the dark, where he parked his car and waited for the sun to rise. Michael ordered the technician to freeze the frame as the sun crested the horizon.

"What do you see?" Stan inquired.

"The sun," Michael answered.

"The sun?"

Michael faced Stan, "We have two accounts that conflict. It should be obvious that one of them is a lie. You've confirmed that the informant is trustworthy, yet Mr. Bradley's memory proves his innocence. Diagnostics prove that the MR isn't malfunctioning, so there are only two answers. First, your informant is lying. Second, someone has rearranged Mr. Bradley's memories."

"I didn't know that was possible. How did someone do this?" Stan frowned.

"You can use the Mind Reader to shuffle memories and even create them. Initially, the Mind Reader could only read a few seconds of memory. Later, the government asked me to improve it. During my research, I found a way to superimpose memories. The Regime used it on agents and sent them to other countries with undercover assignments.

"It made it easier for them to blend in. Also, if the foreign government apprehended the agent, the superimposed memories were a reality to them. If they stuck to the truth that we implanted in them, they would pass any lie detection test on the market today. Due to the obvious danger of the technology getting into the wrong hands, we kept it a secret."

Michael pointed to the big screen monitor, "With this memory, we can check when the sun was supposed to rise in this location on this date. If they don't coincide, we know that someone superimposed this memory over the original one for December 15."

"If what you suspect is true, our technology is in the wrong hands," Stan remarked.

"How could they have gotten the schematics for the MR?" Michael inquired.

"I don't know, but I'll need to inform Supreme Commander Porter at once. It could be a breach of our security."

"Wait! Before you go, I will need at least twenty lab techs with level eight security clearances to review the scan. Finding the splice will be tricky."

"They'll be here within the hour. Anything else?"

"No, that should do it."

Without another word, Stan left the room, and as the door closed, a memory from Michael's first day in school popped into his mind. The first lesson taught to all children was that the Regime did not tolerate crime. The government did not bend for all severe offenses such as murder, rape, illegal drugs, theft, etc., and sent these criminals to the Moon Penal Colony if found guilty. It also applied to government officials who abused their power and tried to circumvent the law. They never released them.

"No one is above the law," Michael whispered.

The Mind Reader first brought him to the attention of General Saunders. Michael did not create the Mind Reader to help the judicial system; he created it as kind of a joke. It was like a parlor game for fun. General Saunders pointed out that by making a device that could record and playback a person's memories, he ensured the sentencing of the guilty and vindication of the innocent because the Regime's advanced technology made it increasingly difficult to prosecute crimes that lacked physical evidence.

When Supreme Commander Porter first announced to the public that the Regime planned to use the Mind Reader as evidence in court, there was a great debate on its merit. At first, most Regime citizens were against its use, but as increasing numbers of victims allowed the MR to scan their memories, conviction rates rose. The public felt safer, so their opinion of the MR changed. If it became known that it is possible to superimpose memories, Michael knew that 'Mind Reader' testimony would no longer be relevant in any court in the Regime. Also, Lawyers could have prior convictions overturned, which would bring chaos.

Sentries brought a very uncooperative Mr. Bradley back to the testing room. Michael watched as the technicians scanned and recorded the past year of Mr. Bradley's life. The human brain stores a massive amount of information in a year, making him grateful for the staff. He copied Mr. Bradley's memories, divided them equally among the personnel for review, and worked on the superimposed impression to uncover the truth of that day's events.

His success depended on whether the overlying images compromised the neuron cells that held the original memory, but it would still be a mystery if the overwrite damaged them. He scanned Mr. Bradley's brain at the slowest speed, so it would pick up every detail his neuron cells stored. He worked with the file for a few hours with only a snowy video and static sound of that day to show for it. The recovered information showed that during Mr. Bradley's lunch, a man with short, dark hair approached him. The man wore a black suit, white shirt, red tie, and sunglasses.

Michael took a snapshot of the man from the screen, stored it in a folder, and reviewed the file, but the computer could only save bits and pieces of video and sound. He heard the man say, "Good d- Mr. -, I would - to – with - a." Michael played it repeatedly, adjusting the settings yet could only get a few words, so he prepared the best quality video manageable, electronically transcribed the conversation, and reviewed it.

Many words were missing; the ones that stuck out were "payment," "Mind Reader," and "contract." It was not much to go on, but at least he had something. He checked government records, looked for contracts set before the committee around the date in question, and found three. First, there was a five-year contract for replacing and supporting all the current government androids with the latest model by *Integrated Robotics;* second, there was a building contract for a new Market Place in the Regime; third, there was a competitive bid for the replacement of government androids by a company called *Latest Innovations.*

As Michael finished imputing the information for his report to Supreme Commander Porter, Stan walked in, "How are you progressing?"

"I've found a few things already," Michael played the gritty video for him.

Stan frowned, "Not much to go on."

"I know. I could only make out a few words here and there. Still, I did find a few clues that may help the Regime Bureau of Investigation with their inquiry."

"Show me."

Michael opened the transcript, showed Stan the few words he found, and gave him the list of companies that sent bids.

"You think *Integrated Robotics* or *Latest Innovations* propositioned Mr. Bradley," Stan guessed.

"It's the only thing that makes sense. Their bids are close, and we're talking about a long-term contract and millions of Regime Talons."

"Money is almost always the reason."

"There's still a possibility he saw this person before. He may not have recognized him, but I'll have my team looking through his memories to see if his face shows up anywhere."

"Excellent idea. I'll have the RBI start an investigation into these companies right away. In the meantime, if you find anything, don't hesitate to call me."

"I won't. We need to find whoever has this Mind Reader/Writer before they do severe damage."

"Supreme Commander Porter gave it the highest priority, so trust me, we'll find them soon," Stan assured and left.

Michael thought of everything someone could do with his invention, sitting back in his chair. People could copy their entire life and superimpose it into someone else's mind, killing that person and taking control of their body. A person could also download a subliminal or a prevalent command, turning a passive person into a heartless killer. He shivered at the thought of having his conscience replaced by another's. What troubled him the most was how his invention's schematics got outside the Regime's server. The central server had no internet connection for obvious security reasons, which meant someone had to break in and steal it. *We have a traitor in our midst.*

Chapter 20

Earth
The United States - Texas - Houston
May 8, 2452

Jared set a chip down on his pillow. It was the twin to the one implanted in his back. He needed to be invisible tonight. Using the mini transmitter, he simultaneously activated the chip on his pillow and deactivated the one in his back. He verified everything was working correctly, dressed in street clothes, grabbed his bag, went to Tim's room, and knocked. Tim opened the door wearing his pajamas and raised an eyebrow seeing Jared.

"Where are you going?" Tim wondered.

"Supreme Commander Porter is sending me on an errand. I need to speak with the head of the resistance, a General Bailey, to be precise."

"I hear his base camp is west of Houston; it's mobile because he never stays in the same place for long."

"Our latest intel gives me the proximity of where he should be."

Tim furrowed his brow, "Wait. What about your chip? Won't the computer know where you are?"

"There's a duplicate on my pillow, so the computers will think I'm in bed sleeping."

"I guess you plan to drive."

"I must. The US scans for portal activity in their territory. If I contact him, I'll set up a portal signature disrupter. Otherwise, they might find its signal and send in troops."

"Ok, let me get dressed, and I'll be right with you."

"I appreciate the offer, Tim, but it's best if I go alone on this one. Also, you don't have a secondary chip to leave behind that can fool their computer."

"You will be driving through gang territory at night! Are you insane? Don't you remember what happened on our way here, during the day?"

"It must be done. Besides, you must be a little crazy to do what I do, which explains why I'm here. Is there a vehicle you can spare, something that you don't need, something I may not be able to return?"

Tim thought for a moment. Vehicles were hard to come by and expensive to support. After what happened to Jared's motorcycle, he did not want to hand over the keys to his new car.

"Let me call my employer."

Tim disappeared into his room, leaving the door ajar, but Jared did not enter out of respect; Tim returned a few moments later.

"He's sending something over now. Go downstairs and wait in the lobby. Someone will be over shortly."

"I appreciate it, Tim."

Jared headed straight to the lobby. About an hour later, someone finally showed up. The man carrying the keys was full of grease and grime. As he approached, Jared smelled gasoline and oil. Jared stood to introduce himself as the man stopped.

"Here," the man tossed the keys with a disapproving gaze. "It may not look like much, but it's mechanically solid."

"Thanks."

"By the way, I *would* like it returned," the man emphasized and left.

"I'll do my best," Jared answered, moving toward the door.

Outside, he found the vehicle the man left for him. It was not surprising to see the dilapidated condition of the car. Dents covered every panel, and some of the rust holes were big enough to put his fist through. As he pulled the door open, it creaked loudly. *This thing's been in a few fender benders.* The seats had rips in several places, but they still had enough foam to support his weight.

He tossed his bag onto the passenger seat, sat, shut the door, strapped on the seat belt, and started the engine. It sprang to life without any hesitation. *You've got to love grease monkeys. They know how to keep 'em purring, and there's a full tank too! How thoughtful.* He activated his GPS with his destination already coded in. His foot smashed the gas pedal, and he sped off.

Having driven for half an hour, Jared checked his location with the GPS. He stayed off the main roads. Sadly, the backstreets changed from blacktop to dirt several times. For the last several miles, the throughway stayed dirt and gravel. It was pitch black outside. The only light came from the crescent moon, which barely illuminated the night sky. The speedometer showed that he was only moving at thirty miles per hour. Although he wanted to drive faster, the road was too bumpy.

A bank of white lights lit up on his left and blinded him. He heard a big throated engine, and the spinning of oversized tires echoed as the lights came toward him. Adrenaline shot through his body, automatically causing his subcutaneous body armor to release into his system. When the truck hit him, his body was ready for it. The vehicle slammed into Jared's left rear fender, spinning his car around 180 degrees. *They've done this before.* Jared hit the gas to speed away, but his engine stalled. *Damn, I don't need this.* Jared keyed the ignition; it would not start.

"Buenas Noches, gringo," the voice was menacing.

Jared stopped trying to start the car and grabbed the steering wheel to keep his hands in sight, "And how are you this wonderful evening?"

He turned into the lights and looked at the backlit shadow of a tall, thin man.

The man chuckled, "I'm doing fine, but you, on the other hand, are not doing so good, I think."

Jared heard laughter coming from behind the lights and guesstimated that there were five or six other men.

"I was just on my way to the countryside."

"And trespassing on our turf!"

"And you are?"

"I am El Diablo," he answered.

He stepped to Jared's door and positioned himself so that Jared could get a good look at him; he extended his right arm toward the lights.

"And these are my *Demonios.*"

Well-rehearsed, Jared thought.

"Is there anything I can trade for safe passage?" Jared queried.

"If this car is an example of your wealth, you have nothing to trade by the looks of it."

El Diablo pointed an old-fashioned six-shot revolver at Jared's chest and cocked the hammer back with his thumb.

"Would a diamond be enough?" Jared blurted.

El Diablo chuckled again, "Where did someone, who drives such a poor excuse for a car, get something as valuable as diamonds?"

"Not diamonds, just one big one."

El Diablo studied him for a moment, "Ok, let me see it."

"It's in my bag."

"Don't make any sudden moves gringo, and keep your hands where I can see 'em."

Jared reached across the seat and pulled the bag into his lap.

"No tricks gringo, or we'll fill you full of more holes than this poor excuse for a car has!"

"Relax. No tricks, I promise," Jared pulled out a small case, opened it, and handed it to El Diablo.

Carefully, Jared sneaked a large caliber, two-shot derringer-like pistol into the palm of his left hand while El Diablo focused on the diamond.

"Who did you kill to get it?" El Diablo asked.

"Does it matter?"

"Not really, but I can't tell if this is real or not. Hey, Carlos! Come here, man, and bring your loupes."

Crap, I would have to run into the only gang with a diamond expert. As Carlos approached, Jared noticed two more vehicles with banks of bright lights assume a position behind his car. *If they continue to illuminate this place, it'll be like sitting on a tropical beach at noon.* El Diablo motioned for Jared to get out of his car, so Jared kept his hands up and stood. El Diablo kept his gun pointed at Jared.

"What you got, boss?" Carlos walked up beside El Diablo.

"This gringo is trying to buy safe passage with this. Tell me; is it *wort* anything?"

Carlos took the diamond, held it up to the light, and laughed.

"What's so funny?" Jared inquired.

"This ain't no diamond. It's Zirconia," Carlos answered.

"He's lying," Jared countered.

"Why should one of my trusted lieutenants lie to me?" El Diablo frowned.

El Diablo pulled the trigger, and his old-fashioned six-shooter exploded with a loud pop. The bullet slammed into Jared's chest momentarily, knocking the wind out of him. Its force slammed him back into the rusted-out car.

"Idiota!" El Diablo exclaimed.

"Damn it! That hurt!" Jared yelled.

He raised his left hand with blinding speed and put one bullet into El Diablo's forehead and the other into Carlos' temple. Both men fell to the ground with small fountains of blood spurting up through the new holes in their heads. Jared jumped into the front seat, pumped the gas, and turned the key. His engine sprang to life. He hit the gas and sped out, moving out of their light and toward the road.

He thought that losing their leader would slow them down; he was wrong. A vehicle with bright fog lights came up behind him and fired a heavy caliber machine gun. His back window exploded into a thousand shards and disappeared into the night. The road was too narrow for him to swerve effectively. Bullets riddled the car's panels, doors, and trunk. His back took several hits, but his body armor kept him alive. Jared pressed to put more distance between them. The road led to a steep hill, and as he crested the top, the car went air-born for a few seconds. He landed, slammed on his brakes, and swerved, trying to avoid the battle tank sitting in the middle of the road.

"What the hell!" Jared yelled.

The car skidded sideways and stopped several yards from the armored vehicle. His engine stalled again. There was complete silence until he heard the electric motor moving the tank's barrel downward. Jared felt sick to his stomach and wondered if his body armor could stop a cannon blast at this distance. Before his thoughts moved further down that line of thinking, the other vehicle crested the hill. Jared heard the engine revving high as it went airborne, and the tank commander fired. Jared ducked.

The other vehicle took a direct hit in midair. It exploded, and Jared felt the intense heat from the flame. His ears rang from the almost simultaneous blast of the cannon and the explosion of the truck. Searchlights lit everything up around him. Jared saw several men with guns trained on him, and a man with white hair, who smoked a cigar, walked out from behind the tank. Another man, who appeared younger, stood beside him.

The white-haired man studied Jared for a few moments before speaking, "You don't look like a gang member."

"I'm not."

"Who are you?"

"My name's Jared. Supreme Commander Porter of the Regime has sent me to speak with General Bailey."

"Oh yeah? What does the Regime want with him?"

"Sorry, it's for his ears only."

Gunfire erupted from on top of the hill. The white-haired man ducked back behind the tank and yelled, "Return fire! Return fire!"

Jared got out of the car, ran over, and crouched near the white-haired man.

The younger man pointed his pistol at Jared, "Don't even breathe funny."

Jared raised his hands, "In my pocket is a video of Supreme Commander Porter verifying my identity."

He pointed to the pocket. The younger man reached in and took out the device. He pressed *play* and held it up for the white-haired man to watch. Porter verified Jared's story.

The white-haired man waved his hand at the younger man, "It'll have to be good enough."

A grenade exploded near the tank.

"What the hell did you do to piss them off?" the white-haired man yelled at Jared.

"They tried to stop me, and I had to kill two of their men," Jared answered.

"Shit, who did you kill? El Diablo?" the younger man wondered.

"Yes, and someone named Carlos," Jared confirmed.

"You killed El Diablo?" the white-haired man marveled.

"Um, yeah… he left me no choice."

"Great, they think you're one of ours. Nice job, kid; now we've got a battle on our hands, maybe a war."

"Why not just use the tank and wipe them out?" Jared suggested.

"I would, except I used the last shell to save your hide."

"Wait. Are you telling me there are no more shells for the tank?"

The white-haired man laughed and looked at his friend, "Do we have any shells, Colonel Scott?"

"No, General. Still waiting on supply to get more."

Stunned, Jared looked at the white-haired man, "General Bailey?"

General Bailey frowned, "Yeah, it's me."

"What the hell are you doing out here? You should be back at Headquarters."

General Bailey laughed, "Headquarters? Are you sure you're from the Regime? I mean, if anyone would know that we ain't got a headquarters, it would be them. They've got satellites everywhere."

"To be honest, the intel didn't indicate that you had one, so I assumed you built it underground, or it was well camouflaged."

"Oh, we camouflaged it, all right. It's completely invisible, even to us."

A bullet ricocheted off the tank near the General's head, "Damn it! I'm tired of this. Colonel, where's Sergeant Burke?"

"His squad is about two clicks to our south."

"Get him on the radio and tell him we need support now!"

"Yes, Sir!"

"Is there anything I can do to help?" Jared inquired.

"I think you've done enough. Just sit tight."

General Bailey's men returned fire, but shooters at the top of the hill took out their searchlights and pinned them down with a constant barrage of small-arms fire.

"How many do you think, General?" questioned Colonel Scott.

"Can't tell for sure; I would guess about thirty, maybe forty."

"They have us outgunned four to one."

General Bailey smiled, "Not for long."

As if on cue, gunfire erupted from the north.

"'Bout damn time, Larkin!" General Bailey mumbled; he faced Jared, "It won't be long now."

"Won't be long till what? They get us?" Jared quipped.

General Bailey chuckled, "No, till Larkin…I mean, Sergeant Burke kills 'em all."

He turned back to his entrenched squad, "Hold your fire, men; we don't want to hit him accidentally."

Jared listened intently. It was hard to tell at first, but the noise of gunfire decreased. At one point, he heard a few faint screams until there was silence.

"Is it over?" Jared queried.

"Yep, he got 'em. Every one of 'em, I'm sure."

A chill ran down Jared's spine, "You said he, don't you mean they?"

"Nope." General Bailey stood and yelled, "Sergeant Burke, is your mission accomplished?"

"Yes, Sir!"

"Excellent. Now get down here."

"Colonel, tell Sergeant Murphy he's in charge of the platoon until Sergeant Burke returns. After that, they're to dispose of the bodies and resume their patrol. Also, I want someone to get me a light, now!"

"Yes, Sir!"

Moments later, undamaged lights lit up the area.

"There, that's better," General Bailey paused briefly, "Now, I need you to put your hands behind your back, son."

He pointed his pistol at Jared's head.

"But General, I showed you the video!" Jared protested.

"Until I'm fully convinced, you're just going to have to be uncomfortable."

Jared frowned and put his hands behind his back, "I understand."

Sergeant Burke arrived, but Jared had his back toward him and General Bailey, making it impossible to see him. He felt plastic restraints close in around his wrists.

"What do you want to do with him?" a deep, throaty voice asked.

"Put him in the jeep. We'll take 'em to the farm."

Chapter 21

Akil
Argi City
The 22,272[nd] Terrestrial Rotation of the Second Summer

In his private dressing room, Zorion heard the noise of the crowd. The arena's overseer entered earlier to inform him that citizens from each city filled every seat. This group of attendees would be a vastly different type of Akilian than had attended the last celebration. Other than the four families involved in the competition, this sort consisted of religious zealots because Gau's justice drove the event.

Zorion nodded to his aide. As Ring Master, he had to wear an eccentric costume. He refused at first but conceded because his public relations advisor explained that it would help with his popularity. The aide brought him the sacred Mask of Gau, which rested on a red pillow. They chose a mask painted with a fierce expression for this ceremony, portraying Gau's power at its highest.

Zorion reluctantly removed the mask from its resting place and secured it on his head. The eye holes were big enough to see through, but they blocked much of his peripheral vision; he hated wearing it. While his attendant fussed over him, Zorion noticed Thea putting on the Mask of Izar, Gau's mate. *I wonder how many other masks you wear, my dear.* His assistant attached the black cape that completed the ceremonial costume and led him before a large mirror.

Zorion frowned behind the disguise, staring at his reflection. *I look like a monster in a child's bad dream.* The cover kept his face hidden, so his unenthusiastic approval went unnoticed by his helper. Grimly, he walked over to the doorway and assumed the ceremonial pose. Thea placed her hand on Zorion's left arm, and wordlessly, they stepped out into public view.

The crowd greeted Gau and Izar's arrival with a loud ovation that shook the arena's walls. Behind the mask, Zorion grimaced. He had no idea that Gau was this popular. Hundreds of musicians were waiting at the entrance of the arena. They lined up in four rows. Zorion, wearing Gau's mask, gave the signal for the ceremony to begin. *There is no stopping it now.* The musicians started playing, so they marched into the arena. Zorion focused on a secured monitor out of the public's sight, sitting behind a low wall at his feet.

The display showed, in high resolution, the musicians as they marched around the stadium in four rows, which turned into eight and finally sixteen. They marched with slow, measured steps, slightly out of sync with the music (dictated by tradition), and formed the revered symbols, standing for victory to the strong and death to the weak. An elite regiment of Zorion's special guard (all dressed in black and carrying black flags) formed two lines at the arena entrance. The song ended, and everyone stood still. There was complete silence.

Not one of the hundreds of thousands of spectators dared utter a sound upon pain of death. The silence dragged on for many heartbeats, making everyone uncomfortable, which was the point. Zorion wanted everyone to feel as uneasy as he did. They needed to understand the seriousness of the upcoming events. It was not something to celebrate. It was not a game. Yes, there would be a winner; but the losers would pay the ultimate price.

Zorion gave the signal, and the musicians broke the eerie silence by playing their city's anthem. The crowd cheered so loudly that Zorion felt his mask vibrate against his face. He had to steady it with his free hand until the noise dissipated. He could see his warriors' stride in circles behind the musicians on the monitor, marching in counter-rotation. The two bands formed two circles beneath the hovering, clear-wall battle chamber. Later, they would lower the eye to the arena's surface, ensuring no escape for the opposing parties.

When seen from above, it was the Eye of Gau. The soldiers and the musicians made up the iris, and the clear battle ring was the pupil. At that precise moment, the music stopped. The soldiers and musicians were now in place and began the slow beat of a monotonous drum. Simultaneously, two rows of honor guards, carrying Zorion's house flags, made their way from the entrance and formed a circuitous path to the platform, where Zorion would oversee the ceremony. The footway curved along the outside of the arena. Gau and Izar had to walk the whole circumference before sitting as part of the celebration. Their journey would bless the battle-ring and sanctify the ritual bloodletting.

Zorion could feel his heart pounding, but the tense and nervous emotion was not for himself. Instead, it was for the four stubborn and foolish eligible females who stayed in the Eye of Gau during the first ceremony. The music started playing, snapping Zorion out of his brooding. *That is our cue.* Striking the required pose, Gau led Izar between the two rows of warriors. As they walked past, the soldiers pivoted one hundred eighty degrees and brought their flags up and over, meeting in the center.

Along the way, Zorion could feel a slight breeze from the flags. Many from within the crowd waved and begged Gau's blessing, but conventional protocol forbade Zorion to acknowledge them because he could only bless the winner for this ceremony. As he approached the dais, he noticed his youngest son, Va'ron, seated beside his sister Yetta. A wave of disappointment hit him, seeing her. He had heard from his sentries, who gave details about her quick temper. She also flaunted her privilege over those who attended to her.

Another disappointment. Where did I go wrong? As in the prior ceremony, Garbi sat alongside her in the stands. Reports from the Science Lab showed that she was ambitious and had her eyes set on being Chief Administrator. Zorion did not frown on that kind of aspiration but would never allow her to have Yanamai's position. Garbi did not have the correct character for the job.

Gau and Izar reached their special viewing booth and sat. The honor guard turned and formed another spiral around a ceremonial chair set twenty forearms from the ring, opposite Gau and Izar. The musicians paused and started playing again. Otsoa took his cue and entered the stadium, walking to the ceremonial seat within the spiral. The crowd cheered.

Following the proper protocol, Otsoa ignored the crowd. As much as he wanted to wave and accept their acclamation, the ritual demanded that he keep his thoughts only for those who would die and live for him on this Terrestrial Revolution. Even with all the distractions, the only one he could think about was Yanamai. The moment Otsoa sat, the music stopped, and the soldiers marched out of the auditorium in a single file, their boots hitting the ground in perfect synchronization. Once the soldiers were out of sight, the musicians began playing "The Melody of the Female Warrior."

It was a powerful and robust piece that sent chills down Zorion's spine as it played. The four challengers marched onto the Eye of Gau, two by two, and each female adorned themselves in the traditional, tight-fitting, but flexible bodysuit. They decorated their clothes with the fighter's family crest to make recognizing each fighter in the battle enclosure easier. They bound their long hair tightly within a net to secure it during the fight.

The music stopped, so each competitor went to her assigned location and began preparing for the confrontation. Zorion's thoughts drifted back to his younger times. Sword fighting and self-defense were standard curricula in his society, especially for someone of his status. Every school cycle, he sparred with Broll. They competed to be the best in their class. Zorion gently stroked his left wrist, remembering how he nearly lost it because they practiced with live swords.

Broll got past his defense, and Zorion instinctively held his left hand up to ward off the blow. He closed his eyes as the memory of the injury came flooding back; the shock, the pain, the disbelief, the sight of the blood pulsing from the stub where his hand had been. Had Broll not grabbed it off the floor and held it tightly to his wrist, the loss would have been permanent. Zorion still did not know what he admired most about Broll, his skill with a sword or his quick thinking.

Since it had been his prerogative to reward or punish, Zorion chose to repay Broll's quick thinking by putting him in charge of his security team. Hearing the door creak open behind him, he knew who it was. Broll took a position at the rear of the dais. Behind the mask, Zorion smiled. *He is still the only one I would allow to stand behind me with a naked weapon.*

As the fighters warmed up, each performed a series of stylized moves signifying her school of combat. Zorion noted that none of the competitors had similar training, as evident by their different techniques, but all showed equal poise and grace. *It is a shame to think that three will die before the Terrestrial Rotation is over, and one will become my daughter. Will I ever look upon her without remembering the other three?*

After a short delay, Zorion stood to begin the second part of the celebration. He reached the podium, and everyone became silent. The quiet hung in the air like a stench. It had been a long time since he felt this nervous in front of a crowd. He walked to Gau's eye, where the four competitors stood side by side, and paced back and forth, examining each competitor.

He spoke the ceremonial words in a deep, forceful voice, "You have chosen to place your fate in the hands of Gau. I salute you. At the end of the challenge, three of you will have died with honor. The other will have earned the right to be *Gau's Chosen*."

Having completed the introduction, he moved toward his seat but stopped before sitting. Instead, he gazed at each of the four through the forbidding disguise. He could feel the weight of their imminent loss resting upon him like a large stone, so he ignored protocol and lifted the mask to rest it on top of his head, exposing his face. There were gasps from the crowd from devout acolytes.

He dealt with problems that affected millions of lives every work cycle, but this was different. The moment he shared with them right now was tangible. These would be the last few heartbeats for three of them. Their loss would take them away forever, and that knowledge connected them. Akilian historians would remember them, always, by this defining moment.

Saddened to the point of tears, he approached each fighter one at a time, kissed each one on the forehead, and hugged them tightly; it was his way of coping with the dire situation. He returned to his place before them, put his hands behind his back, straightened his body, and with a loud, caring voice, shouted, "Fight well." The crowd went wild, cheering, screaming, and waving their banners and flags. Zorion pulled the mask back down over his face and turned to go back to his seat; the cape swirled behind him in a grand flourish. Seeing it on the monitors, he disapprovingly rolled his eyes beneath the mask. It was not the way he wanted to exit. *I feel ridiculous.* Still, the crowd loved it.

Zorion sat the exact moment Yanamai burst through the door at the back of the dais. "Zorion! Zorion!" she yelled, her voice barely making a dint above the crowd's noise. In her excitement, she forgot the protocol. Knowing where he would sit, she chose the quickest path to him. Before Zorion could say a word, Broll plunged his unsheathed sword into Yanamai's belly. Seeing her eyes widen in shock and fear, Zorion catapulted from his seat.

At first, she did not understand the reason for his attack but realized her mistake as she collapsed to her knees; she had run past the Screener without stopping. Broll pulled his sword from her stomach and raised it to behead her, continuing with the execution.

Zorion ran toward him, yelling, "Broll. Nooo!"

Hearing his words, Broll stopped mid-swing yet kept his sword poised, just in case.

"Yanamai!" Zorion yelled, flipping up the mask. Before he could reach her, Broll's guards stopped him. A small crowd formed in the doorway.

Broll faced them, "Send for the Screener."

Otsoa, thinking that his potion had finally taken effect, sprinted across the arena from the ceremonial chair.

"Broll! You fool! Why did you do this?"

Otsoa knelt beside her and lifted her into his arms.

"Because it was my duty," Broll replied.

Otsoa stared down at Yanamai's yellow shirt and gray tunic, soaked with blood, "You are all right, Yanamai. You will recover within a quarter of a Terrestrial Revolution or so."

He tried to sound hopeful. Despite the excruciating pain, she struggled against Otsoa's hold but was too weak to escape him because the injury was too severe. She had not received a wound like it since her early school cycles fighting Addien. Her reflexes were the fastest Yanamai had ever seen. Barely ten heartbeats into the practice, Addien plunged her sword into Yanamai's side. It took Yanamai about a quarter of a Terrestrial Rotation to recover.

Yanamai looked at her stomach and realized it would take at least that long but looked down again and thought, *maybe longer.* Broll's guards kept Zorion back until the Screener verified her identity, and Zorion knelt at her side, frowning at her injury.

Otsoa looked up at Zorion, "She remembers!" Tears formed in his eyes. "She remembers! She came here to stop the ceremony before it was too late!"

Zorion gazed at Otsoa with wonder. *How could he believe that?* "Let us see what she has to say."

He looked down at her, "Yanamai. Yanamai. Can you hear me?"

She opened her eyes and nodded her head slightly.

"Tell me what happened."

"P - Planet - I - I have found a planet."

Otsoa listened in abject disbelief as his hopes faded away. She did not come here to stop the ceremony. She was not even thinking about him. Gently, he lowered her to the ground and walked back to his seat. For a moment, he allowed himself to feel joy and happiness, but now numbness and emptiness replaced them because the one person he adored confirmed she would never care for him.

Zorion knelt by Yanamai, placed her head in his lap, and stroked her forehead in Otsoa's absence. Although he desperately wanted to stay by her side until the Recovery Attendants arrived, there was nothing he could do for her. The thought of postponing the challenge did cross his mind, but it was much too late for that. He nodded for Broll to take her from the crowds' sight and returned to his place on the dais.

He stood before the four competitors, who did not move during the disruption, and lowered his mask to speak into the voice magnifier, "I apologize for the disturbance. The injured Argian will be fine. Now, without further delay, the ceremony will begin. Fighting first will be Lore and Lomah."

There was polite applause from the crowd as the combatants walked to the center of the arena, and as assistants lowered Gau's thick, transparent pupil to encompass them, they took their positions. It was forty strides across and five times the tallest combatant's height.

Lomah's heart pounded with nervous excitement, performing the last of her pre-fight stretching routine. During the earlier ceremony, she danced by Otsoa and did not find him attractive. She planned to leave with the crowd, but her parents frowned, so she stayed on the Eye of Gau. They had insisted that the position of being by his side would offer her greater rewards than love, and by their actions, they had not changed their minds, so when Otsoa left his fate to Gau, she remembered thinking, *I hope they are right. I am risking everything.*

During Lomah's upbringing, her parents often told her that she was born for greatness. From her youth, they trained her to be beautiful and deadly. She spent many yellow harvests perfecting her fighting skills for this very scenario. If they did their job right, her training would save her life during this Terrestrial Revolution. She glared at her opponent. *She is simply another training exercise.*

At first, Lore did not look at her opponent, placing all her mental focus on preparing for the fight. The contender was simply an unknown object in her path to greatness. *I will move the object out of my way.* Lore had confidence in her ability to fight yet had a weakness like any combatant. She could never win against someone familiar. Her instructors made her fight only with close friends to overcome that vulnerability until she became a remorseless fighting machine.

Lore glanced at the nameless obstacle in her path. It stood four finger-widths shorter than she, but height did not always guarantee victory. Zorion, still dressed as Gau, gave the signal, and the musicians played a fanfare. The competitors met in the center of the battle arena. They bowed to each other, turned, and bowed to Gau. A few heartbeats later, Zorion yelled, "Fight!" The amplifier made his voice eerily echo around the massive arena.

Their swords met with a loud crash. The collision of the two metals caused sparks to fly. Lomah used an array of high and low swings in her attack. Lore effortlessly blocked each one. Lomah had quick reflexes, but Lore practiced against faster opponents and spun, swinging her sword toward Lomah's neck. Lomah ducked just in time; the sword cut the net that held her long hair in place, and it flew about wildly.

Lore took advantage of the situation and started her flurry of attacks. Lomah went on the defensive, but her long hair kept getting in the way and tangling around the sword and her arms, causing her to miss a block, and she took a deep cut on the shoulder. Frustrated, Lomah grabbed her hair at the base of her neck. Her sword moved up and over in one smooth motion, removing the cumbersome strands. There were gasps from the crowd; she did not care because her hair would grow back, her head would not. Without looking, she tossed it aside.

Lore grimaced, seeing Lomah cut her hair. Having just started their fight, she hoped to exploit her disadvantage to end the match. Now, Lomah was back in the competition but had not recovered from her injury. That would change soon because within seventy to a couple of hundred heartbeats, the cut would close. Lore swung her sword in a constant barrage of slashing attacks, driving Lomah backward.

Having slipped on the hair she previously cut and discarded, Lomah unexpectedly fell to the floor. Seeing an opening, Lore swung and thrust aggressively, hoping to injure her. Lomah blocked most of Lore's slices, but several got through, hitting her legs and abdomen. Although Lomah rolled and stood to put distance between them, Lore did not relent. Seeing another opening, she took it.

Lomah saw the attack coming and missed the block. Lore's sword pierced through her upper abdomen, and the tip protruded from her back. Blood sprayed across the battle-ring floor. Paralyzed from the stab, Lomah dropped her sword and fell to her knees. Instinctively, she grabbed Lore's sword with both hands, trying to keep her from pulling it out of her torso. During the struggle, she heard her parents wailing from the other side of the transparent barrier.

In her peripheral vision, she saw them running toward the ring, but the sentries prevented them from reaching it. Lore held her sword firmly until Lomah was too weak from blood loss to respond to an attack. If she withdrew her sword too early, Lomah's body would begin to recover, and the fight would continue, so Lore waited until Lomah blacked out and yanked the sword out.

During her last heartbeats, Lomah had trouble concentrating. *I should not have listened to them. I should have left the arena when I had the chance.* Time seemed to slow down as she remembered the grueling training program her parents enlisted her into, but her thoughts drifted to her youth, which was a much happier time before her parents began constantly urging her to prepare to win the celebration.

Now it is over. Lomah grew angry, thinking of what her parents' ambitions cost her. *For what? Sovereign Cubes. Prestige?* Searching the crowd, she found them, held back by guards. "Why?" she mouthed to them. Of course, they were crying, but it was of little consolation. In her peripheral vision, she saw Lore move to her right side. *It will be over soon.* With her eyes fixed on her parents, she took one last breath and waited for the inevitable. They briefly turned away; Lomah hoped they would summon the courage to watch her pay the price for their scheming. They turned back, and their eyes met. She almost smiled, seeing the agony on their faces. *Good, now live with what you have done; I do not have that luxury.*

Lore brought her sword down swiftly, and everything went black for Lomah. Her head tumbled to the floor, but her torso stayed upright. With its few last beats, her heart pumped blood high into the air, some splashing on Lore's face as she watched Lomah's torso fall to the ground with even more blood gushing onto the floor near her feet and over the painting of Gau's eye. Lore loudly exhaled in relief.

Lore's parents were the first to cheer their daughter's victory. The excitement on their faces confirmed that it was over. As the thick, transparent pupil of Gau lifted into the air, the sentries let Lomah's parents enter as the walls were still rising. They crawled on their knees to get underneath them. As they did, their daughter's blood dripped down off the glass onto their hair and clothes.

Keening like some pre-ice, four-legged beast, they crawled to Lomah's body. Her mother desperately grabbed Lomah's head and placed it back onto her torso, hoping for a miracle. Nothing happened, and her cries echoed around the arena, quieting the cheering crowd as she clutched the corpse to her breast. Zorion saw her running for the ring and watched her pitiful efforts to resurrect her daughter. With the Mask of Gau firmly in place, he fought against tears at the horrific sight and met them on the floor.

Zorion knelt beside the bereaved mother, "Her spine is severed. The body cannot recover."

At first, she would not let go, so Zorion patiently waited until he had to move her.

"I am sorry, but you must let her go now," he lamented.

Still weeping, she nodded, gently laid down her daughter's body, and stood. Zorion waved for his aides to escort her from the Eye of Gau. As he retreated to his assigned seat, a dozen of Gau's acolytes rushed in to retrieve Lomah's body and prepare the pupil for the next combat. Zorion sighed, watching them work. The image of her trying to reattach the head and her scream of agony would haunt him until his death.

He tried to soothe his conscience because Otsoa put this in motion, not him. Moreover, he warned Lomah not to stay on the image of Gau's eye, but she did not listen. Nevertheless, he still felt guilty and scolded himself. *I should have found a way to stop this!*

The acolytes finished cleansing the blood from the floor, so Zorion called for Durnah and Neeka. They walked to the battle ring without looking at each other. Again, the assistant lowered Gau's thick, transparent pupil as the competitors prepared to fight.

Durnah briefly meditated on the earlier match and tried to imagine herself in the same situation. A few options sprang to mind, and she set them aside, just in case. She looked at her family's assigned seats and found her parents. They were close and had tried desperately to talk her out of attending the ceremony. Even as she stood in the Eye of Gau, they waved at her, hoping to dissuade her.

Also, before the fight, her patriarch spoke with a shaky voice, "If you withdraw now, I am sure Zorion will accept it. Just give him a reason to spare your life."

She knew he was up all night, worrying. A smile touched her lips because she loved him very much. Her desire to stay on the Eye of Gau was not out of greed or ego; Otsoa was suitable for her. Even she did not expect to feel such a powerful connection toward him. Nor did she ever dream of finding herself in a deathmatch, but she stood with sword in hand, risking her life for some unknown. She took a deep, cleansing breath and turned to face her opponent.

Neeka stretched in preparation for the event and summed up her opponent using her peripheral vision. Durnah was a hand width taller than her. *Size does not matter.* Like all the other competitors, who took part in the ceremony, she prepared for this festival from her youth. Neeka had been born into poverty, so her family saw an opportunity to join Zorion's house. They knew there would be a celebration for him and began the arduous task of preparing her for it.

Her parents sacrificed and saved to buy her the proper clothing and instruction needed to succeed. Her uncle, a soldier in Zorion's army, trained her how to fight. He showed her moves and techniques that most fighters could not teach, making her a deadly warrior. In her peripheral vision, she saw Zorion stand. *It will not be long now.* She moved to the center of the pupil and bowed.

Zorion yelled, "Fight!" Durnah pressed her attack first, hoping to end the fight, but Neeka deflected each strike easily. Although Durnah tried the different moves that her instructors taught her, they did not produce the desired effect, so she combined them. Neeka smiled. *Is this your best?*

Neeka recognized that Durnah was fighting by the numbers. She lacked the fluidity of a real fighter. *Form one - form two - form one - form three - form two - form four. It will be too easy.* Neeka allowed Durnah to drive her into the pupil's arc, where the transparent wall protected her back. She could almost hear her uncle screaming at her not to make such a foolish mistake, but in this case, it was not a miscalculation.

Her opponent was a mechanical fighter. She had no sense of a sword's true artistry. Anyone else would have disengaged and retreated to the center of the pupil. They would have recognized her superior skill and would not waste time trying to pummel her into submission. A smile touched the corner of Neeka's mouth because Durnah had made a fatal mistake. *Never give it your all right away. You must pace yourself.*

Soon Durnah was exhausted and stopped her attacks. Her arms ached, and her shoulders burned. Her hands felt slippery from sweat. Tired, she retreated to the center of the pupil. Neeka seized the opportunity and rushed in. Her swings were fast and precise. Her uncle taught her to attack from odd angles, making them awkward to defend.

Durnah struggled to protect herself. *Where did she learn these moves?* The attacks were keeping her off balance. She kept retreating to avoid the sword pounding her until nearing the pupil's wall, where she shifted to her left and tried to move back into the center of the fighting floor. The fourth time she moved, Neeka kicked her knee and dislocated it.

Durnah screamed, landed on the ground, rolled, and rose to her uninjured knee. She struggled against excruciating pain to keep her mind focused and her sword high enough to block the inevitable onslaught. Durnah felt each heartbeat, striving to stay alive; it did not look promising after receiving cuts on her right forearm, shoulder, cheek, leg, and hand. Blood soaked the right side of her bodysuit, but her knee mended, and she stood.

Neeka snarled as Durnah got back up, having never seen such persistence. *That attack should have taken her down!* Durnah's strikes were aggressive and sloppy. Neeka waited for her to make another mistake, it did not take long. Durnah raised her sword high in the air and brought it down with all her might, hoping to power through Neeka's defense, but she was weak, and her attack was slow.

Neeka saw an opening and took it. She grabbed Durnah's wrist as it came toward her, then twisted and flipped Durnah over her shoulder. Durnah turned, forcing Neeka off balance. They hit the floor at the same time, dropping their swords. Durnah's body slammed hard on the Eye of Gau, knocking the wind out of her. She lay stunned and tried to pull in a fresh breath of air. *Gau, save me!*

Neeka raised herself with her hands, looked over at Durnah, and saw her struggling to breathe. *I have won*! *All I need to do now is finish her off!* As she tried to stand a sharp, debilitating pain in her left ankle stopped her. Looking down, she saw the broken joint. *Oh, no! No! No!* She struggled to stand on her uninjured leg and hopped over to her sword.

Durnah opened her eyes. She wanted to fill her lungs with air, but her muscles would not respond. Concentrating, she finally started taking short breaths. As time passed, she wondered why Neeka waited, so she craned her head in Neeka's direction and saw her hopping toward her sword. Adrenaline shot through her body because she realized there was a chance to survive, so she rolled over, picked up her sword, and stood.

There was not a heartbeat to spare. Durnah took advantage of her opponent's broken ankle before it had the chance to recover. Durnah approached Neeka with her sword held high. Neeka's eyes widened, raising her sword to block Durnah's attack. Hopping on her unharmed leg, Neeka recognized Durnah's stylized assault and tried to counter but failed.

Durnah swept Neeka's unscathed leg out from underneath her. Neeka tried to catch herself with her bad leg. Pain shot through her. She screamed and fell to the floor. As Neeka tried to rise, Durnah jammed her sword through Neeka's chest, pinning her to the Eye of Gau. Using her sword for leverage, Durnah swung herself across Neeka's prostrate body and kicked the sword out of her hand. Neeka grabbed Durnah's blade, holding it tight to her chest even though the pain was excruciating.

She had to keep the sword in her and get her own back. She still had a chance to kill her opponent and remove the sword later. She found herself pinned to the floor as Durnah tried to remove her blade, which only pulled Neeka into a sitting position. She pulled on her weapon, but her opponent held it firm, so Durnah placed her foot on Neeka's chest and pulled the sword from her body.

Blood poured from the wound, and Neeka gurgled, trying to breathe. Durnah stepped to Neeka's left and swung her sword with all her might, removing Neeka's head. Blood squirted upward, fifteen to twenty forearms in the air as her head rolled away. It splattered on Durnah's face before turning her head. The torso hit the floor with a thud, and Neeka's head rolled to the wall and stopped, facing the crowd.

The mob's roar shook the arena. Durnah heard Neeka's parents screaming at the horrific sight despite the din. She felt a cold chill, considering how close it came to her being the one losing her head but pushed the thought away. *I cannot doubt myself or my opponent has already won.*

Chapter 22

Earth
The United States - Texas - West of Houston
May 8, 2452

Sergeant Burke carefully guided Jared to the jeep, and at the door, Burke pushed his head down to keep him from hitting it. Colonel Scott took the driver seat, General Bailey sat to his left, and Sergeant Burke sat to his right, putting a sack over his head. Sergeant Burke guided Jared into a barn at the farm, where he tied his limbs to a wooden chair and removed the sack.

As his eyes adjusted to the light, Jared could only see a blur walking away from him; his training kicked in, and he surveyed the room. It was clear they had taken him to a barn. The light dimmed and brightened from time to time, a visible sign that they were using a faulty generator for electricity.

"Headquarters," Colonel Scott quipped, standing near General Bailey.

Once his eyes adjusted, Jared saw a mountain of flesh standing near the exit. *Sergeant Burke.* The man was tall, about six and a half feet, but he was also thick, without an ounce of fat on him. His muscles were so large that they appeared as if trying to burst out of his camouflage fatigues. Although appearing youthful, scars on his cheeks showed he saw the worst of humanity.

"Is this the idiot who drove through El Diablo's territory and nearly killed us all?" Sergeant Burke scoffed.

Burke would be difficult to subdue even with his subcutaneous body armor, so Jared ignored his comment and turned his attention to General Bailey, "May we talk privately, Sir?"

Jared hoped that General Bailey would tell the other two men to leave, allowing him to continue his mission, but Bailey ignored him and played the video Jared gave him earlier.

"I didn't get a chance to listen to the whole thing," General Bailey responded as the device continued to play Porter's message.

He shook his head, "We've been fighting for years without help from the Regime. So why does Porter want to talk now?"

"There are events in motion you need to know about, which is why I'm here."

"Whatever you need to tell me, you can say it in front of my men. I trust them with my life."

"I respect that, Sir, but my orders are clear."

Before General Bailey could reply, Jared saw the barn door open, and a beautiful young woman stepped through.

"Larkin. General. Colonel. What are you doing out here?"

"Sarah, go back in the house," Larkin demanded.

"Not until you tell me what's going on!" she insisted.

"Sarah, I *will* carry you to the house. You *know* I'll do it," Larkin threatened.

"Daddy! Daddy!"

A young girl ran through the barn doors. Her hair was dark, long, and curly. Jared noticed that she looked like her mother but with a few of Larkin's features.

"Sable, what are ya doin' out of bed, darlin'," Larkin gently scooped her up with one arm and hugged her tightly.

"We heard the jeep pull up. You didn't come inside, so I came out here to see what was wrong. I told Sable to stay inside; she didn't listen," Sarah frowned at her.

"Yeah, just like her mamma, right, sweetie," Larkin joked.

Larkin smiled at Sarah and kissed Sable on the cheek. Sable giggled and hugged him tightly.

"Why is he here?" Sarah nodded toward Jared.

"We're questioning him," Colonel Scott answered.

General Bailey and Larkin flinched.

"Didn't I tell you not to bring those damn gang members to our barn?" Sarah yelled.

"Now calm down, Sarah," General Bailey replied softly.

"Don't tell me to calm down, dad! The man broke free the last time you did this and almost got away! He could have hurt Sable!"

"Don't worry, baby. I won't let anything happen to you or Sable," Larkin promised.

"You can't be everywhere all the time, Larkin."

"Ma'am, I'm not a member of a gang. My name is Jared, and I'm a Regime representative here to speak with General Bailey."

Sarah looked at the General. He nodded.

"If you know he's a Regime representative, why is he still tied up?" she demanded.

"We were still trying to determine whether he was lying," Colonel Scott added.

"Well, dad, are you convinced yet?" she inquired.

"Yeah, he brought a video confirming it. I just needed a moment of peace to make sure it was on the up and up. Kinda hard to make these decisions with someone shootin' at me," General Bailey quipped, with sarcasm in his voice.

"Untie him, dad!"

"We were getting to it, Sarah. Calm down," General Bailey paused and nodded at Larkin. "Go ahead and untie him. I believe him."

Larkin set Sable beside her mother, instructing her not to move, and pulled out a Bowie knife covered with dried blood, and Jared's eyes widened with surprise, "Did you kill all those men with that?"

Larkin stopped in his tracks. There was a look of dread in his eyes. Jared had said something wrong, which would somehow get the man in trouble, but it was too late.

"Dad, may I speak to you outside, please," Sarah spoke calmly.

"Look, I had to send him. Jared attracted attention on his way over here. We were takin' fire," defended General Bailey.

"Ok, if you won't come outside to discuss this privately, we'll do it right here. You promised you wouldn't put Larkin in those situations again."

Sarah glanced at Sable and hoped she didn't understand her meaning. Instead, Sable just looked at her and smiled, so she returned her attention to the General.

"It takes him days to calm down!" she yelled, facing Larkin, who held his head down.

"Sarah, you know I wouldn't have done it unless it was an emergency. There were forty armed men out there. Sending Larkin saved lives," General Bailey insisted.

"There were thirty-two," Larkin added.

"Shut up; you're not helping," General Bailey snapped.

Sarah and her dad continued to argue, so Larkin walked over and removed Jared's bonds.

Jared interrupted their quarrel, "Sarah, I'm sorry for all the problems my visit has caused, but General Bailey isn't exaggerating. There were many, and they were *very* persistent."

"I'm hungry, mommy," Sable pulled on her mother's dress to get her attention.

Sarah sighed, "Let's continue this in the house. Are you hungry, Jared?"

"Starved."

At the table, everyone watched with amazement as Jared inhaled several plates of food.

"This is delicious, Sarah. You're a wonderful cook," Jared mumbled, with a mouth full of food.

"Thanks; I guess that's one of the reasons Larkin stays with me."

He walked over to her and gently wrapped his massive arms around her, "I stay with you 'cause I love you, Sarah. You saved me."

"Saved you from what?" Jared questioned.

"Larkin used to be the *Outlaws'* leader. They're a gang that controls eighty percent of the suburbs. The blood you saw on his Bowie knife is nothing compared to how it used to look. With so many wanting his position, it was only a matter of time until somebody killed him," General Bailey explained.

"Those were tough times. I fought every day to keep my position. Everyone wanted to be at the top, but together, me and my brother kept most of 'em in line," Larkin added.

"How did you meet if you were in a gang, and she was out here?" Jared raised an eyebrow.

"It was my idea to trade with the resistance. Our food supply wasn't the best, so we sneaked into the city and stole medical supplies, gasoline, and whatever else we could grab; we would meet with the resistance and exchange it for food," Larkin stated.

"One day, I begged my dad to let me go with him during an exchange. I wanted to see what it was like," Sarah remarked.

"Yeah, she annoyed the hell out of me, but I only agreed to let her go if she promised to stay in a jeep with the motor running. Also,

I assigned three armed men to be by her side and kept her fifty yards from ground zero."

"I remember that day like it was yesterday," Larkin gazed upwards and replayed the events in his mind. "The jeep caught my attention right away. I was, of course, suspicious of its location and contents. General Bailey saw me lookin' and told me it was his daughter. I let my men continue the trade. I returned to my car, retrieved a pair of binoculars, and saw her sitting in the front seat. I couldn't believe how beautiful she was. I asked General Bailey if I could meet her. He said no."

"I said, 'Hell, no!'" General Bailey yelled.

"I knew if I was to ever have a chance with her, I had to change, so I decided to break away from the gang and join the resistance."

"Later that night, he snuck past our defensive perimeter to ask me out on a date," Sarah smiled.

Jared's brows puckered, "A date, really?"

He faced General Bailey, "Please tell me you didn't know about it?"

General Bailey's lip twitched, "She kept it from me at first; it made me mad as hell when I found out about it, trust me. Sarah invited me over for dinner one night and told me what was goin' on. Larkin was hiding in the barn, waiting for Sarah to tell me. After explaining everything, she told me where he was. I stormed in, ready to shoot 'em, but he fell to his knees and asked for forgiveness and permission to marry my daughter. Kept sayin' how much he loved her."

He paused, and Jared saw his hand caressing the pistol resting in his holster.

"What did you do?" Jared queried.

"I held my gun on him. Only God knows how close I was to killin' 'em. Son of a bitch snuck past my border patrol and into my home with my daughter!"

"Calm down, dad. It's ok." Sarah soothingly interrupted.

General Bailey exhaled loudly, "He swore his allegiance to the resistance. Promised to give vital intel on the gangs and fight to the death anyone that would try to hurt Sarah, me, or anyone in the resistance."

"Did that convince you?" Jared inquired.

General Bailey laughed, "Not even close. I told him that before I would give my approval, he had to agree to a few tests."

An evil grin grew as he remembered putting Larkin through his trials.

"That was *the* worst month of my life. I didn't think I was going to make it. The only thing that kept me goin' was knowin' that Sarah would be waitin' for me at the end of the tests," Larkin frowned.

"You best believe I put him through hell to prove his loyalty, but eventually, I was convinced, and now..." he paused to look at Larkin. "Now, I trust 'em with my life."

"I can only imagine how hard those tests must have been," Jared speculated.

"No, you can't," Larkin shook his head.

Sarah grabbed his hand and kissed it. She knew the tests scarred him emotionally,

"You're all right, baby. You made it through."

She faced Jared, "Once dad finally gave his approval, we got married, and Sable was born nine months later."

She caressed her daughter's hair with motherly pride.

"How old is she?" Jared questioned.

"I'm six," Sable held up seven fingers.

"She's six, but she's having some trouble with her numbers."

Jared finished pouring the last drink down his throat and set the glass on the table, letting out a quiet burp, "Ah, that was delicious."

"You can really pack some food away. If you're not careful, you'll be carrying around a big belly in no time. It'll make it hard to run from a gang," Sarah joked.

"I have a high metabolism. Trust me; I'll burn it off," Jared assured.

"What's Porter want with us lowly, Texas rebels?" General Bailey queried.

"I'll be more than happy to tell you, Sir. Once we're alone," Jared insisted.

"Larkin, help me put Sable to bed," Sarah picked up her daughter from her seat.

Larkin looked at General Bailey, who nodded his approval.

"Colonel, why don't you wait for me in the jeep? I'll be right there," General Bailey politely ordered.

Jared furrowed his eyebrows in thought, "The reason Supreme Commander Porter has been hesitant to help you in the past is due to lack of support."

"I'm guessin' there's support now?"

"Yes. Things are changing fast. The Supreme Commander sent me here to speak with you."

"I see, so you're here to size me up."

Jared nodded, "In a manner of speaking. I've read your dossier, General. It's impressive, up until you deserted."

"Porter doesn't think he can trust me."

"You've been on your own for years. *You* don't answer to anyone, and *you* make all the decisions."

"Porter thinks if he helps us, I'll turn on him like I did the governor."

"We have to consider the possibility."

"How much does the Regime know about me?"

"I'll admit we don't know much. Your dossier included a photo from about ten years ago."

"Well, I'm better looking now, as you can see."

Jared smiled and recited, "News reports from 2445 say that Governor Sonya Gonzales signed a bill into law, raising the land tax in the rural areas surrounding Texas's cities. They also said that her dad, President Martinez, decided to pay off the U.S. debt to China with Texas land."

"Ah, but what the news reports didn't say was that the journalist, who leaked the story, was killed the day before publication, and the following day, someone in power shut down the news agency that leaked the story," General Baily explained.

"I see. You believe the governor had a hand in his death."

"My gut tells me she had something to do with it."

"Why did you rebel?"

"Did you read the article?"

"Yes."

"You should know what happened."

"The article didn't tell everything. I would like to hear it from you," Jared remarked.

"Fine. The government had to raise taxes to get the land, making it impossible for its citizens to pay for it. Once they defaulted, it was legally justified to take it."

"I read in the article that the government would reimburse anyone who was displaced."

"Ha!" Bailey laughed loudly. "They were reimbursed all right, but those government thieves only offered a tenth of what the property was worth!" He paused, took a deep breath, and exhaled loudly to relieve his tension, "My orders were to evict anyone who couldn't pay their taxes. I can't describe how dirty I felt, and even worse, it didn't happen at once. In the first month, they only took a couple of farms. By the second month, they took another twenty, and six months later; the state confiscated ten percent of the farms surrounding Houston."

"Why didn't everyone band together to try and stop it?"

"They did! I helped them file a petition to repeal the law, and the locals put together enough money to hire lawyers to fight it in court. They lost, of course, because the judge rejected the petition."

"Rejected? How? I thought the state constitution."

General Bailey interrupted him, "Those damn politicians take turns wiping their ass with the constitution, state and federal! They do what the hell they want, especially if it suits 'em."

"That's why you rebelled?"

"Me and my men protected this area from those gang members for years."

"Yeah, I met a few…nice people."

"During that time, I got to know a lot of the locals. As you would expect, some of my soldiers married during our long-term occupation and had children. These people are our family!"

"And, you were ordered to remove them."

"There's only so much a man can take. I couldn't look another neighbor in the eye and tell 'em they had to leave their home."

"I understand; your orders were tough."

"No, my orders were unconstitutional! The politicians are breaking the law, not the farmers, but since I swore an oath to defend the constitution, I knew what I had to do."

"Desert?"

"Bitch called *me* a terrorist!" fumed General Bailey; he smiled. "But it was worth it. A week before it happened, I had a meeting with my staff. We all agreed. I didn't force a one of 'em. In turn, they met with the soldiers, and word came back saying everyone was with me. I ordered as many weapons, ammunition, medical supplies, tanks, and vehicles as they would allow. I told 'em the gangs were attacking more often. I received the shipment the following day, so I phoned the governor, told her I would no longer do her dad's dirty work, and hung up."

"So she called you a terrorist."

"Yep, she even blew up a few buildings and blamed us for it."

"Was anyone hurt?"

"They said several people died. I sent soldiers to verify the story. They couldn't, so I guess that was a lie too. Put it on us so we would look bad."

"It worked."

"I know. Outside of our little group, they hate me."

"How have you survived for so long? Your supplies must be low."

"Yeah, she made sure of it because the gangs started attacking us more often. They must have had a supplier giving 'em weapons and ammunition. I lost a lot of good men that year. We hit 'em hard a few winters back, so they started keepin' to themselves. Our supplies became critical, so we started dealin' with some of Houston's businesspeople. They gladly took our food in exchange for whatever we needed. The problem was getting the shipment past the gangs until Larkin approached me, so out of necessity, I made a deal to give them a part of each shipment for safe passage."

"I wish I would have gotten in on that deal," Jared mused.

General Bailey laughed, "You seemed to handle 'em." The General paused, "So, did I pass your assessment?"

"That depends on your answer. If the Regime decides to help you, are you willing to obey orders?"

"Porter's orders?"

"Ultimately, yes."

"I'll need to run your offer by my staff, but I don't think there'll be a problem. Besides, I've never had an issue with obeying orders if the government I'm serving obeys its laws and treats its citizens with respect, so if Porter agrees to do that, I'll carry out any order he gives," General Bailey responded.

"I've worked with Supreme Commander Porter for several years now. I believe he's an honorable man."

"Only time will tell, Jared."

"Just remember, both sides must earn trust, General."

"Are we done?"

"No, not yet. I'm also here to let you know that Texas will undergo a major change."

"I see. What sort of change are we in for?"

"What I'm about to tell you is highly classified, and if the wrong people find out prematurely, many Texans could die."

"You have my word. I won't tell a soul unless you approve."

Jared nodded, "Recently, the Regime has been approached by some of Texas' citizens asking for help."

"What kind of help?"

"They want to secede."

"About damn time. I was wonderin' when those pasty bastards were gonna step up to the plate."

"I take it that you agree with their decision?"

"Hell, son, I've been trying to get those city fellas to grow a pair for years. It must be worse than I thought for them to make such a bold move."

Jared agreed, "It's pretty bad."

"What do you need from me?"

"Although we're hoping for a peaceful transition, we still anticipate gang resistance, and you know them better than anyone."

"They're definitely an ornery bunch. Thanks to the governor, they fight dirty and are heavily armed, and my ammunition is dwindling. Porter's gonna have to start sending us supplies if he wants our help."

"We anticipated your needs, but Supreme Commander Porter won't make a move until you sign an agreement with him."

"You mean, join the Regime?"

"That's what this interview is all about. Now, do you want in, or would you rather continue to go it alone?"

"That all depends; what happens if Texas finally secedes?"

"The Regime will drop flyers in every city and surrounding areas telling them that we are now in control. They must report to a nearby station for processing."

"The gangs aren't going to like that at all."

"Agreed, but that's where you come in. We will need your help. Since you're in contact with all the other commanders surrounding Texas's different cities, we will put you in charge of each division. You will be working with us to coordinate keeping the peace. Consider it a police action."

"You realize this won't be a police action. It's going to be an all-out war. No gang member will voluntarily lay down his weapon and submit to the Regime."

"We agree, but someone must do it. Once the Regime takes control, things will move swiftly. We'll be coordinating with you every step of the way."

General Bailey rubbed his chin in thought, "The governor's gonna make it hard on us. What you're proposing is treason. She'll use her propaganda machine to fight you every step of the way. She still controls segments of the National Guard that didn't desert with us."

"You leave the governor to us."

"Ok, Jared, I'll talk to my staff and contact you after deciding."

"I'll wait for your call," Jared paused. "Next time we meet, it'll be via a portal."

"That's fine with me. I don't know why you didn't use one to get here in the first place."

"The U.S. monitors portal activity, especially within its border state, but I brought a signature disrupter with me, so if you sign the agreement, you simply turn it on before you contact us. It will confuse their sensors. Simultaneously, the Regime will know your exact location and safely open a portal nearby. There's a satellite phone in the trunk of my car. If the gang hasn't shot it to pieces, you can use it to contact our Assistant of Defense once you've made your decision. If you believe that your men are on board, I suggest making a list of the things you'll need and let him know."

"I'll do just that, and once Larkin returns, we'll take you back to your vehicle. Speakin' of which, how do you plan on getting back to the city? Do you plan to use the disruptor?"

"No. I'll leave the same way I came in. Using the device too many times could alert them that something is going on here."

"I'll send an escort with you, and hopefully, the gangs will think twice before tryin' to hit you again. You came at the right time, son. Until now, I've bluffed 'em, but we're nearly out of ammo, and a lot of our vehicles need parts that the motor pool can't get."

"I greatly appreciate the escort, General. Don't worry; if you decide to accept the Regime's offer, you'll have everything you need and more," Jared clapped his hands and rubbed them together. "Now, before I leave, can I have some more of that pie Sarah made?"

"Damn, son, where the hell do you put it all?"

Chapter 23

Akil

Argi City

The 22,272[nd] Terrestrial Rotation of the Second Summer

Zorion checked his timekeeper. The protocol dictated that the last two fighters have a couple of thousand heartbeats to recuperate. *That gives me just enough time to check on Yanamai.* Broll and his security team followed Zorion to the Recovery Station, where he stood by Yanamai's side. Gently, he took her hand. Yanamai was tired from the loss of blood, but the touch of his hand woke her. She opened her eyes, saw Zorion, and struggled to talk.

"Shh - do not try to speak."

"I am fine, really," she spoke with a raspy voice and tried to sit up.

"Relax. I am just here to make sure you are all right."

He gently pushed her back down. At first, she tried to resist but collapsed back to the bed, feeling a sharp pain in her stomach.

"Ouch! That hurts!"

"Stop being so stubborn and rest."

"I will, I promise, but what I must tell you is important."

She winced as the pain went through her belly, so he summoned an aide to bring water, and she drank it.

"I still cannot believe you did not stop for security. You know I almost lost you."

He felt tears welling up in his eyes, "I have never told you this before; you are like a daughter to me."

"What about Yetta?"

"You are the daughter I should have had. Now, tell me what was so important that you nearly died over it."

"We have located a planet in sector 1-5-6-9-2-4-1. It is good that you decided to use the sector Otsoa gave us. It saved us hundreds of Terrestrial Rotations of searching, maybe thousands."

"I wonder how the Akilian, who gave him that sector, knew there was a hospitable planet there?"

"Maybe they have a lab too?"

"I guess it is possible. Elzer did receive a considerable sum of Sovereign Cubes with no record of where he spent them. I will pass the information along."

"We discovered the planet because they are trying to reach a neighboring world with a portal machine, which created a strong signature for us to track."

"That is good and bad news."

"What is the bad news?"

"Sentient life inhabits the world and they may not allow us to live there; we have no choice, we must pursue it because time is running out."

Yanamai nodded but was barely awake. The earlier attack, combined with her recent conversation, had taken its toll. As she fought to stay awake, Zorion touched her cheek with the back of his fingers.

Although unsure if she was still alert, he whispered, "I want you to rest now. You have told me what I needed to know."

Upon hearing his words, Yanamai allowed herself to relax, succumbing to exhaustion, and went fast to sleep. Before leaving, he kissed her forehead and walked toward the auditorium, where Broll stopped him. The look on Broll's face told him everything.

Zorion put his hand on his shoulder and looked directly into his eyes, "You were doing your job. Think no more of this."

Broll politely smiled but still felt guilty. As Zorion left the room, Broll signaled the security team to take their positions.

*****

Durnah saw Zorion leave the arena and felt relieved, hoping that his absence would give her more time to recuperate. Since her lungs continued to burn, she took deep breaths and exhaled; it was a technique her trainer taught. She felt a gentle tap on her shoulder, turned, and saw an unfamiliar young socialite standing beside her with water.

"One down, one to go," the unwelcomed visitor handed her a cup of water.

Durnah studied the cup.

"Do not worry. It is only water," the debutante smiled.

176

Her parents taught her to be wary of strangers, so she hesitated but felt compelled to drink for reasons unknown to her, and without thinking, she gulped the liquid down.

"You have fought well so far," the stranger noted.

"Thanks… I guess," Durnah frowned, not knowing how to take the backhanded comment.

"Tell me, Durnah, how badly do you want to win the match?"

"Why would you ask me that? If I lose, I am dead."

"I only meant to ask if you would be willing to accept advice."

"Sure, but I will not promise to use it."

"Fair enough, yet knowing your rival's weakness would certainly give you the advantage. Would it not?"

"I have known Lore from childhood. I know her moves, strategy, and style, so I seriously doubt anything you tell me would give me an advantage."

The socialite leaned close to Durnah's left ear and whispered. A few moments later, the socialite stood, took the cup from Durnah's hand, and walked away, leaving Durnah to stare absentmindedly in disbelief. *Could it work?* The idea never occurred to her. The advice reminded her of something her instructor mentioned a long time ago. *She must have overcome it by now.*

As she continued to ponder the debutante's suggestion, Zorion returned, wearing the mask of Gau. She saw him looking around on the dais, speaking to his guards, and could only guess the subject of their conversation. Thea walked in, wearing the mask of Izar; she must have slipped out too. The moment she returned to his side, they sat.

"Sorry I am late; I needed to use the facilities at the last moment," Thea commented.

Zorion nodded absentmindedly and looked at his timekeeper. It was past time for the fight to begin, so he stood. Durnah and Lore took the cue and headed for the center of the pupil, where they found their marks. Durnah reached out and gently grabbed Lore's shoulder. Lore faced Durnah quizzically.

"We have been good friends since we were young. I want you to know that it is an honor to face you in battle. May Gau smile upon you during this Terrestrial Revolution."

Unexpectedly, Durnah hugged Lore tightly and let go, with tears in her eyes. Expecting a response, she waited, but Lore did not speak nor change her facial expression. Instead, she turned away from Durnah as if nothing had happened. Durnah cursed under her breath. *I should not have listened to that socialite; Lore did not believe me and will fight harder if that is possible!*

As Durnah suspected, Lore fought furiously, attacking with precise strikes. It took all Durnah's concentration to keep her from getting through her defenses. As the fight progressed, Lore backed Durnah to the arc of the pupil. Again, Durnah found it hard to concentrate. She was still berating herself for using the stranger's bad advice, which cost her.

Lore swung at her head, and Durnah ducked at the last moment, avoiding decapitation. Durnah saw an opening and took it. She parried one of Lore's swinging attacks, swept Lore's sword aside, and kicked Lore in the stomach. Lore grunted because Durnah's foot forced all the air out of her lungs. Stunned, she backed away from Durnah, who went on the attack; now Lore was on the defensive but easily kept Durnah's strikes from connecting. Many heartbeats later, she went from defensive back to offensive.

Lore's strikes made precise cuts at every opening. Whenever Durnah managed to parry an attack, their swords sparked between them. Lore recognized that something distracted Durnah. *There is no use in getting fancy. Not with her.* Lore pushed Durnah's sword downward and spun. The edge of her sword cut Durnah's throat leaving a deep gash.

Durnah staggered backward in shock. She could not believe how good Lore's fighting skills had become. Durnah felt the blood seeping down her chest into her fighting suit. She tipped her head forward to aid in the recovery process. As Lore watched Durnah retreat, memories of their childhood came to her mind. One memory stood out during a practice session, Durnah nearly fell over the guard rail on the hundredth floor. Had Lore not grabbed her tunic in time, she would have fallen to the bottom. *Did I save her then, only to kill her now?*

The contradiction made her waver. Other memories flashed through her mind until Durnah was no longer an obstacle in her path, she was a friend. She remembered what Durnah said before the match, and there was no more fight left in her. *I cannot kill my friend.* Durnah felt her wound steadily closing. She held her sword, ready to defend against the final attack, but it never came. Lore seemed distracted, lost in thought.

Durnah lunged at her and plunged her sword through her chest. Lore fell to her knees, dropping her weapon. Durnah pulled her sword from Lore's chest and stepped to her left to deliver the final blow. Lore turned to look at Durnah with tears in her eyes. Durnah raised her sword, ready to strike, but stopped seeing Lore's face. *What am I doing? I cannot kill Lore.*

Thea moved to the edge of her seat with anticipation, waiting for Durnah to claim her prize; she froze. *Kill her, you fool!* Everyone was yelling for her to kill, yet Durnah did not move. Heartbeats passed, and Thea saw that Durnah could not win independently, so she intervened. Using her Skean powers, she gripped Durnah's hands with invisible ones. Durnah felt the sword tug and thought it was a hallucination. It was as if it moved of its own accord.

The sword swung down through Lore's neck with such force that Durnah stumbled forward. As Lore's heart pumped for the last time, it shot blood directly onto her face. Durnah became horrified as some of the blood got into her mouth. Gagging and spitting, she tried to rid herself of the red liquid. Stunned, she reeled backward from the gruesome sight. *What have I done? Oh, what have I done?*

Thea smiled behind her mask.

As Zorion watched Durnah, something caught his attention. To his left, he saw Thea moving her hand upward. Durnah froze, so Zorion believed she could not go through with the kill because she and Lore were friends, and it would be a shock to see Durnah decapitate her. Allowing his curiosity, he turned somewhat to look at Thea's hand. Holding it slightly open, it appeared as if she held something invisible. *A sword?*

With Durnah still in his peripheral vision, he saw Thea's hand and Durnah's sword move downward simultaneously. Turning back to the battle ring, he watched in horror as Lore's heart bathed Durnah with its blood. In addition, the force of her strike noticeably set her off balance. It looked as if someone or something either pulled or pushed her forward. The two events, occurring at the same time, troubled him.

Zorion did not believe in coincidences but did not understand how Thea could know when Durnah would strike. *Unless she somehow controlled it. No, that kind of power does not exist. Does it?* The coincidence continued to bother him. It also brought back memories from his childhood. His patriarch hired entertainers for one evening. They brought dolls with strings attached to them, moving them about, hiding behind a small stage.

Occasionally, he could see their hands as they controlled the doll's movements. It made him wonder if Thea was a puppet master like them. *Where are the strings?* The match was over, so the aids raised Gau's thick, transparent pupil. Zorion removed his mask and walked to Durnah. Having collapsed, she lay face down in a pool of Lore's blood, weeping.

"Come, Durnah. It is over. There is nothing you can do to help her," Zorion whispered somberly.

He extended his hand, but she hesitated at first and took his arm as he helped her stand. She accidentally glanced at Lore's body and buried her face in his shoulder, moaning loudly with tears. Zorion held her tightly, trying to comfort her. Blood covered her from head to foot, so he motioned for an aide to bring a towel. Gently, he wiped her face and neck until wiping away most of the blood.

"I am sorry, I got blood all over your clothes," she lamented.

"Do not worry; I plan to burn them once we finish here," he halfheartedly smiled, carefully dabbing around her eyes, soaking up droplets of tears and blood.

"There, that is better. Now we can see your lovely face."

Although she wanted to smile, it was simply impossible. The pain of what happened was too much for her to bear. Zorion comforted Durnah until it was time to complete the next phase of the ceremony. Zorion held out his hand. She took a deep breath and put her hand, still freckled with blood, on top of his, and he guided her to Otsoa's seat.

As they approached, Otsoa stood. The closer she came, the tighter Nayrah's noose felt around his neck. Nayrah won again. *She always wins. I am sure she is already controlling Durnah, which* means her control over my entire life will be complete. I will never escape her now. Zorion and Durnah arrived and stopped.

"I present to you a warrior worthy of joining houses," Zorion yelled for the crowd to hear.

He took her hand and placed it on Otsoa's hand, who sighed inwardly.

"It is my honor to receive such a one," Otsoa yelled, bowed, and stood at attention.

In keeping with protocol, Durnah moved beside him. Simultaneously, the crowd stood and cheered their approval. The noise was deafening, and her victory was bittersweet. Selfishly, she was happy to win because she belonged at Otsoa's side, but everything had a price. She saw Gau's acolytes removing Lore's body in her peripheral vision, and another wave of grief hit her. At what should have been her happiest moment of the ceremony, she fought against tears.

Moving forward with the following ritual, Zorion handed her the fertility bag. Durnah welcomed the distraction. She opened the top of the sack to its maximum and walked around the arena. Before the ceremony began, greeters handed everyone a flower made of moss, dyed black. As Durnah came close to each attendee, they tossed the flower, hoping she would catch it in the bag.

According to tradition, Durnah must capture one hundred or more flowers for Gau to find her worthy and bless her with a child. If less than a hundred, his judgment would fall on the new couple, cursing them. She tried to focus, but her thoughts turned to Lore, and the distraction kept her from filling the fertility bag. There were thousands of spectators tossing their flowers toward her. Most did not make it to the front row. She walked the arena and handed the bag over to an acolyte, who counted the number of flowers.

He approached Zorion with a worried look, "Sir, she only caught ninety-nine."

Not willing to let Durnah's union begin with a fabled curse, he told the acolyte to bring him a flower and the voice amplifier. He returned to Otsoa and Durnah with the flower in hand and pulled Gau's mask over his face.

"The acolytes have counted ninety-nine."

Durnah went pale at the number, and the crowd began to mummer.

"It is not over yet. I have not had a chance to toss my flower."

The spectators went quiet as he handed the bag to her. This time, she gave the ritual her full attention and opened the sack again. Standing twenty to thirty paces from her, Zorion tossed the flower. He threw it high, but its shape caused it to fall short. Not willing to allow Gau's curse to settle on her union with Otsoa, Durnah ran and dove for the flower as it fell toward the ground. Her body slid across the floor as she held the bag up with her right hand.

The lip of the bag caught the flower midway, and as Durnah came to a stop, it teetered on edge. Everyone watched with anticipation. It wobbled back and forth for several heartbeats until finally, it fell into the bag. The spectators filled the auditorium with loud cheering and applause as they stood. Durnah sighed in relief, stood, waved at the crowd, and thanked Zorion for his gift.

The last song of the ceremony started to play, so Otsoa walked over to her, and they danced before everyone. As they spun around, Durnah remembered practicing it from her youth. It had always been a fantasy, but it had become a reality now. They whirled around the arena until the song finished; Otsoa reluctantly kissed her. It took a great deal of effort to keep his lips firmly pressed against hers. Although, for Durnah, it meant everything, so it was easy. At the end of the celebration, they walked toward the exit.

Along the way, the crowd tossed brown and green moss woven into flower-like blossoms and repeatedly yelled, "Gau has made you worthy!"

Outside, they could still hear their chants echoing down the boulevard. Thea took her place beside Zorion at the center, where Gau's acolytes encircled them inside the arena. Still wearing their costumes, they waited for the final ritual to begin. All the lights dimmed except for one, which shone down on Gau and Izar.

Musicians menacingly beat bass drums as acolytes poured the blood of the fallen over them, soaking their costumes, as they chanted, "Gau has bathed himself with the blood of the weak! His justice will reign supreme forever!"

Zorion frowned beneath the mask, disgusted by Gau's rituals. He would outlaw all of them if it were up to him, but his counselors had recommended against it because most Akilians believed in Gau. Even speaking against it would lower his approval ratings to their smallest numbers. *I cannot wait to get out of this ridiculous costume and take a bath.*

Otsoa and Durnah left the arena and arrived at their apartment, where his guard opened the door for them. Durnah was still grieving the loss of her friend but allowed herself to embrace the moment because it was the reason she fought.

"You have a beautiful home."

"Thank you."

"Or…I should say, *we* have a beautiful home," she forced a playful smile, which faded, seeing her sleeve soaked in blood. "I need a bath and new garments."

"You will find everything you need there," he pointed at a closet down the hall.

"I will return soon."

There was a knock on the door. Otsoa opened it to find a few of his assistants holding Durnah's bags.

"Put them in her dressing room."

As the procession of luggage handlers walked by, he started feeling claustrophobic, and it felt like all the rock surrounding his apartment was crashing down upon him, and his breathing became labored. He could not catch his breath, so he stepped outside to get some fresh air. Looking out over the city, he wondered if things would have been different if he had met Durnah first. *Nayrah was right about one thing; she is beautiful.*

However, it was simply too late. Otsoa already gave his heart to Yanamai, even though she did not want it. His mind drifted to the first time he saw her at school. He thought she was more beautiful than any other female. It was around his thirteenth yellow harvest. Since she was a little less than two Yellow Harvests older than him, they only shared a couple of classes. Being tall for his age, he looked older than those in his group and had hoped it would give him an advantage in attracting her.

He finally worked up the nerve to sit across from her during lunch, and to his surprise, she invited him to stay, and they talked during the whole break. After school, he walked her home, and she introduced him to her parents, who invited him in for dinner. He spent the entire evening with her and her family; the visit was pleasant, and he did not want to leave.

As time moved on, they became close. During walks home from class, every school cycle, they held hands, but on one Terrestrial Rotation, Yanamai invited him inside her home because her parents were out. She led him into her bedroom, where she professed her love for him, and they coupled. He remembered that Yanamai was very enthusiastic during intercourse. If he concentrated hard enough, he could still smell her hair, taste her lips, and feel her soft skin against his. *I did not imagine this!*

Afterward, she acted as if nothing had happened between them, and her indifference haunted him. Since their relationship had been secretive, he had no evidence to support his claim. Even Nayrah could not find a video of them together on the walkway to and from school. Laughter brought him out of the trance, so he turned and saw two of the luggage handlers leaving.

Returning to his thoughts, he sighed. Their intimate encounter was his favorite memory, but he paid a high price for it. He arrived an eighth of a Terrestrial Revolution late for his appointment. Nayrah never asked him why he did not show up on time. Instead, she gave him the beating of a lifetime, and it took several Terrestrial Rotations to recover fully.

To cover his secret life with Nayrah, he told Yanamai (while they were still together) that he had fallen down some stairs. It was not a lie. Nayrah regularly threw his body around like some child's toy. Falling down the stairs was a part of the punishment, but Yanamai was worth it. Zorion warned him about childhood romances. They sometimes ended in disaster. Sadly, his prediction came to pass.

Since Yanamai continued to deny their relationship existed, he tried a different strategy. Rather than insisting they were together, he tried to convince her to join houses with him. She refused, telling him they were not compatible. His persistence got him in trouble with Zorion and Nayrah. Not knowing what went wrong left him in constant agony, and now, he needed to hear her say, *"I love you."*

Absentmindedly, he walked toward the elevator and selected the three hundred fifteenth level. Zorion's guard, Allon, followed him. Thoughts of Yanamai occupied his mind, leaving his subconscious to guide him; the doors opened, and he headed straight for Adirah's apartment.

"Are you sure you want to be on this level?" Allon inquired.

"As long as I do not visit the second level, it is my business where I go," Otsoa snapped.

"Fine, it is your reputation."

He knocked on the door, and Adirah answered, wearing a sheer gown that depicted her occupation.

"I see you have been thinking about her again," Adirah flirtatiously gazed at him.

"Yes. Are you available?"

"For you, I am always available," she smiled, stepping aside to let him in.

She closed the door behind him and held out her hand. He placed a few thousand Sovereign Cubes in it. Adirah walked to her dresser, put away her fee, and transformed into Yanamai's image. Satisfied that her cubes were secure, she walked to the bedroom, seductively removing the gown. Her body was precisely the way Otsoa remembered it during their first encounter. He watched her untie long yellow hair from the other room as she walked to the bed and posed, sweeping her hair over her hips.

She waved him over with her index finger, saying, "Come to me, Otsoa."

Chills ran down his spine at hearing Yanamai's voice. Adirah always did an excellent job imitating Yanamai right down to her walk.

Desperate to satisfy his urges, he ran to her, knelt at the side of her bed, looked up, and begged, "Tell me, Yanamai."

"I love you, Otsoa," Adirah replied.

Tears streamed down his face as he gazed into her eyes, trying to memorize how her hair flowed over her hip, her blue eyes looking back at him, her thick eyelashes batting at him, and every curve of her body. Lust consumed him, so he pulled her close and kissed her passionately.

A few thousand heartbeats later, Otsoa left Adirah's apartment and stopped at a fountain to bask in the afterglow of his encounter with her. He paid for her company often for more than a yellow harvest now. He met her while running an errand for Nayrah. Down here, Sovereign Cubes could buy anything. She needed the cubes, and he needed companionship. If it were not for his responsibility as Zorion's heir, he would have offered to join houses with Adirah but was unsure if she would agree to accept him.

She understood him like no other and was willing to fulfill his heart's desire. Something he was sure Durnah would never agree to do. He inhaled deeply, but the gleam in his eye vanished, replaced with panic and fear. The air held a pungent smell that reeked of Nayrah. Lights flickered and went out. He realized Allon was not with him, which meant she had subdued him. Now, he was on his own.

He bolted forward, running for the elevator. Along the way, he realized the avenue was empty. He pushed his body to run faster, passing fountains in a frantic dash until nearing the elevator, and not a moment too soon because he was getting tired. *Only fifty paces more, and I am there!* Pushing off with his left foot, he leaped to the door and summoned the next available car. Panting nervously, he waited for it to arrive.

From above, he saw the car lights fast approaching. *Come on! Come on!* As the doors opened, he looked behind and carefully scanned the darkness. *Ha! I have outrun her!* He spun around to step inside and stopped because a hooded figure was waiting for him. Otsoa jumped back and screamed, but no one could help him. Her eyes pierced through him like daggers.

He retreated from her, but it was no use. His body lifted from the ground with a wave of her finger and flew inside the carriage. As the doors closed, he knew there was no escaping her. He dismissed the thought of pleading for mercy because there were no words that would prevent the inevitable, so instead, he stood to face her defiantly. His boldness made her smile.

"I am through doing your bidding. To *Abadose* with you," he spat.

Her smile faded, and through gritted teeth, she spat, "You will regret those words."

Otsoa felt something wrap around his chest, constricting his breathing. He fell to his knees before her, and she unsheathed her sword. The shiny metal blade reflected the elevator's interior lights with a red hue. She ignited it, and the metal instantly came alive and emitted crimson light. The tip of her blade moved to rest underneath his chin. Although it did not touch him, the intense heat burned his skin.

"Your infatuation with Yanamai has caused me a lot of trouble," she growled menacingly.

"Then, kill me!" he struggled to say.

She laughed, "If I were in a generous mood, I would, but I am incredibly angry with you, Otsoa. First, you openly defied me, and now, you have the gall to curse me to my face!"

"I cannot live like this anymore!"

"Oh, you *will* live. Yanamai, on the other hand, may not survive your disobedience."

"No! If you touch her, I will."

"You will what?" she laughed. "Kneel before me and bleed as you are now."

"Please, Nayrah. She is innocent!"

"Her life is in your hands. Disregard my orders again, and I will cut her head clean off! Do you understand?"

Otsoa nodded.

"Now, to your punishment."

*****

Otsoa returned to his apartment about an eighth of a Terrestrial Rotation later. His journey was slow because Nayrah left him with a limp. She always made it a point to maim him. His injuries were in places that made it painful to breathe, walk, sit, or lie down. In other words, he could find no relief until his body recovered in another few thousand heartbeats. The bruises on his legs were so deep it would take more than one Terrestrial Revolution to mend completely. She fractured all his ribs, making every breath a new adventure in pain. Otsoa approached his home and saw Allon speaking into his communicator.

"Someone assaulted me. I have been looking for you since I woke. What happened?" Allon inquired.

"I fell searching for you. I will be fine, but I need your help getting to my bed."

As Allon braced Otsoa with his shoulder, Durnah opened the front door to their apartment and, seeing him, ran to his other side to help.

"I was worried!"

"I am fine; just help me get to bed," Otsoa whispered with a rasp.

"Who did this to you?" she asked.

He paused briefly before answering, "I did because I accidentally fell over the guardrail, again."

"Oh, you poor dear, is there anything I can do?"

"No, Durnah. You have done enough already."

Chapter 24

Earth
Switzerland - Alpine region
May 9, 2452

It was 3:30 AM, and Dragon had almost finished getting ready. Standing in front of a full-length mirror, he pulled down the specially made mask that completely covered his face but allowed him to see. Every part of his attire was black, making him impossible to recognize. *I am the perfect shadow.* Having hidden his identity, he screwed on a suppresser to his weapon and loaded it.

Hearing the clip click into place, he felt the sense of power, that of life and death, which came with a loaded weapon. He jacked a shell into the chamber, thumbed on the safety, turned, and walked to the table where a Portable Vortex Transmitter rested. He picked it up and marveled at its size. *No bigger than a small fanny pack.* Since the Regime vigorously guarded the technology, it made him wonder how his employer managed to obtain it.

He secured it to his waist and admired it, knowing that only Regime Special Government Agents had used the device. If they caught him carrying the PVT, they would send him directly to the penal colony on the moon without a trial. He shivered at the thought. *I must not fail.* He calibrated the device and rechecked the calculations several times per the instructions so that the PVT could open its maximum of four portals per charge. With only three jumps planned, each one had to be precisely timed and correctly aimed.

Opening a portal inside a busy hallway or intersection would attract attention, spoiling his mission. If he had to make more than one random jump, it could strand him somewhere, with no escape. *It would not be a good career move. It's a shame I need this to get to my target.* With that in mind, he entered an emergency jump for the fourth portal, just in case something went wrong.

Having finished his preparation, he took a deep breath, opened a portal, and whispered, "For the love of money."

Chapter 25

Earth
The Regime - Washington, D.C. - Police District - Precinct 5A
May 9, 2452

Dragon heard the whisper of the event horizon closing behind him. Using his wrist GPS, he verified his location, and it confirmed that he landed on target in less than a second, a cell six feet wide and ten feet long. There was a dim light on the ceiling, surrounded by two vents. There were no windows or doors, making escape impossible.

A small sink and a toilet combination sat on one side of the room. On the other, a small bed bolted to the wall was open. Hearing a noise, the occupant stirred and opened his eyes. Seeing a masked intruder, he sat. The face matched that of the picture his employer gave him.

"I haven't told them anything," Comptroller Bradley pleaded.

Dragon removed the gun from its holster.

"Please, I'll give you anything you want if you take me with you," Comptroller Bradley begged, kneeling before him.

Bradley's words did not even make the slightest dent in Dragon's conscience. Without remorse, he pulled the trigger, sending a bullet into Bradley's forehead, splattering the man's brains across the cell's bunk. The body rested in a contorted heap at Dragon's feet. Leaning down, he retrieved the ejected shell casing. He confirmed that the first part of his mission was complete and, leaving no evidence behind, selected the second set of coordinates on the PVT.

A new portal opened, and he stepped through, keeping his gun ready. He landed in a large room full of monitors and computers. He surveyed the area and saw a man sleeping with his head down on a table. *Damn the intel! No one was supposed to be here.* At least the man was fast asleep. He approached a bank of computers, checked the memory logs, and found the one with the Comptroller's memories within a brief time. *It's the right place.*

He removed a device from his belt, set it on the table in the middle of the room, and flipped the activation switch. The instrument sent out an electromagnetic pulse, destroying every computer in the place. Sparks flew when the machines shorted out, but the noise woke the man who slept. *Wow, what a shiner. It looks like he's already had a bad day.*

Dragon did not allow the man's black eye to distract him. Instead, he pointed his gun at the man's forehead and held up his finger, signaling him to stay silent. The other man froze. Dragon mused that it was unnecessary to kill him. He completed his mission; he had the drop on him; the man did not know his identity, and, most importantly, his employer did not put him in the contract. *It's her lousy intel, not mine.* Dragon moved his hand to select his destination, the portal opened, and he carefully backed into the opening, keeping his aim on the other man's forehead. Once through, Dragon closed the event horizon, making a clean escape.

*****

It took Michael several minutes to stop shaking. The man, who destroyed all his work, vanished, yet all he could think about was the gaping hole in the weapon's muzzle that the intruder pointed at him. *How did vortex infiltration happen in the Regime?* The incident left him feeling vulnerable for the first time in his life. He always had a childlike belief that everyone in his native country was safe, but the intrusion had forever destroyed that sense of security. Now that someone broke into their facility and threatened his life, he may never sleep again. Michael regained his composure and contacted security. Stan Hill arrived within minutes.

"While it's fresh in your mind, tell me everything that happened," encouraged Stan.

"About 11 PM, I sent everyone home. I told them to report back no later than 6 AM. I stayed behind to review more of the Comptroller's memories, and I fell asleep until I heard a noise and woke up. Through the smoke of our computers burning, I saw someone dressed in black, pointing a gun at me. He signaled for me to be silent, opened a vortex, and stepped into it."

"Did you recognize anything about him?"

"No, he was covered from head to foot. If I had seen his face, I'm sure he would have killed me."

"On my way over, I had them check the Comptroller's cell. He's dead. Someone blew the back of his head off."

191

The words shook Michael to the core. *That could have been me.*

"Are you all right?" Stan asked.

"No, not really." Michael looked at the computers in the room, "It's all gone."

"Did you find anything before the intruder destroyed them?"

"I'm sorry. No."

As they talked, Alex rushed in, "What's the emergency?" He noticed Michael sitting in a chair beside Stan and ran to him, "Michael, are you Ok? You look white as a sheet."

Michael nodded, and Stan filled him in.

"I need you to trace a portal destination, and I need it as soon as possible," Stan added.

"Where did he open the vortex?" Alex inquired.

"Right over there in the corner," Michael pointed.

"Contact me when you find where the intruder landed," Stan instructed.

"You'll be the first to know," Alex assured.

"Michael, let me take you home. There's nothing you can do for us now," Stan offered.

"Ok," Michael responded, turning to leave, but he stopped to vomit over the nearest bank of computers.

Chapter 26

Akil
Argi City
The 22,273rd Terrestrial Rotation of the Second Summer

Thea had returned home late again, and rather than accidentally waking Zorion, which would start a fight about her whereabouts, she decided to stay in her private chamber down the hall. She had only slept for a few thousand heartbeats before sensing something was wrong. Thea sprang out of bed and felt the power emanating nearby, unlike what she had ever noticed before.

Thea extended her hand, and her Skean sword rushed from underneath her bed into her grasp. The power was so unusual that she believed it originated from a Saiph. *How did one get here without us sensing his or her arrival?* She opened her door with her sword held out, ready to defend or attack. There was a slight creak, and she silently cursed the maintenance worker for not keeping the hinges lubricated.

She stealthily moved down the hall and wondered, *why me? Why did the Saiph not find Gecheana first?* Fear grabbed her, causing the palms of her hands to sweat. She allowed the Night Lord's power, which emanated from the shadows, to flow through her to regain control. Within moments, the fear subsided, and her confidence returned. She scolded herself for allowing such a weakness to control her.

With her strengthened self-assurance, she sneered at the unknown and advanced to Zorion's door, where the power originated. Running her fingers lightly across the door, the thought that Zorion might be a Saiph fleetingly crossed her mind. The idea almost made her laugh. Gecheana would have seen the blue hue around his aura as a child and killed him.

She pushed open his door, and in anticipation of confronting a Saiph, exhilaration made her heart race, and her breathing was deep and quick. She stepped into his room, and her senses were at their highest, searching every dark corner. There was nothing there, so she cleared all the rooms and returned to where Zorion rested. Baffled by the phenomenon, she closed her eyes and used her abilities to scan the room, hoping to pinpoint the power source.

The shadows guided her directly to Zorion. It confused her even more. *Zorion is not a Saiph, so how is power emanating from him?* She noticed his rapid eye moment. Having crept into many a room at night, she recognized the action to mean the individual sleeping was dreaming. *Interesting. The Saiph is communicating with Zorion during the sleep cycle.* She had an idea, and the corner of her lips curled upward into a wicked smile. She hid her sword underneath the bed, slipped under the covers, pulled herself close to him, closed her eyes, and joined in Zorion's dream.

*****

In anticipation of her arrival, Zorion raised his hands to cover his eyes. It did not matter that she was a dream; it was real enough for him. He longed to see her again and to hold her. Within his fantasy, a small light appeared, hovering before him in the avenue. *Finally, she arrived.* The light grew brighter and more brilliant, to the point that he had to close his eyes, and it dissipated. Having lowered his hands, he could see her standing before him.

I have missed you, he says. She opens her arms without replying, inviting him to come closer. *I wish you would talk to me,* he says. As they embraced with a kiss, they sensed something was wrong and stepped back to look around. He sees the concern in her eyes and feels something cold and menacing nearby. Instinctively, he grabbed her hand, and they ran. Before he put ten paces behind him, something tripped him.

As invisible hands dragged him toward the darkness, she returned to help him. *Run*! He yells. For the first time, he heard her voice. *You must wake up now*! She urged. Nodding, he struggled to awaken, but something prevented him. Abruptly, his mysterious dream companion grew brighter and brighter to the point that he had to cover his eyes again, and her illumination penetrated his hands. Although the light burned, it was working. The darkness lost its grip on him, allowing him to break free.

In his dream, he exclaimed, "Ahhhhhhh!"

"Zorion! Zorion!" Thea yelled, shaking him.

194

He found himself trying to stand, but thin arms wrapped tightly around him prevented movement. He craned his neck and saw Thea holding him. It was odd and unnerving that she had the strength to prevent him from getting up.

"What happened?" Zorion relaxed, allowing himself to sink back down onto the bed; she still held onto him tightly.

"You must have had a bad dream. You were flailing around. I tried to wake you, but you would not respond, so I had to restrain you as best I could to keep you from hurting yourself."

He wondered how someone with such a small frame managed to keep him restrained.

"I am awake. You can release me now."

"Oh, of course," she let go.

Zorion got out of bed and looked back at her quizzically, "Your strength is surprising."

He rubbed his sore ribs.

"It was all the excitement. The truth is you broke free several times. I could barely hold on," she lied.

During a quick self-examination, he noticed bruises on his arms where Thea held him.

"What are you doing here? Usually, you sleep in your private chamber if I get to bed before you," questioned Zorion.

"I *was* in my chamber, but I heard you scream, so I opened the door and found you thrashing about in bed. Since I could not wake you, I tried to restrain you," Thea lied.

He nodded for her benefit because something was wrong with her story. *If what you say is true, where are my guards? If I screamed loud enough for you to hear, Broll would undoubtedly be standing beside me by now with his sword drawn.*

"What did you dream? The same as before?"

"Yes, I dreamt that our sun exploded," he lied.

Thea looked at the time, "You still have several thousand heartbeats before returning to work. You should lie down and try to relax. I will massage your muscles to help you get back to sleep."

Her voice was soothing and seemed to wrap around him like a warm blanket. Within the tones of its sound came a powerful seduction that almost forced him to give in to her suggestion. *That is strange. Why are you taking an interest in my sleeping habits? You have never cared before.* He shook off the inviting feeling with focused effort.

"Thanks, but I do not think I can get back to sleep. I have a busy work cycle ahead of me, so I should begin."

Turning, he walked into the bathroom, changed clothes, and left their living quarters. Thea sat in bed, sighing to herself. *He lied to me again.* Over the last yellow harvest, Zorion has drifted away from her control for unknown reasons, and there was nothing she could do to stop it. Even after using her power to coax him back to bed, he somehow broke free of its will. His independence was unsettling. At least now she knew the source.

The Saiph, who communicated with him during his sleep, was powerful. It was something she had never felt before, even in Gecheana's presence, and more frustrating was her inability to see the Saiph. *The blasted light was too bright.* Still, the effort was not a total loss. She did find the answer to how Zorion could resist her. That explanation, however, spawned even more unanswered questions. What is Zorion's role in the Saiph's arrival? Are they working together? Or is the Saiph using Zorion like she is using him? Had the Saiph already arrived, but she is only just now able to detect their presence?

Thea bit her lip in frustration as more questions poured through her mind. At first, Thea planned to let Gecheana know of her discovery but thought better of it. *No, she will figure out some way of making it my fault. I will let this play out and see where it leads.* Thea looked at the time again. *Zorion is not the only one with things to do.* She jumped out of bed with a renewed determination and got ready for work.

Chapter 27

Earth
The Regime - Washington, D.C. - Capitol Building
May 9, 2452

Jay Porter slept soundly until his emergency communicator beeped, waking him. He rolled over to look at his clock. It was 5:21 AM. Sluggishly, he reached over and answered it.

"Sorry to disturb you, Sir. Someone has just assassinated the Comptroller and broken into the memory storage lab to destroy all the computers," Stan reported.

Adrenaline gave Jay a jolt, and he sprang out of bed, "How did the assassin get inside?"

"It looks like he used a Portable Vortex Transmitter."

"I want a complete check of our inventory."

"I've already sent a team to do just that, Sir. I'll let you know if any are missing once they finish."

"You'll need to begin an internal investigation too. We must vet anyone and everyone who is remotely associated with that technology again."

"Understood, Sir, I'll contact Internal Affairs at once."

"What about the Comptroller's memories? Did Michael find anything?"

"The assassin destroyed everything before he could, but I have Alex trying to trace his destination."

"I want you to pursue this assassin with extreme prejudice. If someone does have a PVT," Jay paused, leaving his sentence unfinished to emphasize the serious nature of the situation.

"I understand, Sir. I'll need a good agent to assist me, though."

"Vincent will be there shortly."

"Thank you, Sir," Stan disconnected.

Jay's next call was to Vincent, whom he ordered to report to Stan. When the call ended, he paced in his room. *First, Bradley betrayed us; now, it seems someone else has delivered top-secret equipment to outsiders. I wonder how many people took part in this conspiracy.* It was not the first time someone had tried to sell the technology, but agents stopped them in time. Knowing that someone other than the Regime had the device worried him.

There are only two ways the device could end up in a criminal's possession. First, someone stole a single PVT unit and sold it on the black market. In that case, the thief would be the only one to use it. Without the proper codes, if the robber tried to reverse engineer the machine, sensors would engage the self-destruct failsafe. Second, someone gained access to the schematics. That would be catastrophic. Anyone with enough money could buy it and mass-produce it.

The Regime would need to implement its countermeasures to prevent an invasion. Everyone's safety was at the mercy of that power. Teams of technicians have already discussed these kinds of doomsday scenarios. If Jay discovered that someone had taken the schematics, he would authorize energizing disruptive shields for all government and community buildings.

Its design prevented unauthorized portals from opening inside, but their safety would come at a high cost. The shields require energy, and the number of buildings that need protection would consume a considerable amount of power. Even with all that protection, it left much of the Regime vulnerable because there was no way to protect the entire country. The dilemma made him restless.

Knowing he would not get back to sleep, he got ready for work and stepped into his office. He finished reading the daily briefing at his desk and still felt anxious. He spun his chair around and stared at the camouflaged elevator doors that led to the vault, but it was only 6:32 AM, still too early to go down.

Over the years, Jay developed a love/hate feeling toward the vault. Although it did not always give him the guidance he wanted, it often gave him the direction the Regime needed. He was sure that the anonymous Founder, who built the vault, knew the future. Even though that conclusion seemed farfetched, it was the only logical answer. The Founder created the files hundreds of years ago before much of the technology now used existed.

Only someone with the gift of foresight could conduct such a task, which meant that whatever success the Regime achieved, it did so by cheating. Jay reconciled with that possibility years ago. As Supreme Commander of the Regime, he ensured that they did things decently and orderly for everyone's benefit. He also used the information to keep the Regime on the correct path. *So, where does that path lead us?*

After careful thought, he concluded a few years ago that the Founder should not have built the vault because goosebumps appeared on his neck every time he read the daily file. It was spooky. It knew things no one should know. Sometimes the information made him second-guess his own decisions, going against his instincts. It was like being a pawn in some big cosmic game.

The instructions directed the Regime like a giant ship down a pre-conceived timeline. Whether that timeline was the original, Jay would never know. His mind often spun with questions surrounding the vault's impact, which gave him another reason to hate it. Still staring at the doors, he debated whether to go in early. If the Founder did indeed have foresight, he or she would know of his dilemma.

His instructor trained him for this position from his youth, which demanded that he follow the rules. The rules said that he could only enter once a day, every twenty-four hours. His teacher also trained him to follow his instincts. He wrestled with the idea until finally giving in to his instinct, *to hell with it. Let's see if the Founder foresaw that I would be the first Supreme Commander to break protocol.* Jumping from his chair, he summoned the elevator. The doors opened. *So far, so good.* Nothing nor anyone tried to stop him.

The doors opened deep within the Earth, and he continued, placing his hand on the scanner. The vault door opened. Inside, he walked straight to the filing cabinet and took out the daily folder. Briefly, he glanced at the cases to his right with future dates imprinted on them. Today, the temptation to open those drawers was overwhelming. As his hand drifted to the cabinet, having next year's files, he heard his instructor's voice. *"You are forbidden to open future cabinets. We will remove you from your position, and you will disappear, never to be heard from again."*

His hand stopped inches from the lock, and he spun around, exited the vault, went back to his desk, and opened the sealed file. Inside, he found a sheet of red paper, marking a pivotal time in history. He removed the document from the folder and read it. The timestamp written at the top stated, "6:53 AM." He looked at his watch; the second hand landed on twelve. *6:53 AM, exactly.*

The goosebumps returned. It felt as if someone was watching. Of course, there were cameras in his office, but the Regime saved that video on a secure server. Even if someone were watching him, it would not help them forge documents this precisely. Today's file convinced him that the Founder was indeed psychic. It meant the Founder controlled the Regime's destiny and possibly the world's fate.

Whether it would be suitable for the Regime, he was still undecided. Carefully, he read the instructions, which had nothing to do with the Comptroller's death. It frustrated him, but he did not question it, considering his recent experience. Following the directions, he told his assistant to have Jared contact him. She looked up the proper code for the day, used a standard digital communicator with an encrypted message to ensure the U.S. government could not find their transmission and waited for his response.

Chapter 28

Akil
Argi City
The 22,273rd Terrestrial Rotation of the Second Summer

Zorion approached Yanamai's door and stopped to look over his shoulder. In the lobby, Broll and the rest of his sentries waited. He knocked for a few heartbeats, but no one answered, so he opened her office door, where she sometimes slept. The soft light from her desk lamp created long shadows on the walls. The new sofa arrived a few Terrestrial Rotations before, and she moved it to the far side of the room.

He hated waking her after what happened, but there was much work to do if she had found a habitable planet. He stood beside her and allowed himself a moment to watch her sleep. Her long hair lay scattered about her body, obviously undone by a troubling dream. The blanket only covered half her frame, revealing the blood-stained clothes.

Gently, he touched an area of dried blood. It was rough and flaky. Losing her was unfathomable, and he cringed at how close Yanamai came to dying, yet the sound of her soft breathing gave him comfort. Without thinking, he pulled the blanket to her shoulders. She was lying on her left side, facing him. He saw a tiny bit of drool trickling from the corner of her lip and smiled. *We are all Akilians. We are all the same.* Never had he seen her like this. At every meeting, she arrived prim and proper, but she still held a simple beauty few Akilian females had, even at her worst. *You are the daughter I should have had.*

"Yanamai," he whispered.

Simultaneously, he gently shook her with his left hand. Her eyes opened. By the look on her face, he could tell she did not know what was happening.

She recognized him and sat, "Did I oversleep?"

"No, I woke you early."

Standing, she frantically gathered her hair. Some strands wildly waved above her head.

It took some effort to push down a chuckle, "How do you feel?"

"Much better now. Thank you."

"I am sorry to wake you early, but we have much to do."

"No, I understand."

"Go freshen up. I will wait for you in the lobby."

"That is all right; it will take too long."

He interrupted her, "Stop. It is bad enough that I got you up early. It would upset me if you did not take the time to clean up."

He nodded toward her blood-soaked clothing.

She looked down at her shirt, "You are right. I do need to get out of these. I will only be a moment."

He studied the hologram of her parents. It reminded him of the first time they met after Yanamai's teachers brought him a report of her test scores. Having never seen such high numbers, he knew she belonged in the Science Division. At first, her parents were hesitant, but a few heartbeats later, he convinced them. No matter what happened to the Akilians, he would always be grateful for having met her.

"I hope you know I do not rush for just anyone," she joked.

He saw wet hair clinging to her jacket, "You have time to dry it."

"It will take too long. Besides, I am not going anywhere. You are right. We have much to do."

"Very well. Show me your findings."

She led him into the viewing room. Before leaving for the arena, she had left instructions for her staff to focus on areas of space that had the most portal activity, but due to her injuries, she had yet to see the photos the third shift took. She played the video, and they gasped.

"They look like us!" Zorion remarked excitably.

Yanamai zoomed in on a couple sitting on a bench using a unique enhancement, and the lens they used, combined with the planet's angle, gave them a godlike view. She saw their lips moving and turned up the sound. They listened intently for a few heartbeats but could not hear clearly, so she put her ear close to a speaker.

"I do not understand anything they are saying."

"Me neither," he replied.

As they watched and listened, the couple stopped speaking and started kissing.

"Oops," Yanamai smiled.

"Now that, I understand," he commented.

"Based on this evidence, physical affection is a universal language. I hope they have other customs like ours," Yanamai noted.

"I guess we will find out soon enough," he watched her view the video of the couple in an embrace and, feeling remorseful, continued, "I realize you had to push your personal life aside to perform your duties, but if this works and we finally have somewhere to go, I want you to take time off and enjoy yourself. Find that special someone and live a little."

"Even if they allow us to settle on their planet, it will take many yellow harvests before I finish my work."

"I will find a way to lighten your workload, Yanamai. I promise."

"That would be nice. Thank you."

"Are there any images of their star?" Zorion inquired.

"Yes," she replied, pressing a few buttons on the console.

The image changed to that of a bright, yellow star; they squinted, even though the light was not bright.

"Young and healthy," she commented.

"I can work with it."

"It is beautiful."

"Yes, very."

"How crowded is the planet?" Zorion questioned.

"We have estimated there are roughly one hundred billion inhabitants."

"That is not good; we outnumber them three to one, so our numbers will concern them even if they agree. They may see it as an invasion."

"You are one of Akil's best negotiators, so I am sure you will find common ground," Yanamai assured.

"Thank you for your confidence. However, negotiating with fellow Akilians is one thing, negotiating with aliens is quite another," he paused, smiled, and continued, "But I will do my best."

"I would expect nothing less. Now, here is something you can work with." She opened several images spanning the globe, "The third shift created a full global map. The planet is mostly water, but there is more than enough unoccupied land for us to live." She entered a few commands, and a file scrolled down the screen, "My team highlighted this folder. The notes show that there are many places with extreme temperatures that they do not inhabit, some are cold, and some are hot, so you should ask if we could settle there. I recommend the hotter climate, though."

"I agree if we have a choice, but it is a good start. Thank you," Zorion rubbed his chin in thought. "Bring the information to my office. I plan to call an emergency meeting with the other Sovereigns. We must get started right away on surveillance."

"I will have it for you in a few thousand heartbeats."

As he started to leave, she softly spoke, "Sir."

"Yes, is there something else?"

"I want you to know that Garbi discovered the planet, not me."

"I understand your sentiment. We will note her contribution at some point, but we must ensure our survival to argue about these details; now hurry with that information. We must get started."

"Yes, Sir. Right away."

Chapter 29

Earth
The United States - Texas - Houston
May 9, 2452

Jared's watch alarm beeped; it was 6:08 AM, central time. His training prepared him to come out of a sound sleep, completely alert, among many other things, so he turned on his Regime Communicator and waited for the encrypted message to download. It finished a few seconds later, so he selected the icon and played a video of Supreme Commander Porter.

"Good morning, Jared. Today, we are on high alert. I sent the details within the message you received. Memorize the information and erase the file before you leave. Shortly, you'll receive a handbag that you'll need for your mission. If you're successful, you'll be back in your room before they've noticed you left. Be safe."

Although Porter stayed calm, Jared could see something bothered him. The words 'be safe' held an unspoken meaning. If the enemy captures him, his orders were to detonate a small explosive within the implant that triggered his subcutaneous body armor. He volunteered for the surgery and signed a document that made him the property of the Regime, who did not share technology with anyone; therefore, he had to treat himself like any other Regime resource if caught.

If he did not comply, the Regime would do it remotely. The explosion would destroy his body and any devices he carried, including the implant. Also, it would kill anyone standing within twenty feet. Knowing he might have to end his own life in that way did not thrill him, but he acknowledged the logic and necessity. Besides, that threat tended to bring out the best in him. Going into dangerous situations, as if his life depended on it, kept him from hesitating.

As he reviewed the mission details, a faux leather satchel with a parachute landed in the parking lot, so he ran outside and retrieved it. With the U.S. monitoring portal activity in their territory, it was always best to use the technology as little as possible. A disrupter helped hide the vortex signature, but even that would tip them off if the Regime used it too often. In this case, the Regime opened a portal above the scanners to avoid detection and dropped the bag with a parachute allowing it to descend.

Jared returned to his room, opened the bag, and found Porter's instructions to 'retrieve a disc' and everything needed to complete the assignment. From within the bag, he removed the dossier of a courier, who would have the disc somewhere on his person. The report showed that the runner was a six-foot-three-inches tall, white, broad-shouldered man with cropped blonde hair. He also had a finger-length scar on his right cheek.

There was no information on the man's background, but Jared knew that he was a professional who could handle almost any situation and would die before giving up the disc, which was the size of a dime. Drawing on his experience, Jared believed that he would hide it somewhere on his body, just beneath his skin. He had to intercept the messenger before reaching the U.S. Capitol in California.

Couriers never traveled alone. Since Porter labeled this a high priority, Jared believed he would have a large posse with him. From inside the bag, he removed a Portable Vortex Transmitter with a signature disrupter attached, a .9mm automatic handgun complete with a suppressor and extra ammunition, a small scanner to find the disc, a jamming device for cell phone or radio communication, and a laser pen powerful enough that it could cut through anything.

He memorized the specifics of the assignment and erased the file. Jared expected the target to arrive at the Los Angeles airport at 9 AM Pacific, leaving him plenty of time to freshen up before leaving. He showered and put on a pair of old blue jeans, a white T-shirt, a non-descript faux-leather jacket, and good running sneakers. Downstairs, Jared wolfed down an omelet made of three eggs, ham, bacon, and beef with a stack of blueberry pancakes on the side. Knowing he would use his body armor during the mission, he needed to stock up on carbs and protein.

Jared thought about stepping across the event horizon in L.A, where he would secure a swift vehicle and familiarize himself with each route from the airport to the Capitol. The PVT only had two preprogrammed locations, the L.A. airport's roof and his hotel room in Texas. If he needed to make other jumps, he must calculate them on the spot. Not an easy task if he is under fire.

At least Porter sent the Heads-Up Display, disguised as a pair of sunglasses. They automatically calculated short-distance destinations, which he would need to jump at a moment's notice. The PVT had enough power to make four long-distance jumps (city to city) or six short ones. To make quick jumps using the Heads-Up Display, he had to focus the lens on the destination point, press a button on the frame to lock in the location, and wait for the vortex to open.

Jared finished breakfast, checked all his equipment, secured the PVT to his belt, slid the glasses over his eyes, and adjusted its safety strap that kept them fastened. He also set the twin chip in his back on a pillow, flipped the switch, activated the chip on the cushion, and deactivated the one in his back. Now Jared was free to leave, undetected. As the final part of his ritual, he screwed the suppressor onto his weapon. *There's no need to attract any more attention than necessary.* Having finished his preparation, he hit the encoded setting on his PVT, a portal opened, and he stepped through.

Chapter 30

Earth
The United States - California - Los Angeles Airport
May 9, 2452

Jared kneeled on the LA Airport terminal roof and ensured no one saw him arrive. It was quiet, which was a good sign. On the horizon, the sun began to rise. He paused to take in its beauty and approached the stairway. Before reaching the door, a plane landed nearby. The high-pitched scream of the engines forced him to cover his ears until it landed. *I must remember to bring earplugs next time.*

He opened the door at the bottom of the stairs and mixed in with the crowd. Outside, in the parking lot, he searched for a vehicle. He found a motorcycle, and the corners of his lips curled into a smile. Jared scanned the area to ensure no one saw him and casually walked over, sat on the bike as if it were his, cut into the lock assembly using the laser pen, and started the engine with a small, flat head screwdriver. He moved the bike forward and drove to the front of the airport at the main entrance.

He used the GPS on the motorcycle to guess which direction the courier would take. He punched in Santa Monica, the U.S. Capitol location, since 2216, when the Regime bought the District of Columbia. As he reviewed the GPS map, there were too many courses to the Capitol to cover them all, so setting a trap was not a choice. Instead, he would make his move en route. He sighed. *It's going to get messy.*

Jared turned off the GPS and patiently waited for the courier to arrive. Around 9 AM, he spotted him walking out of the terminal and climbing into a black SUV's second seat. Jared could barely see the four other men inside through the tinted glass. He frowned. *It'll be more difficult than I thought.* The driver pulled out into traffic, but Jared waited until a few cars were behind them before pulling out to blend in with the other vehicles.

As they traveled through the city, Jared caught up with the SUV just as a traffic light stopped them; it was one of those slow lights that held traffic in all directions until all the pedestrians crossed over. Jared pulled up on their right-hand side, filling the vacant space. Acting like a casual motorist, he kept his face forward to avoid suspicion.

He surveyed the area until the light changed; it seemed as good a place as any to make his move. *They won't expect anything to happen in a crowd; the light will change, and there will be a long open stretch of road in front of them with no traffic.* The light turned green, so Jared sped off and veered into their lane. He slammed on his brakes before reaching the next light, spun the bike around, and aimed it toward the black SUV. He throttled the bike with a practiced move, hiking it up onto its rear wheel.

"What's this idiot doing?" the driver of the SUV asked his companions.

"He's here for the data," the courier yelled. "Take him out!"

There were cars on either side of them, so the driver had a choice. He could either bump into a vehicle and take its lane or stop. He chose to slam on the brakes. Ahead, Jared could see white smoke coming from the SUV's tires as it skidded to a halt. Adrenaline triggered his body armor. Simultaneously, Jared drew his gun from beneath his jacket with his right hand. He aimed at the driver's side windshield and emptied the clip.

Although the glass was impervious to bullets, it did weaken. Jared's motorcycle slammed into the SUV, catapulting him forward; he crashed through the windshield like a human spear, killing the driver. The courier and the two guards in the back seat jumped out and ran. Sitting in the front passenger seat, the guard fumbled for his gun. Jared broke his neck using his left hand, enhanced by the body armor.

Jared wiggled and pulled himself through until landing on the front seat. He retrieved a fresh clip from his pocket and inserted it into his weapon. Jared crawled over the dead bodies, opened the door, and followed the others into a nearby restaurant. Inside, he did not see the target. Instead, he saw a trail of patrons lying on the floor, leading to the kitchen.

Jared ran through the kitchen and out the back door into the alley and to the end of the building but found no exits. However, his targets' footsteps caught his attention, and as they neared the corner, he fired at them. One of the bullets struck a guard in the shoulder. The wounded man spun around, simultaneously retrieving a sound disrupter from beneath his jacket, took careful aim at Jared, and released an invisible wall of bone-crushing sound. The surge hit Jared, driving him back more than thirty feet.

His body armor protected his internal organs, still the impact dazed him. Precious seconds passed until he regained his composure; his quarry had moved around the corner, merging into the crowd. *Height. I need height.* Jumping, he grabbed the nearest fire evacuation ladder and climbed. It was only five stories high, but he could feel his legs burn in protest, ascending at full speed. At the top, he ran along the roof's edge, looking for his target, and spotted him entering a hotel across the street.

Using his Heads-Up Display, he focused on a vacant place on the sidewalk. Jared pressed the button on the glass rim, and a portal opened for him to run through. Landing near the entrance out of thin air, he caught some pedestrians' attention. They pointed their phones at him and took pictures. *There's going to be hell to pay for this.* Jared pushed his way through the revolving door and came face to face with the man who shot him with the disrupter. *Not again!*

The man fired another sound wave at him, sending Jared backward through the revolving door's glass windows and steel frames. The rush of sound also shattered every window in the front of the hotel. Outside, the wave hit people casually walking in front of the building, shattering their bones, and causing them to collapse to the sidewalk. Also, the concussion sent glass, steel, and Jared careening out into traffic. Dazed by the impact again, he struggled to stand.

This time the sound of screeching tires surprised him. He turned to see a truck coming straight at him. Jared tried to dive out of the way, but it was too late. The vehicle hit him, causing him to fly into a brick wall and land motionless on the sidewalk. *Ok, this ends now!* Angered, he stood and ran back into the hotel, where a terrified clerk cowered behind the reception desk.

Jared leaned over the counter and shouted, "The man with the disrupter, where did he go?"

The frightened clerk pointed toward the stairs, and Jared took off running. Upon reaching the first floor, he checked the door. *It's locked.* He looked up the stairwell, but they were not there. *The hotel is eighty stories high, so they couldn't have climbed that many stairs yet. They must have broken into another floor.* Using his laser pen, he disabled the lock, sprinted into the corridor, and stopped at the bank of elevators.

There was only one car moving, and it was going up. *They're heading for the roof!* An elevator arrived, so he took it to the seventy-fifth floor and got out. He did not want to risk meeting the sound blaster again. Using the stairs, he hiked the rest of the way to the roof. At the door, he stopped. *It's another place for an ambush.* He put his ear to the door and heard the faint sound of a helicopter.

Damn, they must have requested air extraction! Time is running out! Using the PVT was his only choice. The only problem was that he could not see his landing. Moments later, he had an idea. Carefully, he cracked the door open, just enough to see, but a hail of bullets greeted him. Instinctively, he slammed the door and dove for the ground. Before he could land, bullets ripped through the metal, hitting his body armor and ricocheting off.

They stopped firing, so he raised his head enough to peek out of the lowest bullet hole in the door. On the other side, there was only one gunman. Unable to see the man who used the disruptor, Jared guessed that he was waiting for him at the elevator. As expected, the shooter stood with his weapon ready in front of the building's air conditioning units. Jared focused on a spot behind him and pressed the button on the glass frame to open another event horizon.

The air-conditioning units were running, which drowned out the sound of the portal opening and closing, so the gunman did not hear Jared landing behind him, who pointed his gun and fired, killing him. The helicopter engines were getting louder. He ran to the wall, using the stairwell as cover. Keeping his back up against the brick, he worked his way around until seeing the courier waving at the helicopter.

The other guard was nowhere in sight. *It's another ambush, and he's using the courier as bait. It's a bold move.* Knowing it was a trap, Jared had to spring it. With the courier in his sights, he chased him. Halfway to his target, another disrupter blast hit him from his right side. The impact knocked a hole in the restraining wall, sending Jared tumbling like a ball of dust toward the ledge of the building. Jared slid toward the edge of the roof and let go of his weapon, frantically grabbing anything that would save him.

Before falling, he managed to grab a piece of rebar sticking out of the concrete. Holding on with his left hand, he looked down and felt sick because the ground was eighty floors beneath him. The helicopter landed on the other side of the roof, and the wounded guard walked to the ledge, stopped, and stared down at him. In turn, Jared looked up at his attacker. Blood from the guard's shoulder dripped down his arm and onto his fingers. The wind from the helicopter blew some into Jared's face.

The guard stepped closer, aiming the disrupter at Jared's head. Jared slashed out with his right arm, sweeping the guard's legs from under him. The disrupter fired but over Jared's head. With his free hand, Jared pulled the guard toward the ledge. The man did not have another weapon, so he hammered at Jared with the sound blaster, waiting for it to recharge. As the capacitor built up power, it made a high pitch whine. Once it stopped, the blaster could fire again.

With no other choice, Jared let him go. The man struggled to his knees, so Jared retrieved the laser pen and triggered the thin, intense beam. Jared chinned himself on the ledge using his left arm and struck out with his right arm, holding the pen. The laser moved across the top of the man's head, starting at the base of his left ear and ending at the tip of his right ear. The man was dead before knowing what had happened.

Although his eyes were still open, they were void of any thought, and he fell forward, over the ledge. Jared glanced down and saw the top of the man's head slide away from his body as he tumbled toward the ground. He turned off the laser, put the pen between his teeth, and pulled himself back onto the roof. The helicopter had taken off, but it was still close. The right side of the chopper was still facing him. The door was open, and he could see the courier inside the cargo bay.

Jared found his gun lying on the roof. He ran over, picked it up, and focused his PVT glasses on the inside of the helicopter, running toward it. The software struggled to pinpoint his landing because he and the chopper were moving. Jared pressed the button on the glass rim, but the portal did not open. *Come on! I'm nearing the end of the roof!* The PVT hummed, straining to calculate Jared's request, and even though he did not see an event horizon, Jared leaped off the roof.

Moments before he started losing altitude, a vortex opened. Jared flew through and landed inside the cargo bay; the accumulated momentum caused him to collide with the courier. The other man saw Jared's gun and grabbed his arm. They struggled, and the gun fired a bullet into the back of the pilot's head. He slumped over the controls, and the helicopter spun out of control.

Jared and the courier continued to fight for the gun despite the bucking and spinning. Bullets ricocheted around the cabin; one hit the fuel line, and the helicopter started to smoke. Jared punched the courier in the stomach and drove him back into his seat. Injured, the courier doubled over, releasing Jared's arm. Now that he was free, Jared pointed the gun at him and fired, but the clip was empty.

The courier lunged out of his seat and punched Jared, hitting him in the face, making his glasses askew. Jared beat the courier down with the butt of his automatic, splitting the man's head open. Blood splattered around the spinning cabin. Jared tried to keep focused but was running out of time. He noticed a small, metallic object protruding from a tear within the scar on the courier's face, about the size of a dime.

Jared grabbed it and prayed that it was the disc. Just as he slipped the bloody chip into his pocket, the helicopter slammed into the side of a building, throwing Jared out the open door. The collision broke the blades on the main rotor, and the chopper stopped spinning on its axis. The tail rotor came around as it bounced off the building, hitting Jared's back.

It shredded his leather jacket and tee-shirt, sending him like an ace tennis serve, speeding toward the ground. He grabbed the PVT on his belt with seconds to react and selected the returning pre-coded destination. The PVT hummed again, trying to calculate Jared's position, which continually changed during his fall. *Come on, damn it, the ground's getting closer!* Just as Jared was about to slam into the pavement below, a vortex opened inches above it. Jared moved through the event horizon, spinning out of control.

At the hotel, the portal opened above the swimming pool. Jared pulled himself into the fetal position just before landing. Water splashed to the ceiling, and even though it slowed his descent, he still hit the bottom of the pool hard enough to crack the concrete. He came to the surface, breathed deeply, and smiled. Whoever programmed the PVT knew how Jared usually ended a mission.

Chapter 31

Akil

Argi City

The 22,273rd Terrestrial Rotation of the Second Summer

Zorion entered his office through his private door and asked Shilda to contact his foreign affairs advisor. They spent two thousand heartbeats discussing the situation until they had reviewed all the laws that applied to their unique situation.

Having finished his meeting, Zorion contacted his assistant, "Shilda, please inform the other sovereigns we must meet, and when Yanamai arrives, send her into the conference room right away."

"Yes, Sir." There was a slight pause. "Oh, Sir?"

"Yes, Shilda, what is it?"

"Olan is here to see you."

"Send him in."

Olan stood at the doorway, waited until Zorion nodded before entering, and approached his desk.

"I do not have much time, and I guess you have some bad news for me by your expression."

"Sadly, I do. The informant I used to infiltrate Elzer's financial database is missing."

"Missing or dead?"

"Most likely, the latter, which means."

Zorion interrupted him, "Which means Elzer probably suspects he worked for me."

"Yes, Sir, I had the informant search for a wide range of information, hoping to hide our true target; he disappeared after accessing the financial files."

"Any suggestions?"

"We have agents planted in his city. Some are small business owners, and others work in large corporations. His background checks are extensive, so I have not been able to get anyone planted high enough in his government. Still, I could have a technician try to access his database from one of the corporate offices. Elzer's technicians would find out someone infiltrated their servers, but our agent would leave before the breach. I believe it would be worth the risk to uncover the truth, although it may take some time to get through his intrusion-protection software.”

Zorion exhaled loudly because it was getting messy and he did not see any alternative. Elzer was using those Sovereign Cubes for something, and it was vital to discover what he bought.

“I believe he may have used the Sovereign Cubes to build a portal machine.”

“For what purpose?”

“I am not sure, but if you find the lab, it will at least answer the question of what he did with the funds we gave him.”

“I could send a team during the sleep cycle and break into his office. If we found the information, you would have a case against him, but if we failed.”

“It would mean war. The problem is that it could mean war either way and at a time, we can least afford it.”

“If he did build a portal machine, we can take images of it. The problem is that he will have it heavily guarded.”

Zorion considered his suggestion, closed his eyes, and contemplated the consequences of his actions.

“Have your team look for it. If you can get images, bring them to me. If not, give me the location, and I will use my position to gain access.” Zorion nodded his dismissal; Olan did not move, “Is there something else?”

“Yes. I tried to follow Otsoa, but someone attacked me.”

“Do you think it was another agent?”

“Anything is possible. Whoever ambushed me had skills. The blade must have had a drug on it because I blacked out for a few hundred heartbeats. Also, the guard you charged to watch Otsoa reported someone attacked him on level three hundred fifteen.”

“What was he doing down there? Only seducers occupy that walkway.”

Olan looked at Zorion with raised eyebrows.

“Really, on the same Terrestrial Revolution, he joined houses with Durnah?”

“It seems so.”

“I need to find a way to disown him. In the meantime, find out whom he is working with, and be careful. If this phantom can best you, they may not give you a second chance the next time you cross paths.

"As you wish," Olan bowed and left.

Zorion's communicator buzzed, "Yes, Shilda, what is it?"

"The other sovereigns are ready for you, Sir."

"Thank you."

Jumping from his seat, Zorion moved to the meeting room adjacent to his office. It was circular, and several short, round pedestals were set equally circularly spaced from each other. Above the stands rested the holographic image of each sovereign. Zorion stepped onto his platform so that the others could see him.

"Thank you all for attending this meeting on such short notice. I have some urgent news to share with you."

Elzer interrupted him, "If this is about the funds you have accused me of misappropriating, I want to see your proof!"

The others looked perplexed by his outburst.

"Is this true, Zorion?" Ruvve, the sovereign of Krek, asked.

Although Zorion wanted to smile at Elzer's blunder, he hid it, "It is true that I believe Elzer misused the funds we all donated to his city, but this is not why I called the meeting."

Elzer blushed, and Zorion fought back a self-satisfied grin.

Quok, the sovereign of Nord, spoke, "Tell us the reason you have called us together." He glared at Elzer, "We will all remain silent to hear your words."

"Thank you, Quok," Zorion paused as Yanamai tiptoed in.

He nodded, and she put the data file into the Information Terminal.

"I have some good news. We have discovered a planet."

All the sovereigns became attentive, including Elzer, "Where is this planet?"

"We found it in sector 1-5-6-9-2-4-1. It is on the other side of the galaxy. Yanamai is sending you the information now, so your scientists can review it at their leisure. All the data we retrieved shows that the planet can sustain life."

Elzer reviewed the information, "It is already inhabited!"

"Yes, it is. There is another problem. We cannot understand the language, so I recommend we send a scout to obtain information on it so that we can communicate with them," Zorion added.

"I guess you plan on sending one of your citizens," accused Elzer.

"Yes, but if you want, we can send a scout from any of the cities," Zorion countered.

Gwah, sovereign of Drard, cleared his throat before speaking, "I know someone in my city that would be ideal for this situation."

Zorion nodded his acknowledgment, "I have no objections. Does anyone else?"

Everyone gave his approval, except for Elzer.

"Elzer, you have not given your vote," Zorion noted.

Elzer glared at Zorion and huffed, "Fine."

"Gwah, how soon can the scout be here?"

"I will make sure he takes the next transport to your city."

"Send him directly to my office; once I have something to report, we will convene again," Zorion stepped off the platform, and all the images disappeared.

He faced Yanamai, "When can we send him to the planet?"

Yanamai looked at the time, "The capacitors should be ready within a quarter of a work cycle."

"It does not give you much time to prepare."

"No, Sir. I will begin right away," Yanamai answered and left.

Zorion was about to leave, but she left an image on one of the monitors. The picture showed buildings of all kinds spread out over the landscape. The beautiful, yellow sun burning brightly on the horizon got his attention. Seeing it on a larger screen made it seem more majestic. Yanamai did her part; now, their fate rested in his ability to make a deal with the rulers of this alien world. Yanamai expressed confidence in him, and he wished to borrow that conviction in times like this. *Do I dare hope that we have found our new home?* He heard Shilda calling for him and returned to his office.

Chapter 32

Akil

Krek City

The 22,273rd Terrestrial Rotation of the Second Summer

Sitting cross-legged on a mat in the middle of her apartment, Gecheana kept her eyes closed and concentrated. She diligently tried to regain her foresight of future events. Many heartbeats passed, but she was unsuccessful. Every time she saw some new development, it rapidly changed as before. This time, she latched onto an occurrence that had something to do with a planet. Her video com beeped preventing her from finding an answer.

She motioned with her hand to turn it on, "What do you want, Nayrah?"

Her tone was weary and agitated.

"I have news you will want to hear."

"I already know that Otsoa is with Durnah."

"No, this is a different matter. The science department has found a habitable planet."

"This new world must be the home of the approaching Saiph," she hissed and continued, "I had hoped we would have more time, but since we do not, Zorion must die now so that Otsoa can order Yanamai to search in the correct sector, the one where I saw a vacant, habitable planet."

"Please, allow me to kill him," Nayrah begged.

"Absolutely not. You will not interfere with this part of my plan. If you do, I will take the city from you. Do you understand?" Gecheana threatened.

"I understand."

Gecheana raised her hand to disconnect, but Nayrah stopped her, "You should also know that the scout going to the distant planet is from Gwah's city."

"Do you know his name?"

"No, Gwah did not give it."

"As usual, I must finish your work for you," Gecheana motioned with her finger and disconnected their communication before Nayrah could respond.

She turned the video com back on; this time, Domeka was on the screen.

"Yes, Gecheana, how may I serve you?"

"I have been informed that Gwah is sending a scout to the new planet. Can you tell me who it is?"

"Yes. I have just received the news and was about to contact you. He is my youngest subject, Kraeth."

"Hmm, this may work to our advantage. Refresh my memory. Is Kraeth the one with the Night Lord's venom?" Gecheana questioned.

"Yes, he is."

"Perhaps we can give him a secondary mission before he leaves. It is always good to have a backup plan just in case the primary scheme fails."

"Do you think Elzer will fail to kill Zorion?"

"Without the ability to see the future, I cannot know for sure," Gecheana answered.

"What do you want him to do?"

"Since Kraeth will have access to Yanamai's level, it would help us if he eliminated her.

"How?" Domeka asked.

"Tadra is next in line for Yanamai's position. As her benefactor, I will demand that she search the sector I initially gave to that idiot Nayrah. Once Tadra finds the world I saw in a vision; we can escape to it, hopefully, before the Saiph arrives," Gecheana explained.

"Yanamai has a sister named Garbi. Of the two, Garbi is the better fighter. Kraeth would have no problem pitting them against each other."

"Excellent. Garbi will kill Yanamai, and Tadra will take her place, giving us a better chance of finding our world. Also, if Elzer kills Zorion, it makes my objective much more secure."

"I will order him to use the Night Lord's venom before leaving," Domeka confirmed.

"One more thing, when he returns, I want a full report of his findings."

"As you wish."

Gecheana motioned with her finger, and the monitor went blank. They needed to find the other world, and she only required one of the two plans to succeed in accomplishing it. Seeing how things were going for her recently, she thought it better to contemplate a third possibility. She closed her eyes and meditated on an alternate probability.

Chapter 33

Akil

Argi City

The 22,273rd Terrestrial Rotation of the Second Summer

Yanamai and Tadra worked feverishly to figure out the best place to open a portal for the scout to land. After a considerable amount of deliberation, they agreed on a location. It was far enough away from a city so that no one would see him mysteriously appear out of thin air. It was also a short walk from the nearest inhabited area, where they hoped he could obtain passage to civilization, so Yanamai calculated the precise coordinates where they would open the vortex.

She finished and instructed Tadra to do her own set of computations. This mission was too important to leave anything to chance. Yanamai decided to step outside for fresh air, leaned against the rail, and looked over Argi. A couple of hundred heartbeats later, she checked the time. Since Tadra would be working on the calculations for another couple of thousand heartbeats, she decided to stroll the avenue.

She told Zain her plan, who walked behind her to ensure her safety. It was lunchtime, and a crowd of government employees cluttered the boulevard, rushing to get to their destination. *If they only knew.* She walked along a line of merchandisers, briefly looked at their window displays, turned back to the rushing horde, and smiled, knowing that their lives would change forever. Zorion classified the information so she could not tell Zain. It was going to be one of those defining moments that everyone would remember.

"Where were you when you heard about our new home?"

She sat at a promenade table in front of a local Bistro and ordered some purple moss as a mini celebration. Zain sat at the adjacent table but did not order. Her meal arrived, and she savored the sweet taste as if eating it for the first time. *I will remember this moment.* Just as she shoved the last morsel into her mouth, her communicator vibrated.

"Yes, Tadra."

"I am finished."

"All right, I am on my way."

Yanamai drank the last of her water and walked toward the lab with Zain close behind. Having traveled a long distance, she decided to take the hover bus back to her office and stood in line, where someone bumped into her, knocking her communicator out of her hand. He knelt to pick it up and handed it to her, smiling.

"Forgive me. I did not see you."

Yanamai checked the device to ensure he did not break it, "No harm done."

She returned to her place in line, and the stranger moved behind her, "I am sorry to bother you, but do you know how to get to the city's Capitol?"

"Let me guess; you are from Drard."

"Very good. You know your dialects better than most from my experience."

"No, not really. Tadra, my lab assistant, is from Drard. I hear that accent every work cycle."

"It makes sense; being around a Drardian would make you familiar with our pronunciation."

Although he dressed in business attire, and his manner seemed pleasant, there was much about his outward appearance that she found disagreeable, including his pheromones. Yanamai smiled kindly to hide her disinterest, trying desperately not to be rude.

"It took some time for me to understand every word, especially if she talked fast, but I recognized her pronunciations of specific phrases," Yanamai added.

"I may know, Tadra. If she is the same Drardian I remember, we may have shared a few classes. If I have time, I will try to visit her."

"I think she would like that. She always talks about missing home."

There was an awkward silence between them until Yanamai remembered his first question.

"Oh, I forgot, you wanted directions to the city's Capitol. I am heading in that direction. You are welcome to accompany me."

"Thank you. I am in your debt."

Again, there was an awkward silence between them until she realized no introductions had occurred. It was not that she cared, but it was polite to ask.

"We have not introduced ourselves. My name is Yanamai."

She extended her hand palm forward to greet him.

"It is a pleasure to meet you, Yanamai. My name is Kraeth."

He returned her greeting by placing his hand on hers, palm forward. As they lowered their hands, the hover bus pulled up in front of them. The wind blew a few strands of hair out of the grasp of her fastener and into her eyes. In his peripheral vision, he watched her fix it. *It is a pity I must kill someone as beautiful as you.* The bus doors opened, and everyone walked on. She sat beside the window, and he rested alongside her. The driver closed the doors, and the bus sped off.

Sitting with her hands folded on her lap, she stared out the window, hoping he would sit quietly during the ride. Helping him was not an imposition, but she was not in the mood for conversation. Unbeknownst to her, he prompted his body to secrete a liquid from the palm of his right hand. Turning it upward, he stared at the few droplets with amazement. It was hard to believe that something so obscure could be so powerful.

Once he touched her skin, the drug would enter her bloodstream and go to her brain, awakening the primitive nature that all Akilians had, leaving her open to his suggestion. Gently, he placed his hand on hers and waited for the inevitable. Feeling his touch, Yanamai pulled her hand away. She looked at him angrily until it faded, replaced by a warm, tingling sensation moving up her arm from where he touched her. *He drugged me!* Fearing for her life, she looked for Zain but did not see him; the drug traveled through her whole body until her skin felt hot; Yanamai's eyes turned red and puffy, confirming that it was time.

"You will attack Garbi and forget we ever met," he whispered.

As Yanamai repeated his words, he moved to another seat and watched her. She stared listlessly forward, repeating the command until they arrived at their stop, where Yanamai came out of her trance and exited the hover bus as if nothing had happened. Although he had no reason to doubt its effectiveness, Kraeth caught up to Yanamai and asked for directions; she did not recognize him. Satisfied that the first part of the mission was complete, he continued to Zorion's office. As Yanamai approached her door, Zain yelled her name from a distance; she turned to greet him.

He reached her, panting, "Where have you been?"

Yanamai thought, "The last thing I remember is exiting the bus."

"I thank Gau that you are safe. I lost sight of you at the eatery and cannot understand what happened. You were right in front of me one moment, and the next, I could not find you."

"I am sorry. I do not know what to tell you. I do not remember getting on the bus, only leaving it."

"All that matters is that you are safe. Next time, please give me more notice, so I can request more Argians to watch over you."

"I will. Again, it is my fault. I should have been more careful."

Yanamai returned to her office. Usually, she would sit in front of her Information Terminal, but something drew her to the sword in her bedroom. She removed it from its case and began sharpening it to ensure it would be ready for her confrontation with Garbi.

Chapter 34

Earth
The United States - Texas - Houston - George Bush Park
May 9, 2452

Standing alone in a small clearing, General Bailey waited for the Regime's Assistant of Defense to arrive. Colonel Scott argued that he should not go by himself, but the Assistant's instructions were clear. He had to follow orders, or it would break their agreement, leaving them without a supplier. His men were at least three miles from the meeting site as instructed. Colonel Scott failed to change General Bailey's mind.

He arrived at the site and turned on the disrupter. General Bailey looked at the surrounding scenery. It was something he rarely had a chance to do. Untouched for years, trees and other greenery overran the park, except for the clearing where the General stood. As it began to dawn, he could see rays of warm sunlight piercing through the leaves, and above, scattered across a dark blue sky, white puffy clouds with golden rims floated overhead. *It's gonna be a warm one again today.*

A soft breeze pushed through the lush forest, and the sound of leaves rustling almost masked the whisper of the portal that opened a few meters from his position. Seeing it made General Bailey flinch. When machinery broke down, accidents happened, and if a vortex machine malfunctioned, the event horizon collapsed, cutting anyone walking through it in half. Those are the horror stories that he heard happened occasionally. It made him glad that he did not need them. Several armed men wearing camouflage uniforms rushed through the portal with their weapons raised, scanning the area. One of them looked at his palm computer, then at General Bailey.

"He's clear," the soldier whispered into his microphone.

Once they set up a perimeter around the event horizon, a few men came through and erected a tent, complete with a table, chairs, and lighting.

A soldier approached him and saluted, "Sir, my name is Sergeant 1st class Walker, platoon sergeant for 1st platoon Alpha Company, Sir!"

General Bailey returned his salute, "At ease, son."

"If you would, General, please have a seat inside."

"Sure; which chair do you want me in?"

"Right here, Sir, if you don't mind. Assistant of Defense Long will be with you shortly."

General Bailey nodded. His chair faced the tent's door, which gave him a view of the opened vortex. General Bailey saw a small room filled with soldiers on the other side. Nervous, he rubbed his hands together in anticipation. Moments later, a man dressed in a suit and tie walked out. Underneath his arm, he held a large computer tablet. General Bailey stood as he entered the tent.

"General Bailey, I'm glad to meet you."

"The pleasure is all mine, Mr. Assistant," General Bailey shook his hand.

"Please, call me Neil."

"If you insist."

They sat. Assistant Neil Long scrolled through his tablet, found the contract, and set it before General Bailey.

"I tried to simplify the contract, but you know how lawyers are; they want things iron clad," he smiled, hoping to keep the mood light and friendly.

"I'm afraid I haven't had the opportunity to speak to many. We don't need 'em anymore," General Bailey replied.

"I'm not surprised because I've read that you've had your hands full for quite some time."

"They're getting fuller," General Bailey tried to smile.

"I take it you spoke with your Senior Officers last night?"

"Yes, I did."

"Since you're here, I can assume they agree," Long guessed.

"Yes. Some were hesitant at first," General Bailey answered.

"It's only natural to be suspicious, but are you sure everyone is on board?" Long inquired.

"Yes, I'm absolutely sure."

"Good. All that's left is for us to go over the fine print. Please take your time and read the contract carefully. If you agree to all the terms, sign at the bottom. I want to be clear about this, General; if you or any of your Senior Officers have any reservations, I recommend you don't sign because you belong to the Regime once you do. You will be under our military laws and subject to their penalties if you disobey an order."

As General Bailey read the contract, his hands started sweating. It was an awkward situation at best. Other than his Senior Officers, his men would not know that the Regime was giving the orders, only that they were helping with supplies and ammunition. Signing the agreement could bring them prosperity or death. However, he felt better after reading it because they wrote the contract in layman's terms. Even he understood every condition and procedure listed in it.

The only downside was that the Regime would not give air support until Texas finished seceding. *I would have enjoyed dropping a few bombs on the gang's territory to let them know who was in charge.* Nevertheless, he understood the logic. If the current Texas government spotted the Regime planes flying in its airspace, it would be an act of war. Still, he would receive all the supplies and equipment needed to strengthen his army because having well-armed men would save lives, so he signed the contract.

Assistant Long nodded, "Excellent."

He took the tablet, typed something, set it down, and extended his hand, "Welcome aboard, General. I know we'll make a good team."

General Bailey shook his hand, "I certainly hope so."

Assistant Long stood and smiled, "Come with me. I want you to see this."

General Bailey followed him outside the tent, where several large portals had opened. Trucks of all sizes passed through the event horizon, carrying supplies and equipment. His eyes widened as the tanks rolled in.

"Why do you look so surprised, General?"

"I usually don't see things move so fast."

Assistant Long chuckled, "If you think this is fast, wait until you see your new headquarters."

"I feel like I've just won the lottery."

"In some way, you have."

"Will the disrupter prevent the U.S. from noticing all the portal activity?"

"It's the reason we asked to meet out here. The device will prevent the U.S. from detecting our activity here, but we are also opening multiple vortexes in several other states as a precaution. Hopefully, they'll think it's a solar flare. It's another reason for us to finish quickly."

They watched as hundreds of vehicles, loaded with equipment, men, and supplies, made their way through the clearing. Large machines started taking down trees to prepare the site for his new headquarters. Assistant Long motioned to a Humvee driver, and he pulled up beside them. He got out, saluted Assistant Long, and ran back through the vortex. General Bailey guessed he was going back to fetch another vehicle.

"Here you are, General. It's brand new, right off the assembly line."

General Bailey laughed with excitement, "I don't know what to say, Neil."

"You don't have to say anything, General; just follow orders, and everything will be fine."

"What *are* your orders, Mr. Assistant?"

Assistant Long grinned, "I knew I was going to like you. Follow me."

They walked back into the tent, where Neil showed General Bailey images of Houston and the surrounding areas.

"Your Headquarters will be here."

He pointed to where they stood in the 'George Bush Park,' west of Houston.

"Contact your Senior Leadership and let them know that we'll be arriving soon to set up base camps north, south, and east of Houston. We'll also set up one here to double as your headquarters until we finish the building. If everything goes as scheduled, they should be ready before lunch. By dinnertime, you'll have access to our dedicated Texas satellite. It has night vision, giving you the edge you need. Anything with a heartbeat will show up on your screen, and by tomorrow, all your men should have the tanks, Humvees, weapons, and ammunition needed to secure a tight defensive perimeter around Houston."

General Bailey exhaled loudly, "Wow! That's fast!"

"Get used to fast, General. You need to be ready to fight at a moment's notice."

"Don't worry. I can get used to fast."

"Now, my intel indicates that you have about sixty thousand men under your command. Is that correct?"

"Yes, give or take a few. I haven't had time to make a complete headcount, though."

"Sergeant Walker and his staff will work with you to gather that information. We want a full profile of every man and woman under your command, including their name, rank, years of service, and medical history. Every detail, along with a photo ID."

"That shouldn't be a problem. We'll rotate patrols and have them report to base camp. It should only take a few days, depending on how fast your men can type and how many questions they ask."

"We'll also need intel on the gangs' movements, their fighting tactics, and whatever else you can provide."

"I'll have Colonel Scott work up a full report and have it for you by tomorrow evening."

"I look forward to reading it."

Assistant Long typed on his tablet and studied the page for several moments.

"Once we've finished processing your soldiers, we will need every civilian to report."

"Civilians too?"

"Yes, General, they are future citizens of the Regime. Once Texas comes into the fold, we will need everyone's name; you're protecting them, which means we're protecting them."

"I don't know if they'll be willing to submit to that, Sir, without knowing why."

"Tell them *you* need to know. Explain that if they must abandon their homes because a gang pushes through your border, a record must be on file to reclaim their land. If they don't comply, they will lose their property and have to start over."

"I'll make sure they understand."

"Good. I would hate for anyone to lose what they've worked so hard to achieve."

Assistant Long extended his hand one last time, "General, it's been a pleasure. I'll expect to hear from you tomorrow at 0900 hours via satellite video conference for my daily briefing."

"0900, it is, Sir."

General Bailey shook his hand. Assistant Long left the tent and returned home through the event horizon.

General Bailey got on his radio right away, "Colonel Scott, get your ass down here right now! We've got work to do!"

Chapter 35

Akil

Argi City

The 22,273rd Terrestrial Rotation of the Second Summer

As the elevator moved upward, Kraeth discreetly looked out the cab's transparent wall and saw Yanamai walking away. He had completed the first part of his mission and planned to find her sister, Garbi. His body produced a powerful drug that would eventually leave her system, but not before she and Garbi fought.

Domeka told him that Garbi was the better fighter, yet Kraeth knew that one accidental strike could change the outcome, and Yanamai could win. For this reason, he thought using his gift on this assignment was unreliable, especially since he would not be here to check their progress, but he was not in charge. The elevator stopped, so he stepped out and moved to the Capitol Building's Screening line.

His thoughts drifted to his youth. Domeka was the first to discover his unusual gift. She often yelled at him as a child, and his body reacted by creating the drug. He instinctively touched her hand and told her to stop shouting at him; she obeyed. Kraeth repeatedly drugged her not realizing she had no memory of what happened after it wore off.

Having dosed her several times, she worried about the blackouts, replayed videos of their sessions to figure out what had happened, and discovered what he did. From that Terrestrial Revolution forward, she made him wear gloves if he was around her, preventing him from using the gift against her.

It did not take her long to realize its value, so she taught him how to use it to *her* advantage; she called it the Night Lord's Venom. He removed his communicator and opened a digital photo of Yanamai's sister. The similarities between them amazed him. Her dossier said she worked in the same facility as Yanamai, which made finding her that much easier.

"Next," a guard bellowed, bringing him out of thought.

He turned off his communicator, placed it in the basket with the other items in his pockets, stepped into the screening booth, and waited in the Capitol's lounge outside Zorion's office. Shilda told him Zorion was ready to see him about a thousand heartbeats later. He stood at the door until Zorion acknowledged him.

"Please, have a seat," Zorion motioned with his hand.

"Thank you."

Before sitting, Kraeth handed him a data file with his credentials.

Zorion reviewed it, "I see you are an expert in linguistics, and you have some basic military training, but that seems to be all."

"I thought it would be enough," Kraeth replied with a hint of disappointment.

"To be blunt, no, at least not for this operation. I prefer to send a scout with military training."

"You have already agreed with the other sovereigns to send me."

"That is true, but I will not send anyone who has not earned my confidence. I will contact the others again, and we will discuss someone else, perhaps a soldier."

"With all due respect, Sir, you do not want a warrior for this mission. You want someone who can blend in with the population. Our military only knows how to fight; they do not have my background in linguistics, and due to their size, they will be more noticeable, bringing unwanted attention."

"Let us assume I send you. Tell me about your plan the moment you arrive."

Kraeth stood feeling anxious because if Zorion did not send him, Domeka would be very displeased with him.

"It is reasonable to assume that the inhabitants use markings for their literature as we do. My goal would be to find out how and where they store it. Based on your technician's report, their Information Terminals are like ours, so I developed a small, handheld portable data device to take with me. I will link it to theirs, copy as much information as possible, and return home with it. Once I have enough examples of their dialect, my linguistic software should develop a translation, enabling us to communicate with them. No soldier can do that."

Zorion paused briefly, "It is a solid plan. Very well, I will send you."

Kraeth quietly sighed, "I am glad you approve."

"You will need to meet with Dahmar in the Science Division. He will give you the equipment and clothing you need for your mission."

Zorion walked over and extended his hand with his palm forward. Kraeth returned his farewell.

"Safe journey."

"Thank you, Sir."

Zorion had Shilda call a sentry to escort Kraeth to the Science Division. The guard left Kraeth with the receptionist. She gave him the room number and directions to where Dahmar waited. Before meeting with him, he had to make a slight detour because it was his only chance to finish the second half of his mission before leaving. He got directions to Garbi's workstation from the receptionist and left to find her.

As he approached the Data Analysis Workshop, the door opened, and she walked out. To discreetly dose her with the drug, he asked for directions. Responding to his request, she pointed back down the walkway; he thanked her and held his hand out, with his palm facing forward. Garbi touched his skin and felt a warm, tingling sensation. It started at her hand, moved up her arm, and throughout her whole body. The moment her eyes turned red and puffy, she was ready for his command.

"You will kill Yanamai and forget we ever met," Kraeth whispered.

He heard her repeating his orders as she walked away; the command he gave Yanamai was different from Garbi. Yanamai's orders were to fight Garbi, and Garbi's orders were to kill Yanamai. It was a subtle variation, but it would give Garbi the advantage. He hid behind a corner for a few hundred heartbeats, returned, and asked her for directions again. Having no memory of him, she pointed down the walkway and continued her work cycle as if nothing had happened. Satisfied that he had completed his mission, Kraeth left to meet Dahmar. A few hundred heartbeats later, he saw a tall Akilian approaching the conference room.

"Dahmar?" Kraeth inquired, moving beside him.

"You are late!" he bellowed.

"You are not there yet either."

"I was there, but you did not show up on time, so I left to find you."

"Sorry. I got lost."

"If you cannot find your way around on your home planet, what makes you think you can navigate an alien world?"

"I can do this job."

"We will see," Dahmar commented, opening the door to their room.

Inside, Dahmar grabbed a small bag and set it on the table, "Those are the clothes you will wear. Change now."

Kraeth removed his clothes and put on the strange-looking apparel.

Dahmar set some more items on the table, "You have enough food and water for seven Terrestrial Rotations."

He picked up a small metallic cylinder, about the size of Kraeth's little finger, "This device is your way home. Just point it forward and press this button. It will open a tiny portal and give Yanamai your location, and a few heartbeats later, she will open a larger vortex so that you can return."

If my mission is a success, Tadra will be the one receiving the signal.

Kraeth started to put the cylinder in his shirt pocket, but Dahmar stopped him, "What are you doing?"

"I was putting it away for safekeeping."

"What if someone takes your clothes from you?"

"Where do you want me to put it?"

Dahmar grinned and motioned for Kraeth to stand in front of him. He lifted Kraeth's arms, retrieved a small, sharp blade, and cut a deep gash, starting from two fingers above his elbow to two fingers below his armpit.

"Ow! That hurts!" Kraeth yelled.

Dahmar laughed, "Stop whining; I am just getting started."

Dahmar took the small, metallic cylinder and shoved it into the opening. Kraeth felt a burning sensation as the device moved behind the muscle, and it took all his might to stop tears from forming. Dahmar secured the cylinder and held the flaps of skin together until it mended. Kraeth thought the ordeal was over until Dahmar lifted his other arm. Dahmar ignored his silent plea even though Kraeth frowned and cut his other arm with the same incision. Kraeth flinched from the pain but did not say anything this time. Dahmar shoved another small device into his other arm.

"What was that for?" Kraeth asked.

"It is a laser."

"Why do I need it?"

"It can cut through almost any material. You may not need it, but it is good to have if you get into trouble."

Thirty heartbeats later, Kraeth's wounds recovered, and the devices were now secure behind skin and flesh.

"It is only a precaution. We put these things inside the body in case they search you. It is something Olan taught us."

Satisfied that Kraeth was ready, Dahmar started to leave.

"Do you have any advice to offer me before you go?" questioned Kraeth.

Dahmar stopped, holding the door partly open, paused in thought, and smiled, "Yes, do not get caught."

As Dahmar walked away, Kraeth could hear him laughing. *That was the craziest Akilian I have ever met.* A few heartbeats later, he cracked open the door and looked both ways. *It was all clear.* Kraeth closed the door, locked it, and contacted Domeka via his video com. Moments later, she appeared on the screen.

"Did you complete your mission?"

"Yes. I drugged Yanamai and Garbi. They will hunt for each other and fight. I still believe we should have tried a different way. I will not be here to monitor their progress."

"I will watch the situation while you are off-world; once you return, bring a copy of the data to me, and we will give it to Gecheana together."

"Understood. I will see you when I return," Kraeth replied.

"Stay in the shadows," Domeka disconnected.

Kraeth waved his hand, the door unlocked and flung open, and he headed for the Interstellar Transport Bay.

Chapter 36

Sergeant Larkin Burke barely noticed the sun setting, walking to Lieutenant Blake's tent to report for duty. At first, he was hesitant. Having worked directly under General Bailey from the start, the idea of reporting to someone else was unsettling, but things were changing fast. He saw new equipment and weapons everywhere, even the clothes everyone wore.

General Bailey told him that the Regime supplied everything. Privately, he told him they were also giving the orders. News of the Regime's involvement meant only one thing; Texas planned to join. It did not matter to him. *If they supply us with what we need, they'll have my support.* He approached the tent and heard someone swearing. *Must be our new lieutenant.* He knocked on the door.

"Come in," the lieutenant gruffly answered.

As Larkin entered, Lieutenant Blake slammed a computer tablet down on the table. Larkin sized the lieutenant up quickly; his temper reflected anger issues, just like Larkin. However, at only five feet eleven, he did not intimidate Larkin, but in comparison, the lieutenant's eyes widened, seeing Larkin close. It was a reaction familiar to Larkin. Most people were frightened by his size, and Lieutenant Blake was no exception.

Larkin shut the door and stood at attention, "Sir! Sergeant 1st class Larkin Burke, platoon sergeant for 3rd platoon Charlie Company, reporting for duty."

"At ease, Sergeant."

Lieutenant Blake circled him once and stopped to face him.

"In case you're wondering, you're reporting to me because General Bailey wants us to run more like an army than a band of misfits when we had to spend extra resources to keep up with our supplies. Now, the Regime has resolved that problem, and our orders are to patrol - damn it - I can't get this thing to work!" he pressed one icon and another. "Every time they send an update, it screws things up! Ah, there it is. 'Bout damned time." He motioned for Larkin to stand beside him. "Like I was saying, our orders are to patrol this long stretch of highway west of Houston." He traced his finger along the road.

"I know exactly where we're goin'. I've patrolled those woods a thousand times."

"Good, cause I'm not lookin' to get shot tonight."

"Me neither."

"I realize you have worked directly under General Bailey, so I wanna know right now if I'm gonna have any problems with you obeying my orders."

"You give me the orders, lieutenant, and I'll carry 'em out, but you need to follow my lead in the field. I don't want you gettin' us killed."

"Just remember that I'm in charge, and we'll get along fine. Now assemble your men and brief them. I'll meet you outside my tent in fifteen."

"Yes, Sir!" Larkin replied and left to gather his men.

Fifteen minutes later, Lieutenant Blake stepped out of his tent. Larkin had his men in formation and ready to go.

"I've assembled the men, and we are ready for patrol, Sir!" Larkin yelled.

"All right, let's get started."

Lieutenant Blake marched toward the border, and his platoon followed behind him in a single file. By the time they reached their destination, it was dark.

"Platoon, stagger formation, and night vision goggles in place! Keep your eyes and ears open! Nobody, and I *mean* nobody, gets past us, or you'll answer to me!" Larkin bellowed.

Lieutenant Blake gently grabbed Larkin by his arm, guiding him off to the side.

"What about you, Sergeant? Where are your NVGs?" he whispered.

"Don't need 'em. I see fine in the dark."

"They're designed to show a green signature to represent our soldiers, so if you're not wearing 'em, you could accidentally shoot one of your own during a fight."

"As I said, I see fine in the dark. I know who my men are and who the enemy is."

Larkin turned and walked at the head of the line to take point, leaving Lieutenant Blake with a bewildered look. He shook his head. *Why do I always get the crazy ones?* Larkin led his platoon through the woods and scanned the old highway, which used to be the Sam Houston Tollway that circled Houston's city. His whole body was tense and alert. Moving across the broken blacktop, he caught every sound and movement. Nothing escaped his senses.

A twig snapped, so he raised his arm to stop his men and focused on the area where the sound originated. Anger burned inside him, and everything around him became clear; it was a deer, so Larkin allowed the anger to drain from his body and waved his men forward. Minutes later, he heard a hand smacking skin. *Mosquitoes.* Grinning, he remembered what General Bailey told him.

"Texas has a buffet of mosquitoes. Every season brings another species."

Larkin knew they were a nuisance to his men, but they never bothered him for some reason. General Bailey used to joke, saying they were afraid to get within five feet of him.

"Sergeant," the Radio Telephone Operator whispered to get his attention.

Larkin signaled his men to stop, "What is it?"

"I just got a call from HQ. They're picking up heat signatures, a lot of 'em, one klick south of here, heading straight for our border. Our orders are to intercept."

"Can they tell if they're human or animal?"

His RTO whispered into his radio first and answered, "They can't be sure, but they're movin' at a slow, steady pace."

"Damn, it sounds human. Who else they sendin'?"

"4th platoon Charlie Company, but they're more than sixteen klicks south of us."

"Shit, they'll never make it in time."

Larkin signaled for his men to gather around him. Lieutenant Blake took a position on his right side.

"Listen up; we have a new FRAGO. There's movement about a klick down the road to our south, heading straight for our border. 4th platoon Charlie Company is on their way, but it doesn't look like they'll make it in time, so we're on our own. Murphy, take your squad and scout ahead. I want to know for sure what's out there. I want everyone else in a straight line. We need to hustle if we're to get there in time."

After the briefing, Murphy's squad sprinted ahead of the platoon, and the rest ran steadily, arriving a few minutes later. Murphy came running out of the woods and stopped in front of Larkin.

"Sergeant, armed men are approaching from the east. They don't have NVGs; they're using flashlights and lanterns.

"How many?" Larkin asked.

"Two, maybe three hundred."

He sighed and signaled for his platoon to gather around him.

"All right, this part of the highway has hills on either side. If we let 'em get to the road, we should be able to box 'em in. I want claymores laid up and down the highway where they're gonna cross, everything we've got. Lock the frequency to my remote detonator. Put snipers at the top of the hill on their side of the road but out of their path. Tell 'em to hold their fire until they see my signal. The moment I give the Ok, I want 'em to take out as many as they can from behind.

"Murphy and Nelson, you'll take your squads to the other side of the road. Murphy, you go north, Nelson, you go south. No more than fifty meters. Turner, take your squad to the top of the hill. Stay out of their path. As the last one crests the top, you come in behind 'em. We'll catch 'em in a crossfire. Once I detonate the claymores, I'll take care of any that make it over to our side; when it blows, unleash hell."

"Sergeant, what about tank support? I hear we just got a whole bunch of 'em," Murphy inquired.

"Nah, if they spot the tanks or hear 'em comin', we'll lose the element of surprise. Now do what I said so they don't catch us unprepared."

"Sergeant," Lieutenant Blake motioned for him to approach.

"Yes, Sir."

"In the future, if we receive new orders, I expect that you check with me before giving them to our platoon."

"We don't have time to discuss this, lieutenant. Two to three hundred armed men will be over that hill in a matter of minutes."

"I understand, but I want the men to recognize that the orders they're receiving are coming from me."

"General Bailey never had a problem with me giving my men orders."

"I'm not General Bailey, and things have changed. You need to respect the chain of command."

Larkin fought back the urge to hit him. *God damn officers!*

"Ok, I want everyone to stop what you're doing!" he yelled.

"Sergeant, what the hell are you doing? They will hear you yelling!" Lieutenant Blake whispered a yell.

"Apparently, our lieutenant needs to issue you all an order, so nothing moves until he says so."

"Damn it, Burke! Men, go back to what you were doing," Lieutenant Blake ordered.

Larkin looked at Lieutenant Blake and growled, "You better go find a place to hide. They'll be here soon."

Lieutenant Blake returned his glare and left to get into position with Murphy's men. Having received their orders from Larkin and Lieutenant Blake, Murphy, Nelson, and Turner ran to meet their squads. They laid all their claymores on the road. In less than ten minutes, everyone was in place. Larkin sat in the dark waiting, and his thoughts dwelt on the approaching band. Adrenaline rushed through his body, so he chewed gum to help keep his mouth from getting dry.

His heartbeat increased, and sweat formed on his forehead. It was not nerves. It was anger, no, fury. He could not wait to face them. They threatened everything and everyone he loved, and they would receive no mercy. Gazing through the darkness, he saw his men scattered about the hillside. With a little more concentration, he could see the position of the three snipers. The dark hid nothing from him.

Often, Larkin wondered how or why he had such extraordinary abilities and knew it had something to do with an event that happened to him and his brother in a cave when they were young. Before his parents died, they took him and Tucker on vacation to Australia. They were on a beach, went exploring, and discovered a cave, but the only thing he remembered was waking up as his parents working frantically to revive them.

Later, his parents told him they ate something poisonous; they did not elaborate. Although his memory was sharp, he did not remember eating anything in the cave. He often thought it might have been a mushroom or something like it but could never be sure. Whatever it was, it had changed him and his brother forever. Since that time, Larkin felt a presence. Having discussed it with Tucker, he discovered they could feel something nearby, watching, and waiting, yet they did not know why.

At the age of ten, his parents died, and there were plenty of hard times that followed. Homeless, he and his brother wandered the state of Texas until they finally made a home in the abandoned suburbs of the Houston area. The constant fight for survival made them strong, and each time they fought, they became more powerful. By the time Larkin turned eighteen years old, he and his brother had killed more men than Larkin cared to remember; it had become a way of life for him, and he started liking it at some point.

Branches broke in the distance, and his instincts focused on the top of the hill, where he saw the silhouettes of men carrying flashlights, lanterns, and weapons. They were coming straight toward him. *They'll be sitting ducks with those lights.* Patiently, he waited for them to make their way to the road. *The scout was correct; there's a few hundred of 'em - jeez, they're not even in a staggered line but bunched together.*

Their ignorance did not surprise him because they did not have formal combat training. They were thugs, street fighters. The thought enraged him, and he gritted his teeth. *They're animals that need slaughtering.* The group made their way down the hill, using their lights to search the surrounding areas. They spread out upon reaching the road, focusing their illumination forward and to their side.

Larkin's snipers watched through their night vision scopes on the hill, waiting for his signal. He held his breath and ducked behind a tree as the beams from their brighter lights swept past him. He removed his Bowie knife from its sheath, poked his head out from behind the tree, looked directly at the snipers, and made a cutting motion in front of his neck with his blade.

That was the signal, so each sniper picked a target and fired. The suppressors kept the noise of their bullets down to a whisper. They fired multiple rounds since it was a target-rich environment, taking out the intruders. They focused on killing the stragglers at the back of the group first, but someone noticed and yelled that they were under attack.

The invaders raised their weapons and started firing aimlessly into the night. Larkin smiled and squeezed the detonator. The ground shook beneath him, followed by the heat from the explosion. Balls of fire engulfed the area. The eruption shredded bodies and threw them in every direction; the flames vanished, so Larkin's men returned fire, and chaos ensued. The raiders ran for cover; Larkin's men shot many, killing some and wounding others. Their cries aroused his predatory instincts.

Hiding in the tall grass like a lion, he waited for any that might make it across the road. Despite his soldiers' efforts to stop them, some did make it through, and Larkin went after them. The night gave him cover, but they could not hide from him. His instincts told him when to duck, jump, and turn. At one point, he felt compelled to lower his right shoulder. He spun around in one smooth motion, turned, and watched as the bullet flew by him as if moving in slow motion.

Once he was in this zone, the entire world moved that way. To him, the people he hunted were practically standing still. Larkin closed in on one of the men who crossed the road. The intruder only took a few steps before he was on him. Larkin grabbed the man's hair with his left hand and lifted him off the ground. While struggling to break free, the man screamed from pain, fear, and surprise. Larkin made a quick work of him.

It was as if some unseen hand guided his Bowie through the man's spinal cord, between the L1 and L2 vertebra, and the man instantly went limp. Larkin tossed him aside without a second thought, looked for another target, and hunted in the same fashion. His rage gave him clarity, allowing him to see everything. Anyone within his killing field did not survive. He loved the hunt and the satisfaction of taking a life but would never tell Sarah because of her disappointment in him.

He justified the emotion by telling himself and others that it was necessary to protect his family, but he knew the truth. It made him feel alive and powerful. Having eliminated everyone within his kill zone, he took a moment to check on his platoon. The gang outnumbered them four to one, and his soldiers gave their best effort. Larkin scanned the area and heard several cries for a medic; it was something every leader dreaded to hear.

Still, he could see that they *were* prevailing. A quick scan of the area showed more of his men than intruders. Survivors hid in the bushes near the road, hoping to stay undetected, but Larkin knew their plan. They would remain concealed until morning, wait until his platoon moved on, and continue their mission. *Not on my watch.* The thought enraged him, and he ran to flush them out of their hiding places.

First, he focused on the nearest ones, positioned himself between them, and yelled, "Fire!" He moved aside. They reflexively turned and fired but shot each other dead. The fighting ended, and everything was quiet except for his heartbeat. Believing the battle to be over, he made his way to the street, where his platoon checked bodies to ensure they were dead. A gunshot drew his attention. He turned to see that a soldier had put a bullet in a pretender.

"Good work, Peterson."

Returning his attention to his work, he saw the lieutenant approaching. Blood dripping from his shoulder showed that he had caught a bullet during the chaos.

"You ought to get that looked at, lieutenant," Larkin advised.

Seeing Larkin, Blake shook his head in disbelief, "You don't have a scratch on ya. How the hell did ya manage that?"

Larkin ignored his question. The truth was, he had no idea. Larkin sensed someone nearby and allowed his instincts to guide him toward the road's edge, where he found a drain underneath the street. It had a small stream running through it. He jumped down into the water and saw a man cowering inside. *No wonder I didn't see you.*

"What is it, Sergeant?" Lieutenant Blake asked.

"I missed one."

"Don't kill 'em; take 'em back to be interrogated."

"We don't interrogate or take prisoners, but I want to know who's behind this," Larkin mumbled under his breath, picked him up by his collar, pinned him against the tree, and brought the Bowie knife to his neck, "Who sent you?"

Seeing the blade, the man froze, unable to speak.

"Answer me," Larkin growled, pressing the knife harder into the man's throat, drawing blood.

"Perez," the man blurted.

"I don't know, Perez. Who is he?"

"He's El Diablo's brother. He sent us to avenge his brother's death."

Larkin pressed his total weight onto the man's chest, nearly suffocating him.

"Give Perez a message for me. Tell him to forget about any delusions of retribution. If he doesn't, the next time he attacks the resistance, I'll personally hunt him down and kill him! You got that!"

The man nodded nervously, "Who do I say the message is from?"

Larkin forcefully threw him down into the water, where he hit his head on a rock and started bleeding. Larkin did not have mercy and shaved the back of his head with his knife, close enough to see the skin, and carved the initials LB. The man screamed as Larkin cut him.

"You tell 'em, Larkin Burke!"

"Sergeant Burke, what the hell are you doing?" Lieutenant Blake demanded.

Larkin threw the man upward, out of the drain, and onto the road.

"Now, get goin' before I change my mind!" Larkin yelled.

"No! We need to interrogate him!"

"I just did. Perez sent them."

"Nelson, tell your men to stop him now!" Lieutenant Blake yelled.

"Belay that order!" Larkin roared.

Nelson did not move.

"Damn it, Burke! We can get more out of 'em than just a name! We can find their base location, routes, and where Perez lives!"

"He doesn't know. They change locations and routes constantly. The moment Perez sent him, he moved everything to a new location. This way, Perez will get my message and think twice before attacking us again."

"Damn it, Burke! You disobeyed a direct order!"

"No, Sir. Our orders were to intercept, and that's exactly what I did."

Murphy ran up to him.

"Report," Larkin demanded.

"We've got five dead, another fifteen wounded."

"Damn it!" Larkin whispered under his breath.

He felt goosebumps on his neck, looked toward the south, and sensed a considerable number approaching. He reflexively brought his weapon up and aimed at the approaching horde. Seeing that Larkin drew his gun, his men did the same. At first, Lieutenant Blake looked at them quizzically, thinking they were all paranoid but raised his weapon, too, just in case. There was silence for a few seconds until someone yelled from the woods.

"Don't shoot! I'm Sergeant 1st class Dunn, platoon sergeant for 4th platoon Charlie Company!"

Larkin lowered his gun, "It's all right, men. Stand down."

"We've been running full out since HQ notified us," Sergeant Dunn panted.

"You missed the party, but we could use some help with our wounded and cleaning up the mess."

Sergeant Dunn nodded, "I'll get my men on it right away."

"This ain't over, Sergeant," seethed Lieutenant Blake, walking past him.

"It better be."

Chapter 37

Akil
Argi City
The 22,273rd Terrestrial Rotation of the Second Summer

As Yanamai sharpened her sword's blade, Tadra knocked on her bedroom door, looking for her. She put the sword back in its case and answered.

"Yes, Tadra, what is it?"

Tadra noticed her eyes were red and swollen, "Are you feeling all right?"

"Never better. What do you want?"

"The scout will be here at any moment."

"Good. I want to get this over with," Yanamai replied and entered the lab. "Have you run the simulation?"

"Yes, three times. The results were positive."

"Good, we are ready. Now, all we need is the scout," Yanamai commented.

Moments later, Kraeth walked into the room. Tadra met with him to see if he had any questions, but he did not, so Tadra nodded toward Yanamai, who opened the vortex. Since their landing was on the other side of the galaxy, the portal required millions of volts, shaking the floor as the energy passed through thick cables underneath the room. The event horizon appeared with a clap of thunder. On the other side, there was an array of colors. Their sun was also in the distance, filling the Interstellar Transport Bay with an other-worldly yellow light.

Tadra stood beside her and remarked, "It is beautiful."

"Yes," Yanamai agreed but barely noticed.

All she could think about was attacking Garbi.

Chapter 38

Earth
The Regime - Washington, D.C. - Capitol Building
May 10, 2452

Supreme Commander Porter stared at the data chip in his hand. A few hours before, Jared had sent it to him. In his report, Jared spared no space describing how many people died or the number of times *he* almost died trying to obtain it. Supreme Commander Porter smiled despite himself, reading Jared's elaborate story because he was obviously hinting at a vacation. *You'll get one soon enough.* Sighing, he shook his head. *Whatever is on this disc must be essential because many men died for it.* As he contemplated the implications, Ms. Bradshaw buzzed.

"Yes, Ms. Bradshaw?"

"Assistant of Defense Long is here to see you."

"Send him in."

Supreme Commander Porter put the disc in a plastic case, set it in his drawer, and casually closed it as Assistant Long walked into his office. He did not choose his Assistant of Defense but still admired the man greatly. During their tenure, Assistant of Defense Long showed courage, loyalty, and, most of all, intelligence. Assistant of Defense Long stopped before the Supreme Commander's desk and waited for his acknowledgment.

Assistant of Defense Long was at least ten years his senior but was always deferential, a man who understood the 'chain of command.' Jay often drew on his experience to decide on military actions or ensure that any sanctioned decision was within the Regime mandates. Since he was a busy man, Jay knew that a personal visit usually involved terrible news. Standing, Jay extended his hand to greet him.

"Neil, it's good to see you again; please, have a seat."

"Thank you, Sir." Neil sat, "I'm sorry to inform you that someone destroyed our International Transportation Station in Frankfurt, Germany."

"Destroyed? How?"

"An anti-tech group called the *'Tech Revolutionaries'* has claimed responsibility."

"Yes, I remember hearing about them." He laughed, "Diederich Schmidt, their leader, uses the name 'Tech Revolutionaries' to goad us. If you've noticed, it has the same acronym as 'The Regime.'"

"I agree it's a taunt, but his propaganda videos have accrued quite a following, about one million worldwide, outside the Regime. In them, he says we plan to use technology to destroy the world."

"I wonder if his followers realize they are using technology to spread their message."

"I would be surprised if they did."

"I understand he has many supporters. I've wanted to meet with him for years, but, up until now, it's only been words, so tell me, what happened at the facility?"

"They hid an explosive within a container. It had a protective barrier, which gave the Scanner a false reading, and just as the box passed through the event horizon, it exploded."

"I see," Jay tapped his chin in thought briefly, "Did I miss something?"

"Only a Portal Technician would know that detonating a bomb within the event horizon increases the power and force of the explosion. Unless, of course, it was an unhappy coincidence," Neil answered.

"Do you think Diederich Schmidt worked for us?"

"Anything is possible. Did our camera pick up any images?"

"Yes, we have a profile of one of the Revolutionaries."

"Put it through our facial recognition software. If he worked for us, his photo should be in the system."

"Already on it."

"How much damage did it do on our side?"

"Although our people followed protocol, having the blast shields in place wasn't enough; the terrorists destroyed the whole facility."

"Loss of life?"

"The combined numbers for both facilities: One hundred fifteen, with another sixty seriously injured. They're still digging through the rubble because several employees are missing."

"Well, Diederich, you have my attention now, but I don't think you'll like it," Jay whispered to himself and faced Neil, "How do you want to proceed?"

"To cover our public relations, you should openly demand that Chancellor Scholz capture and turn over those responsible for the attack."

"You know as well as I that he won't do it."

"Or he could cooperate, as described in our mandate. The Regime Rules of Engagement authorize us to execute an operation to find, capture, or kill those responsible."

"This use of force could lead us to war."

"Perhaps, but that assumes they can prove we are involved. If we execute the operation correctly, we can either retrieve or kill those at fault without the public knowing we were there. Chancellor Scholz can posture all he likes. He will look good to his people, and we will have punished those responsible. It's a win/win situation."

Jay agreed with him. The Regime held the position that an attack on one was an attack on all. The Regime never started a war, but neither did it shy away from protecting its interests, as some learned the hard way. Still, committing human life always deserves careful consideration because the price of war was human lives. At the same time, they had to stop anyone willing to take human life indiscriminately.

Supreme Commander Porter took a moment of quiet contemplation and replied, "Very well, I'll have Ms. Bradshaw set up a video com meeting with him today. I'll let you know the results after we talk. I want your proposal on my desk as soon as possible."

"I already have an idea. Once I work out the details, I'll bring it to you."

"Thank you, Neil," they stood and shook hands again.

"By the way, I read your report on Texas, so tell me, what kind of man is General Bailey?"

"He seemed… how shall I put it… cooperative."

"Do you think he's trustworthy? Can we depend on him to follow orders?"

"I don't trust anyone outside the Regime, Sir, but I think he'll stand with us as outsiders go. We're saving his hide now. I think if he had the opportunity to eliminate the gangs threatening his territory, he would jump at it."

"Good to know. I'll see you soon."

Assistant of Defense Long left, so Supreme Commander Porter buzzed his receptionist, "Ms. Bradshaw, I'll need a video com meeting with Chancellor Scholz as soon as possible."

"Yes, Sir, and by the way, Danny is here to see you," she answered.

"Good, send him in."

A moment later, Danny walked in. Right away, Jay could tell he was nervous. Body language often gives away a person's thoughts. He imagined himself in Danny's position and realized that he would be worried because it cannot be easy standing before the Supreme Commander of the Regime without knowing why. Besides Michael and Alex, he did not often speak with civilians, but the sensitive situation needed immediate attention, so he felt obligated to oversee it personally.

As a pragmatist, he always tried to keep things in perspective. He was a high official but still only a cog in a much larger wheel. *One that the council can easily replace.* With that in mind, he respects everyone's place, no matter how high or how low their perceived status is. For example, he did not have the necessary skills to decode what was on the disc in his drawer as Danny did. Without that cog, the wheel would not turn. Jay retrieved the disc from his drawer as Danny stopped a few feet from his desk.

"Do you see what I have in my hand, Danny?"

Danny squinted, "It appears to be a very tiny disc, Sir."

"Correct. I called you here because I want you to discover what is on it."

"Me? Supreme Commander, I appreciate your confidence, but surely there are others more qualified."

"I've read your dossier. You're just as qualified as anyone else, if not more. You simply haven't had a chance to shine. Now's the time."

"Thank you, Sir. I'll do my best."

"I know you will."

"Do you have any idea what's on it or what I'm looking for?"

"No, but whatever it is, six men died protecting it."

Danny swallowed hard, "Protecting it? You mean we stole it?"

"Danny, as you age, you'll discover that sometimes it's necessary to do something wrong to make things right. This is one of those times," Jay replied.

"I understand. I think."

"I've assigned two android sentries to be with you at all times. They're programmed to protect you and the disc."

"Protect me?"

"Don't worry. Standard protocol dictates that the Regime must protect everyone involved with this data just in case the people we took it from are trying to take it back."

Supreme Commander Porter paused to let the seriousness of the matter sink in, "Now, I suggest you get started."

He handed him the disc, and Danny left without saying another word.

Ms. Bradshaw rushed in, "President Martinez wishes to speak with you."

Supreme Commander Porter sighed, "Put him on the main monitor."

Within moments, he stared at an enlarged image of the President of the U.S. His face seemed chubbier than the last time they spoke, and his hair had more grey strands. Bags under his eyes showed a lack of sleep. *The office takes its toll, no matter where it is.*

"Santiago, how are you this morning?" Jay asked in a practiced pleasant tone.

"Let's skip the pleasantries, Porter. You know why I'm calling."

"No, I don't. You'll have to inform me."

"The disc, Porter! I want it back now!" President Martinez spoke with an edge of frustration and anger in his voice.

"What disc?"

"Don't pretend to be ignorant! I lost six good men because of you!"

"I'm sorry for your loss, but I don't have this disc you're describing."

"I swear, Porter. If you don't return it to me now, I'll."

"You'll what? Send in a special ops team to kill me? You've already tried that and failed."

Santiago's face turned blood red with rage, "You won't get away with this, Porter! I know you open portals inside my country. Oh, you claim you're delivering humanitarian aid, but we know it's to hide your true objective."

"What is that?"

"To spy and perform subversive operations to destroy this good nation."

"I don't *need* to destroy your nation. Political corruption has done that. It saddens me to see representatives come and go, yet each is satisfied with the state of their nation. Hundreds of years ago, you were accountable to the public, but now, helping your constituents is a thing of the past. None of your elected officials seem to care about the millions of homeless and jobless citizens under your well-fed thumbs, or they would do something to change it.

"Knowing how desperate your citizens are, we send food and medical supplies to rural areas for their survival. Have you ever been outside the Capitol? Your people are dying, yet all you do is raise taxes and misdirect government funds into your bank accounts, so you'll forgive me if I refuse to do nothing while you systematically kill your citizens with starvation, neglect, and oppression."

"My people are my concern! What I do with government funds is none of your damn business! I swear I will bring this issue to the United Nations!"

"Go ahead, but I suggest you bring proof and not accusations. Also, you might want to pay the two percent GDP you owe, or they may not even listen."

"One day, Porter. I will rally every nation against you. When that day comes, you'll regret ever crossing me!"

"You do that, Santiago, and I promise I will direct my first attack at you, personally. Remember that wherever you are in the world, I will find you, and you can be sure that you won't live to see whether the Regime survives or not."

"Don't threaten me, you son of a bit."

Supreme Commander Porter disconnected communication. He was not about to listen to any more of Santiago's ranting. Instead, he sat behind his desk to continue his day's work as if the conversation had not taken place.

Chapter 39

Akil
Vlor City
The 22,274[th] Terrestrial Rotation of the Second Summer

Behind his ornate, antique desk, Elzer rhythmically tapped his fingers near the bottle Kemena gave him. Across the room, he saw his reflection in a brightly polished display case and almost smiled. He liked the way he looked. The image of power suited him. He was an imposing figure, and his desk was just as striking. Before their sun changed into a red giant and drove everyone underground, an expert artisan built it for Vlor's sovereign.

Since then, each ruler has passed it down, and now it is his. The craftsman used fiber from the *Baobatin,* an enormous plant that grew on the surface. The legend surrounding the desk said that it took a team of twenty laborers just to cut one down. Elzer studied the grain's three-dimensional quality and felt the fiber's smoothness. He gently allowed his fingers to explore the carved reliefs and decorative edges. Even after all this time, the desk was still perfect.

He would never admit it but admired their gift. It is a work of art. His image matched the skill and artistry it took to shave the edges, cut each piece, and fasten them together. *One Terrestrial Revolution, I will be the Supreme Sovereign.* He knew that achieving such a title required risks, and one of those uncertainties caused a knot in his stomach, which kept him up during the sleep cycle.

His attention returned to the bottle on his desk. Simultaneously, his fingers stopped tapping, and he gently picked it up. He opened the report his top scientist gave him with his other hand. Within the details of his findings, he confirmed what Elzer thought it to be: a camouflage potion, but at least now, Elzer knew it was not just a bottle of smelly water. He closed the report, pushed his fingers through his hair, and sighed. His hand returned to the desk, so he studied it and remembered.

Just a few Terrestrial Rotations ago, he lacked a few fingers; now he had them back. He wiggled them as if trying to convince himself that they were real. *How did Kemena do it?* He could not trifle with someone that had her power. Disobeying her would translate into him losing more than a few digits, but her instructions put him in a dangerous position.

Though he had no moral objection to her mission, killing Zorion was a considerable risk. If he failed or if someone linked him to the assassination, it would plunge his city into war; a war Vlor could not afford to fight. Moreover, if there were a conflict, he would not be sure if the other three sovereigns would side with him.

He regretted not spending more time building closer relationships with them because this attack could force him out of his position. He did not want to do it but had no choice. Beneath the top of his desk, he found the switch for the voice-activated recording device and turned it off. *I must keep this a secret.* Elzer contacted Igon, his Chief Administrator of Intelligence, and woke him.

"I need to see you now!"

"I will be there shortly," Igon sluggishly replied.

He disconnected, sat back in his chair, closed his eyes, and imagined Igon rushing to get ready. He perversely smiled because giving orders and making Vlorians jump gave him immense pleasure, especially those who thought they were better than everyone else. The knot in his stomach left. Igon was a tool, and like all tools, each one had a specific place in the order of things.

Elzer knew that Igon would rush to get ready and find the quickest way to make it to his office, and he would take a heartbeat or two to regain his composure to ensure that his sovereign would never see him flustered. It was a game they played to perfection. A few hundred heartbeats later, Igon appeared at the doorway, wearing the regulation uniform, and Elzer permitted him to enter without playing his usual waiting game. Igon walked up to the desk. He stopped and stood at attention at a respectful distance, waiting for instructions.

"I want you to handpick one of my sentries. One you believe capable of performing a special task," Elzer whispered.

Even though the recording device was off in his chambers, there were others outside, and he did not want to risk them picking up his voice.

"May I ask what the objective is?"

Elzer hesitated. The knot in his stomach returned.

"Sir?" Igon whispered.

Igon's voice brought Elzer out of his thoughts.

He moved to Igon's side, leaned in, and whispered into his left ear, "Zorion's assassination."

Igon gulped loud enough for Elzer to hear, "You realize the dangers of committing such an act?"

"Of course, I am not stupid," Elzer replied with an angry whisper.

Igon knew Elzer well enough to know that there would be no talking him out of this dangerous decision.

"Why do you want a guard to perform this mission? We would have a better chance of success by using an agent."

"This will not be a hit-and-run assignment. I need to make sure that no one links me or anyone under me to this kill, so we must replace Zorion's guard with our own. If the time is right, he will take Zorion's life and leave the original guard to take the blame."

"How will he get past security?"

"With this," Elzer retrieved the bottle from his pocket.

"What is it?"

"It is a concoction that will imitate Molo's pheromones," Elzer handed him the bottle.

Igon held it up to the light and saw that the liquid was as clear as water. To evaluate it, he removed the cap and sniffed.

Igon wrinkled his nose, "It smells like the wardrobe room at the stadium."

"Yes, to us, but it will make a Screener think it is Molo."

"May I ask where you got it?"

"It was given to me by someone who will remain anonymous."

"Do you trust this Akilian?"

"No."

"That complicates things. If we cannot fully trust this potion," Igon shrugged his shoulders and left the rest unsaid.

"You better figure out a way to test it before our guard goes through Zorion's security."

"I will need time to develop a plan."

"No, you do not. I know you. You already have two or three contingency plans for the assassination of every sovereign, including me, tucked away in that masterfully devious mind of yours. I want the Vlorian in place by the first changing of Zorion's guards."

"The first changing of the guards?" Igon blurted out incredulously.

"You are supposed to be the best. Now prove it."

Igon bit back a retort and sighed, "I better get going."

Elzer nodded, "Dismissed."

Igon bowed, left Elzer's presence, and rushed to his office, where he opened every file on Zorion's guards. He hated Elzer for rushing him on such a sensitive operation. Still, he smirked. Elzer was right. He already had all kinds of contingency plans, including one for himself. *If things go wrong, I have a private apartment in every city and enough Sovereign Cubes put aside to support me comfortably for the rest of my life.*

The information appeared, so he accessed Molo's dossier and read it. There was nothing special about him because Broll hired him more for his brawn than his brain like all the others. Elzer had guards just like him on his staff; they were the common, dependable ones. *The kind of sentry you see but never notice.* He accessed a list of safe homes his department bought in Argi under assumed names.

The closest was fifty tiers below the guard's dedicated living sector. *Now, how can I get him down fifty levels without anyone noticing me?* He checked the list of current undercover agents living in Zorion's city and saw a laundry service company. *Excellent, I can place him inside a large bin and take him down on the service elevator.*

Igon sent a coded message to the agent, giving him specific instructions on when and where to meet. *Now, to choose a guard.* He scanned the employee list, hoping to find an ideal candidate that met all his criteria; he found one named Shafe and stopped. The subject was still single. His parents died in a hover bus accident several yellow harvests before, and there were no siblings. *Good. If he fails, no one will miss him.* Igon transferred his information to his data device, stopped at his apartment to change into a business owner's attire, and retrieved a few supplies needed to bind and gag Molo once they subdued him.

He packed a black carrying bag and hurried to Shafe's apartment. Having heard the door chime, Shafe stirred in his sleep. He blinked his eyes, trying to decide if it was a dream or if it was real. The chime sounded again. It was real, so he opened the door. Seeing Elzer's Chief Administrator of Intelligence, his jaw dropped. Briefly, Igon waited for Shafe to invite him in.

The invitation was not forthcoming, so Igon asked, "May I come in?"

"Of course, forgive me. I just woke up."

Igon stepped inside, closed the door behind him, and spoke calmly, "I understand. I was also sleeping only a brief time ago, but Elzer just gave me a high priority, highly classified mission."

Igon inspected Shafe's home. The condition of the room confirmed that Shafe did live alone.

"Mission? Forgive my ignorance, Sir, but why are you speaking with me?" Shafe queried.

"The assignment requires someone with your background. I will need someone who can fit in with guards without drawing any attention."

"What would you have me do?"

"Before I tell you, I need to know that I can count on you. The mission is dangerous. If Zorion's guards catch you, they will torture and kill you, but if you are successful, I will greatly reward you with," Igon paused, purposefully looking around his room, "enough Sovereign Cubes to purchase a better apartment and a maid to take care of it. Perhaps you might even find someone willing to join houses with you and fill the apartment with offspring."

"How many Sovereign Cubes are you offering?"

Igon smiled to himself because greed was always an ally, trying to manipulate someone. *No matter how bad the risk, you put enough Sovereign Cubes on the table, and they will do anything.* However, Igon had no intention of paying him because even if Shafe succeeded, Igon would kill him before stepping off the intercity transport, leaving no loose ends.

"Does a million Sovereign Cubes sound like enough?"

Shafe's eyes perked up, "A million? Whom do I have to kill?"

"I will tell you on the way. Now get dressed. Do not put on a uniform. Instead, wear traveling clothes, like you plan to visit a relative," Igon advised.

Shafe changed, and they traveled to the nearest Intercity Transportation Station. On the way, Igon changed his appearance. Igon secured a private booth on the train to Argi. After the carriage started moving, he gave Shafe the details of the mission. Shafe almost balked when Igon told him the target was Zorion, but Igon added another million Sovereign Cubes to sweeten the pot, and Shafe was willing to take the risk. *He would kill his parents for two million Sovereign Cubes if they were still alive.*

The trip took longer than expected, leaving them with no time to spare, so Igon had to improvise if something went wrong. Shafe memorized the roster of Molo's duties and his patrol route, and Igon contacted his agent and arranged to meet. They arrived at Argi and took the shortest route to the level where the guards lived. Igon's agent discovered a blind spot behind the fountain near the guards' residences on that tier. He waited for them with a mobile hamper half-filled with laundry.

"The data file said that the sentries leave as a unit at precisely the same time to prepare for their shift," Igon reported.

"How can we separate him from the others and subdue him?" Shafe asked.

"I will lead him over here. You two will disable him. Remember, do not kill him. We need him alive."

Igon told his agent to stay put, changed his appearance again, and led Shafe over to a spot near the elevators.

"Watch this. They have become complacent," Igon whispered, directing Shafe's gaze toward the guard's housing units, over to their left.

All the sentries opened their doors around the same time.

"Pretend you are asking me directions as you study him. You must be perfect. You cannot miss a hair on his head. Once you are ready, slip out of sight behind the fountain."

As the guards made their way to the elevator, Igon spotted Molo leaving his home. He nodded to Shafe, who intently studied Molo while discreetly looking over Igon's shoulder. Shafe turned and hid near the fountain. Igon changed his likeness, matching a schoolteacher where Molo's offspring attend; he planned to tell Molo that his heir fought another student during the prior education cycle. It would be enough to get his attention. Molo stepped at the end of the line, so Igon approached him.

"Excuse me, but are you, Molo?" Igon queried.

As he spoke, the elevator arrived, and the other guards boarded.

"Who wants to know?" Molo grumbled.

"I apologize for disturbing you so early, but we need to discuss your heir fighting at school," Igon commented.

One of Molo's fellow guards held the elevator and yelled, "Are you coming?"

Molo sighed and waved for his colleagues to go without him, "I will get the next one."

The guard let the door shut.

"What has he done now?" puzzled Molo.

As other Akilians began to queue at the elevators, Igon moved toward the fountain. Molo followed him.

Once they were out of sight from prying eyes, Igon faced Molo, "I am sorry to report, but your heir tackled another young Akilian and injured him."

Molo sighed, "I will talk to him when my shift is over; I promise he will not...."

As Molo spoke, Shafe stepped behind him and stunned him with a quick two-fingered blow to the nerve junction behind his left ear; it was fast and silent. As Molo's body went limp, Igon's agent slipped behind him with the mobile hamper. Igon smiled. It was over in a heartbeat. They removed Molo's uniform, secured his hands and feet, and covered him; the agent left with him in the hamper as Shafe put on his clothes.

Shafe dressed, and Igon watched out for danger. They were invisible to anyone heading toward the elevators. To anyone who might have seen them, it would merely appear that a guard forgot his uniform, and a laundry worker delivered it to him at the last moment. It was an incident that if anyone saw, they would forget. Shafe changed into Molo's uniform, shape-shifted to match Molo's physical appearance, took out the concoction, and, using a transfer cylinder, put two drops on his tongue.

He gagged, "This stuff is nasty."

"You will need to take two drops before every work cycle. Do not forget," Igon warned.

Shafe nodded.

"Now, we must make sure it works. Here is a schematic of the living quarters. Hurry back to Molo's apartment and see if his partner can identify you. If she believes you are Molo, hide the vial behind a dresser in the bedroom. If she knows you are someone else, kill everyone, and return to me."

Shafe studied the layout, handed it back to Igon, took a deep breath, and walked to Molo's home. Inside, Molo's family sat at the table, eating breakfast.

Molo's partner saw him, frowned, and walked to him, "Is everything all right?"

Shafe waited for her to get close, and he just stood, looking at her for a moment.

She did not notice the switch, so he smiled, "Everything is fine. I just forgot something."

Turning, he walked to the bedroom, removed the bottle from his pocket, and placed it behind a dresser, per Igon's instructions. He pushed the furniture back to the wall and left the bedroom, pretending to find the item. She blocked his path to give him a long kiss goodbye on his way out. Their offspring giggled, seeing their parents embrace; Shafe ignored them. Since it was his first kiss, he allowed himself to enjoy the moment and ignored the distractions. She pulled away, and Shafe gazed into her eyes, waiting for some adverse reaction but hoping none would come.

"Hurry, or you will be late again. You do not need to give Broll a reason to fire you," she smiled.

Shafe nodded, gave her a final kiss goodbye, walked to the elevator, and saw Igon in the corner. With a nod, he signaled that everything was going as planned. The elevator doors opened, and Shafe entered, thinking how easy it was to fool her. The taste of her kiss was still on his lips. *It is a shame I only have one bottle of that stuff.* The elevator doors opened, so he moved to the back of the line, where two of Molo's colleagues waited for their turn.

"What was the problem?" one of them asked.

"My heir fought in school," Shafe replied.

"I cannot keep mine out of detention either," the other complained.

Shafe grunted his understanding, and they waited in silence until their turn. Shafe's thoughts dwelt on the possibility of someone discovering him. It was true that Molo's mate did not detect anything, but a Screener would be another matter entirely. As he approached the head of the line, panic set in, causing him to hesitate, which got the attention of the Screener. "What is wrong?" she questioned.

"Nothing."

"Step into the booth. You are holding up the line," the Screener snapped.

Shafe handed his sword to the guards and walked into the stall, where they restrained him. The Screener walked over to him to check his pheromones and returned to her post. Everything seemed to be going well until she stopped; Shafe felt his stomach lurch into his throat. She turned around, and he saw her frown.

Nervously, he inquired, "Is there something wrong?"

Although he tried to keep his voice steady, it was not easy because a storm of fear raged inside him.

"Have you eaten some bad moss since I last saw you?" she wondered.

"Not to my knowledge. I do not feel sick," he replied.

At that moment, his stomach growled and gurgled. *Shut up! You will give us away*!

This time the Screener took her time examining him. *It is all over*.

She returned to her information tablet, "If you are not sick now, you probably will be soon. It should go away in a few hundred heartbeats, but you should be more careful with what you eat."

Without looking up, she turned and waved him in. He retrieved his sword and personal belongings and walked to his post, where he looked around to ensure no one was watching. Satisfied no one could see him, he collapsed against the nearest wall and laughed. *I have done it!* Having noticed his hands shaking, he took some time to regain his composure. A few hundred heartbeats later, he felt well enough to start his rounds and made mental notes of hiding places to prepare for the next operation phase.

Chapter 40

Akil
Argi City
The 22,274[th] Terrestrial Rotation of the Second Summer

Zorion woke with Thea nestled close beside him. At first, he was indifferent to her presence, but it occurred to him that he did not dream of the beautiful female during the sleep cycle. Zorion craned his neck and looked at Thea suspiciously. During his sleep cycle on the prior Terrestrial Revolution, Thea had restrained him. Her presence coincided with the darkness felt during his dream. Now, when he slept, there was only darkness. Zorion knew that Thea somehow prevented him from seeing the yellowed-haired beauty in his dream. Frustrated, he got out of bed, making a special effort not to disturb her. He dressed and headed out the door in less than his usual time.

Broll greeted him with a puzzled look, "Is everything all right?"

"No," Zorion grimly replied.

"What is wrong?"

He looked at the door, "I am not sure yet."

"Is there anything I can do?"

Zorion thought, "Did you hear me screaming two sleep cycles ago?"

"Of course not. You know I would have been by your side in only a few heartbeats if I did."

Zorion nodded. *I thought so.*

"Why? *Did* you scream?" Broll asked.

"No, I do not think so, but Thea said I did."

"You must not have screamed very loud."

Zorion walked toward his office, contemplating Broll's remark until something caught his attention, "What is that noise?"

Putting his hand behind his right ear, Broll listened carefully, "It sounds like the clashing of swords."

They dashed to the railing that overlooked a private promenade. On the next level, they saw two females fighting.

"Is that Yanamai and Garbi?" Zorion inquired.

Broll squinted, "I believe it is."

"I need to stop this at once!" Zorion exclaimed, moving toward the elevator.

Before reaching it, Broll jumped ahead of him, blocking his path, "You cannot. It is a private matter between them. You know the law."

Zorion walked around him, "Do not quote the law to me! I am your sovereign! I will not allow them to die this Terrestrial Rotation!"

"You stay here. I will stop them," Broll turned and ran for the elevator, unsheathing his sword along the way.

Zorion ran behind him, ignoring his advice and entered the car.

Broll was not pleased, "Please. Stay here."

"I am your sovereign. I have heard your advice, and I have chosen to ignore it."

Knowing Zorion's stubbornness, Broll selected the next level, and the doors closed, "At least do me a favor and stay a good distance away. I will be busy enough with the two of them. I cannot protect you at the same time."

"Agreed, but I want them alive. No beheadings," Zorion warned.

Broll sighed, "It would be easier if I killed Garbi to protect Yanamai; the fight would be over, and we would have a better chance of not being seen."

"Absolutely not! No one dies this Terrestrial Revolution, Broll! Understand?"

"Yes."

"Good."

The doors opened, and they ran toward the dueling duo.

To end the fight before they spilled blood, Zorion yelled, "Yanamai, Garbi, stop fighting this instant!"

Chapter 41

"And another thing," Santiago yelled.

"Sir," Alonso Sanchez, his advisor, carefully interrupted.

"Not now! Can't you see I'm yelling at Porter?"

"Sir, he disconnected."

"What? Damn him!"

Santiago lifted his desk and turned it over in a fit of rage. Alonso stepped to the side as Santiago threw books, pens, paper, and whatever his hands could find until collapsing into his chair, panting.

Alonso calmly walked over to him, "Perhaps we should return to the source and obtain another copy."

"I'll have to pay for it again! The last one cost me a billion dollars!"

"It will pay for itself in time. That was the reason you bought the software in the first place."

"How did he know, Alonso?"

"We must have a mole or one of the men in charge of transporting the data chip betrayed us."

"You think Porter repaid him with death instead of Regime Talons?"

"It sounds like something he would do."

"Still, I must pay for it again."

"It is inconvenient, Sir, but it's still worth it even if you must repurchase it."

"Do you truly believe it will work?"

"I do, Sir. I've seen a demonstration."

Santiago sighed, "Very well, hand me the phone."

Alonso picked up the one Santiago threw across the room earlier and handed it to him.

"Ms. Diaz, get General Ming-tun Fu on the video com at once!" Santiago shouted.

"Right away, Sir," his assistant replied.

A few minutes later, the Chinese General appeared before him on a large monitor set on the east wall.

"Good day, President Martinez. I trust you've received the package," General Ming-tun Fu smiled.

"No, I haven't. Someone intercepted it."

"I'm sorry to hear it. My agent told me that he made the transfer to your courier successfully."

"Somehow Porter found out and stole it before I received it."

"Are you certain *he* took the disc?"

"I don't have proof, but my gut tells me it was him. He's the only one who could have stolen it without leaving one spec of evidence behind."

"Without proof."

"I know. I have no case against him; still, someone leaked the information about the purchase."

"I can assure you that it did not come from my people. It would be bad for business."

"It seems I'm at your mercy, General. I'll need to purchase another disc."

General Ming-tun Fu grimaced, "I would be more than happy to sell it to you again, President Martinez, but I'm afraid it's impossible."

"Why?"

"My scientist disappeared, along with any copies of the schematics delivered to you. Even the originals are missing."

"I thought you kept him in a secure facility."

"We did, but he disappeared without a trace."

"It sounds like Porter's been very busy today," Santiago guessed.

"Yes. We're at his mercy until we can build our portal machine."

"Meanwhile, I'm out a billion dollars."

"There may be another way," General Ming-tun Fu tapped his desk in thought.

"Do you have another scientist?"

"No, but I have something just as good, the agent who stole the original schematics. Two years ago, I managed to infiltrate the Regime."

Santiago's ears perked up, "Are you telling me you have an agent living in the Regime?"

"Not currently, but I can get her back in, and she had access to the lab where they will keep the disc if they have it."

"Is she good? I mean, Porter will have it guarded well."

"Don't worry, Santiago. My agent will figure out a way to retrieve it."

"How much is this going to cost me?"

General Ming-tun Fu smiled and rubbed his hands together, "I'll give you a good deal since you're a valued client. If my agent doesn't retrieve the disc, you pay nothing. If she does, you pay half a billion."

Santiago stood and yelled, "What? That's outrageous, Ming-tun! I've just paid you one billion for schematics I still don't have!"

"Which is why I'm giving you a discount."

Santiago's face turned red, "Give me a minute; I must discuss it with my advisor."

"Take all the time you need."

Santiago walked to Alonso and whispered, "I can't afford this. I've already paid him a billion for the original. It nearly wiped out all the liquid assets in my offshore shell companies."

"You still have enough money to invest in the stock market."

"Isn't it too risky?"

"Not for us. We have access to non-public information on companies, and we can influence the prices as well; it's all perfectly legal, at least for us."

"How long will it take?"

"I have some friends on Wall Street that can help us. You'll have half a billion in just a few weeks."

Santiago rubbed his chin in thought, "Sounds like a solid plan. Make it happen."

"I would suggest one thing."

"Yes?"

"Have his agent kill Porter as part of the price because if she can get in the Regime, she should get close enough to take him out."

Santiago smiled, "Good idea, Alonso - good idea."

"Even if she only brings back the data, we'll have proof that Porter took it, so we'll have a solid case against him."

"You're right. I'll take the evidence and rally the United Nations to go to war against him."

"It's what you've always wanted, Sir. Take back America!"

"I like the sound of that! We could use that in our propaganda commercials," he patted Alonso on the shoulder and walked in front of the video camera.

"Well? Do we have a deal?" General Ming-tun Fu asked.

"We have a deal on two conditions. First, if your agent retrieves the disc, she brings it to me; I want it in my hand before I pay for anything."

"Very well. What's the second condition?"

"I want her to kill Porter."

General Ming-tun Fu smiled, "You *are* wicked, Mr. President. Still, I cannot make any promises. It will be hard enough to get the disc. Only certain officials have access to the Supreme Commander."

"I'm sure if this agent is half as good as you claim, she can pull it off."

General Ming-tun Fu sighed, "Tell you what I'll do. I'll instruct her to do both, but you'll have to settle for the data if she can't get to Porter. Fair enough?"

Santiago groaned, "Very well."

"Excellent. I'll let you know when she has completed the mission. Good day, President Martinez," General Ming-tun Fu disconnected and smiled. *Santiago didn't even try to negotiate.*

Santiago turned to his assistant, "I hope his agent is successful. That disc can ruin Porter and make us kings, Alonso."

"Yes, it would, Sir."

Chapter 42

Akil
Argi City
The 22,274[th] Terrestrial Rotation of the Second Summer

Startled out of a sound sleep, Thea sat up in bed, feeling a nudge from the shadow universe. The last time, it was a warning, one she ignored. *I will not make that mistake again.* She jumped out of bed, threw on some clothes, grabbed her sword, and ran outside. As she followed the flutter, it led her to the railing overlooking the promenade, where she saw two females fighting in the second-level courtyard.

As they grappled, two males ran out of the elevator. She heard one of them yell, "Yanamai, Garbi, stop fighting this instant!" *Well, that answers the question of whose fighting.* Nayrah recognized Zorion's voice right away, and the fourth figure was Broll. A wave of jealousy hit her. *Zorion would never allow anything to happen to Yanamai. He gives her more attention than his offspring.*

The thought made her angry and heightened the connection to her powers. As her attention turned toward the fight, she frowned. Everyone knew that Garbi was the better fighter. It would only be a matter of time until she killed Yanamai. At Zorion's command, the two stopped fighting, and Thea thought it was over, but before taking another breath, she saw Yanamai and Garbi lunging at each other.

"End this at once!" Zorion yelled.

Thea could hear a mixture of anger and panic in his voice. Yanamai and Garbi completely ignored his command. Thea felt another ripple from the shadow universe, and dread overcame her. *Why do I feel this way?* She felt a cold and chilling wave wash over her. The hairs on the back of her neck stood up. Reflexively, she unsheathed her sword, expecting to see an opponent nearby; no one was around. *There is something wrong here, but what?* Bewildered, she focused her thoughts on the fighters, trying to access their emotions.

Her lips curled upward into a smile sensing their hatred for each other. Their emotions were primal. With the strength and prowess that earned Broll the title 'Chief Administrator of Security,' he jumped into the mix, demanding their attention. Thea snickered. *He will have no problem handling these two amateurs.*

It occurred to Thea that Zorion gave them two commands to stop fighting, but they ignored him. *Yanamai should have obeyed him, even in this situation. So why did she disregard his command?* The revelation troubled her, and she nervously tapped on the rail with her index finger, trying to unravel the mystery. As the fight continued, Broll grabbed Yanamai's wrist and smacked the back of her hand with the flat side of his blade.

The pain from such a strike caused her to drop her sword. Clenching her wounding limb, she sobbed from the discomfort. *Why are you whining? He could have cut your hand entirely off. It is what I would have done.* Seeing her opponent vulnerable, Garbi attacked, hoping to take advantage of the situation, but Broll did not allow it. Instead, he blocked her strike with little effort and unexpectedly kicked her. It stunned her, sending her back several paces.

Fluidly, he spun around, picked up Yanamai's sword, and tossed it to Zorion. Without her weapon, Yanamai resorted to fists. Lunging out with her right arm, she punched Broll's jaw, breaking it. Thea could hear cracking bone even from her lofty position. *You do not cause Broll pain and not pay for it.* Broll punched Yanamai in the nose with his off-sword hand, stunning her, and kicked her in the stomach. The force lifted her off the ground and sent her careening into a nearby wall.

She slid down into a stupor, exposing her neck. With her senses heightened, Thea felt the force of his attack, making her cringe. Having recovered, Garbi saw her opponent helpless. Charging, she yelled and swung her blade downwards, hoping to sever Yanamai's neck. Before her sword could make contact, Broll turned and parried her attack, knocking her off balance. Again, he snatched her victory away. It enraged her.

With bloodshot eyes and an insane look, Garbi attacked Broll wildly. She screamed obscenities, swinging at him sloppily and blindly, like an offspring having a tantrum. It puzzled Thea; their primitive emotion, tireless, aggressive attacks, and unwillingness to obey authority left only one answer. *Someone drugged them. But who? And why?* To Thea's surprise, Garbi finally wore out and surrendered.

"Wise choice," Broll commented.

Kneeling, she presented her sword above her head as a sign of submission. *I guess I was wrong.* Satisfied, Broll sheathed his blade and moved to retrieve Garbi's sword until she changed her position, flipping it around and driving it straight into Broll's chest. Feeling the attack, Thea fell back two paces. With wide eyes, she watched, amazed at such a quick turnaround. Broll fell to his knees, and his face portrayed his shock. He grabbed the blade and tried to extract it using both hands, but his breastbone held it in place.

The move was perfect; it gave Thea chills. Again, she felt a warning from the Shadow Universe. *I was right! Someone drugged them! I wonder what potion would cause this.* Kraeth's image flashed in her mind's eye. *Now it makes sense! Only the Night Lord's Venom could induce such insanity.* Before she could ponder the new revelation, Garbi retrieved Broll's sword from his belt and marched toward Yanamai, who remained slumped forward.

It was dishonorable to kill an unconscious opponent, but Garbi did not care. Thea only had a few heartbeats to decide whether to save Yanamai or allow Garbi to kill her. *If Kraeth dosed them, the order must have come from Domeka, who would have received her command from Gecheana.* Now the attack made sense. By eliminating Yanamai, Gecheana could replace her with Tadra, who was indebted to Gecheana for her schooling, obligating her to do whatever Gecheana demanded. Simultaneously, by killing Yanamai, Gecheana would claim that she put Otsoa in line, not Nayrah (her alter ego), and use the situation to demote her. *Not in this lifetime!*

Knowing what she must do, Thea returned her focus to Yanamai. Garbi held Broll's sword over her neck and was about to swing; before Garbi's blade touched Yanamai's skin, Zorion's sword blocked it. Angered that someone had yet again taken victory from her, Garbi's rage turned to Zorion, and she attacked with the same berserk zeal used against Broll. *I know Zorion can beat her, but I cannot take a chance; she might trick him too. I must stop this now!*

Desperately, Thea looked for something to use. Seeing that Broll was still on his knees, with his head slumped forward, she had an idea. Although his right hand was on the hilt, he was not moving.

Concentrating, her mind's eye saw beyond clothing and flesh to where the blade rested, just to the side of his heart. *If I pull the sword out, he should recover enough to fight.* Using her powers, Thea grabbed the sword with her mind, and with a smooth motion of her hand, the blade jerked forward out of his chest, pulling Broll with it.

Falling face forward, he remained motionless. Precious heartbeats passed while Thea waited for his wound to heal. *Come on, get up, get up*! The sudden silence caught her attention. Looking over, Thea saw Garbi pretending to be tired again. *Do not allow her to trick you too!* Again, Garbi surrendered like before. *Zorion will die; I know it.* Broll moved and stood. By now, Zorion had placed his sword on Garbi's shoulder, with the sharp end facing her neck to keep her in check. Broll grabbed Garbi's weapon that had rested inside his chest moments before and staggered toward Zorion. *He is not going to make it in time*!

"Put the sword down, or I will remove your head!" Zorion demanded.

Garbi dropped it, "I am unarmed."

The hairs on Thea's neck screamed a warning.

Zorion kept his sword resting on her shoulder, "Now, back away."

Garbi smirked, "As you wish."

She took a measured step backward with her left foot, planted it firmly on the ground, and kicked out with her right foot, lifting the sword she had just dropped moments before into the air. As it came back down, she grabbed the hilt and lunged at Zorion, but Broll plunged his blade through her upper back in the middle of her attack. The tip came out of her chest, about three fingers wide above her left breast; Garbi grunted and collapsed to the ground.

That was close. Thea looked to the shadow universe again; it was quiet. *Things are right again.* Trusting the darkness and seeing that Broll had things under control, she returned to her apartment. Before leaving, she saw Domeka hiding in the shadows. They briefly glared at each other until Domeka disappeared into the darkness. Thea returned home, went straight to the guest room, collapsed on her bed, and fell fast asleep.

Chapter 43

As Broll plunged the sword into Garbi's chest, Zorion heard bones breaking, giving way to the metal blade. Surprised, her eyes widened with shock until she looked down to see a sword protruding from her chest. She grunted and collapsed to the ground at his feet. With a nod, Zorion thanked Broll for his help.

He noticed movement on the level above in his peripheral vision and saw a distant figure turn and walk away. He did not see her face but recognized the cloak. It was a gift he gave to Thea several yellow harvests ago. *What do you have to do with this?* Zorion pondered her presence for a few heartbeats and faced Broll.

"Bind them and put them in separate cells on independent levels."

"They have not broken any laws," Broll protested.

"It is for their protection. Did you see the look in their eyes?"

"Yes. They appeared deranged."

"I do not know what has happened, but something is not right."

To ensure everyone's safety, Broll summoned a team of twelve to meet them. He removed two restraints from his belt and secured their hands behind them. The guards arrived and carried Yanamai and Garbi away.

Once they were alone, Zorion reached over and touched Broll's shirt at the site of his wound, "I thought she pierced your heart."

"She was close."

"I saw you try to remove it, but you were unsuccessful and collapsed."

"Yes. I am glad you removed it."

"I did not remove it. I was fighting Garbi."

"If so, I have no idea how it came out. I fell forward and caught myself. I could not move to see who helped me, so I assumed it was you."

Zorion craned his head to the spot where Thea stood moments before.

"Did you see anyone else around?" Broll asked.

Zorion faced Broll, "No, my friend. You must have unconsciously removed it before you blacked out."

Broll laughed loudly, "Hah! That must be it! I am resourceful, you know!"

Zorion smiled, "Yes, I know you are."

Chapter 44

Earth
The Regime - Maryland - Farming District
May 10, 2452

Kraeth stepped through the event horizon and heard the portal close behind him. New fragrances, sights, and sounds assaulted his senses. Every breath brought fresh and intoxicating aromas. It was overwhelming. Before taking two paces, he became dizzy and collapsed to his knees, waiting for his body to adapt to the alien planet. A few heartbeats later, his eyes adjusted to the brilliant sunlight.

The bright, yellow orb hovered just above the horizon, and its light made his eyes water. Its heat felt good on his skin, yet it made him feel weak as a Skean. The Shadow Universe urged him to destroy it, leaving Kraeth bewildered because he had no idea how to accomplish it. Pushing aside that feeling, he caressed the green vegetation that surrounded him. The sun prevented him from seeing far, but he noticed the green plants everywhere, covering the ground like a carpet. He felt one side was rough and the other smooth between his fingers.

His eyes adjusted, allowing him to see, so he scanned the landscape and noticed many assorted colors of greens and browns. Also, he saw multi-colored flowers with yellow, purple, and pink peddles; images of his homeworld museums came to mind. The exhibits offered dioramas of what Akil was like before the frost, but those displays lacked the texture, smells, and sounds associated with the environment.

The historians omitted details like tiny insects, which were in an abundant variety around him, and the small, winged mammals flying from one large tree to another. Their chirps made it seem like they were singing to each other. A few hundred heartbeats later, he stood and continued his journey. With the sun on his left, he headed south.

According to Yanamai's instructions, he had to travel straight to find a portal machine. Along the way, he discovered many different small, flying insects. One started buzzing around his head. Instinctively, he swatted at it. For reasons unknown to him, it attacked him, leaving his hand sore and bumpy, but within a few heartbeats, the pain and the lump it left behind disappeared. *At least the yellow sun has not affected my recovering abilities.*

He came upon a fence blocking his path. Since it extended beyond his sight in either direction, he climbed over it, landed, and walked. A hundred paces in, he noticed large mammals grazing. They reminded him of the *Boonines* from the dioramas back home. If he remembered correctly, Akilian historians believed that *Boonines* were docile creatures, despite their enormous size. Since they ignored him, he was sure they were deferential as well.

He ventured farther into their territory and heard an unusual sound. Turning, he saw one charging at him. This *Boonine-like* creature had large horns and a ring in its nose, and it stood taller than the rest. It would run him down at its current pace in less than twenty heartbeats. The Shadow Universe sent him a warning, so he ran and approached another fence.

Although it was not far away, it seemed unreachable, with the angry mammal rapidly closing the distance behind him. The beast gained on him, so he called on his Skean powers. Unlike Akil, this new world did not have many shadows, at least not now. Still, darkness was always around. The vegetation cast small shadows beneath it, and the larger ones cast even more shade. From it, he drew strength and increased his pace.

Despite his new surge in speed, he could still hear the beast's hooves beating hard against the ground. As it came closer, he could hear air blowing out its nostrils until he finally saw a stream at the bottom of the hill. He launched himself into the air without losing his stride, but his leap fell short, and he landed in water up to his knees. He saw the beast pull up short, stopping at the water's edge.

Kraeth froze, waiting to see what it would do; they stood, staring and panting. The hairs on his neck rose moments before the creature lunged forward. He turned and sloshed his way to dry land. Drenched by the stream, his pants clung to his legs, slowing his pace. In the distance, he heard a female's voice. Briefly, within his peripheral vision, he saw her standing on the other side of the fence, shouting and waving. He could not understand her.

Ignoring her for now, he focused on the fence. He would be safe if he could get to the other side before the beast reached him. It was all he wanted. He called on his power to give him another burst of speed in one last effort. His pace increased, but it was too little, too late. The beast finally caught up with him. Simultaneously, he felt pain in his buttocks and felt himself abruptly lifting off the ground. His body flew over the fence with such power; it reminded him of Gecheana's wrath.

A few heartbeats later, he saw an aerial view of the fence flying over it. Nothing he learned in his Skean training prepared him for anything like this. He used his powers to soften his landing, but it was insufficient. He landed hard on his back, knocking the wind out of him. His muscles froze, preventing him from taking another breath.

Struggling against pain and shock, he tried to fill his lungs until everything went black. At that moment, he imagined himself floating away from his body but heard a female voice. She gently smacked his cheeks as he regained consciousness.

"Come on, Kraeth. Breathe!"

He gasped, filling his lungs with fresh air, and a few hundred heartbeats later, his breathing returned to normal.

"Are you out of your mind? I told you that bulls are dangerous. He could have killed you!" Relief and anger replaced the panic in her voice.

The only thing he understood was his name, which confused him. *How does she know who I am?*

"Are you all right? Are you hurt?" she inquired.

All he could do was stare at her quizzically.

"What's wrong with you? Why won't you talk to me?"

He stood and checked his extremities and torso to ensure the beast did not cause severe injuries. There were a few scrapes and bruises, but nothing too serious. The wounds would heal within a few hundred heartbeats. He could not find his backpack nearby because it landed several paces away, so he jogged to retrieve it.

"Why don't you come inside and lie down?"

Still dazed from the attack, he did not have the strength to interpret what she said. However, he knew that meeting a local could mean trouble even in his weakened condition, so without delay, he turned on his heel and ran South, hoping to find a portal machine.

"Where are you going?" she yelled as he disappeared.

Kraeth walked for about ten thousand heartbeats and stopped because the sun began to set. By his calculations, he should have found the portal machine by now. *In my haste, I must have run in the wrong direction.* If he did not see the facility soon, he would have to camp. After traveling a few hundred more heartbeats, he found an isolated building. It was well lit, with small hovering transports parked by walkways that led inside.

From a distance, he watched several locals exit one of the vehicles. Since none paid any attention to their surroundings, he merged into their small group. He kept a position close enough that the casual observer would consider him part of their crowd but not so close as to catch their attention. Inside, he separated from them, moved to the shadows, and watched them pass through a sustained event horizon. It did not go unnoticed that each alien swiped a card through a machine to gain passage. *It is never easy.*

Above the portal's opening, he saw symbols, which had to be their language. Unable to understand its meaning, he watched the traffic a little longer before acting. The group he followed gathered on the other side of the event horizon. They appeared to have entered a vast building. To keep his anonymity, he had to steal a card. Returning outside, he hid at the corner of the building.

When it was dark, he moved toward an unsuspecting elderly couple. Now that it was night, his powers returned to their norm. Drawing on them, he put them to sleep, caught them, and gently laid them down on the pavement as they started to fall. Now armed with a pass, he re-entered the facility, swiped it, and walked through. On the other side, he found himself standing in an extensive complex filled with lights and music, which assaulted his senses.

Aliens filled the building, but no one gave him a second glance since he looked like them. *My disguise is exact. I am blending in well.* Satisfied there was no threat, he moved forward, hoping to find literature. Upon reaching an emporium, he saw symbols like the ones above the portal opening. *Now, how do I decipher it?* He wandered the broad boulevards for a few thousand heartbeats and noticed a pattern.

Unlike the stores on his planet, these did not have a centralized location, but it did appear that each one specialized in a specific item; for example, some stores sold food, and others sold clothes. It was like this throughout the establishment. He needed to find one that sold information if such a thing existed. Near a store that sold a pungent, black liquid was another that seemed to sell nothing.

Kraeth watched aliens pick up small devices from a table, browse shelves of pictographs until finding something they liked, and lift handheld devices that transferred information. Afterward, they returned to the store that sold the pungent, black liquid and sat, looking at the screens on their handheld devices. Following their lead, he entered the store and walked around.

He saw aliens sitting in chairs in several places, examining items from the shelves, so he walked up behind one and looked over its shoulder. He saw symbols like the ones on the buildings on the device's screen, but he could not buy anything without the local currency, leaving him with only one choice; he would decipher the language here in the store.

Kraeth picked up one of the devices and selected an item on the shelf. It took several tries until he chose the correct image, and the transfer began. With the information in hand, he explored the building to find all the exits. In the back of the store, he noticed aliens coming and going through a couple of doors. They seemed gender-specific. Walking behind a male, he entered the room. The scene was familiar to that of the restrooms on Akil.

Finding himself alone, he looked for another way out. Although there were no other doors, he found a tile that left a gap in the ceiling above one of the stalls. Entering the booth, he stood on the seat, pushed up on the tile, and found that it moved quickly. Looking in the space above, he discovered that it was not an exit, but it had enough space for him to hide. He replaced the tile and explored the rest of the store.

Having found all the exits, he returned to the seating area and started working. A few thousand heartbeats later, he realized the store was almost empty. *They must have a curfew here. Perfect. I can hide in the restroom, wait until the store closes, and continue my work.* He placed the device back on the table and calmly walked to the bathroom.

Standing on the seat, he slid the ceiling tile to one side, pulled himself into his hiding place, and waited. It was uncomfortable and cramped, but the discomfort was manageable. For a long time, it was silent, so he let himself down and peeked out the restroom door. Aside from a few lights, the store was dark. Skeans did not need lamps to see, so the darker the room, the better it was for him. Cautiously, he returned to the table, picked up his device, sat, and continued deciphering.

Chapter 45

Akil
Argi City
The 22,274[th] Terrestrial Rotation of the Second Summer

Zorion canceled all his early work cycle appointments and sat alone in his office to think. The fight he and Broll stopped, and Thea's unexpected presence at the event bothered him. *I found her beside me after my dark dream, and she appeared during a clash between my best scientist and her sister.* Something about her troubled him, but he could not make any accusations without proof.

Turning to his Information Terminal, he pulled up the database that held Thea's vetting information. *Security thoroughly investigates anyone who joins houses with a ruling family.* The dossier showed that Thea had little to no Sovereign Cubes when they first met. It was not a surprise because she told him that her parents died early in her life, leaving the city responsible for her care. Until this moment, he never thought to question it.

He reviewed the official record and discovered that everything was as she claimed. He also examined the databases the investigators used but could not find anything out of order. Again, everything was as she said. *Still, there is something off about her.* Zorion thought long and hard. *Was every database consulted and cross-referenced?* He requested the Information from the Terminal. Several heartbeats later, it answered, "No." The auditors overlooked Housing Reclamation. Since they lived underground, the government accounted for every iota of space.

Zorion studied the Housing database and looked for Thea's parents' listing of residences before their deaths, but there were none, so he requested a list of homes for everyone named in Thea's data file, from relatives to her parents' birthing assistant. The Housing database was empty, which could only mean one thing; none of these people existed. A chill ran down his spine. *If these people do not exist, who is living with me?* The communicator on his desk beeped, interrupting his thoughts.

"Yes, Shilda."

"Sir, Noka requests to see you."

“Send him in.”

Noka stood in the doorway, waiting for Zorion to grant permission to enter, and sat in front of his desk.

“What news do you have for me?” Zorion inquired.

“I have brought the estimate you asked for,” he handed him the invoice in a small, portable information device.

Zorion frowned, reading the list until frustration took hold of him.

“This is nearly double what it cost the last time!” he exclaimed.

“Please remember that it has been a long time since we have built energy consoles. The price of materials and labor has increased. We will need more maintenance vehicles to keep the ice and snow from forming on them, and it is necessary to replace some of the ones that are already in use.”

Zorion sighed. Sometimes he hated his job.

“For now, replace the maintenance vehicles. That is all I can afford. Perhaps in about sixty Terrestrial Rotations, I might have enough for you to build another console.”

“Very well, Sir. I will put the order in right away.”

“How is rotating the grid working out?”

“Not satisfactory. We have had many complaints from businesses and homeowners. We have tried to reassure them that it would only be temporary, but they have not taken it very well.”

“I am sure they blame me.”

“Our service representatives confirmed that some had communicated that very thought.”

“I do not have a choice. Our science department must have access to the power they need. It is vital to our survival.”

“It would help if Elzer contributed,” Noka cautiously added.

“I am still working on it.”

“Have you considered…” Noka paused.

“What?”

“If you cannot find proof, you could bring him before Gau’s judgment seat.”

Absentmindedly, Zorion brought his hand to his chin, contemplating Noka’s suggestion. Zorion’s parent/sovereign brought Benat, Vlor’s sovereign, before Gau’s Judgment Seat during his youth. As heir, it was his responsibility to fight for his city, and fight he did. He killed Benat's first heir, Edur, so Gau's law compelled Benat to yield to Argi's sovereign's demands or suffer the same fate as Edur.

Elzer took Edur's place as heir, becoming Vlor's sovereign after Benat's passing, and he held a grudge against Zorion for killing his sibling. If Zorion brought Elzer before Gau's judgment seat, Otsoa would have to fight a death match with Elzer's heir. In the event Otsoa won, Elzer would have to start sending the promised electricity, no matter how it affected his city. He did not doubt that Elzer misused the Sovereign Cubes they gave him, but proof had made itself elusive again. If Otsoa won, what Elzer did with the currency would not matter anymore.

He had to ask himself: *Am I willing to risk Otsoa's life?* For a long time, he watched Otsoa grow increasingly irrational. *He lacks the character needed to rule a city.* The thought of replacing Otsoa as his heir gave him hope for Argi. *If I do this and Otsoa loses, Va'ron will take his place as heir. He is still young, so I would have time to train him. I could ensure no other influence except mine.*

"I will consider your suggestion," Zorion replied.

"Really?" Noka was unmistakably surprised.

"I think it would show the citizens of Argi that I am fighting for them and that I am willing to make a personal sacrifice on their behalf."

"Indeed, Sir. It would. I am glad to hear you say it," Noka smiled.

Standing, Zorion paced behind his desk. The more he thought about the idea, the more he liked it.

"Yes. I will present the matter before the other sovereigns before this work cycle is over." He paused and faced Noka, "Do not repeat this to anyone. I do not want this news leaked before I have had a chance to speak with the other rulers."

"Of course, Sir, I will not say a word."

"Very well, that will be all for now, Noka. Perhaps we will not have to worry about rotating the grid during future Terrestrial Rotations."

"I am confident that Otsoa will win, Sir. He is the strongest and quickest fighter I have ever seen," Noka extended his hand, palm up.

Zorion returned his farewell, smiling at his compliment, "I think Broll is faster. Still, you are right. Otsoa is a strong fighter. He has a good chance of winning."

"Argi needs a win right now."

"Akil needs a win."

Noka bowed and left to return to his office, where he contacted his supplier and ordered the new maintenance vehicles. Of course, he doubled the price. It was his usual practice, and since he was the only supplier in the city, who made those specific items, Zorion had no idea. If times were desperate, if the science department could not get the power needed to save their planet, Noka would have included the energy consoles with the price, but he saw no need to sacrifice a significant profit because Zorion still had other options.

The businesses and homeowners suffering did not affect him because Zorion was on the receiving end of their anger. For Noka, it was a winning transaction with no risk and a great reward. Noka thought Zorion was too honest. One lesson Noka remembered from his parents: Honesty did not always make the most Sovereign Cubes.

He had suggested bringing Elzer before Gau as a test and thought Zorion would fail. However, since Zorion agreed to put Otsoa's life at risk, it gave Noka pause. Had Noka known Zorion was this bold, he *may* not have charged him so much for the maintenance vehicles. For just a moment, he wondered what Zorion would do if his inflated prices came to light. The thought made him shiver but knowing he would make an excellent profit soothed his conscience.

Chapter 46

Akil
Argi City
The 22,274[th] Terrestrial Rotation of the Second Summer

Once Noka left, Zorion called a special meeting with all the sovereigns. Shilda worked frantically to arrange it. Some were still in their sleep cycles, but she finally had their holographic image over their designated pedestals, so Zorion stepped onto his platform, allowing the other sovereigns to see and hear him.

"My friends, I have called a special meeting because I want to bring Elzer before Gau's judgment seat."

There was chatter among them, except for Elzer, who simultaneously stood and slammed his fist on his desk, "This is outrageous! You have no grounds to bring me before the judgment seat!"

"I do. Since you refuse to give your share of electricity, you leave me no choice. I am asking the other rulers for their approval."

The chatter diminished, and each sovereign approved Zorion's request.

"You will all regret this," Elzer spat.

"Zorion is right, Elzer; you have taken Sovereign Cubes from all of us, but we have not received anything in return," Ruvve accused.

Elzer collapsed in his chair, "Why would you do something so foolish?"

"I am tired of your games, Elzer. It is time you accept responsibility for your actions."

Zorion ended his communication and sent a copy of the meeting to the Information League. *Now all Akil will know of your betrayal.* Elzer sat speechless in his chair, shocked by Zorion's bold move. *Damn you, Kemena, look at what you have done. Now, I may lose Tuso, my oldest heir.* He ordered his assistant to summon Tuso to give him the news himself.

*****

Otsoa sat in Zorion's waiting room, feeling nervous. It reminded him of when he was young and had done something wrong. Zorion did not call him to his office unless it was for disciplinary reasons. He wondered which one of Nayrah's horrible schemes Zorion discovered. Otsoa could never divulge her name, so its responsibility would fall on him; the door to his office swung open, and Otsoa jumped to his feet.

Zorion glared at him for a few breathes, "Come in, we need to talk."

Otsoa felt a cold sweat pierce his skin while walking into his office.

"Have a seat."

Otsoa sat. *This meeting will not be good for me; I can feel it.*

Standing behind his desk, Zorion contemplated how best to give Otsoa the news.

"There is no gentle way of saying it, so I will just come out with it. I am bringing Elzer before Gau's judgment seat. You will fight Tuso within two Terrestrial Rotations."

Otsoa jumped out of his chair, "You did what?"

"Do not worry. I know you will win. We have right on our side."

Otsoa laughed nervously, "Right? It has nothing to do with it! I have seen Tuso fight; he is better than me; he is better than most!"

"Nonsense, I have seen you fight. You are quick and strong. I would not have done this if I did not think you could win."

Otsoa thought it was a nightmare. *This predicament cannot be real; it cannot be happening!*

Zorion saw the look of fear on his face, "I am not asking you to do something I have not done myself. When I was your age, I fought before Gau's judgment seat. I was victorious, as I am sure you will be too."

"If you are so sure of victory, *you* should fight him!" Otsoa yelled.

"That is not how it works, and you know it; you must fight Tuso because we need the extra electricity if we are ever going to get off this planet."

285

"I only see *my* life at stake."

Otsoa paced for several heartbeats, trying to think of a way out, and thought of Nayrah. Due to his blunder during his ceremony, she had every reason to kill him, but since he was still alive, it was clear she did not want him dead. *She will do something to stop it. I am sure.*

"No, Otsoa. There are billions of lives at stake here, not just yours. We must get off this planet, and for some reason, Elzer is playing a deadly game that is slowing our progress. It is the only way to force him to do what is right. I need your help. *Every* Akilian needs your help. It is your chance to shine."

"I do not want to help them! I do not want to shine! Cancel it at once!"

Zorion groaned, "I had hoped you would have accepted this with dignity, but I can see now that it will not happen. In any case, I cannot withdraw my request, and even if I could, I would refuse. It is too important. You have a chance to change Akil's future. Instead of running away from it, you should be running toward it."

Otsoa collapsed in his chair, defeated. Any comfort he felt earlier, thinking Nayrah could stop it, left him. *Even Nayrah cannot get me out of this one.*

"I suggest you go home and get some rest. We leave in two Terrestrial Rotations for the Main Arena."

Otsoa left Zorion's office without saying another word and headed straight for Nayrah's home.

Chapter 47

Earth
The Regime - Maryland - Police District
May 10, 2452

Sam sat in a small break room at the tenth precinct with his colleagues, Nick, Gerard, and Reece, playing poker. He was about to raise the bet until a dispatcher told him that his wife was on the video com in the adjoining room. Since policy prohibited personal communication devices while on duty, Sam had to leave the game. He grabbed his cards, left the table, and smiled. The look of fake injury on his friends' faces did not fool him.

"That's right, I don't trust none o' ya," he chuckled.

The fact was he trusted them with his life, but poker, well, that was a different matter. On his way to the communication room, Sam thought about the amount of downtime they had. It was due to the Regime's strict laws and no tolerance. This hardline approach to crime meant that if a dispatcher sent Sam and his team on a call, it was usually a false alarm. He was glad the Regime took a firm position against crime because many citizens felt safe doing the things they needed to do or wanted to do, day or night.

The courts sent convicted, violent criminals to the moon's penal facility. It was a one-way ticket. Thinking of the moon-penitentiary brought back memories of when he worked as a prison transporter for five years. It was a mandatory requirement to join the police force. Once, he asked to see the inside of the prison. His clearance got him approved for a brief tour. He remembered it as if it were yesterday.

Before going into the main entrance, he had to put on weighted boots to compensate for the moon's light gravity. Everyone in the facility, including prisoners, had to wear them to maintain maneuverability. One of the guards told him that as the Regime grew, the need for more prison space increased. As a result, the government built several prison blocks and buried them in the Taurus-Littrow region on the moon's surface. The blocks were large, stainless steel, sealed boxes that held sixty thousand cells, eight feet high, six feet wide, and ten feet long.

The facility was twenty cells high, fifty cells wide, by sixty cells deep. They overlaid the stainless steel compartments with thick plastic, making them easier to clean. Each cell had a toilet, sink, light, mattress, and air ventilation. The prisoners had nothing to do except eat, sleep, and ponder the decisions that led them there. He walked the narrow hallway of level one, section four, with several guards making their rounds during his tour.

Everything was sterile. It reminded Sam more of a psychiatric hospital rather than a prison. The cell doors did not have bars. Instead, they were solid steel. About five and a half feet from the floor, they installed an oval window made of thick glass. It enabled the guards to perform a quick visual inspection of the prisoners while patrolling the quiet halls. At lunchtime, the supervising guard ordered his men to open the cell doors, one at a time.

They handcuffed ten prisoners to a mobile steel bar and escorted them to a small dining area on the same floor. Only the guards had keys; the architects did not automate anything. Two sentries secured a prisoner, and another two stood outside the cell with tasers ready to fire. The Warden prohibited firearms because discharging a weapon inside a steel box would cause a ricochet, killing anyone in its path.

The guards watched over the prisoners for their fifteen-minute break, ensuring obedience to the rules. Since they did not allow utensils, the prisoners ate with their hands and used a wet cloth to clean them. Afterward, the guards handcuffed them to the mobile steel bar, escorted them back to their cell, and selected the next row of prisoners in the same fashion.

Using this standard operating procedure, the prisoners only saw each other during breakfast, lunch, and dinner. After that, they spent the rest of their time alone. The Warden also prohibited visitation from anyone. The prison excursion left him feeling bleak, and he could not imagine spending the rest of his life there. For that reason, they made sure everyone knew what would happen if they broke the Regime's weightier laws.

To date, no one has escaped the moon's penal facility, and Sam understood why. The guards rotated shifts and sections every month to avoid familiarity with the prisoners. In addition, the Regime limited every position at the prison to a five-year term. During their off-hours, the employees lived in a secluded area, away from the general population on Earth. This strategy kept their identity a secret, and, just on the chance that a prisoner's family member may have somehow obtained their name, it would be impossible to gain access to the guards.

Without access to family and friends, prisoners had no chance of bribing a security officer. Nor did their relatives or companions have an opportunity to hold an officer's family member hostage in exchange for release. Direct access to the facility was by a portal, but they had emergency procedures in place. For example, if they could not open a vortex, they would launch a space shuttle and land on the prison facility's dock, where it would connect to an escape hatch to either bring in supplies or transport personnel.

Even if someone were rich enough to buy or build a private space shuttle, hoping to free an inmate, defense systems already in place kept them from getting close to the moon without authorization. If one prisoner could overpower the twelve guards on his level, he or she would have more to deal with in the Transportation Station because the portal only opened at another secure facility on Earth.

Assuming they got this far, Earth's gravity would make it impossible to run or fight, giving the Earth Security Force the advantage. Furthermore, a prisoner can only leave the facility by obtaining the Supreme Commander's approval, which is not easy to get. As Sam entered the communication room, his wife's beautiful, smiling face caused his thoughts of the moon prison facility and its procedures to vanish.

"How's your day been?" she asked.

"Quiet," he answered.

"Quiet's good."

Sam nodded in agreement.

"I'm sorry to bother you at work, but we're out of milk. Would you mind stopping on your way home to pick up a gallon?"

"Sure, no problem."

"Thanks, I've been busy today, so I haven't had time."

They continued to talk until Sam heard his colleagues becoming restless, so he reluctantly ended his communication.

On his way back to his seat, his friends made kissing noises, "Yes, dear, anything you say, dear."

"Knock it off, you idiots!"

Sam sat, raised the bet, and won the pot on a two-pair bluff. His colleagues moaned in disbelief.

"Serves ya right, actin' like children."

As he pulled in his winnings, the siren sounded.

"Someone has activated a silent alarm at Griffin's Book Store at 19412 Market Place," the dispatcher announced.

"A bookstore?" Reece queried.

"Must be a mouse running across the floor," Nick quipped.

"I don't want anyone taking this lightly. That's how someone ends up dead," Sam warned.

He understood Nick's point. Most calls ended up being a faulty alarm system or, as Nick remarked, some rodent setting off the motion detectors, but Sam knew that complacency kills. Several years ago, his cousin, who used to be a police officer, got a call just like any other. This time, a robber surprised him and wrestled his disruptor from him, set the setting to kill, and unleashed its power on him.

The weapon crushed every bone in his body. An internal investigation uncovered that his cousin and his team were indifferent. Before leaving, they joked and laughed, thinking it was routine, but their conceit cost his cousin's life. Sam had no intention of that ever happening to him or his team. It took them twenty seconds to put on their 'jumpsuits.' They punched in the store's coordinates and arrived moments later.

Each officer had a predetermined entry point. Gerard was at the back door, Reece covered the front, and Sam and Nick landed inside the store. Sam was holding an electric taser, and Nick held a disrupter. Nick set his weapon to immobilize, not kill. The two split up and walked down the aisles. A couple of minutes later, they made their way to the lounge area, where they saw the suspect sitting on a sofa, reading. Sam moved right and signaled for Nick to approach from the left.

Usually, Kraeth's Skean abilities would have alerted him to any intruder within fifty paces from him. Instead, after everyone left, he checked the store and found all the doors locked. Feeling safe, he directed all his focus on the task of deciphering the language. It left him vulnerable, but he did not foresee any danger. Now, seeing movement in his peripheral vision, he realized his mistake. He jumped to his feet and ran to his right, where someone waited for him.

"Get on the floor now!" Nick yelled, pointing his weapon at the suspect.

Kraeth could not believe his stupidity. As the officers approached him, he remembered the rear exit, so with a slight motion of his hand, he flipped over the table in front of him and made a run for it. Sam fired his taser, and the needles hit the table instead of his intended target. Kraeth ran and motioned with his hand again, knocking over a whole shelf of stories, taking Nick down with it.

Nick recovered and fired his weapon, knocking over some shelves in Kraeth's path. Kraeth stumbled but regained his stride. Within moments, he reached the back door. Sam radioed Gerard that the suspect was coming out the back. Kraeth opened the door, and Gerard fired his disrupter, hitting the target hard and knocking him down on his back. Stunned, Kraeth lay motionless as officers put electric restraints on him, made him stand, frisked him for weapons, and read his rights.

Sam called it in, "Dispatch; we have a suspect in custody, so please open the door to a holding cell."

"Roger, Blue Raider," the dispatcher replied.

Within moments, a portal opened in front of them. Sam and Nick motioned for their prisoner to walk through the event horizon. Having no choice, Kraeth stepped through, and the vortex closed behind him. Kraeth landed in a small room. On the floor lay a small foam mattress. He craned his neck to check every space. Sadly, there were no doors or bars, leaving him with no options. Above, he saw two vents, but they were too small for him to squeeze through.

A few hundred heartbeats later, a portal opened on the other side of the room. Two males, wearing strange uniforms, stood on the other side of the event horizon; they were not in the store from where he had just left. Instead, they were standing in a well-lit room, from which he could see no exit. One kept a weapon pointed at Kraeth, and the other walked into the room with him. The officer frisked him a second time and uncuffed him.

Kraeth rubbed his wrists and considered using his powers to subdue them. He realized it would not do him any good because without knowing his location, he had no way of figuring out how to escape. *Am I underground or on the surface?* Being underground meant he would need an elevator, stairway, or portal transmitter to get out. He knew how to use an elevator but not a vortex machine. *Better to let things play out a little longer. I might have a chance to escape later.*

He remembered leaving his backpack on the sofa. *Great. That is all I need.* There were so many officers rushing at him that he did not think to grab it and hoped they did not bring it with them. *Yeah, they were smart enough to catch me. I am in big trouble.* The guard returned through the event horizon. Kraeth leaned against the wall and watched the vortex close, leaving him trapped inside the four walls. In his mind, he could hear Dahmar laughing at him. *Do not get caught.*

Chapter 48

Akil
Argi City
The 22,274[th] Terrestrial Rotation of the Second Summer

Gecheana summoned the five Skeans to Krek, and Nayrah rushed to meet with them. Nayrah already knew the topic of discussion. The Information League continually broadcasted Zorion's meeting in each of the five cities, where he asked to have Elzer brought before Gau's judgment seat. She planned to ask for Gecheana's help to prevent the fight from happening. As the elevator descended, her thoughts drifted to the last time Nayrah spoke to Otsoa. Her threat to kill Yanamai if he continued to see her has worked so far. At least, she believed it had, but the thrashing she gave him could have also kept him in line.

The elevator doors opened, and she hastened to Gecheana's apartment, resolved to find a solution to her dilemma. She planned to ensure that Otsoa would not die by Tuso's sword, causing her to lose a valued asset. She arrived at Gecheana's apartment as the others were settling down. Nayrah hastily took her seat, waiting to hear what Gecheana would say.

"As you are aware, Zorion will bring Elzer before Gau's judgment seat. This battle will put Kemena's subject against Nayrah's."

"We *must* stop it!" Nayrah exclaimed.

"Silence!" Gecheana snapped. "Events are already set in motion. I have meditated on the matter."

Kemena and Nayrah perked up.

"And?" quizzed Kemena.

"There is nothing we can do without revealing ourselves," Gecheana replied.

Kemena and Nayrah stirred in their seats.

"I will not let Tuso die at the hands of her *seta*!" Kemena hissed.

Nayrah thrust out her hand in a surprise attack, sending Kemena flying into the wall. Before Kemena could retaliate, Gecheana stepped between them.

“Stop it!”

“Gecheana, you cannot allow this to happen. Otsoa is part of the plan, remember? He is to take Zorion’s place, so we can tell Yanamai where to look. He is a valuable asset.”

“I have already discreetly instructed Tadra to search the sector I gave you earlier. Besides, if Otsoa dies, we still have Va’ron. Being younger, he will be much easier to manipulate.”

“How can you allow this to happen?” Nayrah asked, bewildered.

“I am not the one who cannot control her subjects. Zorion and Otsoa do their own will, not mine. Now, you must suffer the consequences of your failure.”

“I will show you how much control I have,” Nayrah growled, racing for the door and angrily stomping her feet.

Before she left, Gecheana stopped her, “Neither you nor Kemena can use your powers to help your subjects during the fight.”

Nayrah did not reply. Instead, she turned and slammed the door behind her.

Chapter 49

Earth
The United States - Texas - Houston - Western Suburbs - Gang Territory
May 10, 2452

In an abandoned school cafeteria, Marco Perez ate breakfast. His girlfriend, Clara, used the remaining instant pancake mix they stole from the city a week ago. Today, he would send his 'hunters' back to Houston to take more supplies. Unlike Tucker, his gang did not have an arrangement with General Bailey, so scavenging became a way of life.

Over the years, he and his men accumulated a few generators, which they hooked up in the school, providing him with specific amenities, but nothing like those the city offered. After eating the last pancake, he swallowed a glass of creek water that Clara had boiled and filtered the night before. As Perez set the glass down, his guards entered with one of the men he sent out last night to avenge his brother's death. The man fell to his knees and wept.

"Tell me what happened, Blanco," Perez spoke soothingly.

"Señor Perez, we took the path as you instructed, but they waited for us and killed everyone except me."

Perez's demeanor changed, "I sent three hundred fifty soldiers, and you're telling me that none are left alive!"

"He only spared me so that I could give you a message," his voice was shaky.

"He?"

"Larkin Burke, Señor. He warns to forget about any delusions of revenge, and the next time you attack the resistance, he'll personally hunt you down and kill you."

Perez stood, enraged, "Larkin has been a pain in my ass for far too long! I'll have his head for this!"

In frustration, he swept his plate and glass off the table, shattering them.

"Maybe Señor Tucker could help," Blanco suggested.

Perez walked over to Blanco and put a gun to his head, "I don't need anyone's help, especially Tucker's, and you should have died with the others!"

Without hesitating, he pulled the trigger, sending the bullet through Blanco's head, splattering brains and blood across the floor and on the wall. His body fell to the floor, making a soft thud on the concrete.

Perez paced for several minutes and motioned to one of his guards, "Get this scum out of my home and send a messenger to Tucker. Ask him for a meeting."

"Right away, Señor Perez."

"You need to control your temper, Marco. You could have learned more from Blanco," Clara counseled, standing near him.

Marco sighed, "I can't help myself because I have no patience when it comes to the Burke brothers. They're arrogant sons-a-bitches, who've been a thorn in my side for years."

"Why are you meeting with Tucker?"

"Larkin is out of my reach, but I'm hoping Tucker has a way of getting to him."

"Even if he does, do you think he would betray his brother?"

"I'm going to find out."

"What are you going to give him in return?"

"Something I know he wants. Something he won't refuse."

Chapter 50

Akil
Argi City
The 22,274[th] Terrestrial Rotation of the Second Summer

Sitting in a bistro, Olan finished eating and headed for the avenue, where he saw her signal to meet at the corner table. He walked to the back of the restaurant and sat with his back against the wall, waiting for her. Within a few heartbeats, she came over, sat in front of him, and removed her hood.

"I did not think I would see you again," Olan smiled.

"I was not sure myself because you did lie to me."

"I did not lie. I told you I would delay the mission. I just did not tell you how long."

"It only proves that you do not love me. You are playing games with me."

"I do love you, Nayrah, but I will not commit treason, even for you."

"I should find someone else to love me. Maybe Zorion would be agreeable."

She used her powers to push the thought into the most primitive part of his mind, where jealousy and anger lived. Her energy washed through him, and he blinked rapidly as his intellect accepted her premise.

"Zorion? How long have you been seeing him?"

"We have met a few times. He has shown interest."

The thought of sharing her body with Zorion sparked rage in him, "I do not want you to see him ever again! You are mine!"

Although he whispered, she felt his rage. He was almost ready; just a little push would send him over the edge.

"If Zorion wants me, he can have me. He is sovereign, and what he wants, he gets."

Olan's rage peaked at its highest level, and he struggled against the irrational emotion, but it was too much for him to quench. How could Zorion do this to him? They were friends from their youth. *How could he throw it all away over Nayrah?*

"You would betray your oath to me? Our promise to each other unites us!"

Fighting tears, Nayrah paused before sealing his fate. It would be the last time they met, so she committed his image to memory. Tomorrow, Zorion will be dead, and Broll will have executed Olan for killing him. It was a sacrifice, but one Nayrah had to make to save Otsoa, and it would prove to Gecheana that *she* was still in control. Unable to hide her sorrow, a tear appeared in the corner of her eye and trickled down her cheek. *Forgive me, my love.*

Her voice quivered, "I think you are confused; you and I are simply acquaintances, but if Zorion were no longer sovereign, perhaps we could be more."

Olan stared at her quizzically, "Are you suggesting I kill him?"

"No. Of course not. That would not solve anything. At least, I do not think it would. All I know is that by this time on the following Terrestrial Revolution, I could be Zorion's paramour. If that happens, our relationship will be over."

Jealousy, anger, rage, and confusion dominated his thoughts. Though he struggled against it, the intense emotions would not leave him. Zorion would soon take Nayrah from him, and he could not allow that to happen. He had to stop it.

"There is only one course for us. I will kill Zorion."

"You will need this," she retrieved a small dagger from her belt. She slipped it into his hand and continued, "Use it to pierce his heart, and while he is unconscious, you can remove his head. Do this, and we can be together."

He saw Nayrah's reflection in the shiny, metallic blade of the knife and slid it into his jacket pocket. Having set things in motion, she stood to leave, but he gently grabbed her arm.

"Will you come to my apartment and stay during the sleep cycle?"

"I must prepare myself because Zorion will call for me if you fail."

Nayrah smiled pitifully at him and returned to the avenue, leaving him alone with his new thoughts. As she walked away, he felt empty inside. One image dominated his mind, Nayrah. He wanted her. No, he *needed* her in his life and would not hesitate to kill a thousand Zorions to have her.

Chapter 51

Earth
The United States |- Texas - Houston - Western Farmland - Burke
Home
May 10, 2452

Sarah stepped into her kitchen, carrying a basket of eggs from the chicken coop, and put them in cartons. She heard Sable scream, it was a high-pitched cry, and she instinctively ran upstairs but found Larkin holding her, gently patting her back.

"It's ok, baby. I'm here. Nothin's gonna hurt you," Larkin consoled.

Sarah looked at him knowingly, "The dream again?"

He nodded.

"The bad man is coming, momma. He's coming!" Sable cried hysterically.

"It's just a bad dream, Sable," Sarah opened the blinds and motioned for Larkin to bring her to the window. "You see. There's no one out there."

"I saw him, momma! I swear. He's *going* to hurt us!"

"Listen to me, Sable," Larkin's voice was firm but gentle. "I'm not going to let anyone hurt you. I promise."

"You weren't there, daddy, only mommy and me, and the bad man hurt us."

Larkin embraced his daughter tightly, "It's just a bad dream, Sable. I swear."

It took about half an hour before Sable calmed down; Sarah and Larkin took her downstairs for some warm milk.

Sarah motioned for Larkin to step outside, "I don't like this, Larkin. She keeps having the same dream. I don't know what's causing it."

"Maybe we should ask your dad to send over an army doc."

"You mean a psychiatrist?"

"Yeah. There's nothing wrong with that."

"They're not pediatric psychiatrists. They trained to help soldiers."

"I know, but he could still help."

Sarah thought about it, "I guess we have no choice. We need to know what's upsetting her."

"I'll call and see if he can send someone over today."

Just as they started to walk inside, a vehicle approached. Sarah looked at Larkin apprehensively.

"It's not what you think," he tried to reassure her.

"Get your gun anyway."

Larkin retrieved his weapon and returned before the vehicle arrived. When it stopped, he saw General Bailey in the back seat.

"It's your dad."

Sarah hugged him when he stepped out, "Dad, I'm glad you're here. I need to speak to you about Sable."

"Sable? What's wrong?"

"The nightmares are back."

"What do you want me to do?"

"Would you send a doctor over to talk with her? We need to know what's upsetting her."

"I'll see if Dr. Grant can come by tomorrow."

"Today, dad."

"Look, Sarah. We've got a lot going on right now. Everybody's scrambling to get things organized. Tomorrow's the best I can do."

"All right, send him tomorrow. Now, why are you here?"

"I need to speak to Larkin alone."

Sarah gave him a quizzical look, "What's wrong, dad?"

"Sarah, you go inside. This is the military's business."

"It'll be fine, Sarah. Go on, take care of Sable."

Reluctantly, Sarah went inside. Larkin and General Bailey walked to the barn.

General Bailey shut the door and started yelling, "Are you out of your God-damned mind?"

His sudden outburst startled Larkin, "What do you mean, Sir?"

"I've *heard* that you disobeyed a direct order!"

"I always follow orders, General. You know that."

"Why did you let that gang member go after Lieutenant Blake gave you a direct order to hold him for questioning!" He kept his voice raised.

"It wouldn't have done any good. He was just a foot soldier, so they don't receive any valuable information."

"So, you carved your initials in his neck and sent him on his way!"

"I gave him a message to take to Perez."

"What was that?"

"I told him that if he attacked the resistance again, I would hunt him down personally and kill 'em."

General Bailey picked up the wooden chair they used for interrogations and threw it across the room into a stall, breaking it into pieces. He noticed one of the chair's legs lying on the ground, retrieved it, and walked back to Larkin, holding the wood firmly in his grasp.

"Let me make something clear to you since you're too stupid to figure it out on your own. The resistance is an army. Granted, we're not a big army, and until recently, we haven't had enough supplies and equipment to help us hold the line, but now that the Regime is backing us, we're finally able to function normally. That means I cannot patrol the line anymore because I have a base to work from now. In my place, there are officers, and if one gives you an order, I expect you to obey it as if I gave it myself!"

General Bailey swung the wooden leg without warning, hitting Larkin's left arm between the shoulder and elbow. Even though he sensed the attack, Larkin didn't move. It made contact, and his arm throbbed in pain.

"Now tell me, Larkin. What happens to soldiers who disobey orders?"

"They're court-martialed, Sir," his voice was soft and repentant.

"That's right, you idiot! What if you end up in prison for five years? Who the hell's going to take care of Sarah and Sable?"

"I don't know, Sir."

"I am, you moron! That means I'll have to send soldiers to the farm to watch over them while you're wasting away in prison! I'll have to stop by every night to ensure they're safe. I don't have time for that!"

Again, he swung the wooden leg, hitting Larkin's left arm in the same spot. This time Larkin flinched.

"I ought to bust your ass down to private, you boneheaded, dimwitted idiot! You don't deserve those stripes!"

Larkin held his head down and solemnly replied, "Yes, Sir,"

"You better understand something, soldier! You're not in a cell *only* because you're married to my daughter! Right now, I regret ever allowing you to be with her!"

"Please don't say that, Sir."

Again, he sensed the wood approaching his left arm. His instincts urged him to move or block; he willed it away. Instead, he stood motionless until the wooden leg smacked the same spot on his arm. This time, he put his right hand over the injured area and fell to his knees in submission, hoping General Bailey would not strike him again. General Bailey stepped in close, but due to Larkin's height, even on his knees, he stood about as tall as General Bailey, who only had to bow slightly to speak into his ear.

"You need to remember that your decisions affect everyone who cares about you. Did you ever think about what Sarah would do for the five years you could be spendin' in prison right now?"

"No, Sir."

He yelled in Larkin's ear, "I didn't think so, you imbecile! That's five years of raising Sable alone! Five years, you cretin!"

Instead of hitting him again, General Bailey threw the wooden leg into the stall with the rest of the chair and returned his attention to Larkin.

"I ought to let Lieutenant Blake file charges against you, and after a year or two, Sarah might meet someone else. Maybe an officer this time."

Although Larkin could take corporal punishment to its extreme, hearing the General say that he hoped Sarah would find someone else hurt him more than twenty strikes with the wooden leg.

"No, Sir, please don't. I promise. I'll do whatever the Lieutenant says."

"You better, cause you ain't gettin' any more chances; you stupid son of a bitch!"

Seeing Larkin about to cry, General Bailey believed he understood his point. Over the years, General Bailey grew to care for Larkin, but he could not allow him to continue disobeying orders. The

Regime would severely punish him. If Lieutenant Blake filed charges, they would undoubtedly put him in prison. Satisfied that Larkin understood, he spun around and left without saying another word.

Chapter 52

Akil
Argi City
The 22,274[th] Terrestrial Rotation of the Second Summer

As Nayrah approached her door, she saw Otsoa sitting in front of it, "What are you doing here?"

"Waiting for you. Where have you been?"

"I have been busy trying to find a way to prevent the fight from taking place."

"So, you have heard."

"Of course, I have heard. It is *my* city. I know everything that goes on here," she snapped, opened the door, and entered her apartment.

"I did not mean to offend you. I just…"

She cut him off, "Get inside before someone sees you."

Otsoa walked in and closed the door behind him, "What am I going to do?"

"Do not worry. I have put something in motion to keep Zorion from bringing Elzer before Gau's judgment seat," she sat in her favorite chair.

Cautiously, Otsoa walked over to her. She did not drive him away, so he knelt, hugged her knees, put his head on her lap, and wept.

"Thank you, Nayrah."

"None of this would have happened if you had obeyed me," she grumbled, but her anger vanished as quickly as it came.

She felt an odd sensation of parental care and stroked his hair, "You must be mentally prepared to fight, just in case."

Three Terrestrial Rotations ago, he wanted to die after Yanamai left him because of his debacle with the potion. He still did, but not like this. Everyone knew that Tuso would win, and his humiliating demise would be videoed for all to see; it was a fate worse than death.

"You will not fail, Nayrah. You never do."

"No, Otsoa. I have failed before." *I have failed you as a parent.*

Lifting his head, he faced her with tears, "If so, I have never seen it. You always get what you want."

Nayrah stared into Otsoa's eyes and allowed herself to feel parental warmth for him for the first time in her life. It was a strange emotion that she pushed away. *Skeans do not love.*

Otsoa stayed quiet for a few heartbeats, "Even if I do have to fight, you will be there to help me, right?

"I will be there, but you will not see me, and I am forbidden to use my powers to help you."

"Why? By whom?" *Are there more of you?*

"It does not matter who. The simple fact is that I cannot help you. Now, go home. You need rest."

"I am facing death; how can I sleep?"

Gently, she pushed him off her lap, stood, walked over to a cabinet, retrieved a small bottle, and handed it to him, "Drink this, and by the time you reach your bed, you will fall right to sleep."

Otsoa drank it and handed the bottle back to her.

"Now go before you fall asleep on the avenue."

Otsoa left, leaving Nayrah to sit alone in the dark. Her thoughts drifted toward Olan, bringing tears to her eyes. Although Gecheana forbid it, Nayrah still loved him, and if Gecheana found out, she would kill her and Olan. To accomplish her goal, she had to sacrifice the only Akilian that made her happy which deeply hurt her. Zorion's death must be public and by a trusted friend. It was the only way she could prove her worth to Gecheana.

I am a Skean, and Skeans do what they must to complete the mission. Gecheana made her rehearse the phrase to strengthen her will for many yellow harvests, yet it did nothing to soothe her conscience. A tear rolled down her cheek, visualizing what would happen to Olan after the attack. She wiped it away but more followed. *Oh, my love. What have I done?*

Chapter 53

Earth
The United States - Texas - Houston - Western Suburbs - Gang Territory
May 10, 2452

Marco and several of his men drove to a clearing where the messenger said they were to meet. It was 5 PM and still light out. Marco would not have met him any later. To do so would be suicide. Before leaving, he ensured all his men were well-armed in case Tucker decided to betray him. His driver got out of the vehicle, but he stayed inside. The rest of his men stepped out of their cars simultaneously. They searched the area, making sure it was safe. His second in command, Rico Soto, gave him a nod several minutes later. Marco opened the door and got out.

"Tucker will approach from the north," Marco informed Rico. "I don't want anyone to shoot unless I give the order."

Rico nodded. Fifteen minutes later, he saw someone approaching. His men pumped shells into their shotguns to prepare because the click action intimidated anyone on the receiving end. Tucker appeared out of the shadows. He led the 'Peacekeepers,' the largest gang in the Houston area, and feared no one. Many dreaded Tucker even without his soldiers because of his brute strength and willingness to use it.

The only way Marco and his men stayed alive all these years was to keep moving, avoiding any ambush Tucker might send. Now, it seemed that Tucker would end up getting what he wanted. Marco motioned for his men to lower their weapons and walked out from the shade to meet him in the clearing. Marco stood five feet ten inches tall, with a thick frame that made him a terrifying sight. Still, he was insignificant compared to Tucker.

Like his brother, Larkin, Tucker was six and a half feet tall, and his frame was twice that of Marco's. Tucker extended his hand to greet him and smiled boyishly, but Marco knew that youthful grin was deceptive. Behind the pleasant mask lay a crafty reptile that would kill without remorse. Knowing this, Marco carefully extended his hand, and they shook.

"I was surprised to hear from you, Perez," Tucker remarked.

"Like my messenger told you, I'm willing to negotiate an agreement between us, but I want something in return."

Tucker laughed, "Of course you do. Nothin's ever free, so tell me what you want."

"Just so we're clear, the deal is: I become your second, and my men take orders only from me," Marco reiterated.

"That is the agreement. I'm in charge, and while you're alive, you'll be my second."

"Just remember, if someone kills me, the deal is off, and my cousin Rico will take control of my soldiers." Marco's expression changed before continuing, "And I promise you; he will avenge my death, just as I'm sworn to avenge my brother's."

Tucker raised his hands defensively, "Marco, please, there's no need for idle threats here. I only meant to stipulate all the terms of our deal. You have my word. I won't try to assassinate you, nor will I order it. Now, tell me what you want in return."

"I want you to kill Larkin."

Tucker frowned, "I have no love for Larkin because he betrayed me, but he *is* my brother." He paused, shoving his hands into his pants pockets, "I'm sorry, I can't kill him."

"The deal's off," Marco spun around and started to leave.

"Wait! You haven't heard my counteroffer."

"Counteroffer? I don't want anything else."

"I said *I* couldn't kill him, but I would be willin' to capture him for you."

"I'm listening."

"I'll bring him to the warehouse, where it'll be up to you and only you to kill him. In the pit."

"No deal. I can't take him one-on-one. You know that. I know that."

"I admire you, Perez. Few men would be willin' to admit their limitations. I tell ya what I'm gonna do. I'll capture him and restrain him with thick chains, five feet long. That ought to even things up."

"I don't know," Marco frowned, thinking about his offer.

Tucker groaned a few moments later, "Ok, what if I hand you his weapon, the Bowie knife he uses to kill. You'll be fighting a chained, unarmed man. I can't make it any easier than that, Perez."

Marco looked at Rico, who shrugged, so Marco faced Tucker, "Ok. Let me know when you've captured him. I'll face him in the pit."

Tucker extended his hand, "I've wanted this for a long time; it'll be good to have you with us, Perez."

Marco paused, looking at Tucker's extended hand, knowing what it meant. He was honor-bound to avenge his brother's death. It was the only way Marco could repay Larkin for killing a family member. Reluctantly, he shook Tucker's hand, sealing their agreement.

Chapter 54

Akil
Argi City
The 22,274[th] Terrestrial Rotation of the Second Summer

Alone in his office, Zorion scrolled through endless digital images, continuing his search for the female in his dreams. During his inquiry, he found some who were close but not exact. He moved their photos to a folder for review by dragging his finger across the monitor. That gallery had become significant and continued to grow.

Due to his uncertainty, he did not want to leave out any that could be her. *If only you would tell me your name.* His timekeeper chimed, so he turned off his Information Terminal. It was time to go home. At his door, he paused, hoping that Thea would not be there to greet him. *Am I now hesitant to return to my apartment?* He turned the handle but stopped because his assistant buzzed him.

"Yes, Shilda."

"Broll is here."

"Tell him I am going home. He can meet me on the promenade."

"He has Yanamai and Garbi with him. You said to bring them to your office once they calmed down. Shall I send them in?"

Zorion collapsed back into his chair. *I am not in the mood to deal with them now.*

"Yes, send them in."

He felt his facial expression turn into a scowl as the door to his office opened. They stood at the entrance, expecting his invitation, but he studied Yanamai and Garbi before speaking. They perfectly resembled each other physically. Identical twins were rare on Akil, and it was even more uncommon for a younger sibling to resemble the older one exactly. Zorion suspected Garbi of changing her likeness to match Yanamai's for many yellow harvests, yet her reasons were a mystery to him.

A few yellow harvests earlier, he felt nostalgic and asked Yanamai to show him their pictures. In some of the images, she and Garbi posed together. Even at such an early age, he could barely tell them apart, but they were opposites in every way except their appearance. As evidence of that fact, Yanamai stood in the doorway, with her head held down, ashamed to face him. In comparison, Garbi looked him in the eyes, unabashed.

Yanamai embodied the attributes he wanted in a daughter in almost every respect. She was selfless, kind, and caring, and she put everyone else's concerns above hers. It made him very protective of her; on the other hand, the thought of his daughter, Yetta, brought a twinge of pain. *Where did I go wrong with her?* He had not spent as much time with Garbi but knew her well enough to recognize that she was outspoken, forward, and ambitious. Traits that were not necessarily bad if appropriately used, though she tended to employ them only for personal gain and did not mind hurting anyone in her way.

"Sit down," he spoke sternly.

They moved to a seat. Zorion stood and walked around the desk until his frightening frame loomed in front of them. They watched him closely as he moved. He glared at them for several heartbeats, hoping to use all the intimidation his office held.

"I am very disappointed in both of you."

"I do not understand. What have we done?" Garbi inquired.

"What?" Zorion frowned and faced Yanamai for her answer.

"The last thing I remember was stepping onto the hover bus, and I woke up in a cell. Please tell me we did not hurt anyone," Yanamai replied worriedly.

"You do not remember trying to kill each other?" puzzled Zorion.

"What?" they spoke in unison, looking at each other quizzically.

"The last thing I remember was walking the lab hallway," Garbi replied, confused.

Pressing a button, Zorion replayed the video the cameras recorded of the promenade where the fight took place; Garbi and Yanamai watched in horror as the scene unfolded. Zorion noticed that their eyes had returned to normal, and they did not have the crazed looks as before. When it was over, Garbi and Yanamai cringed.

"What are you going to do with us?" Garbi inquired.

"Do you expect me to believe that you do not remember anything?" Zorion questioned.

Concentrating, they frowned, trying to remember, but shrugged their shoulders.

"Zain should know my whereabouts," Yanamai offered.

"He is recovering," Broll interrupted. "Someone drove a sword into his back."

"Did I do that?" Yanamai gasped, horrified.

"Yes. I reviewed the video. You attacked with his back turned toward you. It was disgraceful."

"I swear, I have no memory of it!" Yanamai exclaimed.

Frowning, Zorion looked to Broll, who shrugged.

"I will resign right away. If I am capable of this kind of madness, you cannot trust me to oversee the Science Division," Yanamai lamented.

"I planned to send both of you to prison for such recklessness, but it is clear that someone drugged you," Zorion remarked.

"It would explain our actions and memory loss," Garbi confirmed.

"Why would someone do that to us?" Yanamai queried.

"I am not sure, but one of you would have lost the fight," Zorion replied.

"Which means one of you was a target," Broll added.

"Someone tried to kill one of us?" Garbi gulped.

"Tell me, which one is the better fighter?" Zorion asked.

"I am," they responded in unison.

Yanamai faced Garbi, "You know I used to beat you in every match."

"That was several yellow harvests ago. I have improved," Garbi countered.

"She has," Broll offered. "She surprised me and almost ran you through."

"That means someone tried to kill Yanamai," Zorion concluded.

"That does not make sense. I do not socialize with anyone because I do not have the time, and Otsoa's persistence has ensured that I cannot leave the second level, so why would anyone want to kill me? I am trying to find a planet for us to live on!" Yanamai shouted.

"Remember the change in the sector?" Zorion inquired.

"Yes," Yanamai nodded.

"What?" Garbi interrupted.

"I think that whoever gave him that sector is the one who tried to kill you," Zorion surmised.

"Why?" Yanamai questioned.

"What are you talking about?" Garbi interjected.

"What if he gave you the incorrect sector?" Zorion proposed.

"We did find a planet," Yanamai noted.

"It is inhabited. What if the correct sector holds an uninhabited world?" speculated Zorion.

"All right, so why does this Akilian want to kill me?" Yanamai queried.

"Tadra is next in line," Zorion moved to his Information Terminal.

"Will someone please tell me what you two are talking about?" Garbi insisted.

"There it is," Zorion said.

"What?" Yanamai and Garbi spoke in unison.

"Tadra has a benefactor. Someone paid for her education," Zorion explained.

"That is not unusual," Yanamai countered.

"True, but if her sponsor approached her after she took your place, he or she could try to persuade her to look in a different sector while we work with the current world," Zorion expounded.

"Do you think Tadra knows?" Yanamai wondered.

"It is possible. I will put an agent on her to watch her movements. In the meantime, I will make Thixi your replacement. Hopefully, we will never have to use her, but I cannot allow Tadra to have that position now, even if she is innocent," Zorion stated.

"I should be her replacement," Garbi chimed in.

"They already tried to kill Yanamai. If they find out you are her replacement, what do you think will happen?" counseled Zorion.

"Oh," Garbi shook her head.

"Until we find whoever tried to kill you, I want both of you to remain on the second level. You will live in your offices under guard," he paused to face Broll, "I want twenty guards on each of their residences beginning now."

"Right away!" Broll yelled.

"What about our parents? They could be in danger too," Yanamai worried.

"I will move them to my guest area. No one will get to them. I promise."

"Thank you," Yanamai smiled.

"Now go home, clean up, and rest. I need you back to work as soon as possible," Zorion commanded.

Zorion signaled Broll to stay behind as they left, "Someone is getting past your security."

"I will resign at once," Broll frowned.

"No. I need you by my side, but you must consult with Olan. Someone bested him as he followed Otsoa," Zorion added.

"I will increase security and have Screeners perform routine checks throughout the work cycle. I will not leave your side from now on," Broll declared.

"Thank you, my friend."

Chapter 55

Earth
The Regime - Washington, D.C. - Fort McNair
May 11, 2452

Michael sat at his desk, reading e-mails. Most were from colleagues, except one that was from his mother. He sighed profoundly and moved his fingers with a lethargy that mirrored his inner emotions to find a dinner invitation. The last one he attended was months ago, and he had only spoken to her a couple of times. His reason for avoiding her was personal.

From his earliest memories, his stepdad always showed great disappointment no matter what he achieved. Finally, years ago, he gathered enough courage to ask him why, but his stepdad refused to admit there was a problem. It frustrated him because he could not fix the issue without knowing what bothered him.

Michael composed a short response to his mother, recalling his last visit. He had stepped through the front door and saw him glance over. Their eyes met; his stepdad turned away and faced the entertainment center without greeting him, making him feel unwelcome. He mentioned it to his mother, who dismissed the idea as a figment of his imagination. *I know better.*

He responded, *"Thank you for the invite, but things are hectic around here. I don't think I can get away from work. I'll call you sometime next week."* He sent the e-mail and spent ten minutes going through the rest. *There's nothing from Chu Lian.* Later, he stepped out of his office and into his workshop. He put on a lab coat, headed toward the incubator, and stopped, hearing a knock on the door before reaching it.

"Come in."

An android entered, carrying a sealed glass container marked as evidence, and there were hazard stickers all over it. There was also an envelope.

The android smiled, "Good morning, Sir. Where would you like me to put this?"

"Who sent it?"

"Officers from the tenth precinct arrested a man last night. They found this odd-looking substance sitting on a table where he sat. They want to know what it is and ensure it is not dangerous."

"Why send it to me? Don't they have labs to take care of this kind of thing?"

"They did not give that information, Sir."

He found two documents. The first was the police report. The second was a brief letter from Assistant of Defense Long's office, ordering him to run a battery of tests on the unknown plant.

"Put it over there. I'll get to it in a few minutes," Michael pointed to a table on the far side of the room.

"Thank you, Sir." The android put the container on the table and inquired, "Sir, do you have anything that needs to be delivered?"

"No, thank you."

"Have a nice day, Sir," the android answered and left.

Michael inspected the incubator to see the progression of his latest experiment and examined his checklist to note the time, temperature, and changes on the tablet fastened above the incubator. Everything looked normal, so Michael examined the container the android delivered, and within its transparent sides, he found an assortment of colored mosses. He opened the lid and wafted his fingers over the top, trying to detect an aroma, but there was none.

His computer beeped as it displayed the results of his latest test on the microorganisms. Setting aside the evidence container, he walked to the terminal and reviewed the outcome. *Hmm. Hmm. What the - yes!* Excited about his findings, he contacted Supreme Commander Porter's office, where his assistant put him through at once.

"What did you find?" Supreme Commander Porter asked.

"It's just as I suspected. The microorganism..." Michael began to say, but Supreme Commander Porter cut him off.

"I don't want to discuss this over an open line. I'll be down in your lab in about an hour."

Michael disconnected, turned his attention to the odd-looking moss, and read the police report. They apprehended the suspect, who had the moss in a bookstore while reading a tablet after hours. *It doesn't sound like a serious crime, so why am I looking at this?* The police found moss and a water container on the table near his seat.

They wanted to know if they were dealing with a new drug or drug delivery system. *It makes sense; there are hallucinogenic mushrooms. Someone may have created a hybrid of moss that did the same thing.*

Using a pair of tongs, he removed several colored moss samples, placed them in individual Petri dishes, and put them under a microscope. They looked strange. He accessed the library, opened images of every known moss species, and transferred them to the screen above his worktable to compare them. He saw that each color's leaves were more significant than the average moss plant. He heard the door to his lab open and saw Lisa, his assistant, returning from her vacation.

"You're late."

"Sorry. I got held up at the - whoa, what happened to you?"

"What? Oh, my eye. I was in a scuffle. You got held up at?"

"The International Transportation Station."

"You must have arrived during rush hour."

"I did. I'll stay late to make up my time."

"Not a problem. Did you have a good time?"

"It was nice," she smiled.

"I can tell you met someone."

"Yeah, I did."

"Well, tell me about him."

"I was at the Natural History Museum, and I physically bumped into Ethan. Of course, he apologized. As I started walking away, he struck up a conversation. We talked, and before I left, he asked me to dinner."

"Let me guess; you said no," Michael joked.

"Stop being silly. Of course, I agreed to meet him. I just love that British accent."

"How did it end, or did it?"

"He doesn't have a Regime visa, but I can visit him on the weekends. There's a direct transport to London, so it'll only take about fifteen minutes to get through customs, leaving us the whole weekend."

"Still, long-distance relationships are hard."

"I want to give him a chance. You never know what might happen."

"I'm glad you enjoyed yourself."

"What's on the screen?" she wondered, putting on her lab coat.

"It looks like moss. I think. Honestly, I've never seen anything like it before."

"A new species?"

"That's what I'm thinking. Here, look."

Lisa examined the moss, "This does appear odd."

"I know this will sound strange, but I want to do a nutritional analysis."

Lisa looked at him quizzically, "Why would you want to eat it?"

"Not me. The police confiscated it. They want to ensure it's not a new drug, and before I test it for hallucinogens, I want to see if it has any nutritional value."

"Ok, I'll start working on it right away."

Lisa made herself busy outlining a series of tests for the moss, so Michael made a separate nursery bed for each color, removed a section from each moss, and placed them in the nursery. With everything in place, Michael watered the moss and put it under a grow light in the back room of the lab. He returned to find Supreme Commander Porter standing over Lisa's shoulder, looking at the moss.

"Where did you get this?" Porter asked abruptly.

"The tenth precinct sent it over," Michael replied.

"I see," Porter mumbled distractedly. "You have some good news for me?"

"Yes." Michael handed him the results of his tests.

"Interesting, Michael. Your report says the microorganisms we retrieved from Mars communicate information about population size and metabolic state through pheromones?"

"Yes, that's correct."

"Isn't that the way most bacteria from Earth convey information?"

"Yes, Sir, it is, but after I separated these bacteria from each other, they continued to communicate telepathically."

"They don't have brains, so how can they make such a connection?"

"They have receptors on their surfaces to determine their surroundings. They grew into a small colony, so I separated them and placed them in different rooms. Some of their receptors changed into transmitters within a few minutes and began emitting signals. During my tests, I located and deciphered their signals."

"What is the farthest distance you've assessed so far?"

"During my last test, I sent one colony to the lab in Maine, one here in Washington, D.C., and the other in Florida."

"You were able to pinpoint their location?"

"Yes, I can find their exact position."

"How long will these colonies live in a human body?"

"I don't have any conclusive proof yet, but I believe they would continue to reproduce inside the tissue from what I've seen so far."

"Will the bacteria cause any ill effects to the host?"

"All my tests have shown that they never exceed their population once they've set up a colony. I guess that it's a survival instinct. They seem to know that overpopulating will kill their host, killing themselves, so I believe they're harmless, but I need to do more testing to be completely sure."

"Are they resistant to antibiotics?"

"There are a few that kill them, so I've made a list."

"What is the frequency of their communication?"

"It can't be heard on any radio receiver if that's what you're asking, so I had to develop a special sensor to listen in on their conversations because it's a bio frequency."

"You said you could decipher their signals. Do you know what they're saying to each other?"

"They don't communicate as we do. It's like Morse code. The signals they send are in short and slightly longer transmissions. I can even name each colony. They each start with a different pattern, unique to themselves. It's repeated along with the message a couple of times. Afterward, the other replies in like manner."

"Excellent; I want to do a test run on a human subject."

"Sir, I must remind you that these organisms are alien. I still need to do more tests."

"You'll complete them all, but for now, I want to see them in action, so be prepared to insert the bacteria into a host. I'll have a volunteer here by tomorrow."

Abruptly, Porter turned and headed for the door. Along the way, he glanced at the tray of moss on Michael's table. Michael frowned. Had he known Porter would put his research into action before thoroughly testing it, he would not have alerted him to his progress. A lesson he would remember in the future. *This reckless action hurts or even kills. You can't inject an alien organism into a human body and expect nothing to go wrong.* Michael had to obey his order, so he prepared a colony for implantation.

Chapter 56

Earth
The Regime - Washington, D.C. - Civilian Prison
May 11, 2452

Kraeth meditated, sitting crossed-legged on his bed, hoping to find a way of escape. Although he preferred the dark, the room was dim, which allowed him good access to his Skean powers. In his mind's eye, he could see that the walls surrounding him were an arm's length thick, all the way around. There were other cells on his level, rows of them, side by side. He saw several corridors between the cells, but they were too far away for him to reach. *How am I going to get out of here?* He explored the area and sensed a ripple in the wall in front of him. Even with his eyes closed, he could see the portal open with his mind's eye.

"Wake up, sleeping beauty. Time to face the judge," the guard quipped.

Kraeth did not understand him but could tell by his mannerisms that it was time to get up. He opened his eyes, uncrossed his legs, and stood. The guard motioned for him to turn around, put handcuffs on him, and led him out into the hallway, where he saw a control panel on the wall. As Kraeth walked away, he craned his head to get a good look.

"Turn around," the guard nudged him from behind.

It did not take a genius to know what the guard wanted him to do, so he faced forward. Farther down the hallway, two more guards joined them. They walked through a series of passageways to another cell. This one, however, had a door made of metal bars. The guard had to open it physically so that Kraeth could step inside. The door made a loud banging sound when it shut. There was a rectangular opening about waist high in the door. The guard motioned for him to turn around; the sentry reached in and removed the handcuffs.

"We'll call you in a few minutes."

Once they were out of sight, Kraeth checked out his new surroundings. There were no chairs, but it had a long bench and an exposed toilet. Sitting down on the board, he closed his eyes and connected to his powers, trying to find the guards and retrace his steps to the control panel. He saw only one sentry at the transmitter in his mind's eyes. Farther down the hallway, he sensed the other three that escorted him to his present cell. The rest of the prison within his vicinity was vacant.

One will not be a problem. He prodded his arm, looking for the cutting tool Dahmar inserted before he left Akil. He found it and flipped the switch while it was still inside his body. A laser beam shot through his skin. Carefully, he rotated it, making a small incision big enough to remove it, turned off the laser, and pulled the device out. A few heartbeats later, his skin closed over the wound.

He cleaned the tool, cut through the metal bars of his cell, and quietly laid them on the floor under the bench. Kraeth poked his head out of the cell and looked to ensure it was clear before stepping outside. He did not see anyone, so he headed down the hall and retraced his steps toward the transmitter. He neared the corridor corner, felt a warning sensation, and heard someone yell, "Halt!"

Turning, he saw the three guards standing at the junction behind him. They each pointed a hand-held weapon at him. With only one choice, he ran for the console. The sentries released a barrage of shots from their handguns. Using his powers, he ducked, twisted, and jerked out of their path. As they flew by his head, he could hear the projectiles cutting through the air. Now, he had heightened senses and could hear the thud as they hit the wall near the transmitter corridor.

He rounded the corner and saw the lone guard at the console. Having heard the shots, he stood with his weapon drawn; seeing Kraeth, he fired. With his powers at their peak, Kraeth saw the projectile leave the muzzle of the sentry's gun. *I can beat this.* Dropping down on his left leg, he slid toward the guard. The slug cut the air above him, where his head was moments before.

The sentry's expression changed from anger to disbelief. Kraeth did not wait to give him a second chance, so he reached out with his mind and grabbed his weapon. The other screamed in pain as an invisible force tore the gun from his hand, breaking his fingers. Kraeth stopped sliding, stood, grabbed the weapon out of the air, and pointed it at the guard's head.

Calmly, Kraeth motioned for him to move out of the way and randomly selected icons with his free hand, hoping to open a portal to escape through. He had a little time to figure out how it worked and improvised. Precious heartbeats passed. In his peripheral vision, he saw the other three turn the corner. Using the guard as a shield, he fixed his weapon's muzzle against the sentry's head. The others stopped moving forward, but they trained their guns on him.

Keeping his hostage between them, he moved the guard to the console and motioned for him to select the correct icons. Reluctantly, the sentry did what he wanted. Kraeth memorized the sequence for future use. The transmitter powered up, and a portal opened. On the other side, he saw another hallway.

He edged his way over to the event horizon, keeping his hostage between himself and the others. Just before Kraeth reached the event horizon, his hostage elbowed him in the stomach, causing him to release his grip, just enough for the guard to break free and dive for the ground. Exposed, Kraeth turned and jumped toward the vortex. Just as he crossed the event horizon, one of the other sentries fired an electronic weapon.

"No!" the Sergeant yelled.

It was too late. The energy pulse hit the portal, generating feedback to the transmitter, which exploded in a shower of sparks and arcing electric surges, causing the vortex to collapse with a rumbling sound. The Sergeant raced over to the guard on the ground.

"Where did you send him?"

"I followed protocol and sent him to the penal colony on the moon. That dumb bastard will be in for one big surprise. He broke my damn fingers."

The Sergeant moved over to the destroyed transmitting console. The other two sentries had already grabbed fire extinguishers and fogged the area. He saw that communication was still intact and toggled the switch, "Moon One, come in."

"Moon One here," the dispatcher replied.

"Please confirm the arrival of the prisoner," the Sergeant continued.

"Negative, we had an open portal for a few seconds, but it closed," the dispatcher answered.

"Damn it!" the Sergeant shouted.

"Is he dead?" the guard, who fired the electric pulse, asked.

"What do you think, rookie?"

"I'm sorry. I didn't intend for that to happen."

"Why did you use your pulse gun?"

"I don't know. Everything happened so fast; I figured it was the best weapon to use for the situation."

"You shouldn't have even been wearing it in here. Don't you know you're never supposed to use an energy weapon anywhere near a vortex?"

"Yes, Sergeant. But I thought."

"You're a damn rookie! You're not supposed to think! You're supposed to follow orders!"

"Wasn't he getting away?"

"Didn't you recognize the location on the other side of the event horizon?"

"No, where was it?"

"It was a hallway in Moon Colony One. He wasn't escaping. He was heading to another secure facility, but now he's dead!"

"I'm sorry. I thought he was getting away."

"I don't think sorry will help you, rookie," the Sergeant paused, looking at the smoke rising from the transmitter, "The Captain will not be happy with you after hearing about this."

Chapter 57

Akil
Argi City
The 22,275[th] Terrestrial Rotation of the Second Summer

Zorion woke to the soft music playing. During most of the sleep cycle, Thea argued with him, trying to convince him to withdraw his request to bring Elzer before Gau's judgment seat. It left him very tired. The longer the argument continued, the viler she became. It was a side of her he suspected existed but never saw before. Later, she realized that her verbal reasoning would not change his mind, so she became physically violent.

Not willing to accept her abuse, he called Broll. By the time he arrived, with four guards by his side, she had worked herself into an insane rage, and it took all the sentries to remove her. Their struggle lasted for a few hundred heartbeats until they managed to restrain her and the event prevented him from getting his usual sound sleep. Sitting on the edge of his bed, he rubbed his belly. *She is petite but hits very hard.*

Inside the refreshing room, he splashed water on his face. Looking in the mirror, he frowned. *How did I get here? How did things get so out of control?* Since the last yellow harvest, he began seeing the real Thea and did not like her. Most couples would have reached a symbiotic relationship, where the two functioned as one, but they were far from it. An ancient poem flashed into his mind. *The heart of her spouse safely trusts in her. She will do him good all the Terrestrial Rotations of her life. She is not afraid of the snow, and her partner is known at the gates, sitting with his advisors.* Zorion shook his head. This last outburst convinced him that he needed to separate from her.

Without thinking, he whispered, "I do not love her, and it is clear she does not love me, so I do not want to be with her anymore."

He felt a weight lift from him. *Why did I wait so long to come to this conclusion?* The thought of leaving her felt good. Memories of his life flashed in his mind's eye. Sadly, he could not remember ever being happy with her. It always felt forced. Within a few Terrestrial Rotations from the sudden death of his first partner, Thea took her place. *I wonder why she inserted herself into my life. She should have known we were not compatible.*

Their recent fight proved she deceived him by staying within the image of Gau's eye throughout his celebration that occurred many yellow harvests ago. She made herself available to him, hoping for prestige and Sovereign Cubes. In doing so, their relationship was one-sided until now. Spending so many wasted Terrestrial Rotations with her and so many wasted heartbeats when he could have been with someone who genuinely cared for him made him angry.

His attention drifted to the one in his dreams, and the anger drained from his mind. He closed his eyes and tried to imagine her. *I have not seen you in ages. Please come back to me.* With so many things going wrong in his life, he wanted her to appear again soon. He sighed because his timekeeper chimed; it was time to go to his office. Shilda greeted him with the work he had to complete before leaving for the Main Arena.

"Before you start, Olan has been asking to meet with you," Shilda commented.

"Is he in the lobby?" Zorion peeked out the door from his seat.

"No, Broll has the whole area locked down. Only essential personnel have been allowed up."

"I do not have time. Tell him I will speak to him once I return."

"Very well."

A few hundred heartbeats later, Zorion completed the work Shilda gave him, just as his timekeeper chimed. He left his office, and Shilda joined him, with Broll close behind.

"Your formal suit for the event is in the last carriage. I prepared your lunch; it is waiting for you in the dining area," Shilda walked beside him.

"What would I do without you?

"I do not think you would get anything done," Shilda answered bluntly.

"I believe you are right," Zorion chuckled.

"Otsoa and Thea will ride in the first carriage. I cleaned and pressed his fighting attire. There is food for him as well. You also have a change of clothes for your return trip. I took the liberty of setting clothes out for Otsoa's return."

Zorion stopped walking and looked at her, "Thank you for everything."

"He will do fine; you will see."

"Have you heard anything from Thea?"

"I have not heard from her this work cycle. Besides, Thea is too fussy with her clothes, so she must select her attire. I have already been down that avenue."

"I am sure she is on the train already."

"Here."

"What is this? I finished all my work for the early part of the work cycle."

"I am sorry to disappoint you; that was for the prior work cycle. Now, you must finish what I just gave you, or you will be behind again," Shilda insisted sternly.

Zorion smiled, "Of course, I will start on it soon as we depart."

Shilda turned to leave but stopped to face him, "You will come home victorious, Sir. I know it in my heart."

Zorion nodded and watched her leave until she disappeared. *What would I do without you, Shilda?* It did not escape him that his assistant seemed to know more about him than Thea. Broll's hand moved to his ear communicator in his peripheral vision.

"Is there something wrong?" Zorion asked.

"A disturbance at the security post," Broll answered.

"Go take care of it."

"I am not leaving your side."

"Broll, relax. You have sealed off the whole area, and there are guards everywhere. Go and hurry back. I will ensure the train does not leave until you are on board."

Reluctantly, Broll obeyed and left. Zorion turned around, strolled to the terminal, and reviewed the list of things Shilda gave him to complete during his trip. *I will never get this finished.* Nearing the train, he saw Thea approaching the front carriage. She looked at him with a knowing, smug grin. It gave him a chill down his spine. *What is she up to now?* Since Otsoa was not present, he used his communicator to ask the head guard at the security post to see if he had checked in yet.

"No, Sir. We have not seen him," the guard replied.

You better get here soon, Otsoa, or I will take you kicking and screaming to the Main Arena.

Chapter 58

Earth
The Regime - Washington, D.C. - Capitol Building
May 11, 2452

Stan Hill waited outside Supreme Commander Porter's office. His eyes were heavy with sleep because, for some reason, it took Alex most of the night to find the assassin's destination. Stan had waited for the results, thinking it would only take a brief time. That decision cost him a good night's sleep, but during the early morning hours, Alex found it. Believing the Supreme Commander would see him right away, he rushed over to give him the news personally.

His assistant told him to wait. *If I had sent him a video, I could be in bed right now.* He stared at the four androids programmed to guard the Supreme Commander to occupy himself. They looked human but stood motionless, giving away their robotic insides. Sensors continually watched everything within a hundred yards of their position within their human-like frame. Even walls could not prevent them from spotting danger. If anyone set foot on this floor without clearance, the androids would move into action. Just as he closed his eyes to rest them, Ms. Bradshaw called for him. Startled, Stan stood, trying to compose himself. Adrenaline sent his heart racing, so he shook off its effects and walked into the Supreme Commander's office.

"Good morning, Mr. Hill. I hope you have good news for me," Porter gestured toward a chair in front of his desk.

"I do, Sir. Alex has finally located the assassin's landing," Stan sat.

"Excellent," Porter pressed a button on his communications console. "Ms. Bradshaw, contact Vincent and have him here ASAP."

"Right away, Sir," she answered.

"Where did he go?" Porter inquired.

Stan retrieved a small holographic projector from his coat pocket and set it on his desk. A flip of a switch produced a three-dimensional image of the Earth. Stan made a few selections on the console and magnified the spot.

"He transported to an unpopulated mountain in the Alps, Switzerland."

Stan pointed to the display.

"We can transport an agent to within 100-yards of the assassin's landing, but that's as close as Alex can get."

"Interesting, he must be using their neutrality for refuge," Porter surmised.

"Agreed. You must be discrete."

As they talked, the door opened. Turning, Stan saw Vincent entering. In the background, he also saw two of the androids that guarded the Supreme Commander. One uncharacteristically moved its head. *That's odd.* Before Stan could voice his concern, the Supreme Commander started a conversation with Vincent.

"As I'm sure you've already guessed, I have an assignment for you."

"What is it?" quizzed Vincent.

"I want you to find the assassin who killed the Comptroller and bring him back for questioning."

"How do I identify him?"

"The intruder wore a mask, so there are no pictures. However, he did land in a remote area in Switzerland, which means he's either alone or part of a small group. If you find more than one, bring them all in. How you capture them is up to you, but I want them alive."

Vincent examined the display for a few moments, "I'll get my gear together and leave at once."

Stan stood as Vincent left, "I'll be returning home if you have no further need of me."

"Get some rest; you've earned it," Porter reached for the console. "Ms. Bradshaw, is Jared here yet?"

"No, Sir. The Governor of Texas summoned him to a meeting," she replied.

"Very well, let me know when he arrives," Porter disconnected the phone and smiled. Everything was going according to plan.

Chapter 59

Earth
The United States - Texas - Houston
May 11, 2452

Jared held a knapsack full of food, waiting for Tim to arrive in front of the hotel. It was early, so early that it was still dark. Their journey to the State Capitol Building would take about five hours, so they were up at dawn. Since they planned to travel through dangerous territory, Tim asked for a small National Guard convoy to escort them to Austin for protection. An invitation sent to Jared from Governor Gonzales spurred the trip. Hearing the squeak of a vehicle's front brakes, he turned and saw Tim approaching.

After Jared sat, Tim greeted him, "Good morning, Jared."

"It would have been nice if I could have slept in a little longer," Jared yawned.

"Sorry, but it's a long way between cities, and there's no way I would go without protection."

"Why couldn't we just fly there?"

"There isn't a city-to-city flight in Texas. The government reserves fuel for import and export only."

"She knows we're coming. I could get portal transport for us."

"As much as I would prefer it, Governor Gonzales could not allow it because it would violate the Portal Treaty of 2356. Also, any link to the Regime is political suicide."

Jared nodded, "Where do we meet up with them?"

"At the city limits on I-10."

"I haven't seen this SUV before."

"It's bulletproof. I told my boss I wouldn't travel without it."

"Good idea."

"I hope the Governor has some good news for us," Tim smiled optimistically.

"I only received an invitation; she didn't give an agenda. If she cooperates with us, this will go smoother and faster," Jared offered.

"With her history, it's unlikely. Even if she does, she'll ask a high price for her help."

"I know the Regime will do its best to give her what she wants if it's within reason," Jared assured.

"Good, we need this change. Things have declined so badly that we've become wards of our employers. In exchange for our labor, they feed and clothe us, give us a place to live, pay for our utilities and give us company scrip to buy items from stores they own, which keeps us from paying taxes on those items. The government has given us no other choice. It's the only way we can survive. Salaries have become outdated. Instead, we barter and trade. The government is aware of the loophole, so I don't know how much longer they'll allow it."

"If you're not paying taxes, who is?"

"Our employers. Only large corporations can afford the exorbitant taxes and survive, but even they see the writing on the wall. Every corporation is struggling, yet Governor Gonzales signs more bills that increase the taxes without fail. Everyone says she's never met a tax she didn't like."

"It's a sure way of destroying commerce."

"Even worse than the taxes are the limits they set on the amount of money a company can earn. If a business makes more than they allow, the government confiscates it. That law forced us to barter and trade to survive."

They arrived at the city's security wall, and Tim pulled beside the lead vehicle. They got out, and Jared showed security his invitation. Tim and Jared returned to their SUV. Moments later, the convoy started moving. They stopped several times during their trip because armed drifters attacked. Most of the outbreaks were lone snipers, hoping to disable a vehicle and use it for parts. There were a couple of attacks from small groups of renegade gang members, but the National Guard hunted the attackers and killed them before moving on.

With their help, Jared did not have to leave the comfort of the SUV once. Also, not using his armor prevented the deep hunger that followed. For that alone, he was grateful. They finally reached the State Capitol Building's parking lot six hours later. As Jared opened his door, Tim placed his hand on his arm.

"Be careful, Jared. We don't know why she invited you. Just remember, she's an intelligent person. I wouldn't be surprised if it were a trap."

"If it is, I'm getting ready to spring it," Jared smiled.

Jared climbed the front steps of the State Capitol and walked through the front door. He met a security detail that searched him for weapons. He emptied his pockets, and a guard scanned him. Before allowing him inside, the sentry asked him the reason for his visit. Jared retrieved his invitation and gave it to him; the guard pointed him in the direction of the governor's office. While walking the State Capitol Building halls, the lush carpet absorbed any noise his shoes would have made.

Classical music played in the background complementing the exquisite furniture, historical paintings, and antiques set about the hallway. A few minutes later, he reached the governor's office, gave his invitation to the assistant, and waited in the lobby. About ten minutes later, the door to her office opened. As her guest walked out, Jared recognized him as the Lieutenant Governor. Out of respect, Jared stood as he walked by. Turning, he saw Governor Gonzales standing in the doorway, smiling.

"Please come in."

Inside, he saw that the décor in her room exceeded that of anything in the hallway. A large, beautiful chandelier hung from the ceiling, giving off a soft light that caressed the whole room. A large oak desk sat near the west wall between two large windows. All kinds of elegant furniture sat strategically around the room, with historic paintings decorating every wall. As she walked away, his eyes followed her, but she did not sit behind her desk. Instead, she retrieved a manila folder and rested it on the front of her desk.

"Please, have a seat," she pointed to a chair while examining the folder's contents.

He studied her, hoping to set up a profile. His first impression was that she was more attractive than in her photo. Her hair was straight, black, and lengthier than her dossier showed. The ends stopped just below her shoulders. Her eyes were a rich brown, and her olive-colored skin was smooth with no blemish. He could only see the beginning signs of aging around her eyes from his seat. *You're between thirty-five and forty.*

She had a small frame, but her arms' muscle tone meant that she worked out, which her perfect posture revealed. *I bet there's a private gym in the adjoining room.* Jared's eyes moved up and down her body and did not ignore the tight-fitting white shirt with lace design and a tight gray skirt that stopped just above her knees. *You're proud of your body or clinging to your youth. A sign of desperation?* She read the folder's contents, set it on her desk, cleared her throat, and extended her hand for him to shake. During her greeting, he felt a firm grip. *You're competitive too.*

"I want to thank you for coming to meet me, Jared."

"You're welcome, Governor Gonzales. Although I must admit, I wasn't sure why you wanted to see me."

"Please, call me Sonya," she smiled pleasantly at him.

You are trying hard to make friends. "As you wish. Sonya, why did you call me here?"

"I have it on good authority that you're the man behind House Bill 10996."

"You mean the bill that will allow Texas to split into multiple states?"

Her smile widened, "Yes. That's the one."

"I thought Representative Hastings is supporting that bill?" Jared queried.

"Yes, he is, but he also gave me your name."

"I see."

"Let me be direct, Jared. Your bill doesn't have enough support to make it to my desk."

"You brought me here to brag?"

Sonya laughed softly, "No. I brought you here to make a deal."

"I don't understand. If the bill doesn't pass, you've won, so you don't need to make a deal with me."

"I have one year left in my second term. As you know, I cannot run again for another four years."

"You could always run for President."

Sonya chuckled loudly, "Run against my dad in his third term? You don't know just how ruthless he is."

"I can guess."

"Four years is a long time, and I'm not getting any younger."

"You're thirty-seven."

"How did you know?" she raised an eyebrow, surprised at his accuracy.

"You must be thirty to be governor. It is the third year of your second term. Your dad must have helped you get elected just as you turned thirty."

"Excellent, Jared. I'm impressed."

"You shouldn't be; it's simple math. What did you plan on doing in the four years you have off?"

"That's just it. The last seven years have been difficult. I've made some mistakes along the way."

"You mean like trying to take peoples' homes?"

Sonya smiled wryly, "Yes. I owed my dad for helping me win the governor's office, but my political debt to him cost us."

She paused. Jared thought she would cry until she regained her composure. Her dossier said that her husband died during a robbery, but Jared believed someone had killed him to keep the story behind what she and her dad did to the people of Texas from getting out. Sonya cleared her throat and continued.

"The reason I asked you here is: I know you will need help with getting this legislation passed. If it does, the President will veto it, which will give Texas legal grounds to secede, so you will need a new bill submitted so congress can vote on it, and the entire process could take years."

"I see you've figured out what we hope to accomplish."

"I know the President very well, Jared. He will not allow Texas to secede without a fight."

"We expect a fight."

"Yes, but fights can cost lots of money and, in many cases, lives."

"The business owners of Texas are willing to do whatever it takes to accomplish the mission."

She picked up the file from her desk and began reading, "Your name is Jared Stewart. You were born and raised in the Regime, and you are a member of the Inner Circle, where you became an agent. Now you're here in my state, pretending to be a Texas businessman," she paused to look at him with a raised eyebrow, "Sound familiar?"

Interesting. Her people have hacked our system and found the false dossier on me. Supreme Commander Porter will need to hear this. Turning, he looked at the door, expecting several armed officers to rush in and arrest him.

"Don't worry. I'm not going to arrest you. I brought you here to negotiate."

"Ok, so you know who I am and my employer. You obviously want something from the Regime. What is it?"

"I am willing to hand over Texas to the Regime. If on the day I sign the bill for secession into law, Porter guarantees *in writing,* with his Supreme Commander seal, that he will move me to the Regime, grant me citizenship and give me a bank account with a million Regime Talons."

"A million Regime Talons? That's equal to a billion U.S. dollars! Sheesh, you don't want much," he replied facetiously.

"I think it's a small price to pay for a state as big as Texas."

"I'll have to speak to Supreme Commander Porter first, but I'm sure there's room in the Immigration District for you."

"I'm afraid that's unacceptable. I want to live in the Inner Circle." She spread her hands apart, looking at her surroundings, "As you can see, I've become accustomed to a certain lifestyle."

"I can see the kind of lifestyle you're accustomed to, but I'm afraid it's impossible, outsiders are not permitted to live there, and even visitation is limited."

"The deal is off. Have a good day, Jared," she responded flatly, walked toward her chair, and sat behind her desk. Jared stayed seated. "Our meeting is over, Jared. You can leave now," she dismissed.

Inwardly, he sighed. This mission was vitally important, and he didn't want to fail. Now, Sonya just dangled a carrot in front of him. Although her demand for the Inner Circle residency would be out of the question, he had an idea she might accept.

"Perhaps a separate home could be built for you. You could design it exactly the way you want, and I could get you certain Inner Circle amenities."

"Sorry, not good enough."

Frustrated, he stood, "What you're asking for is impossible! Supreme Commander Porter will not allow it! He *can't* allow it! You need to work with me here! You said it was a negotiation! Negotiate! People's lives are at stake!"

His outburst was for her benefit, and he hoped it reached some small part of her humanity if she had any left. Besides, she still had not revealed her genuine desire. Moreover, the dossier proved she researched Regime law, which clearly states that Supreme Commander Porter could never honor her request.

"There is a way," she raised an eyebrow.

"There is?"

"Yes, if someone from the Inner Circle, let's say you, were to marry an outsider, let's say me, it would automatically make me a citizen of the Regime. Since you are an Inner Circle resident, I would be as well. Oh, and I want at least one child."

"Are you asking me to marry you?"

"Oh, don't look so sad," she smiled playfully, "I can be a lot of fun once you get to know me."

"Look, there are a lot of other men in the Inner Circle who would be happy to consider your offer. I can compose a list of backgrounds and photos and deliver them to you as early as tomorrow."

"I've already made my choice."

"Yeah, but you haven't even seen the list yet! Wouldn't you rather marry a movie star or CEO of a company? I'm sure I could arrange it."

"Oh, please… movie stars are so phony, and CEOs are more concerned about making money than forming intimate relationships, but you're different. I knew it the moment we met. There's a certain connection between us. Certainly, you've felt it too?"

Her statement took him completely off guard because he was not ready for this situation. Never would he think she would target him for a husband. Although she was attractive, he did not feel any connection to her. Yet, for the sake of the mission, he played along.

"Sure, I sensed something, but I thought it was your negotiation style, trying to distract me."

"I've used my charm for that in the past, but this is personal. I'm looking toward the future, and I would like to have you in it."

"Marriage *is* personal. What we're negotiating is business."

"Oh, please, Jared. Marriage is a business too. If it weren't, why do they make it a legal contract?"

"You truly know how to be romantic."

"I know you've never married. Your dossier was clear on that, so I know I'll be your first wife, hopefully, your last and only one."

"I've never been married because I'm only twenty-one."

"If it's our age difference you're worried about, I can assure you; I have many good years left."

"Sonya, you're sixteen years older than me."

"Yes, but we have so much in common!"

I must have Supreme Commander Porter rewrite that dossier.

"Look, I'm flattered, really I am, but I'm not interested in getting married, let alone being blackmailed."

"I realize I'm forward. I'm sure it seems like an ambush, and if circumstances were different and I had the time, I would be much subtler than I am now. I would take the time to play the traditional cat and mouse game with you, but life seldom gives us the time we need, so I must improvise."

Why do I get the feeling I'm the mouse in this scenario?

"How could you possibly think either of us would be happy in a relationship started by extortion?"

"This isn't extortion. I'm making you an offer. I have something you want. You have something I want. Hopefully, our desires will be the same."

"I've seen too many friends get caught up in a loveless marriage. I certainly have no intention of joining them."

"Why don't you take some time to think it over?" she paused and slowly, seductively, walked toward him, leaned over, and whispered in his ear, "While you're thinking, keep this in mind: I promise that if you agree to my proposition, you'll have romance and much more."

Gently, she kissed him on his cheek, which brought unexpected chills down his spine, making him cough nervously. It was not the first time a woman tried to seduce him, but for reasons unknown to him, he started to feel that connection she mentioned earlier, and it concerned him.

Is it her confidence, her style, or the way she talks? Admittedly, she has a certain je ne sais quoi, but is it worth the risk of getting personal with her? Seeing him waver, she seductively smiled and walked to the front of her desk. Jared found himself captivated by her every move. Stopping to face him, she caught him staring at her figure.

Embarrassed, he moved his gaze to the chandelier above. *That was smooth, Jared. I'm sure she missed you gawking at her ass.*

Sonya paused for a long time; when Jared did not respond, she faced him, "I'm calling a special session to vote on this bill in five days, so I'll know your answer if I haven't heard from you."

Jared cleared his throat, "I'll contact you after speaking to Supreme Commander Porter."

He tried unsuccessfully to keep his response emotionless, giving up any negotiation advantage, so he stood to leave with what little dignity he had left until Sonya walked in front of him. Looking down at her, he fixed on her beautiful, brown eyes that glared back at him, demanding his attention. There was a desire in them; Jared had seen that look before but never felt like this about someone. *Is this love? No, it can't be. I don't even know her. Is it infatuation? Whatever it is, it's frightening.*

Pushing herself up on her toes, she put her arms around his neck, pulled him close to her, and kissed him passionately. The move surprised him, and he stood frozen in place for the first few seconds until giving into her advance, returning her affection. They remained locked together until Sonya finally stepped back.

"That's a small sample of what you could have, what we could have together."

Her voice was soft and seductive as if it were a musical instrument. The silkiness of her tone excited him. His face was flush, his heart raced, and he felt warm to the point of perspiring. Now, he was worried. Compromised by his feelings, it precluded him from going any further on the mission. *My own emotions have betrayed me!* Upon returning, he would tell Supreme Commander Porter what happened and ask him to remove him from the assignment. He did not want to jeopardize the mission.

"I promise. I'll consider it carefully."

Gently, she took his hand and walked him to the door, "I hope we'll meet again."

He saw her eyes yearning for him. Reflexively, he smiled walking away, and at the corner, he looked back to see Sonya still standing in the doorway, smiling. *Why is she so happy?*

Chapter 60

Akil
Argi City
The 22,275[th] Terrestrial Rotation of the Second Summer

Outside Nayrah's apartment, Otsoa knocked for about a hundred heartbeats, but there was no answer. Now, he was more worried than ever. *Where could she be?* His timekeeper chimed; delaying his departure any longer would make him late for the train. Even so, Zorion would not leave without him, which was no comfort. For a few heartbeats, he considered running away. Going to another city and living like an ordinary citizen suddenly had appeal. *I could change my appearance. I have enough Sovereign Cubes to live for a long time without work.*

Any hope of leaving vanished because he knew that Zorion would never stop looking for him. To make matters worse, he did not have the potion Nayrah had given him, so a Screener or some random Akilian could find him and turn him in. It gave him chills to contemplate the possibility that Zorion would escort him to the Main Arena, under heavy guard in front of everyone who knew he had tried to run.

Every Akilian would know he was a coward, and even if he became the victor by chance, no one would let him live it down. *Public humiliation would be a fate worse than death. I have no choice.* He fought back tears and returned to the Sovereign's Level, where the train would take him to meet his doom.

Chapter 61

Earth
The Regime - Washington, D.C. - Fort McNair
May 11, 2452

Standing in his closet, Vincent removed two large bags, containing clothes for various occasions. *For this mission, I will need something warm. The snow-covered Alps will be cold, and since I don't know where the assassin went after he stepped through the event horizon, I must prepare for the worst.* He put on a warm coat and checked the small nuclear generator implanted in his chest. As a Special Agent, the Regime allowed him to choose an enhancement made possible by its Science Division.

Surgeons ran wires through his body using the laparoscopy procedure, making him an electronic weapon. The embellishment allowed him to release an electrical charge with his right hand, which could disintegrate a human being. In addition, he could create a shield strong enough to withstand almost any kind of bombardment with his left hand.

He confirmed that his implant was working correctly and headed for the supply room, where he signed out a Portable Vortex Transmitter and a utility belt, having several finger-sized electronic tools to help him with his search. He secured the devices and continued to the International Transportation Station, where the technician entered the coordinates. Seconds later, a portal opened before him, and a cold, crisp breeze blew through the event horizon, encircling his body. The smell of pine reminded him of home.

He walked through the portal and whispered, "Ready or not, here I come."

Chapter 62

Earth
Switzerland - Alpine region
May 11, 2452

Once clear of the portal, Vincent heard it close behind him. His landing left him at the base of a mountain near a lake. Due to the six-hour time difference, it was only a few hours away from sunset. Reaching into his utility belt, he retrieved a scanner and searched the area for any residual trace of a vortex. It led him to footprints that headed up the mountain.

The tracks started in the middle of a field, in the middle of nowhere, so he was confident they belonged to the assassin. Since the killer did not try to hide his route, Vincent could easily follow his trail but could not decide if the operative was careless or overconfident. *Either way, this murderer has no idea how viciously the Regime protects its technology.* He traversed the rough terrain and stopped for a break an hour later.

Vincent took out his binoculars and scanned the area. In the distance, he saw a cave and approached from the left side, stopping about a hundred feet before the opening. He found several security sensors secured within the rock near the door using his scanner. The binoculars allowed him to pinpoint their location visually. *Damn, wireless motion detectors. They will slow me down.*

He only knew of two ways to defeat it. First, walk toward it at a snail's pace. The downside was that it would take hours. Second, disrupt the frequency, so the sensors cannot alert the occupant. Choosing the latter, he held out both hands and directed power to each. His left hand produced an invisible buckler, and his right hand became fully charged. Using that power, he touched the shield giving it a steady stream of electricity.

They produced a high-pitched, disruptive signal inaudible to human ears. Vincent held out his hands and continued the energy stream, walking toward the entrance. He reached the door and powered down because he was out of the motion detector's sensor range. The cave entrance was dark, so he removed a finger-sized flashlight from his utility belt and saw a large, steel door blocking his path about five feet inside the cave opening. *No wonder you don't care if someone follows you.*

Holding the flashlight in his teeth, he used his scanner to look for a secondary security system. The device showed an electrical sensor on the door. Opening it without using the proper security protocols would break the circuit, setting off an alarm. Carefully, he examined the door. It was smooth all the way around. There was no effortless way to open it, and there were no handles or edges because it was set tightly into the rock wall of the cave.

Ok, Vincent, think like your prey. He's someone like you. How would you design this door? You would have to open it quickly if someone was chasing you, yet it would have to slow your pursuers up so you would have time to stage a defense. Using his scanner, he searched the surface of the surrounding wall. On the left side of the door, about eye height on the wall, he discovered an electronic touchpad hidden behind a false rock face.

The touchpad had twelve symbols, four across and three down, but the symbols meant nothing to him. He changed the scanner to a different setting and found that the occupant only touched five of them. *Now, what's the combination?* There were too many sequences to try each one. Add to the fact that if he got it wrong the first time, potentially all kinds of bells and whistles would announce his presence to whoever was inside. He stared at the pad until the answer came to him.

He removed his glove and hovered his hand a finger's width over the five symbols. *It can't be that simple.* Carefully, he lowered his hand, making sure all five fingers touched the pad simultaneously. The door clicked open. *Brilliant! If you are in a hurry to get in, you contact all five simultaneously. Someone following you will spend a hell of a long time figuring out which five you touched and in what order, giving you enough time to prepare a very hot welcome for them.*

He pushed the door open to a finger's width and inserted the tip of his scanner. It picked up energy signatures about fifteen feet on the other side of the door and about eight feet in the air. *It must be a camera.* Reaching to his side, he retrieved his weapon. He pushed the door open, aimed, and fired in one smooth motion. The bullet shattered the optical lens of the camera.

If anyone is watching, I will face resistance shortly. Vincent checked the room to make sure no one was in the vicinity. Satisfied it was clear, he closed the large steel door, pressed his back against the wall, and waited for an attack. No one came, so Vincent continued down the corridor and used his scanner to check for any internal security systems but found none. Upon finding a room, he stopped to clear it.

There were several along the way. Some were storage areas for food and clothing; others were supply closets. One was full of weapons, including four deactivated militarized robots. Their model number, C500, showed they were first-generation combatants, and they did not have human-like synthesized flesh used on androids because there was no need. Instead, they were metal skeletons, made to look as intimidating as they were deadly.

The adjacent room's light emanated from the space beneath the door at the end of the hallway. Standing at the entrance, Vincent faintly heard voices on the other side. Carefully and quietly, he retrieved a listening device from his utility belt, stuck it to the door, and began recording. Vincent inserted an endoscope through the gap at the bottom and discreetly scanned the room. The small, thumbnail-sized monitor showed an image of a man he presumed to be the assassin, sitting in front of a computer display.

Holstered in the small of his back was the latest .9mm automatic. The grip faced to the left. Since the man looked away from him, he could not see his face but did see a young woman somewhere in her mid-thirties on the video screen. Her hair had two tones, dark at the top and changing to blonde around her ears. A black jacket covered most of her torso, exposing only a small 'V' shape of an orange top underneath. With a stare that would make most men turn away, she glared at the man sitting before her. *There's no doubt she's serious.*

"Finally, you've returned my call," the man commented irritably.

Vincent recognized the mandarin accent.

"I've been busy, Dragon. You're not my only employee," she responded sternly.

Where have I heard that name before?

"I've completed the task, and I expect prompt payment," Dragon demanded.

"The Comptroller's death was supposed to look like he had a heart attack. Instead, you put a bullet through his head. Now, the Regime is aggressively looking for you. If they succeed, they can find me, and for that, you get half of what we agreed," the woman insisted.

"Unacceptable. There were cameras in his cell. They would have known his death was unnatural."

"I loaned you a PVT, which gave you unlimited access. You could have drugged his food in the kitchen."

"They were close to figuring everything out, so I had to act, or the Regime would be looking at your image from his memory right now, Dawn!"

"I don't accept your excuse. Now, I'm opening a small portal near you; toss the PVT through the event horizon, and I'll transfer your payment."

Vincent heard the faint sound of a vortex opening in the room, but Dragon did not return the PVT as expected, and Dawn became angry.

"The PVT is my property, Dragon. Return it, or else," she threatened.

Dragon chuckled, "What are you going to do?"

The PVT started beeping. Dragon removed the device from its denim bag and saw numbers counting from forty with every beep.

"You have thirty seconds to return it. If you don't, I'll close the portal. Ten seconds afterward, it will explode. You won't survive."

Watching the small screen from the endoscope, Vincent saw Dragon tapping the device with his fingers contemplating his next move. *What the hell are you doing? Return the damn thing before you kill us!*

"You're bluffing. You wouldn't destroy advanced technology like this."

"Ten seconds," she replied flatly.

Vincent's eyes widened. He counted down from ten, hoping the idiot in the other room did not call her bluff. Vincent opened the door to send the bag through himself with only five seconds remaining. Simultaneously, Dragon tossed it through the event horizon. The portal closed, and Dawn disengaged the self-destruct. Dragon reached over to disconnect their communication but stopped.

"I hope our little disagreement won't keep you from using my services in the future."

"You may not have one."

"Why do you say that?"

"Because the Regime has found you. Turn around," she advised and disconnected their communication.

Dragon spun in his seat when the monitor went black and saw Vincent standing in the doorway. Reflexively, he stood, grabbed his weapon, and fired. Although his fast reflexes engaged the shield, Vincent was a second too slow. The first shot nicked his left shoulder, but the buckler stopped the other bullets that followed. They ricocheted around the room, posing as much danger for Dragon as for him.

Realizing he was fighting a Regime special agent, Dragon lunged for a table near the monitor and grabbed a remote control. *Have fun with this, you son of a bitch.* He thumbed the switch, which activated his four militarized robots. Dragon continued to fire at Vincent as the C500s came alive in their storage room. In a short time, they were in the hallway, moving toward Vincent. Dragon stopped firing, smiled, turned, and ran.

Vincent was about to follow, but hearing servos in motion made him stop. Turning, he saw the C500s moving toward him. Their red eyes projected laser beams to sight their target. Looking down, he saw several red dots on his shirt. *Uh, oh.* Vincent raised his shield just as they unleashed a barrage of high-caliber bullets at him. The sound was deafening, and the projectiles' force drove Vincent backward into the room from where Dragon fled.

After about two minutes of continuous fire, they ran out of ammunition and brought their sound disrupters to bear on him. They made a high pitch whine as the capacitors built up a charge. Vincent added more power to reinforce his shield and waited for the attack. Moments later, the C500s released bone-crushing sound waves in sequence to cause the most damage. The buckler took the brunt of the blows, but the sheer force of the sound lifted him off the ground, slamming him hard against the wall, and held him there.

With their target pinned, the C500s moved forward for the kill. *I must end this, or I'll never catch Dragon.* He sent more power into the shield, braced himself against the wall, and directed a surge of energy to his left hand. The burst expanded his buckler rapidly. The concussive force of the expansion hit the C500s, knocking them over. Vincent stood, channeled power to his right hand, and unleashed a devastating blast of electricity.

Their alloy bodies shook from the voltage as their metal skeleton frame began to glow; the excessive heat melted them and shorted out their CPUs. He shut off the power to his right hand, and the C500s lay in an unrecognizable, hot, molten blob. With them out of the way, he headed in the same direction Dragon left. The back exit led to a platform and a tunnel with tracks. *Great. Hundreds of years ago, this must have been a ski station, which means this whole mountain might be hollow. Well, there's only one way down.*

There was a small, bubble-like vehicle parked on the rails, so he jumped in, pulled the glass cover down, and hit the accelerator. It took off, forcing him back against the seat. The lights on the tunnel's ceiling sped past him in a blur. A few minutes later, he entered another station with a platform. His vehicle came to a stop behind another, just like it.

He jumped out of the car and followed the hallway, which led him outside. *I'm on the other side of the mountain.* Nearby, he saw several Hover Snowmobiles lying on the ground but did not find the keys in them. *Don't think this is going to stop me, Dragon.* Using a cutting tool from his utility belt, he bypassed the vehicle's ignition system, which sprang to life. Now, all he had to do was figure out which direction Dragon took.

On the horizon, the sun was setting, just a hair's width above the top of the mountain. *It will be dark soon. There's nothing like a little pressure.* Using his binoculars, he scanned the area, but the forest gave Dragon perfect cover. He searched a little longer and saw some branches in the distance without snow. *That must be where he went.* Vincent revved the engine, kicked in first gear, and sped off in pursuit.

Chapter 63

Earth
The Regime - Washington, D.C. - Capitol Building
May 11, 2452

Supreme Commander Porter and his guests heard a commotion outside in the waiting room. He called for his assistant, and the doors to his office burst open, but one of the androids entered instead.

Supreme Commander Porter stood, "Seven-four-three-one, what is the problem?"

The android did not reply, so he told his guests to hurry behind his desk and hit the emergency button underneath it. A one-inch-thick transparent aluminum wall lowered to the floor, surrounding them. The android reached the barrier and began pummeling it. Again, Supreme Commander Porter called for Ms. Bradshaw but did not hear her answer.

"Seven-four-three-one, override command Echo-One-Alpha, shut down at once!" Supreme Commander Porter yelled.

The android continued to ignore his command, so he reached under his desk and pressed the distress alarm. *Help will be here soon.*

Chapter 64

Earth
The United States - Texas - Houston
May 11, 2452

Jared left Sonya, returned to his hotel room, sat on his bed, and replayed their conversation in his mind. Staring at the floor, he tried to figure out why Sonya could tempt him when others failed. He felt embarrassed and dreaded facing the Supreme Commander but had to give a report. Using his remote, Jared asked for passage home. Within seconds, a portal opened in his room, and he stepped through it.

"Welcome home, Jared," the technician remarked.

"Thanks, James," he replied, raising his hands so that James could scan him.

"All clear."

"Thanks."

Jared headed straight for the Supreme Commander's office, and his wristwatch vibrated. Its face flashed a Level One emergency code. Knowing the Supreme Commander was in danger, Jared ran toward his office and found Ms. Bradshaw on the floor, unconscious. He checked for a pulse. She was not in any immediate danger, so he moved toward the office door, where three androids blocked his path.

"Shut down, authorization Jared-six-four-nine-eight-one!" he yelled, but instead, the androids attacked.

"Ok, I guess we do this the hard way."

Adrenaline released the chemical in his body, making his skin an impenetrable barrier. The androids shot at him with their weapons, and the bullets ricocheted off his body. Jared worried that one might hit Ms. Bradshaw, so he ran toward them and jumped, throwing his body horizontally. His speed and weight were enough to knock them down, but he knew they would not stay there for long.

He got on his feet and headed for the android, hammering away at the transparent aluminum wall inside the office. Porter and the others stayed behind the wall, showing no signs of panic. Instead, he looked annoyed at the inconvenience as his guests cowered behind the desk. As Jared approached the android, it turned and hit him with its left fist, knocking him backward, and returned to hammering the barrier.

Again, Jared got up, as the other androids entered to keep him away from the one trying to break through the wall. Jared kicked and punched for several minutes, trying to reach their manual shut-off switch but failed. Even one on one, their strength and reflexes were superior to his, and facing three made it an impossible task. Finally, another special agent arrived named Oliver, a weapons specialist, and Jared prayed that he had something formidable in his arsenal.

"Distract the others, so I can stop the one hammering the wall!" Jared yelled.

Oliver nodded and tossed four ping-pong-sized orbs into the air. The spheres moved as Oliver directed them. *Now you're going to get it.* Each one housed a weapon, which Oliver controlled wirelessly through an implant in his brain. The spheres scattered throughout the room, about a foot below the ceiling. A powerful burst of energy shot from each of them at the androids.

The attack did not affect them, but it did get their attention. It was enough of a distraction to keep them occupied. Jared resumed his attack on the android, trying to break through Supreme Commander Porter's enclosure. He charged at his target and heard other androids shooting at Oliver's orbs. Jared leveled out his body and slammed into its midsection, knocking it down. He reached for the manual shut-off switch at the base of its skull; its metal hand stopped him.

By sheer mechanical strength, the android kept a firm grip on Jared's hand as it grabbed his belt with the other and pushed Jared off, sending him flying toward the wall. His skin protected him, and he got up.

"Focus all four spheres on one android for two rounds!" Jared yelled.

Oliver nodded, aimed the spheres toward the closest android, and targeted its optical sensors. Smoke poured from its head, and sparks shot out of its mechanical eye sockets, taking it out of the fight; the small victory came with a price. Oliver had focused on one android, but it gave the other two enough time to zero in on one of the spheres. They shot it down, leaving Oliver with only three.

Jared continued to kick and punch the one still trying to take down the protective wall, while Oliver used the remaining three orbs to keep the other two androids occupied.

Jared found the manual shut-off switch and flipped it, but it did not turn off the android.

"What the hell happened to all their safety protocols?"

"I don't know. Where the hell is Vincent?" Oliver yelled.

Chapter 65

Akil
Argi City
The 22,275[th] Terrestrial Rotation of the Second Summer

Just outside his carriage, Zorion waited for Otsoa to arrive on the platform. He gave his full attention to the hand-held information device Shilda gave him earlier. Unable to leave without Otsoa, he began working on it. In his peripheral vision, he saw someone approaching; it was Olan.

"I am surprised to see you. Shilda told me that Broll blocked off the whole level." Olan did not respond, so Zorion continued, "I sent you a message. I guess you did not get it. I do not have time right now, but you will be the first I see once I return. I promise."

Ignoring his comments, Olan kept approaching and growled, "You will fit me in now."

"What is wrong, my friend? Why are you so upset?" Zorion asked, seeing his angry mood.

He also saw a look of confusion in his eyes, and without another word, Olan attacked with the blade Nayrah gave him. Before Zorion knew what hit him, Olan plunged it into his chest. Sudden pain and shortness of breath made him gasp. He tried to cry out, but it came out as a faint whisper; Olan repeatedly stabbed him until the pain overwhelmed him. Zorion still noticed that Olan appeared dismayed by his actions. It was as if he could not believe the attack was happening either.

Shafe, posing as Molo, was on duty nearby. His post kept his line of sight focused away from the attack, but in his peripheral vision, he saw Olan stabbing Zorion. Without turning his head, Shafe froze, not knowing what to do. If Elzer ordered another to attack and he interfered, Elzer would punish him. If someone else was attacking him for other reasons, and Shafe interfered, Elzer might still punish him for being stupid.

Knowing the security monitors would show that the event was out of his line of sight, he kept his face forward. Since Zorion did not scream for help, Shafe would use his silence as an excuse. Shafe did not move until the siren sounded, believing that the best action to take was no action. When that happened, everyone had to move, including him. He ran to Zorion's position and was first on the scene.

By the time he arrived, Zorion was lying in a puddle of his blood. Olan was still kneeling over him, with his knife raised to strike again. Before he could, Shafe threw himself at him from behind and grabbed his wrist. The two struggled for a few heartbeats, but Olan got the better of Shafe and flipped him onto his back, slashing at him with the short blade, putting the dagger between Shafe's armor, and cutting him underneath his left arm.

Shafe grabbed the knife and removed it; Olan stood and unsheathed his sword. Shafe rolled away and stood, drawing his weapon. Olan attacked first, and the two combatants fought fiercely. Although injured, Shafe took the initiative to drive back Olan, keeping him on the defensive. However, Olan was no mere guard; he was the Chief Administrator of Argi's Intelligence Department. To reach that position, one had to be the best at everything, and he was.

Those skills allowed Olan to turn the fight around and put Shafe on the defensive, driving him backward until reaching a wall. Now, Shafe had nowhere to turn. In this battle, Olan's victory would mean his death, so in a desperate move, Shafe responded wildly. It was not pretty, but it was enough to make Olan take two steps back. The moment he had the advantage, it disappeared.

Pain shot up Shafe's arm as Olan snapped his wrist, disarming him, a move Shafe had never seen before. The sound of his sword dancing on the ground made Shafe sick to his stomach. It was as if it mocked him. The moment Olan raised his sword, he knew his life was over. He closed his eyes, not wanting to see the end come, and as he waited for the final blow, time seemed to slow down. The last few heartbeats of his life were dragging out, and it tormented him.

There was enough time to contemplate what it might feel like to lose his head. Would he feel pain as the blade cut through flesh and bone? Instead, Shafe felt a sharp pain in an unexpected place, his chest. He opened his eyes and saw Olan's face, frozen in an expression of shock. Shafe looked down and saw the sword still in Olan's hand but turned to the side. To his surprise, there was another blade that penetrated his chest.

As his eyes followed it, he saw that it originated from Olan's upper torso. He looked at Olan quizzically until he saw Broll and several other guards standing behind him, which made sense. His fight with Olan distracted him until the others arrived to stop him; he unexpectedly felt a tug, which could only mean one thing: Broll was pulling the blade out. *Oh, no. It is going to hurt.*

With a quick pull, Broll removed the blade from both bodies. Shafe collapsed to the ground. Although he tried to stay awake, his wound was too severe. Within a few heartbeats, everything went black. Olan, on the other hand, fell to his knees. Before he could react, Broll kicked his weapon out of reach.

"I should remove your head, but I am sure Zorion will want to interrogate you first," Broll whispered into his right ear.

Olan succumbed to his injury and blacked out. The sentries, who came with Broll, bound Olan's hands and feet and carried him away. Having apprehended the culprit, Broll searched for Zorion but could not find him. Instead, he saw aides at the scene, sopping up his blood with their distinctive yellow rehabilitation towels. *They have taken him to a Recovery Station.* Several stations were on the elite level; he knew they would take him to the closest one, so he ran to the nearest one.

"Where is he?"

An attendant pointed toward the adjoining room, where caretakers frantically worked on Zorion. They cut his coat and shirt off and applied pressure to his wounds, which were still bleeding. Zorion had many lesions, making it hard to see an area on his torso that Olan did not cut. Due to the enormous blood loss, Zorion's skin was pale, like the dead. Footsteps coming toward the front door of the station caught Broll's attention. He saw stewards carrying the blood-soaked rehabilitation towels in a container where Olan attacked Zorion.

"Hurry! Lay them on his stomach," one of the bedside attendants ordered.

In his line of work, Broll saw this scene play out many times; the caretakers gathered the victim's blood within the towels, which they placed on their belly, so the skin could absorb it back into their body and use it to generate more. However, with so many gashes, it would take a few hundred heartbeats for them to close. Plus, he would need moss and water to make a full recovery.

"He is awake," one of the stewards shouted.

Pushing them out of the way, Broll moved beside him. Zorion could not talk but nodded, letting Broll know he was all right. Thea came running into the room.

"They just told me what happened. Is Zorion alive?"

"Yes, he survived," Broll replied.

Thea hid her disappointment because they might suspect her involvement, so she faced Broll.

"Where were you during the attack?"

"He sent me to manage a situation at the security post," Broll ignored her hidden accusation.

"You should have never left his side," she spat.

In his peripheral vision, he saw Zorion roll his eyes. It was his signal to *get rid of her*. Moving from Zorion's side, he took Thea's arm, turned her around, and guided her out of the station. She protested the entire way.

Chapter 66

Earth
Switzerland - Alpine region
May 11, 2452

Sitting on the hover snowmobile, Vincent dashed through the forest and accelerated the small jet engines to their top speed, causing his adrenaline to spike; one little mistake could end his life. The trail took him up the mountain, where the temperature dropped quickly. The frigid temperature made his eyes water without goggles and burned his cheeks. He followed the thinnest of trails and often spotted branches without snow, signifying that something or someone had recently passed. He hoped it was Dragon.

Why would he lead me up the mountainside? Moving beyond the edge of the tree line, he drove out of the mountain's shadow into the sunlight and stopped. *Come on. Where are you?* He aggressively searched but did not see him. *I'm not giving up.* Vincent spotted a small black dot cresting a ridge several hundred feet above him. *That must be him.* He opened the throttle and the hover snowmobile shot forward like a rocket.

In less than twenty seconds, the speedometer read 150 mph. The hovercraft could easily follow the ground's contours beneath it at a lower speed, and at the vehicle's fastest pace, it was like being on a small boat during a storm. The machine bucked beneath him. Everything, except for the ridge ahead of him, was a blur. Upon reaching the last known position of the other hover snowmobile, he stopped to search again.

He saw him disappear behind a large boulder covered with snow. *I'm catching up!* Rather than going around it, he decided to go over; it was a risky move, but he needed to get closer. Vincent crested the top of the boulder and discovered, much too late, that there was a considerable drop on the other side. The hover snowmobile started to descend rapidly. During the fall, he cut off the engine.

Vincent moved his weight to the back of the vehicle and pulled up on the handlebars. He turned the bike vertically with his feet on the back footpegs, facing the rear engines toward the ground and turning on the jets. The engine's torque almost tore the handlebars from his grip, but Vincent held on for his life. While falling, he looked below, hoping to find Dragon.

As he neared the ground, Dragon unwittingly moved directly beneath him. Hearing the jets, Dragon looked up, just in time to see Vincent falling toward him. There was no time to shoot, so he dropped his gun, grabbed the throttle, and sped off. Seconds later, Vincent touched down. It was a near miss, and Dragon cursed himself for being careless. Although the jets were powerful enough to counter a fall, he started them too late. He came down too fast, and the hover snowmobile slammed into the ground, damaging one of the hover jets.

It bounced several times before he could level the bike, leaving one of six hover jets disabled, so the snowmobile's left rear leaned toward the ground. Still, the rest kept him afloat. Again, he opened the thrusters to their full power, and now he was within a hundred feet of his target but felt his wristwatch vibrate. He saw a flashing Level One emergency signal on the small screen. *The Supreme Commander is in trouble!*

His orders were clear. Return to Regime Headquarters at once! *I can't; I'm too close!* He knew other agents would respond to the call and decided to continue his pursuit, hoping they would help until he could join them. Dragon tried to evade Vincent by taking them back down the mountain into the valley's wooded area. Both riders had to continually sway from side to side to avoid hitting tree trunks, but sometimes they could not prevent the limbs and vines from smacking them, speeding through the thicket.

Dragon turned his vehicle onto a large stream that flowed between the mountains. They were moving so fast that water sprayed fifty feet into the air behind them. For Vincent, the shower behind Dragon's vehicle made it difficult to see, so he swerved to Dragon's right flank. Dragon saw him move over and did too, using the water as a deterrent.

Taking a chance, Vincent retrieved his sidearm and repeatedly fired at Dragon. He found it exceptionally difficult to aim as they continued to swerve. Vincent had emptied the gun of its ammunition and decided to direct power to his right hand, hoping to disable Dragon's vehicle. As they glided across the stream, he released the electricity from within the capacitor implanted in his body, but tongues of energy went straight to the water, arcing downwards from his hand into the stream below. *Damn it*! Dragon turned his head; Vincent saw him smirk. *You're going down for that!*

Seeing the spray was not enough of a deterrent, Dragon headed back up the mountain. As they climbed higher and higher, Vincent gained on him. Ahead, Vincent saw they were about to run into the side of an extremely high cliff. If they did not slow down, they would die. Vincent reduced his speed, preparing to stop, but Dragon moved forward. Before careening into the mountain, Dragon pulled up on the handlebars and hit the throttle.

His hover snowmobile started ascending beside the cliff. Seeing the maneuver, Vincent duplicated it and followed. The vehicle's jets whined as he climbed straight up the side of the cliff in pursuit. It was clear that Dragon had practiced the move before because his vehicle did not waver. Having never done it, Vincent almost collided with the mountain. It took all his focus to balance his weight, ascending. Leaning too far back would make him fall off, and leaning too far forward would make him crash into the side of the cliff. *He makes it look easy.*

Dragon reached the top of the cliff before Vincent, who arrived moments later. Vincent saw Dragon smiling on his snowmobile, hovering on a ledge nearby. It was not until looking down that Vincent realized they were at the top of the mountain. Deep snow covered everything around them. Playfully, Dragon held his forefinger to his lips, making a shush expression. *He's toying with me, which means it's a trap.* At the top, Vincent could only hear the wind whipping around him.

Vincent felt his wristwatch vibrate. *Not again. I'm sorry, but I don't have time to call home. They'll have to wait.* Returning his focus to Dragon, Vincent saw him holding a switch in his left hand and his thumb pressed down. Vincent heard the dull crack of a buried explosive charge rumble from within the snow beneath him. *Oh, no.* Tons of snow detached from the face of the cliff, starting an avalanche.

Unexpectedly, Dragon pulled back on his snowmobile handlebars, accelerated the rear engines, and shot over the disintegrating ledge, using the falling snow as a base for his hovering jets. Vincent followed, and his stomach lurched, going over the side. At first, it was like free-falling, but he realized his mistake. The snow was swirling around him, making it impossible to see. He had to get out in front of the snow to stay alive, like big wave surfing.

Like staying in the curl, he had to get to where the bow wave of the snowfall was pushing him forward. Staying where he was would suck him back into the avalanche proper and bury him where no one would find him until summer, so Vincent opened the throttle and prayed that there was nothing in front of him. Seconds later, he broke through the front of the swirling snow and saw Dragon only a few yards ahead.

The roar of the avalanche covered any sounds his hover snowmobile made. Dragon focused on outracing the white wall of destruction that his explosive charges released. *I must get close enough to open a portal and deliver him right into Supreme Commander Porter's lap.* At this speed, Vincent realized that they had to be on the same snowmobile for his plan to work.

Dragon remained preoccupied with his survival and did not notice Vincent creeping closer behind him. Vincent looked ahead. The avalanche approached a series of gorges that would channel the snow, like several funnels lying side by side. When the snowfall hits those gorges, it would react like water going through a high-pressure hose. They would condense the energy of the avalanche from a broad front into those smaller openings.

If I line myself up directly behind him, the force of the snow should catapult me forward. He throttled back until feeling the concussive wave of the avalanche teasing at his back. As they entered the center gorge, the blast shot Vincent forward as if take-off rockets pushed him ahead. His vehicle caught up with Dragon's, so Vincent jumped onto his hover snowmobile. The move caught Dragon by surprise, causing him to lose control for a moment.

He regained command of the snowmobile and swayed from side to side, trying to rid himself of his unwanted passenger. Dragon tipped, weaved, and threw several elbow punches at Vincent's head. Still, Vincent held on with purpose. During their struggle, Vincent built up a low voltage charge in his capacitor, put his right hand on Dragon's neck, and released it. Dragon slumped forward, and Vincent leaned over him to grab the controls.

Below the gorge, their descent became almost vertical. Vincent had to use all his focus on maneuvering the snowmobile to keep the avalanche from overtaking them. Dragon regained consciousness and head-butted Vincent during the distraction, stunning him long enough for Dragon to leap off the snowmobile. Vincent grabbed the controls and swore under his breath. Turning, he saw Dragon tumbling down the slope. Dragon grabbed his wrist with his right hand before the rolling wave of snow and rocks swallowed him; a portal opened in his path, and he disappeared into it.

"Damn it! I lost him!" Vincent yelled.

Again, his wristwatch vibrated, flashing Level One emergency, so with no quarry to catch, he set his destination on the PVT and opened a portal directly to Supreme Commander Porter's office. Vincent pulled the nose of the snowmobile up and passed through the event horizon in a near-vertical attitude. On the other side, he flew into one of the androids that guarded the Supreme Commander, pinned it to the wall, and crushed it.

"It's good of you to join us," Jared quipped.

"Sorry, I was in the middle of something important," Vincent replied.

"Will you please stop talking and put these damn androids down!" Oliver yelled.

Programmed with the knowledge of Vincent's ability, the three remaining androids moved to attack him. Vincent built up enough power to stop them. As they rushed at him, he raised his right hand, pointed forward, and released a massive current in their direction. Tongues of electricity danced about their metal bodies until they melted. Only after they collapsed to the ground did Vincent turn off the power. They all stared at the metal corpses as smoke rose from their lifeless, alloyed bodies.

With all the androids disabled, Supreme Commander Porter raised the transparent aluminum wall and contacted the hospital to help Ms. Bradshaw and his guests. Jay apologized, escorted them out into the lobby, and waited with them until the paramedics arrived. Supreme Commander Porter returned to his desk, contacted Adam Rothwell, his lead electrical engineer, and ordered him to assemble a team to determine why the androids malfunctioned. He disconnected, walked in front of his desk, leaned against it, and faced Vincent.

"Now, shall we discuss your tardiness?"

"I was in pursuit of the assassin," defended Vincent.

Supreme Commander Porter searched the room, "I don't see him."

"He disappeared into a vortex as we were falling down the side of a mountain."

"He had a PVT?"

"He did, but he already returned it to his employer, a woman named Dawn," Vincent answered.

"Dawn?" Porter asked.

"Yes. I only got her first name, but I did see her face."

"Without a PVT, how did he open a vortex?"

"He activated something on his wrist. He must have sent Dawn his location because moments later, a portal opened for him."

"Opening a vortex for a moving target isn't easy," Porter surmised.

"It was a hell of a maneuver."

"Every device in our inventory is accounted for, which means Dawn has the schematics and the resources to build a PVT and a Portal machine."

"She could have only gotten the schematics from us."

"Agreed. We have a traitor in our midst."

"I'll have a composite made and start looking for her using our facial recognition software."

"Good. Once you activate that application, I want you to trace the portal she opened. It will lead you to her International Transportation Station. Find it and ensure you get all copies of the schematics and destroy all her technology."

"My knowledge of portal machinery is limited to the use of my PVT. I'll need to consult with a professional to trace it."

"Speak with Alex Sutton. He can help you track Dragon's landing. Now get cleaned up and change into something less arctic."

As Vincent left, Supreme Commander Porter followed him into the lobby to check with the paramedics. They had Ms. Bradshaw and several of his guests on gurneys. He held her hand before they wheeled her out.

"You'll be fine. Don't worry."

He shook Oliver's hand, "Thank you for responding so quickly. Now, go clean up, eat, and report to Debriefing. I want Adam to have a full description of everything you saw and experienced."

"Yes, Sir," Oliver replied.

A few moments later, Porter faced Jared and pointed to a chair, "How are things in Texas?"

Jared picked it up, turned it over, and sat. Supreme Commander Porter returned to his position behind the desk.

"I met with Governor Sonya Gonzales today. She made an offer."

"Interesting, what was it?" he inquired.

Jay removed a water bottle from his refrigerator and poured some into a glass.

"Texas."

"I see," Supreme Commander Porter raised an eyebrow. "And what does she want in return."

"Before signing the bill for secession into law, she wants a written contract with the Supreme Commander's Seal, guaranteeing you will move her to the Regime, grant her citizenship, and an account with a million Regime Talons."

"Sounds reasonable."

"She also wants to live in the Inner Circle."

Supreme Commander Porter sipped his water, "Hmm, that does pose a problem. I assume she knows that we don't allow outsiders to live here. Even I can't permit it."

"Yes. She's aware of the law, so she insisted that I marry her."

Supreme Commander Porter's poker face almost slipped, "Please explain."

"She insists on living in the Inner Circle. She knows the only way we would allow it is if a Regime citizen marries her."

"Are you saying that she has chosen you?"

"I've offered to compose a list of eligible bachelors, but she seems to have made up her mind."

Supreme Commander Porter gently set his water bottle on his desk, "She seems too eager. Why would the daughter of the President of the United States want to live here? There are luxuries within the Immigration Districts that would satisfy her."

"She didn't say but did insist on having at least one child with me."

Supreme Commander Porter almost lost it. He wanted to laugh. Jared's timing was perfect. Even more hilarious was that the young man was so serious about the whole thing. *If only he could see the humor in the situation.*

"You don't have to do this, Jared. I would never insist you make such a sacrifice."

"I appreciate it, Sir, but millions of lives could be lost if I don't."

"What do you want to do?"

"I don't know. I can't explain why she's trying to strong-arm me into marriage. It doesn't make sense because she's attractive enough to find someone on her own. She only has a year left as governor, leaving her the choice of fighting us until next year when she can return to California, which means she doesn't need to come here."

"I suspect she has a hidden agenda."

"Should I tell her no?"

"There is an old saying, *keep your friends close and your enemies closer.*"

"That means I'll be sleeping with the enemy and having children with her."

Porter paused briefly, suppressing another laugh, "I understand your feelings on this matter, so I will not insist that you move forward with her offer if you don't feel comfortable with it. We can continue on our current path, and Texas *will* secede."

"If I don't accept her proposal, she will make it difficult and costly for us. She was clear on that."

"War is always difficult and costly."

"If I accept her offer, I suggest you assign another agent to watch her. I can't remain objective."

"Does this mean you *like* her?"

"I can't explain it. Sonya has a certain appeal, making it impossible for me to read her."

"You're on a first-name basis with her already?"

"She's making it personal, so yes."

"I'm sure I can find someone to watch over both of you."

Jared sighed, "I was afraid you were going to say that. Where would we stay?"

"I would set you up in the cottage near the water."

Jared frowned, "You mean the one with all the bugs and cameras?"

"I promise that whatever our techs record will be in the strictest confidence. Even I won't watch it unless it pertains to national security."

Just what I always wanted: to have my private life recorded and distributed for scrutiny. Jared furrowed his eyebrows, contemplating his future.

Supreme Commander Porter smiled sympathetically, "Remember, the decision is entirely up to you. Just say the word, and I'll replace you with another agent. You will never have to think about Texas or Sonya again."

"I appreciate your understanding, but too many lives are at stake. Besides, if she's planning something, I want to know what it is."

"Agreed."

"I'll go back to Texas and tell her," Jared sluggishly stood as if Supreme Commander Porter had punished him.

"I don't want you to return to Texas just yet," Supreme Commander Porter stood.

Jared turned to face him, "Why? What's wrong?"

"You've had a long day, and Texas can wait, so I want you to get something to eat, go home and get some rest. There's another project I need your help with tomorrow."

"I could use a good night's sleep. I'll see you tomorrow," Jared nodded and left.

When Supreme Commander Porter was sure no one could hear him, he had a full-out belly laugh at Jared's expense.

Chapter 67

Akil
Argi City
The 22,275[th] Terrestrial Rotation of the Second Summer

Otsoa passed through the security post, and two guards met him.

"We are here to escort you to the train," one guard remarked.

"I do not need an escort; Broll has sealed off the whole level," Otsoa replied.

"Yes, you do. Someone attacked Zorion," the guard said.

Otsoa worked hard to hide his excitement, so he acted concerned, "Is he dead?"

"I do not know. Our orders are to take you directly to the train," the guard answered.

Otsoa walked quickly and upon reaching the station, he saw the bloodstain on the avenue and moved over for a closer look. *It looks like Zorion spilled a great deal of blood here. He cannot still be alive. Nayrah, I do not know how you did it, but thank you!* He would now play the role of the grieving heir; it was a small price to pay to become Argi's sovereign. *I will make many changes. My first order will have the scientists figure out the right formula to bring Yanamai's memories back.* He saw Thea approaching. Her face showed grief, so he thought Zorion must be dead.

"I heard the news. I am sorry for your loss," Otsoa pretended to lament.

"He is not dead," she replied flatly.

"What? How? The amount of blood on the walkway looks like there was a beheading!" Otsoa exclaimed, unable to believe his ears.

"His injuries were only to the torso."

"Where is he?"

"He is at a Recovery Station. He should be on his feet within a few hundred heartbeats."

"That means…"

"You should get on the train and prepare to fight."

Unconsciously, she placed her hand on his shoulder, relaying her sympathy. Without another word, Otsoa headed for the front carriage. Again, he briefly had hope, and again some invisible force ripped that hope away from him. Now, he had to face Tuso and fight to the death.

A quarter of a Terrestrial Revolution later, Zorion moved around and soon had the strength to sit. The caretakers gave him plenty of food and water, which he ate and drank hurriedly. Soon, he had the strength to stand. The attendants removed the rehabilitation towels, wiped the dried blood from his skin, cleaned him thoroughly, and presented him with a new wardrobe. Having recovered partially, Zorion dressed and headed for the train again. Broll walked by his side.

"This is not your fault," Zorion offered.

"I am your Chief Administrator of Security. Whose fault is it, if not mine?"

"I ordered you to leave. The fault lies with me."

"What I do not understand is how he got into the station. I had every entrance blocked, and I gave specific instructions that they should not allow anyone, including Olan, on this level."

"Perhaps he managed to trick a guard."

"Or bribe one."

When they reached the train, Zorion looked at the pavement where Olan had attacked him. The surface still had stains from his blood. He looked around for a few heartbeats and saw the hand-held information device Shilda had given him earlier. He walked over and picked it up; there was no blood. Zorion fussed with it to see if it still worked.

"I am sure your team will figure it out, but I need to get to the Main Arena right now."

Using his communicator, he contacted Shilda.

"Please inform the other sovereigns that I will be late. I will explain later."

"Of course, Sir. Is everything all right?" Shilda inquired.

"Yes. Just tell them," he disconnected and turned off the device.

"Are Thea and Otsoa on the train?" Zorion asked a nearby guard.

"Yes, Sir," the guard answered.

"We better get going."

Zorion, Broll, and eight guards climbed aboard the train. Usually, Zorion complained about the number of escorts, but now he welcomed their presence after what just happened. As he settled into his chair, the train left the station. Broll sat across from him and kept an eye on the guards, who stood at the two exits.

Zorion continued to work and glanced up at Broll, "There was something peculiar about Olan."

"Aside from the fact he tried to kill you?" Broll inquired sarcastically.

"Yes. It seemed as if he were struggling within himself."

"He did not struggle hard enough if you ask me. You should have seen your injuries."

"Yes, but he did not kill me. He had the opportunity. His surprise attack had me subdued within moments. All he had to do was sever my head, and it would have been all over."

"You should ask him later."

"Agreed. I suspect he did not act alone," Zorion surmised.

"Tell me who his accomplice is, and I will arrest him or her at once."

"I do not have any proof."

"That is not a problem: he or she can simply disappear," Broll whispered.

"I appreciate your enthusiasm, but no one will ever trust me if I step across that line. You know that. Besides, I could not live with myself if I later discovered I was wrong."

"You should add it to your list of questions."

"I know this may sound odd and perhaps even a little crazy; I believe there are powerful forces at work here."

"Forces? You mean the children of Gau, Skeans, Saiphs, and all that nonsense?"

"I know it sounds crazy, yet I have seen some strange things lately," Zorion stopped before finishing.

"What have you seen?"

"Never mind. We will talk about this later. I have work to do," he returned to the hand-held information device.

Chapter 68

Earth
The United States - Texas - Houston - Western Farmland - Burke Home
May 11, 2452

Sitting at the kitchen table, Larkin fidgeted from the pain in his left arm. It was still sore from General Bailey's chastening the night before. Sarah paced, obviously unable to hide the stress of waiting for Dr. Grant to finish testing Sable in the living room. Not knowing why Sable was having nightmares was troubling, and her imagination ran wild.

"You can come in now," Dr. Grant remarked.

Larkin stood, but Sarah was through the door first. Two seconds later, he was standing beside her, facing Dr. Grant.

"Well?" Sarah demanded.

"Sable is a smart, well-adjusted, six-year-old girl."

"I know that already, Dr. Grant. I want to know what's wrong with my daughter," Sarah snapped.

Dr. Grant faced Sable and smiled, "There's nothing wrong with you, Sable."

Sarah blushed, realizing her mistake, "That's right, dear. Mommy doesn't think there's anything wrong with you. I meant to ask what was causing your nightmares."

"Larkin, why don't you take Sable outside for a walk, and I will speak with Sarah?" Dr. Grant suggested.

Larkin took Sable's hand, "Come on, Darlin'. Let's go for a walk."

"Ok, daddy," Sable jumped up from the couch, and they headed out the front door.

"Ok, they're gone. Now tell me why my baby is having these horrible dreams!"

"Ms. Burke, please try to calm down. Children can sense if a parent is distressed, and your actions could add to whatever is causing them."

"So, you don't know?" she asked, exasperated.

"I told you that I would do my best, but you must remember, I'm not a psychiatrist; I'm a general physician. Last night, I spent a few hours talking with an old colleague named Dr. Shaw, who has an office in Florida. He sent some questions to ask her and gave me some guidelines to follow."

"And?"

"She passed each one. There's no evidence of any recent trauma in her life, physically and mentally. My conversation with her showed that she's normal."

"These dreams of hers are vivid. She sees a man hurting us."

"Yes, I put her in a light trance to keep her relaxed, and she explained it to me. She sees a man wearing a military uniform but is too young to give a good description of the man's face."

"Almost everyone around here wears a military uniform."

"What about Sergeant Burke? He's a large man. Does he sometimes scare her, even if only by accident?"

Sarah shook her head vehemently, "No, he's gentle with her. We've only had to punish her a few times, and I was the one who did it, not Larkin."

"Is there anyone she's in contact with who may be frightening her? Maybe a playmate's parent?"

"No, after school, I bring her straight home, and she has a female teacher. Unless you think someone is lurking around the school?"

"Anything is possible. I'll speak to her teacher tomorrow."

"I'll speak to my dad tonight. By tomorrow I guarantee there'll be someone watching the school grounds."

"Until we can find the reason for her dreams, I don't see anything wrong with it but ensure he keeps a low profile."

"I will. Do you have any idea what's causing her nightmares?"

"No. It's normal for children between three and six to have nightmares. It's the time when their normal fears are developing, and it happens at the same time their imagination is highly active."

"Is it possible that her imagination is getting the best of her?"

"Anything is possible. Usually, children dream of spiders crawling on them or snakes biting them, but Sable's dreams are unnerving for someone her age. That's why I'm trying to find out if she has any stresses in her life, which could likely be fueling the dreams.”

“I’ve never seen her upset. I mean, her demeanor around you is the way she is all the time.”

“It could be that she’s beginning to understand what her dad does for a living and that danger is showing up in her dreams.”

“I guess that’s possible, but it’s not about him; it’s about us.”

“It may be transference.”

Sarah sighed, “Any ideas on how to prevent her from having anymore?”

“There’s nothing definitive. The mind is strong yet easy to manipulate into doing what we want it to do. I know this will sound primitive, but some cultures do things they believe in keeping “spirits” or “evil” away. For example, try putting a glass of water on the night table beside her bed.”

“Really? A glass of water?”

“Do you help Sable say her prayers before bed?”

“I used to, but she wanted to do them on her own.”

“I would suggest helping her again. Try to find creative ways to keep the nightmares away. You could even make a game out of it and create a specific action to keep the bad dreams at bay.”

Sarah nodded, “I’ll try.”

Dr. Grant gathered his things and stood, “There is something else you might want to try if Sable is up to the task.”

“What is it?”

“With all the new equipment we’ve been getting, I ran across an application that will create a person’s face, like a computerized sketch artist. Perhaps if she can describe the man’s appearance, we might be able to identify him.”

“I’ll speak to my dad about getting it. Thank you.”

“You’re welcome, Ms. Burke. I hope my advice will help.”

“I’ll let you know.”

Dr. Grant left, and moments later, Larkin returned, “What did he say?”

“He doesn’t know the cause, but I have a few things I can try to help prevent them.”

She caressed her daughter’s cheek, “Would you like mommy to say your prayers with you tonight?”

Sable nodded, and Sarah faced Larkin, "I'll stay with her until she falls asleep."

"Ok. Let me know if there's anything I can do." He looked at his watch, "I need to get going; it'll be dark soon."

Sarah stepped on her tiptoes, kissed him goodbye, and whispered, "Please be careful, I don't know what I would do without you."

"Don't worry. I'll always come back to you."

Chapter 69

Akil
Argi City
The 22,275[th] Terrestrial Rotation of the Second Summer

Otsoa walked out of the changing room in the front carriage, wearing his fighting attire. He wore black pants and a tight-fitting black and orange shirt, with the family crest emblazoned down the left side. Thea walked over to him with a belt, wrapped it around his waist, retrieved his sword, and fastened it to the strap over his right hip.

"You look fierce," she encouraged.

"Please, do not patronize me."

"A warrior is strong because he believes in himself. If you have no confidence in your abilities, you have already lost."

"I have confidence in my abilities; I am a strong fighter, but Tuso is better than me. He is better than most. I have seen the data streams of his competitions. I cannot beat him."

"Nothing is set in stone. Now is your time to shine. Everyone on Akil will adore you," she used her Skean power to make Otsoa accept it.

The force of her energy made him blink rapidly, "They will adore me?"

Using the light in the ceiling, she made him focus on it, enhanced by her power. With glazed eyes, he stared at it, listening to her.

"You are not afraid."

"I am not afraid."

"Once you win the fight, you will be the envy of every Akilian. They will sing songs to your name. They will celebrate your victory and keep images of you on their holograms. They will name avenues after you. Everywhere you go, they will say, 'There he is. He is the one who saved us.'"

Otsoa smiled, "I am their hero."

"You *will* defeat Tuso."

"He *will* die by my hand."

Sensing the train slowing down, she released him from the trance, "We are here."

He woke and, for the first time, felt confident, "Good. I am ready."

Chapter 70

Earth
Scotland - Dunnottar - Dunnottar Castle
May 11, 2452

Mai Li drove her electric car to Dunnottar Castle, where her employer lived. In the distance, she heard rumbling thunder, and before reaching the fortress, it started to rain hard. Although her wipers moved at their fastest speed, they did little to clear the window. With her pace slowed to a crawl, she crept up to the gate of the majestic estate. She rolled down her window and gave the guard her identification. The massive Iron Gates creaked loudly as the motors pushed them apart.

She drove to the front door and remembered reading an article a few years ago about the castle's purchase from the Scottish government. The figure was in the hundreds of millions. That alone impressed her because it was not an easy task, considering the estate was a tourist attraction, but she learned early on that enough money would buy about anything. She parked the car, dashed to the door, and rang the bell. She struggled against the wind with her umbrella until a butler answered the door and let her in. Standing in the foyer, she shook the water from her clothes.

"Right this way, madam," the butler politely motioned toward the foyer.

"Thank you."

He escorted her up a grand staircase that led to a billiard room, "She'll be with you momentarily."

The butler left and closed the door behind him. Mai walked past the billiard table and absentmindedly pushed one of the balls, resting on the red felt. It smacked into the others on the table, upsetting whatever game was in progress. She looked out the window and saw a lightning flash, a sudden clap of thunder followed, shaking nearby decorations on display.

She moved close to the windowpane and watched the rain beat against the glass with a fury that only a storm coming off the ocean could muster. She stood at the window, mesmerized by the ocean waves crashing violently against the beach below, but the creaking sound of a door opening got her attention. Turning, she saw her employer walking toward her.

"You came alone?"

"I'm sorry, Dawn. There's been a slight snag," Mai cautiously answered.

"Tell me what happened," Dawn demanded, not bothering to hide her disappointment.

"Everything was going as planned. I contacted your agent in the Regime. He connected me with Rachel in enough time for the date. The evening started well. I could tell Michael was interested, and I was within a half an hour from luring him away to London, where I had several men waiting for us."

"What went wrong? Why isn't he here?"

"Max, an old acquaintance of mine from the U.S., saw me. I owed him money."

"Mai, we have an agreement. I gave you an advance to cover the expense of the operation and any lingering debts you had from your former life."

"I hired a private detective to find him in the U.S. because I didn't realize he left."

"What happened next?"

"Max and Michael fought. Max pinned Michael against the wall. Michael kicked him in the shin to break free, and Max threw him into the bar."

Dawn's eyes widened with rage, so Mai held her hand up.

"Don't worry. He's all right. It was just a black eye. I've tried to contact him, but he won't take my calls because the incident embarrassed him."

Dawn paced, obviously upset by the news, "I told you I didn't want him injured!"

"I didn't plan for Max to be there; we met by chance."

"We're running out of time, Mai! You must accomplish your mission soon!"

"Look, the way I see it, I have two options left. I either seduce him into leaving for London, or I drug him and signal for you to open a portal."

"I can't open a vortex within the Regime. It's too risky. Regime technicians have ways of tracking them. You must improvise. Use the tools I gave you and bring Michael to me! I won't repeat this, so listen carefully. If someone hurts him during your pursuit, there's no place on Earth you can hide from me," Dawn raged.

Mai swallowed hard, "I promise. No harm will come to him."

"See yourself out, and the next time we meet, you better have him with you."

Chapter 71

Earth
The United States - Texas - Houston - Western Suburbs - Border of
Gang Territory
May 11, 2452

Larkin led his platoon on patrol and sensed their anxiety because they defended the dark forest near the border between Resistance territory and Gang territory. During the 9 May attack, their unit suffered more than the usual casualties, nine dead and eleven wounded. As their Sergeant, Larkin personally spoke to each soldier's family, injured or killed under his command. The task was emotionally draining, and for the first time in his life, he yawned at work.

His left arm still throbbed, but he ignored it. He had thought about what General Bailey said to him in the barn and acknowledged that he had had anger issues for a long time. Sadly, this was the first time it came close to destroying his family. General Bailey was explicit about there not being any more chances. If he allowed his rage to control him again, it could cost him everything. Larkin did not question the physical attack, even though most men would have been angry.

General Bailey was the only man he respected and trusted. Most importantly, he was the one person allowed to hit him without retaliation. During his shift, Larkin apologized to Lieutenant Blake and assured him it would not happen again. Although things were still a little tense between them, he felt they were on the right path. Larkin felt the hairs on his neck rise, reflexively raised his right arm, and made a fist, signaling his men to stop.

Everyone raised their weapons. They knew if Larkin sensed something, trouble was close. Using his instincts, he searched the forest but did not see anything. Still, Larkin could *feel* something out there. The woods became eerily silent, so he stood still for an exceptionally long time until his RTO crept up beside him.

"Sarge, the Lieutenant wants to know what's wrong."

Without looking at his RTO, he said, "I don't know. It *feels* like there's something out there hunting us."

His RTO swallowed hard, "What is hunting us?"

Larkin retrieved his Bowie knife, "Not what, who. It's my brother, Tucker." Larkin faced his RTO and handed him his gun, "Tell the Lieutenant to set up a defense perimeter. Tell 'em to shoot anythin' that moves."

"What about you, Sarge? Aren't you coming with us?"

"No. I'm going to do a little hunting myself."

"What if we accidentally hit you?"

"You won't. Just make sure the platoon does whatever's necessary to protect itself. Is that understood?"

"Yeah, Sarge."

"Go!"

His RTO fell back and relayed Larkin's message. Lieutenant Blake gave the order to form a defensive perimeter. Satisfied they were ready, Larkin tightly squeezed the grip of his Bowie and let his anger take over. *All right, Tucker, where the hell are you hiding?* He felt a nudge by an invisible hand guiding him in one direction, but another push made him change course. *He's trying to evade me.* He heard gunfire. *Damn it! My men!*

Stray bullets flew past him. He turned and ducked, evading them as a couple of his men screamed, making his anger turned to rage. *They better not be dead, Tucker!* Using all his strength, he ran full out, back toward his platoon, and with a thought, teleported himself forward, landing near them. By the time he arrived, the men had stopped shooting. Larkin visualized his platoon and saw Tucker holding a blade to Lieutenant Blake's throat.

"Put your weapons down, or I'll cut 'em, I swear!" Tucker yelled.

"You keep your weapons aimed at his head," Larkin bellowed.

Tucker gave a gritty smile, "Hello, *brother*."

He did not bother to hide the disdain he felt for him.

"What do you want, Tucker?"

"I came here for you, Larkin. Surrender yourself to me, and no one else gets hurt."

Larkin looked at Lieutenant Blake, "What are your orders, Lieutenant?"

Tucker laughed, "I see they've trained you like a bear in a circus."

He angled his mouth toward Lieutenant Blake's ear and whispered, "Tell 'em to surrender. It's the only way you'll survive."

Lieutenant Blake regretted reporting Larkin for disobeying orders. Larkin apologized earlier, but Blake was still unsure if he could trust him. Now, his life depended upon him.

"Can you get to him before he cuts me?" Lieutenant Blake wondered.

"No, Lieutenant, I can't," Larkin replied.

Tucker pressed the knife hard against this throat, "That's right, Lieutenant. Larkin's fast, but he's not that fast."

Lieutenant Blake swallowed hard, "Can you beat him, Sergeant?"

"I can beat him."

Tucker snarled and yelled, "You've never beaten me!"

Larkin laughed, "You must be thinking of someone else 'cause I've won every time we've fought."

Lieutenant Blake knew Tucker's type: sadistic. Even if Larkin surrendered, Tucker would cut him just for laughs.

"Sergeant, do what you have to, but you don't surrender to him, and that's an order!"

"That's an order, Larkin!" Tucker mocked. "And we know all good dogs obey orders. Woof! Woof!"

"Think before you act, Tucker. Right now, you've got thirty-three guns trained on your head. If you harm Lieutenant Blake, if I even sense you plan to injure him, I'll give them the command to fire. You won't dodge that many bullets."

"I'm willing to take that chance!" Tucker yelled at Larkin and whispered into Lieutenant Blake's ear, "How about you, Lieutenant? You up for a game of chicken?"

Larkin sighed, knowing they were at an impasse. It was only a matter of seconds before Tucker decided to make his move, but he had an idea.

"You know, I was wonderin' if I've never beaten you, why are you hiding behind my Lieutenant? It would seem that someone as tough as you wouldn't be afraid of facing me unless you're a coward."

Tucker growled at the remark, "I ought to cut him just for spite!"

"You cut him, and I promise you won't leave here alive, coward."

Tucker felt rage surge through him. All he could focus on, and all he wanted was to engage Larkin. Tucker threw Lieutenant Blake aside like a rag doll and sprinted toward Larkin without thinking. Lieutenant Blake hit a nearby tree and slumped to the ground. At the same time, Larkin ran toward Tucker. The two collided with a loud thud. The force of the impact caused them to twist awkwardly and flip upward. Gravity soon took over, and they landed on the ground with a thump.

They stood and swung their weapons at each other. Their form seemed wild and reckless, but their aim was precise. Their metal blades repeatedly clashed with blinding speed until Larkin threw his brother hard against an oak tree, shaking its branches. The force caused Tucker's knife to fly out of his hand and into the brush. Now unarmed, Tucker responded with fast, hard punches to Larkin's torso.

Larkin slashed at Tucker's head with his Bowie. Tucker ducked and unleashed several blows to Larkin's arm. When they landed, Larkin flinched and dropped his knife. Realizing that someone injured his brother, Tucker focused all his energy on Larkin's bruised arm. Larkin evaded most of Tucker's assaults, but a few got by his defenses. Now, his shoulder was in excruciating pain. He used it to fuel his anger, and his rage made him stronger.

Tucker swung again, so Larkin disappeared and reappeared behind him this time. Facing Tucker's back, Larkin unleashed punches to his kidneys. Tucker spun around, swinging blindly at him; Larkin teleported himself again. Tucker searched the area and did not see him until he heard branches rustling from above. Looking up, Tucker saw Larkin falling straight toward him. He tried to move a little too late.

Larkin landed on him, pinning him to the ground. Tucker struggled against Larkin's brute strength but was unable to break free. Tucker heard several tanks and Humvees approaching, so he stopped struggling and smiled at his brother.

"We'll continue this later."

Larkin raised his fist to knock him out, but Tucker disappeared before striking, so Larkin stood, trying to sense his location. *Damn it! He's too far away.* He returned to his platoon, and Sergeant Murphy ran to greet him.

"Give me an ACE report," Larkin demanded.

"Three new privates have some bad cuts; they're not life-threatening."

"And the Lieutenant?"

"He's got a minor concussion. He'll be all right."

Larkin sighed in relief as his RTO ran toward him, "Sergeant, General Bailey is demanding a report."

Larkin took the phone and told General Bailey everything that had happened.

Chapter 72

Akil
Argi City
The 22,275[th] Terrestrial Rotation of the Second Summer

Broll and the guards exited first when the train stopped, ensuring the area was secure, and Broll signaled for Zorion to exit. Still sore from the attack, Zorion moved sluggishly but felt much better. He nodded to one of the guards in the first car, who opened the door. Otsoa and Thea stepped out.

"I must meet with the other sovereigns before we get started. Meantime, escort Otsoa to his ready room," Zorion commented before leaving.

"What? No words of encouragement before sending me off to fight your battles?" mocked Otsoa.

He looked at Thea and Otsoa and noticed a dark cloud surrounding them, it disappeared moments later.

"I think we have said all there is to say," Zorion replied and abruptly turned and left.

A few heartbeats later, he entered the five sovereigns' plush and spacious meeting room and saw Ruvve and Gwah whispering near a food tray. Quok, who had just stuffed a handful of brown moss into his mouth, sat at a table on the other side of the room. *No need for etiquette here, I see.* On the other side of the table sat Elzer, sipping from a glass with a rare stimulant made from a fruit plant that existed before the ice, and there were only six containers of it left on the whole planet.

Zorion cleared his throat, "I see you are already celebrating, Elzer."

The sound of Zorion's voice made him gasp, drinking.

A short coughing spell followed until Elzer composed himself, "I thought perhaps you would come to your senses."

Hearing Zorion's voice, Ruvve and Gwah ended their private talk and walked to the table to join the conversation.

"What happened?" Gwah asked.

"I was attacked. The assailant worked me over rather well," Zorion reported.

Hearing the news, Elzer felt the blood rush from his face and broke into a cold, clammy sweat. *Did Shafe attack him without my direct order?*

"Did you apprehend the attacker?" Ruvve inquired.

"Yes," Zorion glared at Elzer. *I do not know for sure, but I guess you somehow play a role in this.*

"Why are you staring at me? I was on my way to the Main Arena," defended Elzer.

"Have you identified the assailant?" questioned Quok.

"Yes, it was my Chief Administrator of Intelligence, Olan," Zorion answered.

"How is this possible?" Gwah inquired, now worried that his staff was untrustworthy.

"I honestly do not know. We grew up together. Olan was a trusted friend and colleague, so whoever turned him must have leverage over him," Zorion surmised.

"If we cannot trust our team, who can we trust?" worried Quok.

"We have no choice. We must keep our confidence in them. If I find out who turned him and why I will share the information with you," Zorion responded.

"I, for one, am glad to see you are alive," Ruvve smiled.

Gwah and Quok voiced their agreements as well. Elzer's silence did not go unnoticed, but none of the sovereigns discussed it.

Quok stood, breaking the silence, "I suggest we tend to the business at hand."

"Zorion, Elzer, please take your seats in the arena. We will follow you out," Gwah remarked.

As Zorion and Elzer entered the auditorium, they heard members of the Information League yelling questions from their perspective seats. It made Zorion happy that none of the journalists could roam free at such an event. In the past, they found them in the most secure locations. *Somehow, they always find a way to sneak past security.* Zorion saw at least twelve data stream devices placed around the ring. *They have added a few more to ensure they do not miss any gore and pain.*

Everything was as he remembered as a young Akilian, fighting for Argi. The engineers had designed the entire arena in the shape of a dome with one hundred bright lights that lit the round ceiling, leaving no shadows in the ring. The illumination covered every space on the ceiling, except for the top center, where a blood-red light eerily glowed to portray the watchful eye of Gau. The sovereigns sat in elevated seats surrounding the circular pit, where the fight would occur.

Gazing at the ring, Zorion could see meticulously groomed green moss on the floor and Vlor's flag hanging over his opponent's door to the ring. The white padded walls were spotless and in much better shape than how he left them. Zorion and Thea took their seats. As they watched the other rulers and their families settling down, Zorion leaned toward Thea.

"How is he doing?"

"He is terrified," Thea stated flatly.

Seeing she was in a mood, he turned his attention to the arena. As with Otsoa's celebration, Zorion had to endure another ceremonial dance ritual before the fight began. Five male dancers, dressed in black, walked into the ring. They wore emblems that portrayed each city of Akil. Masks of Gau hid their faces, and each one had a different expression of his anger painted on it.

Zorion thought the custom ridiculous but knew the other sovereigns would insist on upholding the tradition, so he watched as each dancer drew a sword and pranced about the ring in a pretend fight, swinging them in every direction. The blades were very sharp, and he could hear them cutting through the air as they passed by, but they would occasionally meet in the center of the ring, making their swords clash.

The Information League ate it up. Several supersized monitors placed around the arena made it easy for everyone to see. Following the ceremonial dance, Gau's High Priest walked onto the center of the moss, and with Gau's Chief Representative's appearance on Akil, the crowd became silent out of respect. In the quiet, High Priest Elazar explained the tradition behind Gau's Judgment Seat.

It does not matter what he says. It is all politics. He can couch it in whatever religious phrases he chooses, but in the end, it all boils down to one sovereign needing something from another. Also, he needs it so badly that he is willing to risk his first heir's life to get it.

High Priest Elazar finished and called in the two fighters. Seeing Tuso, Zorion could not believe his size because he had to stoop down to pass through the opening. *What, in the universe, have they been feeding him?* It had been ages since Zorion saw Tuso, who was tall as a young one, except now, Tuso was taller and broader at the shoulders than Otsoa.

There was a smattering of applause from the other families as they faced each other. Otsoa frowned, seeing him. *He will slaughter me.* High Priest Elazar gave the fighters a few hundred heartbeats to warm up before the fight. Tuso paced, staring at Otsoa like a predator. His demeanor was that of focus and rage, with an air of complete concentration about him, something only the most intense warriors had. Otsoa did not look at his opponent but stared at the wall, mumbling. Zorion felt embarrassed for him.

"You better pray to Gau for help," Tuso mocked.

Seeing Tuso's size and anger completely undid Thea's preparation on the train. One look at him, and Otsoa lost all confidence. *I cannot win, no matter how sure I am of myself.*

"Nayrah, I cannot believe you have failed me," Otsoa mumbled, staring at the wall. "I cannot believe you failed to kill Zorion."

He heard her voice in his mind say, "Otsoa."

Although he looked around, she was nowhere in sight.

"Where are you?" he whispered, keeping the conversation inconspicuous.

"I am nearby."

"I do not see you."

"I am hidden."

"I will die this Terrestrial Revolution."

"Do not fret; you will do well."

"Will you use your powers to help me?"

"I cannot. I am forbidden to do so."

"Without your help, I have no hope of winning. You see how big he is."

"How often have I told you: your focus determines your outcome. If you believe you will lose, you will, so I suggest you start believing that you will win."

Otsoa sighed, "I will try."

"I suggest you try *very* hard."

Before Otsoa could reply, High Priest Elazar called them to the center of the arena. Otsoa came face to face with his opponent for the first time, his heart raced, and he struggled to keep his limbs from shaking. Tuso snarled at him, causing his knees to give out, so he doubled over, placing his hands upon his thighs for support. Otsoa took a few quick, deep breaths and stood, but Elzer's section noticed his cowardly actions and laughed at him.

"The fight is to the death, and there are no breaks. The first one to subdue his opponent is the victor," High Priest Elazar looked back and forth at the fighters. "Any questions?"

Both fighters shook their heads.

"Fight!" he yelled, jumping out of the way.

No sooner did the words leave his lips than Tuso swung his sword at Otsoa with precision. Each strike came fast and powerful, backed by his thick muscular frame. Feverishly, Otsoa worked to keep them from landing, but every blocked strike weakened him. Tuso backed him into the wall several times, and even though he managed to escape, it was a struggle.

As the fight continued, Thea watched Tuso closely. It dawned on her that even someone in his condition would not support such a vicious onslaught. *He should be slowing down.* Otsoa had received several cuts to his arms, torso, and legs; some were deep. Thea tried to hide the horror, but her emotions got the best of her. A nudge from the Shadow Universe made her instinctively glance at Elzer's mate, Kemena.

They intensely stared at each other for several heartbeats, and without realizing it, Thea slipped into a state of complete relaxation. *There is nothing to worry about; Otsoa is doing fine.* The thought drained away all her anxieties. Precious heartbeats passed. She heard Zorion speak; it was not enough to bring her out of the trance. At one point, she even smiled uncharacteristically.

Suddenly, she realized Kemena used her powers to lull her into a catatonic state. Anger pushed her happy feeling away, and she returned her attention to Otsoa. By now, gashes covered his body, but one severe cut caught her attention. Tuso had slashed his left cheek deep enough to expose his teeth, causing rage to rush through her, making her powerful.

Reaching out with her mind, she sensed Kemena using her powers to sustain and manipulate Tuso during the fight. *What is she doing? He does not need any help!* She allowed her energy to flow around her, and it became hot enough that Zorion had to remove his tunic. Thea spoke to Kemena through their mental connection - *Gecheana told us not to use our powers!*

You used yours first! Kemena replied.

That is not true!

Kemena ignored her.

Fine, if that is the way you want to play it.

Thea looked to the arena and saw Otsoa on his knees. His sword was several forearm lengths from him, and the fight was about over. Looking at Kemena, Thea saw her smirking as Tuso toyed with Otsoa. Tuso used Otsoa's sword to jab at him, hitting his shoulders and cutting his face and torso. Otsoa wept, knowing his life was at its end. As tears fell from his eyes, they moved over and into the wounds on his face, burning the raw flesh.

They trickled down his chin and mixed with blood, turning them red and appearing as if he were shedding tears of blood. Still, the crowd showed him no mercy. Many laughed. Those who laughed the loudest were sitting in Elzer's section. Their mirth fed her rage to a point she had never been before. Otsoa rested on his knees, waiting for the inevitable. He could not understand why Tuso refused to end it. *You have won, now put me out of my misery, please!*

Since it pleased the crowd, Tuso continued to play with him. This time, he stabbed an open wound on his left shoulder. The attack made Otsoa scream, and it echoed throughout the dome. For Tuso, winning was not enough. He wanted to humiliate him. It was a trait Kemena taught him. Thea knew that Kemena was influencing Tuso to commit these atrocities, which meant that Kemena was trying to embarrass her.

Everyone on Akil would recollect this Terrestrial Rotation because of the way Otsoa died. The other Skeans would recall this humiliation until her dying Terrestrial Revolution; Thea lost control because it was all she could take. *You want something to remember? I will give you something you will never forget!*

Tuso drew his sword back for another demeaning blow, but Thea made a mental connection to Otsoa and allowed her power to flow through him, taking control of his limbs. Before Tuso could hit him again, she balled Otsoa's hand into a fist and forced it to lunge upward. It landed on Tuso's groin with enough force to lift him off the ground. Tuso moaned in pain with a loud female-like whine, falling to his knees. The laughter stopped, and everyone looked on in disbelief.

Even Otsoa could not believe what had happened. *How did I manage that?* A surge of adrenaline raced through his body because he realized that there was a chance to survive. Although he tried, standing was not an option. The loss of so much blood made him pale and weak. *I cannot reach him in time! He will recover and finish me off!* Otsoa stood, but it was not by his power. It was as if some invisible hand had taken control of him. *Nayrah.*

His arms and legs moved, without his command, toward his sword. He picked it up and almost smiled because it was still warm from Tuso holding it. *The things that catch your attention in the heat of battle are strange.* As he spun to face Tuso, blood dripped from the sword and landed on Tuso's back. Tuso leaned forward, desperately struggling to reach his sword, but it was too far away, and he could not move to get it.

With Nayrah in control, Otsoa walked over, kicked the sword even farther away from him, and raised his arms, with the sword grasped tightly in his blood-soaked hands. As his sword hung in the air, Nayrah smiled at Kemena.

Do not dare kill him! Kemena threatened through their mental connection.

The corners of Nayrah's lips curled into a devious grin. Kemena jumped to her feet to defend Tuso, but Thea waved her index finger, releasing an invisible burst of power in her direction. She fell back and over the top of her seat, and with her family's help, she stood to see Nayrah nod her head. Kemena's gaze moved to Tuso, and she raised her hand to stop Otsoa; it was too late because his sword had already passed through Tuso's neck.

His head fell forward and rolled a few paces until it stopped. His torso jolted and fell backward, spraying Otsoa's face and upper body with blood. The crowd gasped as they stood and remained silent, staring at the victor in disbelief; the only sound was Otsoa's heavy breathing.

Stupefied by the sudden events, High Priest Elazar walked to Otsoa and took him gently by the shoulders, "Gau has smiled upon you."

The other three families, who were not directly involved with the challenge, clapped their hands and cheered for Otsoa. Kemena stared at Thea menacingly.

"*You will pay for this*!" her thoughts registered through their mental connection.

Anytime you are ready! Thea replied.

Thea knew Kemena would do nothing here. There were too many witnesses and no dark corners where she could launch a strike, but she would have to confront her in the future. That did not matter right now. All that mattered was that Otsoa was alive, and she defeated Kemena. Aides wiped Tuso's blood from Otsoa's uniform as they returned to the train.

Nayrah used her powers to help Otsoa walk since his body was still too weak to move independently. She instructed aides to support him under his shoulders. Once they took him, she released him from her grip. The aides walked him onto the carriage and laid him on the bed. Once his head hit the pillow, he blacked out. They removed his shirt and wrapped his cuts with rehabilitation towels; Thea dismissed them to tend his wounds personally.

Zorion knocked on the door, but she refused to answer, so a hundred heartbeats later, he gave up. The train started to move, and she examined his wounds. The first injury she worked on was the gaping cut on his face. She took the flap of skin that hung down from his cheek, pushed it back into its original position, and smeared a recovery compound across his skin to hold it in place. Although the wound mended, it left a scar.

She smelled the compound and realized one of the ingredients had spoiled. Tossing it aside, she cursed under her breath and retrieved another jar from her bag. With fingers full of the slimy ointment, she spread it over the remaining wounds of Otsoa's face, and they closed. One look at his torso made a tear form in her eye. *That putok carved you up horribly.*

The rehabilitation towels, saturated with blood, showed her that his wounds were still bleeding. *Kemena must have put an anti-coagulation potion on the sword because these should have stopped bleeding by now.* She carefully removed each of the towels and spread the ointment over all his skin. The bleeding stopped, and several heartbeats later, the lacerations closed. *There, that should do it.* Satisfied that he would be completely whole soon, she sat back in her chair. *I am just going to rest my eyes for a few heartbeats.* In no time at all, she fell asleep.

As the train stopped, the carriage couplers made a loud banging noise. Hearing it, Thea sprang out of her seat. Reflexively, her sword was ready in her hand. She quickly assessed the room and relaxed, confirming there was no danger, but someone started banging on the door.

"Open the door, Thea, or I will have Broll open it," Zorion yelled.

Thea sheathed her sword and waved her hand at the door, forcing the locking mechanism to click open.

Zorion opened it and walked in, "How is he?"

"He is alive, no thanks to you," she spat.

He focused on his injuries, "The wounds are almost gone. He has always recovered quickly."

He does because I help him, idiot. "He almost died out there," she snapped.

"I did not realize Tuso was that large. The last time I saw him, he was tall yet not as muscular."

Kemena has been giving him a strength potion. It is dangerous but effective.

"He will never forgive you for this," she insisted. *I will make sure of that.*

"I hope one Terrestrial Rotation he will look back and see that I did it for our people. Now that he has won, everyone will revere him."

"Revere? Are you joking? Tuso humiliated him in front of the entire world. They will say he won by chance."

"He still won, no matter how it happened. I have seen losing opponents turn a fight around many times. Although I must admit, I have never seen anyone come back from such a thrashing before."

Again, I helped him, idiot. Thea turned from him and focused on Otsoa.

"He will completely recover in a few Terrestrial Rotations, and I will have a dinner in his honor to show my appreciation. I will invite the Argi Information League to interview him. It will give him a chance to describe the fight from his point of view. That should help change any negative beliefs anyone might have of him," Zorion offered.

"Please leave. I need to tend to his wounds," she motioned toward him dismissively.

He groaned, "Very well, keep me informed of his progress."

Outside the car, Broll asked him, "How is he?"

"He will be fine. I am sure his ego sustained more damage than his body; he will get over it, eventually."

"I certainly hope so for his sake," Broll whispered.

Chapter 73

Earth
The United States - Texas - Houston - Resistance Head Quarters
May 11, 2452

General Bailey sat behind his desk, smoking a cigar and reviewing the details of Colonel Scott's operations order for the recon. He recently concluded a special meeting with the Regime's Assistant of Defense to get his approval. Neil was hesitant to authorize the op until General Bailey insisted that Tucker was dangerous. Also, General Bailey reminded Neil that none of this would have happened if Jared had not stirred things up with the gangs. It was enough to convince him, but he was still under orders to keep the fighting to a minimum because the Regime wanted to keep a low profile; Colonel Scott knocked on his door.

"Come in," General Bailey remarked.

"Sir, Sergeant Burke is waiting to see you."

"Send him in."

"Yes, Sir!"

Colonel Scott held the door open, and Sergeant Burke entered the office, "Sir! Sergeant 1st class Burke, platoon sergeant for 3rd platoon Charlie Company, reporting as ordered!"

"Have a seat, Sergeant."

Larkin sat, and General Bailey did not speak for a couple of minutes.

"Since Lieutenant Blake is in the hospital, I've decided to speak to you directly. I need you to do some recon. Are you up for it?"

"Yes, whatever you want."

"I chose you for this mission because you're familiar with the area, so with that in mind, I need to know that you're committed to the outcome."

"I don't understand, Sir."

"Your brother is a dangerous man, and from what you've told me, he's got the same abilities as you."

"Yes, Sir. That's correct."

"The fact that he could subdue a whole platoon by himself while you were chasing him concerns me. Even more troubling is that he wanted you to surrender to him. I can't allow that to happen."

"I agree, so what do you want me to do?"

"I want you to find him and radio HQ with his location."

"And then what?"

"I have access to long-range missiles that will take him out." General Bailey furrowed his eyebrows and looked directly into Larkin's eyes, "Is that going to be a problem, soldier?'

"I wish there were another way, but you're right, Tucker's dangerous. Based on the latest incident, it's clear he wants revenge. Although I don't like the thought of killing my brother, I don't see any other way."

"You have 72 hours to locate his position and return. Choose two men to go with you."

"I can do this alone."

"No, you can't. I told you to take two men with you."

Larkin swallowed hard, "Yes, Sir. I'll notify them right away."

"Good, you're leaving within the hour, so you better get going."

"What about Sarah?"

"I'll let her know you're on a mission."

"Please tell her I love her."

General Bailey gave him a blank stare.

Larkin stood, "Never mind; I'll just be going now."

Larkin returned to his tent to gather a few supplies. Recon missions demanded light packs: only food, water, and enough ammunition for three days. He paused, thinking of Tucker. *Why did you have to attack my platoon? Why couldn't you have just stayed on your turf?* Tucker was his only family at one time, but now he had Sarah and Sable and could not let anything or anyone take him from them, even his brother. A knock at his door brought him out of his brooding, "Come in."

Sergeants Murphy and Nelson walked in. Larkin handed Murphy the radio and the GPS, took out a map, and laid it on the table, "Tucker usually stays at one of three locations. We have three days to find him. He prefers to stay at the Southampton Psychiatric

Center. It's found here at the corner of Bissonnet and Greenbriar. There's an apartment complex across the street we can hide in."

Murphy looked at him quizzically, "Why a Psychiatric Center?"

"He uses their equipment for questioning prisoners."

"Oh."

"Now, his second favorite place is a warehouse located in University Place. It's only a few miles from the Psych Center, and it's close to his third favorite place to stay, which is the old Rice Stadium."

"I've heard those buildings were condemned over a hundred years ago," Nelson noted.

"I'm sure they were, but they're still standing, and he likes the open space."

"What does he need all the open space for?" Nelson asked.

"Fighting and other competitions. He loves a crowd."

"Your brother has an ego, huh?" Murphy inquired.

"Yeah, you could say that. Now, Murphy, you carry the map. I don't need it 'cause I'm familiar with the area. You have the GPS and the radio. If we find him, you'll be the one to call it in."

"Roger that."

"What does he look like?" Nelson queried.

"He won't be hard to miss. He looks like me. We're the same height and body build; only I'm better lookin'."

Murphy and Nelson laughed.

"Ok, we ready?"

Murphy and Nelson nodded.

"All right. I got us a ride to the border at old Route 59. From there, we're on foot. We need to be at the Psych Center before daylight." He looked at his watch. "That gives us six hours. Let's go!"

Chapter 74

Akil
Argi City
The 22,275[th] Terrestrial Rotation of the Second Summer

Nayrah stood in the back room during the early sleep cycle, working on a potion. Her plan: give it to Otsoa without his knowledge. *If it is good enough for Kemena, it is good enough for me.* The drug would make him more assertive and aggressive, like Tuso, but she tweaked the formula to make him more obedient. *Now, you must obey me.*

She poured secretions from the black moss into a bottle and smiled. This secret ingredient grew in a private chamber inside her apartment. It was a place she kept hidden from everyone, including Jadell. The reason for her discretion was that if Gecheana ever found out, she would suffer the wrath of Gau for her disobedience. The liquid bubbled and smoked over a small flame for a few heartbeats until it settled. *There, it is ready.*

There was a knock at the door. Making a potion takes all her focus, so the visitor surprised her. As her hand moved to her weapon, she sensed Otsoa, stopped, and opened the door to find him leaning against the large support pillar outside, staring into the darkness that dominated the lower level.

"You should be resting. You are still weak from the fight," advised Nayrah.

"I wanted to thank you," he still did not face her.

"You are welcome. Now come inside."

He did not move, "I wondered why it took you so long to help me."

"I told you, I was not supposed to help you."

"So why *did* you help me?" Otsoa insisted.

"Because I sensed Tuso's teacher using her powers against you. It was not a fair fight, so I had to intervene."

"He had a teacher like you?" *You have just confirmed my worst fear; there are more than two like you.*

"Yes. We were forbidden to use our powers, but he had already defeated you when I realized it."

“Why did he wait so long to kill me? Why did he humiliate me?”

“Because of me.”

“You?”

“Tuso’s teacher and I do not get along, so I believe she did it to injure me.”

Otsoa finally turned to face her, “I am the one injured.”

Nayrah saw the thick, red scar on his cheek. It was not hard to miss since it began at his left ear lobe and ended a finger width from his mouth’s corner. *Damn that compound*! Nayrah reached up and touched his cheek with her finger.

“His blade left a scar. That is unusual.”

“Is there any way you can fix it?”

Nayrah shook her head, “I do not know of any potion that can take it away. Akilians rarely scar, so there was never a need to make one.”

Otsoa sighed.

“Do not be upset; it makes you look fierce,” comforted Nayrah.

“I do not feel fierce.”

Do not forget your potion! “I will be right back.”

Nayrah hastened inside her home and to the kitchen. She prepared a plate of moss, poured a small amount of the potion over it, and returned with it in her hand.

“Here, eat this.”

“I am not hungry.”

“Eat it!” she snapped.

“All right, all right,” he responded by raising his hands in surrender.

He grabbed a few handfuls and gulped them down.

Nayrah smiled, “That will bring your strength back.” *And more*.

He finished eating and handed the plate back to her.

“Thanks, I am going back home now. I am still tired.”

Nayrah could feel his anxiety, “Otsoa, there is no need to be sad. Even though he may not have known it, Tuso was cheating. Even Broll, with his great skills, could not have beaten him.”

Otsoa nodded, but her words were of little comfort. He turned and walked away, knowing that he would never live down the failure. Nayrah stepped outside and watched him disappear into the darkness. *Your mood will change soon enough.* Turning, she headed toward her apartment. She felt something cold and menacing nearby. *Kemena.* Nayrah unsheathed her sword. *All right, you donag, I am ready for you.*

Instinctively, she directed energy into the power transfer gem, resting inside the hilt of her weapon. Supernatural strength raced through the conduits of the metal. The scarlet blade gave off dim light and heat, which warmed Nayrah's face, holding it in front of her, waiting for the inevitable attack. It was dark, but Nayrah's Skean abilities allowed her to see everything except Kemena, who cleverly hid. Unable to rely on her eyes, she closed them.

Reaching out with her mind, she looked for Kemena. Her neck hair raised, warning her of danger, and her Skean powers covered her whole body, increasing her sensitivity. She yielded to invisible hands and waited for the darkness to tell her when and where to strike. Kemena lunged out of the fog like a ghost; the attack was perfect because she waited until the last moment to ignite her sword.

Nayrah was ready, and invisible hands moved her sword without her knowledge, blocking Kemena's surprise attack. The two scarlet blades danced in the darkness as they swung their swords faster than the eye could see. Trained to make every move count, they ensured that each strike would mean death if not blocked. The heat from their swords created even more fog as they cut through the thick cold mist.

Nayrah could hear the blades cutting through the air with her eyes still closed. Kemena backed Nayrah up against a pillar that supported the avenue above them. Thinking she had the advantage, Kemena swung her sword horizontally, trying to decapitate her. Nayrah ducked and spun at the same time, evading the attack. Kemena had missed, but the momentum drove her blade through the reinforced column.

The sword's extreme heat allowed it to cut without any resistance, and as it passed through, it removed a finger width of the support. With the pedestal's weight and the thousands of avenues above it, the small gap was enough distance to create a rumbling sound that echoed through the fog when it dropped. Even the highest level of the city felt a tremor from that strike. Although it distracted many Argians, neither fighter paid any attention.

As their battle continued, Nayrah remained patient, knowing Kemena would make a mistake. Using her senses, she could feel Kemena using her anger to drive her attack. It was not a surprise because Gecheana taught them to fight that way, but Nayrah discovered that even though using anger made her strong, it also made her reckless. Unlike the other Skeans, Nayrah believed in using a combination of rage, control, and patience.

During the current duel, she noticed Kemena strayed off balance several times. It was not something that even an elite fighter like Broll would catch, but she scrutinized everything as a Skean. Kemena would lose her balance; it was only a matter of time. Her indiscretion allowed Nayrah to take control of the fight by stepping out of Kemena's strike zone, causing her to reach out farther and farther to contact her blade.

If Kemena moved forward to make up the ground, Nayrah moved away and sensed that her moves were feeding Kemena's anger, multiplying her recklessness. As time went on, her attacks were increasingly unsteady until she became frustrated and overextended to land her attack, making her stumble.

It was only a tiny hop, so slight that someone watching in a brightly lit arena would not catch it, but Nayrah was not watching with her eyes. Feeling a nudge from the shadows, she released her rage, which made her powerful, and using that energy, she attacked. The invisible puppet master moved her with precision and grace. Each strike was precise, powerful, and meant to end Kemena's life. The force of her attack drove Kemena back, making her stumble even more.

As they neared the fountain, Kemena hoped to regain her balance. Seeing an opening, Nayrah focused the energy coursing inside her and directed it to flow through her left arm and out of her hand. An invisible wall of power slammed into Kemena, pushing her onto the edge of the water fountain. Bones broke as her body met the hard stone.

With her eyes still closed, she heard Kemena's sword tumbling end over end until it finally settled several paces away. Having left

Kemena's hand, its glow vanished. Nayrah opened her eyes victorious. The invisible hands released her and returned control of her body. The sight of Kemena lying helpless on the fountain seat made her smile. Kemena tried to move as Nayrah approached, but her injuries prevented her.

She broke her neck. Nayrah moved closer, keeping her sword extended, and pointed at Kemena. She stopped with the tip of her blade a hair's width from Kemena's throat. Its heat burned her skin. Kemena's eyes were wide with fear. Nayrah did not want the moment to end; she wanted to savor it like a handful of fresh black moss.

"I will slice you the way Tuso did Otsoa."

Terrified, Kemena shook her head with wide eyes, pleading with her sister, "Do not do this, please! I am sorry!"

Nayrah scoffed at her whimpering, flicked her sword around Kemena's chin, resting it on her cheek near the earlobe, and dragged it down to her mouth's corner, causing Kemena to scream.

"That looked like it hurt," Nayrah sneered venomously.

Paralyzed from the neck down by her injury, Kemena could only suffer through the torture. When Nayrah finished, Kemena felt air moving through the new hole in her cheek. Tears streamed over the torn flesh.

"Why are you crying, sister? You are a Skean. We endure extreme pain all the time. Is that not what Gecheana taught us?"

Before Kemena could answer, Nayrah released a barrage of precise cuts from the neck upward. The assault only took a few heartbeats, and with every cut, Kemena screamed. Satisfied, Nayrah paced, watching her sister writhing in pain. The attack was clean, leaving no blood because the hot blade cauterized each wound, but she knew the gashes were painful. Since there was not enough time, Nayrah decided against taking Kemena back to her apartment to extend her torture.

She needed to satisfy her hunger for revenge, which would only come with Kemena's death. Nayrah raised her sword above Kemena's neck, took a deep breath, and swung downward. Before it touched her flesh, a red and white blade intercepted the blow. The unique colored combination belonged to only one Skean, Gecheana.

"You will not deprive me of my vengeance!" Nayrah snarled.

"You must go through me to get it," Gecheana growled, bringing Nayrah's sword up and away from Kemena's neck.

They faced each other with their swords crossed between them. Tongues of electricity danced from Nayrah's edge to the white side of Gecheana's blade. They stared at each other for a long time. Every fiber in Nayrah's body wanted to fight. *I can beat you and become the Skeans' mistress.*

Fear replaced her anger and confidence. The veil prevented her from acting out her desire. It was like a thick blanket, suffocating her, making her weak. Doubt clouded her mind. *Wait, am I strong enough to defeat her?* Her lack of belief in her ability pushed away her urge to fight. *What if I fail? I always seem to fail.* Finally, Nayrah lowered her sword, turned off her blade, and sheathed it.

Gecheana did the same and leaned over to examine Kemena's face, "What is the meaning of this debasement?"

"I did to her what she did to Otsoa."

"What have I taught you about fighting one another?"

"That it is unprofitable for us," Nayrah replied dryly.

"Why do you disobey me?"

"*She* attacked me! I was only defending myself!" Nayrah exclaimed.

"You call this defending yourself?" Gecheana pointed to Kemena's face and neck.

"She deserved it. Besides, if I had not avenged Otsoa and killed her quickly, she would have been dead before you arrived."

"I saw what happened in the main arena; both of you disobeyed me by using your powers."

"She used her powers first! I only used mine after I discovered it!" Nayrah yelled.

"That is a lie! You used your powers to talk with him before the fight," Kemena accused.

"I only talked with him, I did not control his body, and I did nothing while they fought."

"You see, Gecheana, she has confessed to using her powers. I sensed you talking with him, so I used my powers to ensure you did not take an unfair advantage," Kemena countered.

Gecheana faced Nayrah, "Using your powers to talk with him means you used your powers. Just because you did not use them to control his body is not an excuse; you still used them to encourage him. It is the same."

"Are you judging me on a technicality and saying this is my fault?" puzzled Nayrah.

"Again, you fail to see your mistakes. I have told you this time and time again. You care too much for your subject, Nayrah. It is why you continue to disobey me and why you fail. Now, go home and think about this lesson."

Frustrated, Nayrah abruptly turned and started walking home. She stopped before rounding the corner, "If Kemena chooses to attack Otsoa or me again, I will not hesitate to kill her. The next time, I will do it before you can save her."

She turned the corner, disappearing from their sight.

Chapter 75

Earth
China - Po Toi Island
May 12, 2452

Wu Luli throttled back on the twin outboards as another wave bucked the bow of her boat up into the air. She saw fingers of lightning dancing across the ocean's surface, and seconds later, a loud crash of thunder shook her. As her small craft closed in on Po Toi Island, just south of Hong Kong, her thoughts drifted back to the day her employer, General Ming-tun Fu, found a way for her to penetrate the Regime's security.

*****

"You will replace one of their software analysts in Washington, D.C. Her name is Chu Lian. Here is her photo," he handed it to her.

She examined it, frowned, and handed it back to him, "You made a mistake. That is a photo of me."

General Ming-tun Fu subtly smiled as if enjoying a private joke, "It is, in fact, a genetic anomaly. She is your double right down to the mole on your upper left thigh. The probability of something like this happening is astronomical. We intend to take advantage of it. If you succeed in your mission, you will be the first and, so far, the only agent of any government power who will have ever penetrated the Regime's security."

"How do you propose to make the switch?"

"Chu Lian, get used to the name, is going on vacation. She has scheduled a two-week leave and will be spending her last days at the Mexican resort of Nueva Alma. She will arrive; you will take her place. The cleaners will dispose of her body. It will be as if she never existed because you will be her."

"What about her family?" Wu Luli asked.

"She sees her mother, but irregularly."

"Friends?"

"With regards to that, I sincerely hope your years of training will prove useful."

"How long do I have?"

"As long as it takes. Once inside the Regime, you are to forward as much classified information as possible." General Ming-tun Fu smiled again, "I think you should consider this a long-term assignment."

*****

The boat bucked again, forcing Wu Luli to make a slight course correction. The wind blew against the current, churning the water into a sea of white caps and spray. As the water splashed on her face, she remembered sneaking into Chu Lian's room, dressed as a housekeeper. Chu Lian was taking a shower, and the bathroom door was open. Wu Luli stepped inside just as the water stopped running. Chu Lian reached for a towel, but Wu Luli handed it to her and froze when their eyes met.

It was like coming face to face with herself, and Wu Luli did not know what to do until Chu Lian inhaled to scream. Wu Luli crushed Chu Lian's throat, freezing the scream in her chest, grabbed Chu Lian by the hair, and dragged her counterfeit twin to the other room's bed. Struggling for breath, Chu Lian panicked, preventing her from fighting back.

Wu Luli had everything in her housekeeping trailer. She used sturdy plastic slip ties to restrain Chu Lian's hands and feet and used an injection gun that fired the compound through Chu Lian's skin and massaged her throat until the serum took effect.

"What do you want from me?" Chu Lian asked hoarsely.

"Everything," Wu Luli answered. "I need all your computer identities, passwords, bank accounts, names of everyone you work with, and anyone you might be sexually involved with," Wu Luli went on coldly, holding a micro-recorder to her victim's mouth with her other hand.

"I won't do it."

"Of course, you will," Wu Luli replied. "You won't be able to help yourself."

401

Under the influence of the drug, Chu Lian could not stop talking. She babbled about her apartment, why she came to Mexico for a vacation, about her office, and interspersed in sometimes incoherent chattering. Chu Lian had told Wu Luli everything she needed to know, so Wu Luli loaded another serum into the injection gun and fired it into Chu Lian's shoulder.

"What's that?" Chu Lian inquired.

"Goodnight," Wu Luli responded.

"Goodnight, mother," Chu Lian answered, closed her eyes, and died.

Wu Luli stared at the body lying on the bed for several minutes. A cold shiver ran down her spine. *I've killed before. Why does this make me feel uncomfortable?*

*****

Another loud clap of thunder made her jump, taking her out of the daydream. She slowed the engines near the dock until the boat butted against the pier. As she tied it down, heavy rain fell on her. A hooded raincoat protected her upper body, but the rain made her pant legs wet before entering the building. Inside, she took off her coat, brushed away the rain, and walked through security.

General Ming-tun Fu stationed twenty guards at the entrance and ordered them to keep their weapons aimed at any agent entering until cleared. Wu Luli passed through the metal detector without incident; a sentry waved her in, and she headed directly to his office. Paintings and sculptures from around the world, items she and her colleagues stole for him, decorated the room. Reclining on a leather chair behind a large oak desk, Wu Luli saw the man who obtained her on her twelfth birthday. He was only a mere Colonel then, but now he was the most feared man on all five continents. Wu Luli smiled. *If they only knew.*

"Ah, Wu Luli. Good to see you," Ming-tun Fu commented.

"Please, skip the pleasantries."

Ming-tun Fu smiled, "Very well, I will get right to the point. Nolan Mitchell, who designed the schematics we sold to President Martinez Santiago, disappeared a few days ago, including

402

all copies. Despite our efforts, we have not located him or determined how he got out of the facility without being detected.”

“Sounds like the Regime grabbed him. The only way he could have bypassed your security is through a portal.”

“I agree, which is why I have called on you. Nolan has disappeared, and I believe the Regime intercepted the disc before it reached President Santiago. Since a suspected Regime agent took it from an independent courier, whom President Santiago hired, it conveniently leaves us clear. President Santiago is willing to pay us to retrieve it.”

“Why us? Why doesn’t he send his men to get it?”

“Two reasons. The first is that getting through the Regime’s security is almost impossible. The second is that President Santiago does not want anyone linking him to what is on the disc. If so, he will lose the presidency, and we would lose a valuable client, but if we were to reclaim the disc and prove that the Regime stole it.”

Wu Luli interrupted him, “He would have the support from the United Nations to attack the Regime, but wouldn’t the information on the disc condemn President Santiago?”

“It would fall under the Government Document Privacy Protection Act the United Nations established years ago. If we can obtain proof that the Regime took it, President Santiago can wage his war without fear of prosecution.”

“How does that benefit us?”

“War is always good for business, especially our business, but remember, Santiago will need guns, ammunition, tanks, and the like. Since his country is no longer capable of manufacturing those items, they will need our help.”

“If the Regime has the disc, they’re most likely keeping it in their facility in Washington, D.C.”

“I agree. Our next step is to get Chu Lian back into the Regime.”

A wave of excitement washed over her. Her feelings for Michael had to stay hidden from her boss, so she pushed the emotion aside.

“If I do this for you, I want you to tell me where you are keeping my dad.”

Ming-tun Fu chuckled, "I'm afraid I can't do that. You know the rules. No one can see their parents."

Wu Luli swallowed her growing anger, hiding it behind the impenetrable mask of the perfect agent. Ming-tun Fu trained her well, so she softly asked, "Should I assume that he is dead?" *Of course, you don't threaten Ming-tun Fu and live, but he would do well to remember what he has created.*

"You seem out of sorts."

"I want to know if he is still alive. It makes no difference to our arrangement. I am who I am, but I want to see him if he is still alive."

Ming-tun Fu rubbed his chin in thought, "Very well if you complete this mission, I will make the arrangements."

"No, I want to see him before the mission. I could be in the Regime for a long time."

Ming-tun Fu considered his options. Wu Luli was not the first operative to demand parental visitation, and it surprised him that she did not ask to see him sooner; still, there were risks in letting her know his location. Wu Luli was good at her job, and if she wanted to rescue him, she would be the one agent to succeed where others failed.

"All right, I will let you see him."

"And another thing, I want to be alone with him outside."

"My, you're demanding today," Ming-tun Fu remarked. "Perhaps you presume too much on my goodwill."

"I presume only as much as you allow," Wu Luli countered. "To do more would be presumptuous."

Ming-tun Fu laughed, "You are as dangerous as you are beautiful, Wu Luli. Very well, follow me."

Chapter 76

Akil
Vlor City
The 22,276th Terrestrial Rotation of the Second Summer

Elzer waited for Noka and his team to arrive on the Intercity Transportation Station platform. Thelle, the owner of Vlor Electric, stood by his side. Since his son, Tuso, had lost in the main arena, the law forced Elzer to give twenty-five percent of his city's electricity to the science department in Argi. The thought enraged him. If that wretched Kemena had not forced him to build a Portal Transmitter, which no longer worked, he could have used the Sovereign Cubes to install several new energy consoles. However, since she was too powerful to overcome, he had to succumb to her demands.

On the other hand, if Zorion had not pushed the issue of supplying electricity, he was sure to have had a few energy consoles built within the following few hundred Terrestrial Rotations, which would have resolved their dispute; it felt like the walls of his city were closing in on him. Now, he waited for the arrival of the visible symbol of his defeat. It made him wish he had already given Igon approval to assassinate Zorion. Hesitation had cost him dearly.

Thelle misread the distress in Elzer's face and tried to console him, "Do not worry, Sir. We will figure something out."

"Unlikely, with five consoles down, we are already operating at seventy-five percent. Once we start sending the extra twenty-five percent, it will shut down half the city."

"I have procured several large donations from some of Vlor's bigger corporations. It is enough to build one energy console."

"How much electricity will it provide?"

"Five percent of what we will need, but I had to promise we would not reduce their electricity use during the work cycle." Thelle hesitated, looking for a reaction from the sovereign, "It seemed a fair trade."

"When will it be ready?"

"Fourteen Terrestrial Rotations."

"That fast?"

"The company that builds them is working non-stop to complete it because it is in their best interests to maintain a steady electricity supply."

"It is a help, but I am afraid it will not be enough."

"My team also put together a comprehensive list of ways to conserve energy. With your approval, my company can start implementing the changes right away."

"I will review it after we finish."

Thelle started to ask how his partner was dealing with the loss of Tuso, but the train arrived and stopped, so Noka and a team of five disembarked.

"I want to get this over with," Elzer whispered to Thelle.

As Elzer approached the train to speak with Noka, Zorion stepped off the lead car.

"What is he doing here?" Elzer growled.

"It looks like he brought the Information League with him," Thelle observed.

Once his entire entourage of thirty guards and five disseminators assembled around him, Zorion nodded to one of his sentries, who unfurled Argi's flag and positioned himself behind Zorion.

Elzer was furious, "He is mocking me!"

"Indeed, Sir. It is very disrespectful."

Zorion extended his hand palm-forward to greet him. With the Information League nearby and recording, Elzer had to return his salutation. *I must cooperate because this meeting will be all over Akil by the middle of the work cycle.* As they pressed their palms together, Elzer's expression was neutral, hiding his disdain.

"Welcome to Vlor."

Zorion turned to the Information League with a polite smile, "This is a new Terrestrial Revolution for Argi and Vlor. I came here to put any bitterness between our two cities behind us. I am confident that we will march forward together with the same goal. That goal, of course, is to find a new home. With the added electricity given by the city of Vlor starting in just a few moments, we will have the resources needed to increase our efforts in doing just that."

The Information League shouted questions at Elzer, "Why did it take you so long to contribute?"

Inwardly, Zorion smiled. He told the disseminator to ask the question because he wanted Elzer's response or the lack of it on record so that everyone would know.

"I do not wish to make any statement right now," Elzer replied.

"Why did you refuse to do your fair share, even after Zorion brought you before Gau's Judgment Seat?" another disseminator yelled.

"No comment," Elzer grumbled and turned to give Zorion a menacing look.

"Elzer, what about…" another disseminator started to ask, but Zorion interrupted him, "Please, Elzer has suffered a great loss. Let us focus on the reason we are here." Zorion looked at Elzer, giving him the cue.

"Follow me," Elzer acknowledged, leading Zorion and his companions to his private vehicle.

Everyone boarded, and they headed to Vlor electric. Within moments, they arrived. The Information League stepped out first to chronicle everyone exiting the vehicle.

"Thelle, please show Noka and his team to the power transfer junction," Elzer ordered.

"Of course, Sir," Thelle replied. "Please, follow me," he gestured to Noka.

The Information League followed them, except for one, who hid behind Zorion's guards, where he watched Zorion and Elzer closely as they walked several paces away to talk privately.

"It did not have to come to this," Zorion insisted.

Elzer did not reply. Instead, he stared neutrally at Zorion.

"Now, you are not speaking to me?" puzzled Zorion.

"You got what you wanted from me. Once Noka finishes, I expect you to leave my city."

"I was hoping you would join me for lunch so that we could discuss business and…."

Elzer interrupted him, "I am too busy. This proceeding has put me behind on my duties."

"Very well, since I have your attention, I want to convey my sincerest condolences for your loss."

Abruptly, Elzer turned away, headed to the railing, gazed over his city, and saw lights flicker and go out, just like the light that once shined in Tuso. *You will pay for this Zorion.* Elzer heard the hum of a digital image-collecting device and turned to find a disseminator standing alongside the railing, several paces to his left. *He got a profile image of me while I was mourning the loss of my heir.*

It was an intimate moment, a private moment. Elzer wanted to unsheathe his sword and slice the *Putok* in half, but it would cause a public relations mess, so instead, he swallowed his anger. Frustrated, Elzer returned his attention to Vlor, where more lights flickered and went out. A few hundred heartbeats later, Noka returned with his team. They finished rerouting Vlor's power to the science division. Noka was on his communicator, confirming they were receiving the energy; he nodded to Zorion, letting him know everything checked out. Elzer walked over to where Zorion stood. *What is the next scene in this farce?*

Zorion smiled again for the Information League, "My friends, this is a new beginning. Soon, the citizens of Akil will have a new home, and we will all owe a debt of gratitude *in part* to Elzer for his help."

Again, he extended his hand, palm forward, and Elzer hesitantly returned his farewell.

"Now, it is time for us to return, as I am sure Elzer has much work to do. I want to thank him for his hospitality, and I wish the citizens of Vlor great prosperity in the work cycles to come."

Zorion and his company returned to the Intercity Transportation Station, and Elzer returned to his office, where he allowed himself a temper tantrum. Since no one could hear him, Elzer overturned tables, threw chairs, punched holes in the wall, and screamed in a pure, primal shout.

The outburst ended, and he contacted Igon, "I want him dead! I want it to be a slow, painful death, and I want him to suffer!"

Igon pulled the earpiece away from his ear until Elzer stopped screaming, "I will instruct Shafe to perform the task as soon as possible."

"I should have done this sooner!"

"I must advise you, Sir. If you want his death to be slow and painful, it will take some planning. First, I will need to secure a safe place to take him and buy the instruments of torture so it could take several Terrestrial Rotations. Also, there is a greater risk that a search party will discover us. Every guard and citizen in the city will be looking for him after I abduct him."

Elzer paced in his office and sighed at his conclusion, "I cannot risk having the assassination traced back to me, so do it your way, but just do it!"

"As you wish."

Igon ended the connection and confirmed Shafe's schedule. He was on short-term administrative leave as a reward for the wounds received defending Zorion from Olan's attack. No one would miss him over the following few Terrestrial Rotations. Igon instructed him to meet at their prearranged place. It had to be a face-to-face get-together. There was no telling who might be eavesdropping on their communicators.

Also, he had to give him the keys to the safe house and a new identity because killing Zorion would set off major security procedures shutting down the city: no one in or out, making it almost impossible to leave Argi. Therefore, Shafe had to stay there undetected for at least twenty Terrestrial Rotations until their safeguards returned to normal, making his departure a little easier.

Once Shafe returned, Igon would dispose of him. There could be no loose ends. Shafe was the type who would brag about what he did. Elzer would not allow that. Igon smiled because he would put this matter to rest and reap the incredible rewards from Elzer's generosity.

Chapter 77

Michael arrived at work early to ensure everything was ready for Supreme Commander Porter's 'volunteer.' He triple-checked communications with the organisms, explored his work email, and found one from Lisa with the moss's nutrition results. Aside from its high protein and nutritional content, the moss had several hidden chemicals existing in its leaves. *It looks like the perfect food if the strange stuff doesn't kill you.* There was no sign that the plant was poisonous or had pharmaceutical benefits, which means whoever had it must have used it for food.

Michael went to the tray where he kept the original moss, opened the lid, frowned, and spoke into his intercom, "Lisa, would you come in here, please?"

"Be right there."

Lisa entered the lab a few moments later, "What's up?"

"I just read your results on the moss and planned to run a few more tests, but it appears that all the plants are dead."

"That doesn't sound right."

Michael sniffed the tray, "Come here. Do you smell that?"

Lisa sniffed, "Yeah, it smells like an herbicide."

"Someone destroyed these plants."

"Why would anyone want to do that?"

"We're going to find out."

He abruptly turned and went into the adjoining room, his secondary office. Being familiar with Michael's idiosyncrasies, Lisa followed him, "How? Without any – Oh, I see, you set some aside, you sneaky little…."

Michael interrupted her, "Just keep it quiet. I don't know who did this, so you and I are the only ones who know about it. I want you to take samples and see if you can figure out the properties of the mysterious substance the nutrition test did not show. Don't let anyone know what you're working on."

"I'll get on it right away."

She went back into the central lab with samples in her hands and closed the door behind her. Michael pulled out a chair on the opposite side of the room and sat at the lone desk. *Only two people have access to this lab, Lisa and me.* Using a tablet, he jotted down ideas. *If it wasn't Lisa, who else knew about the moss?* As he wrote, someone knocked on the door. Michael put the pad away.

"Come in."

Jared walked in. They were surprised to see each other.

"How have you been?" Michael finally asked.

"Good, thanks. We missed you at the last family dinner. We haven't seen you for quite a few dinners," Jared replied.

"I've been a little busy."

"Mom misses you."

"I know; we communicate through emails."

"She's having another next week, so tell her you're coming, and she'll plan the day around your schedule."

"I know she told me. Is that why you came by, or is there something else you wanted to talk to me about?"

"I'm your volunteer," Jared affirmed.

"You? Why?"

"Supreme Commander Porter gave me a mission, and from what I understand, these little guys will allow you to track me wherever I go."

"That's what they do. What's the mission?"

"I only know the basics, so it's best if I let General Green tell us the details together."

"All right, take off your shirt."

As Jared removed his jersey, Lisa gasped softly. Michael and Jared looked at her. She was standing in the doorway, blushing.

"Oh, excuse me," she smiled without turning away.

Michael noticed that she kept eyeing Jared's naked torso, "Do you want something?"

"Um - Uh - yeah," she replied. "But it can wait."

She sighed deeply and returned to her desk without closing the door. Michael rolled his eyes, selected a syringe from a nearby bin, filled it with the organisms, and injected them into Jared's back, right above the left kidney.

"Ok, don't move; I'll make sure they're all right."

"Will they make me sick?"

"Oh, I'm sure you'll be fine. Michael's been working on this project non-stop. He's excellent, you know," Lisa yelled from the other room.

Seeing a glare from Michael, Lisa turned around, pretending to focus on her work. Michael turned on the transceiver and sent a message to the organisms. They replied.

"Yep, they seem happy in their new home," Michael remarked.

"Did they really say that?" Jared wondered.

"Oh no, those organisms can't talk or think as we do. Michael's trying to be funny," Lisa giggled.

Again, she had turned from her desk and was facing the open door. Jared politely smiled at her, but Michael turned to face her. Seeing his expression, she realized trouble was not far away.

"Would you like to come in and for me to leave for a few minutes?" Michael joked.

Lisa shook her head and smiled, "No, why would you ask such a silly question?"

"Because you seem to be acting weird, ever since my brother arrived. Obviously, you want to be alone with him based on your mannerisms," accused Michael.

"Jared's your brother! Oh, Michael, you never told me you had a brother," she walked over to shake Jared's hand. "Hi, I'm Lisa, Michael's lab assistant."

Jared returned her greeting, but Lisa just gawked at him.

"Would you like me to take a picture for you?" Michael quipped.

"Do you have a camera?" Lisa jested.

Michael raised an eyebrow, so Lisa spun around, "Ok, don't worry. I get the hint. I'll go back to work."

"As I was saying, I sent the bacteria a basic query to see if they were alive and well. Their reply was equivalent to a yes," Michael explained.

"That's just weird," Jared rubbed his back. "What kind of organisms are they?" "Bacterial," Michael answered.

"I shouldn't have asked," Jared frowned, putting his shirt back on.

"Oh, don't worry, Jared. Those little organisms won't hurt you at all. Instead, they'll find a nice quiet spot to live near the adrenal gland, and you'll never hear from them again," Lisa interrupted again.

"All right, he's put his shirt back on, so the show's over," Michael grumbled.

"No need to be mean, Michael. I'm preparing the test tray as we speak," defended Lisa.

"I would feel better if you looked at the tray and not at my brother," Michael retorted.

Lisa huffed and pretended to return to her work again but winked at Jared before turning around.

"Does that happen to you a lot?" quizzed Michael.

"Sometimes. I've become used to it. She was only doing a little harmless flirting."

"She needs to flirt on her own time, not mine."

"Come on, Mike. Let's meet up with General Green," he hoped to change the subject.

Michael requested an android, and it arrived a few minutes later. It carried the spare transceiver to the Local Transportation Station, where Jared typed in the address.

"Did you create the stuff they put in my body that makes my skin impenetrable?"

"I developed it from a new species of plant discovered in Brazil a few years ago. A friend of mine, a botanist, found it during an expedition. He invited me to the site. They grew wild, deep in the jungle and close to the ground. It took some time, but we duplicated their living conditions. Now, we have a couple of greeneries full of them. I began evaluating them to see if they had any benefits and the rest, you know."

"Huh, well, it's saved my life more than a few times."

"I'm glad to hear it."

The portal opened, so they stepped through and landed at the Military Facility, where guards checked their identifications, and they headed straight to the War Room. It was Michael's first visit. He marveled at the many assorted sizes of computer displays all over the wall, some showed information, and others had live feed from different satellites. Also, in the center of the room, he saw General Green standing near a brightly lit table where holographic maps floated above it; General Green saw them and nodded for them to join him.

"Where should I put the transceiver, General?" questioned Michael.

"On that table."

The android set it down, hooked it into the main computer, and turned on a monitor showing a map and Jared's exact location.

"Impressive. Will it show his location in Germany after he arrives?" General Green inquired.

"Yes," Michael answered.

"Excellent," General Green pressed a button on the table, and a three-dimensional hologram of Frankfurt materialized in front of them. He continued, "Now the plan is simple. Jared, you're to transport just outside the city, right about here," he pointed to a location on the hologram. "From there, you'll make your way into the city on foot. You'll be posing as the brother of the Transportation Station security guard killed last Tuesday. You are on a vendetta. Check into a hotel and ask the locals if they've seen this man," General Green handed Jared a picture of Diederich Schmidt.

"Um, won't that get me killed?" Jared questioned.

"Until now, he's stayed anonymous, but our cameras caught a profile of one of the attackers. Our facial recognition software confirmed his identity as Howard Smith. Our records show that he used to work as a portal technician for the Regime until a power surge killed his wife, stepping through the event horizon. Since then, he has tried to get the Regime to stop using vortex technology. No one would listen, so he left and started the Tech Revolution.

"Later, he adjusted his agenda to get everyone to stop using all technology. To answer your question, since he wants to stay anonymous, we believe the Tech Revolutionaries will capture you first. They will want to know how you figured out his identity. You'll have clues about your real identity on your person, which will make you a better prize. That should get you an audience with him."

"What are my orders if I do meet him?"

"Diederich Schmidt has claimed responsibility for the attack on our International Transportation Station, which killed hundreds of Regime citizens. Now that we know his identity, your orders are to kill him."

"You realize my hands will be tied, most likely behind my back."

"You're a special Regime agent, Mr. Stewart; breaking out of restraints shouldn't be a problem," General Green insisted.

"Not all restraints are the same," Jared jested.

Ignoring his comment, General Green continued, "Once he's dead, contact us. We'll get you out of there and send in a strike team to take out the rest of his group. Just make sure you communicate to us when no one else is around."

"How do I make contact?"

"A doctor will implant this into your ear canal," General Green held up a small chip.

"What's that?"

"It's an earpiece. We will hear everything that's going on while you're there. You need to say, 'Back to Oz,' and we'll transport you home."

"Back to Oz? Who thinks of these phrases?"

"It's necessary to choose words that you normally wouldn't say so we don't withdraw you prematurely."

"When do I begin?"

"Your clothes and passport are in the adjoining room. The doctor will implant the earpiece, so you can change and be on your way."

"I should get started." Jared gave Michael a playful, brotherly punch on the bicep and left to get ready. He turned to face Michael on the way out, "Please, call Mom."

Chapter 78

Gecheana approached Domeka's home and waved her hand, the door opened before her, and a gush of warm, acrid air rushed to greet her. She smiled because Domeka was working on the swords. She waved her finger, and the door closed and locked behind her. In the backroom, she extended her arm, and a large wall moved forward, exposing a narrow tunnel carved into the dense rock behind it.

As she walked into the dark corridor, her eyes adjusted. As a Skean, she did not need light to see in the darkness because it was the Night Lord's territory. Nevertheless, she moved slowly and carefully for several hundred heartbeats until seeing a faint glow, which grew brighter as she came closer to Domeka's workroom.

She found Domeka sitting cross-legged on a pillow in the center of the room. Glowing, hot, molten ore hung suspended in midair, several hand widths in front of Domeka, as she forged the mineral into a razor-sharp blade until satisfied it was ready to begin the cooling process. Gecheana noticed a finished sword sitting on a table against the wall to her left. The blade made a barely audible, clanging noise as she lifted it, but it was enough to distract Domeka. It caused her to drop what she was doing and spin to see who snuck up on her.

"Concentrate," Gecheana turned her attention to inspect the new blade.

"You startled me. You know as well as I that creating these swords takes complete concentration."

"Did the blade cool before you dropped it?" Gecheana asked, ignoring her excuse.

Returning her attention to the edge on the ground, Domeka reached out with her mind to see if it had cooled. It had, so she picked it up with her hand and examined it.

"It is undamaged and ready for the next phase."

"Excellent."

Gecheana ignited the sword in her hand. She rotated her wrist, spinning the scarlet blade in front of her, making the already stifling air in the unventilated room unbearably hot.

"Please, turn that off. I am already sweating," Domeka begged.

Gecheana obliged her request, "Elegant."

"It should be. I made it."

Gecheana smiled at her pride.

"Why did you want them fully operational? Ordinary Akilians cannot direct energy to ignite a blade, yet you had me install the power transfer gems," Domeka queried.

Gecheana ignored her question, "How many do you have ready?"

"Two."

"How many acolytes have High Priest Elazar gathered?"

"Twelve, so far. He is still interviewing the candidates to ensure they fit your description," Domeka answered.

"Very well, I will check with the others to see how far they are with the swords. I will begin their instruction later this Terrestrial Revolution."

"I will have them meet you in the training room." Domeka paused, considering her words carefully, "Is it wise to hand Skean swords over to ordinary Akilians?"

"Extraordinary circumstances require extraordinary measures; for example, Kraeth failed to kill Yanamai."

"It was not his fault. Nayrah interfered with their fight. Garbi would not only have killed Yanamai but Zorion too. If it were not for her, Otsoa would be sovereign, and Tadra would be searching within the correct sector."

"I am aware of her betrayal."

"If you want, I will kill Yanamai," Domeka offered.

"There is no point now. Nayrah's interference has made Zorion suspicious, so he replaced Tadra as Yanamai's second with another and put twenty guards in front of Yanamai's home."

"Why do you allow Nayrah to continue to rule Argi?"

"She has done well but has made many blunders since the past yellow harvest. For example, trying to prove herself, she made a pathetic attempt to kill Zorion by using Olan."

"What a disaster."

"Now, our only hope is for Elzer to kill Zorion. If he fails, we must confront the Saiph at some point. By using a militia, our identities will remain hidden, and we will have a better chance of defeating the Saiph."

"Are Saiphs stronger than us?"

"I killed the last of the Akilian Saiphs a long time ago. I attacked them one by one from the shadows. It is not always the power you wield but how you use it. Our numbers are great and remain hidden, so if we stay unified, we can kill the Saiph whenever he or she arrives."

"Once we defeat the Saiph, will we regain our ability to see the future again?"

"Yes. I only hope it will not be too late. The red sun is coming to its end. If we cannot find another world, we may have only one other choice."

"What is that?"

"I will tell you when it is time. Now, get back to work."

Chapter 79

Earth
The Regime - Washington D.C. - School District
April 14, 2452 (28 Days Ago)

Brook performed her choreographed floor exercise on the center mat as one of several Olympic hopefuls. Julie watched the thirteen-year-old leap, jump, flip, and dance around the square until she reached the end of her routine; Julie turned off the music.

"You're still not landing correctly after the backflip," Julie criticized.

Frustrated by the comment, Brook huffed at the remark, "You're never happy with my performance."

"That's not true. I thought you did well, but you're landing will cause you to lose points."

The snotty thirteen-year-old appeared from behind the mask of the mature athlete, "The landing felt fine to me."

Julie replayed the performance using the computer display found on the nearest wall. Brook watched intently and, seeing her landing, stomped her foot in frustration.

"That can't be! My landing was solid!"

"Video doesn't lie. Now, I want you to practice that move until I come back."

Moving on to another pupil, Julie watched her work on the balance beam. Chloe was standing on her left leg, holding the heel of her right foot above her head, extending her left hand out and upward. She set her foot down, went into a perfect handstand, rolled into an upright position, bent her body backward, grabbed the beam with her hands, and brought her left foot over and back, followed by her right foot. Now, ready for her dismount, Chloe steadied herself and committed to a series of forward-handsprings that led to a double forward flip. She landed and nearly fell backward.

"No - no - no! You must focus, Chloe! You're not pushing hard enough off the beam. That's why you're landing off-balance," Julie advised.

"You're asking me to do the impossible!" Chloe huffed and sat on a nearby chair.

"Where are you going? I didn't say it was time to quit!"

"I need a break."

Julie sprang onto the balance beam and performed the routine she taught Chloe, who carefully watched her perform. *I know she's going to fall.* Julie went through every leap, jump, and flip perfectly, and ended her routine with a double forward flip, landed without a step, raised her arms in the air, and faced Chloe.

"You see, I'm not asking you to do the impossible. Now, get back on the beam and work on your dismount."

Julie walked away, struggling not to limp. *I will not let them see me icing my knee. Some say that those who can't - teach. Well, I could, and it's good for them to realize that now and again.* At the end of a full day of coaching the young, frustrated competitors, Julie put her things in her bag and walked to the Local Transportation Station that brought her closest to her parents' farm on the Eastern Shore. She found her parents' hover vehicle and put her bag in the trunk.

On her way to the driver's door, she looked around. All she could hear were crickets. *It's very peaceful out here.* Taking care of her parents' farm from time to time was not a burden for her; she enjoyed it but preferred to live in the city, where everything was nearby. She started the engines. The vehicle rose several inches off the ground as the jets pushed air toward the Earth; she backed the car from its parking spot and headed toward the farm.

As her hovercar glided over the natural, green roadway, Julie slowed the vehicle to take in the beauty of the lush forest and flora's many distinct colors and smells. She saw one of her parents' androids mowing the house's driveway. Her mother insisted they keep the lawn and surrounding areas manicured to perfection. She parked the vehicle in front of the house, and an android named Ratchet greeted her. Ratchet opened the door and removed her bags from the trunk.

"Did you get the fence up on the south pasture today?" Julie asked.

"Yes, ma'am. The newly purchased cattle are grazing peacefully there now."

"Good work, Ratchet."

"Do you wish to inspect the horses before you eat?"

"Yes, because I don't want to go back outside again once I'm in."

Ratchet went inside the house to put her things away, and Julie walked to the barn. The structure was immense. It was custom built to hold the many prize-winning stallions her dad owned. Inside, it was well lit, and the androids kept the walkway clean because her mother insisted on keeping the farm as mechanically spotless as possible. Julie filled a wheel barrel full of carrots and spent the hour petting, hand feeding, and talking to the horses.

Hearing her singing, the horses poked their heads outside the front of their stalls. They knew about her ritual, so they each patiently waited for the attention she gave them. Julie stood outside of Lex's enclosure and fed him until all the horses in the barn began neighing loudly. Some kicked against the wooden walls, and others started to stand on their hind legs. Turning to see what was causing the commotion, she felt her hair stand up as a small amount of electricity went through her body.

Looking back at Lex, she noticed that his mane was doing the same thing. The ground shook, knocking Julie on her butt. She saw an energy ring form in the walkway, and fingers of electricity reached out to the metal bars on the nearby stalls. The energy ring turned blue, then red, causing a warm wind to move through the barn. Unexpectedly, an event horizon appeared within the circle, and someone dove through the illuminating hoop, but as quickly as the ring of energy appeared, it vanished with a loud clap like thunder. The sound vibrated her body down to the bones.

Julie rested on the floor and heard the horses neighing more frantically now. Smelling smoke, she stood to find a series of small fires inching their way along the wooden walkway. Julie retrieved a fire extinguisher as several androids passed her, going in the opposite direction. With an extinguisher in hand, she returned to help them put out the flames and ordered the androids to calm the horses. After the flames were out, Julie checked on the man lying face down on the floor; she carefully moved him and saw that the ring severely burned his face and arms, so using her communicator, she called Ratchet.

"How may I be of service?"

"Someone is injured! I need you here now, Ratchet!"

"I'm on my way."

Within seconds, Ratchet arrived. Following his programming, he leaned over to examine the injured man.

"Is he going to be all right?" she inquired.

"He has first, second and third-degree burns. I recommend we take him to the house right away."

"Do it."

Ratchet reached under the wounded man, lifted him with ease, and brought him to the farm's emergency room, where he cleaned his wounds.

"Be sure to take x-rays," Julie ordered.

"I already have. I'm reviewing them now."

Julie watched Ratchet work on the patient and became incredibly grateful that her dad installed the emergency medic software upgrade for him.

"How is he?"

"He broke his right humerus. Because of the burns, I can't set it right now, so I'm running an IV with an antibiotic drip."

"Shouldn't you put something on his skin?"

"I can put antibiotic cream on the first and second-degree burns, but the more severe areas must heal on their own. I recommend that you put on this mask to prevent any contamination."

"Oh, of course," Julie took the breathing mask and put it over her mouth.

"How long will he be unconscious?" she queried with a muffled voice.

"Considering his injuries, he may be inert for some time."

"Keep a close eye on him and let me know when he wakes up."

"Yes, ma'am."

Chapter 80

Akil
Argi City
The 22,276[th] Terrestrial Rotation of the Second Summer

Zorion returned from Vlor and headed straight for the interrogation room, where Dolas, Olan's second in command, moved him for questioning. Having arrived at the city's prison entrance, Zorion ordered the jailer to open the gate, and the large, heavy metal doors creaked. The sound gave Zorion chills, imagining what a prisoner must feel like at that very moment. *To live there for more than a Terrestrial Revolution is unthinkable.*

Vul, the prison administrator, met Zorion at the gate and ushered him and his bodyguards to the interrogation room. The prison was at the bottom of the list concerning power distribution, so the corridors were dim. Zorion wondered why anyone would want to break the law and risk imprisonment. He passed through several levels and noticed that more of his citizens had occupied the once empty cells since his last inspection. The imminent threat of their dying sun gave rise to crime.

They take risks because they know we could all die in a heartbeat. The closer he got to the interrogation room, the more depressed his mood became. *We used to be good friends. I want to know what changed between us and when?* It was never good to lose a friend, and with everything going on in his life, he needed as many as possible. Zorion arrived at the interrogation room to find Dolas standing outside with two armed guards. To ensure Zorion's safety, Broll went in first to check Olan's bonds.

Watching Broll from the doorway, Zorion whispered to Dolas, "Have you spoken with him yet?"

"No, Sir. I was waiting for you."

Broll signaled Zorion, who entered the room with the rest of his bodyguards behind him. Seeing Olan bound made Zorion sad. It was still a mystery why he betrayed him.

Zorion frowned, "Turn on the recorders."

Dolas walked over and flipped the switch on the wall, "We are ready, Sir."

Sitting on the opposite side of the metallic table from Olan, Zorion saw bruises on his wrists, where the metal bands confined his movement. Wrinkled and torn clothes covered his body, and his hair was a matted mess. Unable to face him, Olan kept his head down.

"Look at me," Zorion demanded.

Hesitantly, Olan raised his head, exposing cuts and bruises received during his arrest. Zorion saw tears in his eyes, but Olan was a well-trained agent and could easily fake sorrow.

"Do you plan to speak?"

"What do you want me to say?" Olan responded.

"Start with the truth."

Olan spat a laugh, "How can I tell you the truth when I do not even know it myself?"

"Are you telling me you do not know why you attacked me?"

"Yes."

"Now, you insult me after trying to kill me?"

"I am not trying to insult you."

"You must think I am stupid because I remember the savage look in your eyes as you plunged this dagger into my chest several times, so you must have some reason to hate me," Zorion removed the weapon from a sheath behind his back and slammed it on the table.

"I do not hate you," Olan replied, obsessively staring at the knife.

Olan saw his reflection in it, which brought words spoken by a female to his memory. *I should find someone else to love me. Maybe Zorion would be agreeable.* Although the memory of hearing them was clear, he could not remember who said them.

Restless, Zorion stood, paced for a few heartbeats, and continued, "I must say you have failed as an executioner. First, you used such a small weapon for an attack. Second, you did not follow through with a decapitation. Are you getting old?"

Zorion hoped his question would provoke anger, forcing him to divulge some clue as to his motive.

"You know my skills as an agent. If I wanted you dead, you would be dead," Olan replied.

"Are you saying that you did not want me dead; you just wanted to punish me for some reason?"

"I do not want you dead, and I do not wish to punish you."

"There is only one other choice."

Olan looked at him quizzically.

"You are working for Elzer," Zorion commented flatly.

Angered by his accusation, Olan tried to stand; the restraints around his wrist kept him from getting up.

"I would never side with that *putok*!"

"Your protest is very passionate," Broll noted.

"I agree. I think we have found our answer," Zorion concluded.

"No! I am not working for Elzer! You must believe me!" Olan yelled.

"You said yourself that you do not know why you attacked me, yet out of all the questions I have asked, this is the only one with an emotional response. You have interrogated before, so what would you think?"

"That I was working for him," Olan reluctantly agreed.

"There, we see the same outcome."

"I know you do not believe me; I *am* loyal to you," Olan insisted.

His comment brought snickers from the guards, but one look from Zorion shut them up.

"Apparently, my definition of loyalty is outdated." Zorion directed his words to Dolas and the guards and extended his arms to dramatize his words, "I now know that a devoted friend tries to kill you. Thank you for correcting me on this matter."

"Please hear me, Zorion! I have no reason to attack you! I can only say that I fought to stop myself from killing you with all my might!"

"Oh, I hear you," he lamented, sat opposite Olan, and looked him in the eyes. "As you know, it is not my job to interrogate prisoners, so I came here to give you a chance to tell me the reason you tried to kill me and the name of your employer. I had hoped that if I were ever your friend, you would tell me; it is clear I did this in vain, so now, it will be up to Dolas to find out the truth," he stood and signaled for Broll and the others to leave the room. At the doorway, he stopped, "Dolas, do whatever you must to extract the truth from him."

As Zorion walked away, Olan shouted, "I have told you everything I know! I am still your friend, Zorion! I will always be your friend!"

His words deeply cut Zorion, who wondered if it was the right thing to do. He had condemned a lifelong friend to torture if Olan was telling the truth. He thought carefully and decided not to take the chance. Excusing Olan would make him look weak; it was something Zorion could not afford, especially now. Dolas waited in the doorway for Zorion and his entourage to leave; he reentered the interrogation room and deliberately locked the door behind him. The two Akilians faced each other.

Smiling, Dolas leaned against the door and folded his arms across his chest, "Now, what shall we talk about?"

Chapter 81

Earth
China - Po Toi Island
May 12, 2452

Wu Luli followed General Ming-tun Fu down a long corridor and grew angrier with each step. Years ago, the General told her that her dad lived free, in an undisclosed rural area in China, under an assumed name, yet now the General had revealed that he was there on Po Toi Island, a place she had visited hundreds of times. Wu Luli had never trusted General Ming-tun Fu, but she had unwittingly accepted it as truth because he had lied from her youth.

In a million years, never would she think her dad was here on the island, right under her nose. Farther down the hallway, she noticed many doors evenly spaced on each corridor side. Reaching the end, she counted one hundred in total. It was the exact number of agents working under the General. She saw him sitting in a recliner, watching television inside the room to her right.

Instinctively, she searched the room for cameras. Since the General did not bother hiding them, they were visible in every corner. She surmised that every door along the way must lead to the same kind of room but reserved for another agent's family member. Hearing her enter, her dad turned from the television.

Seeing her, he stood and exclaimed, "Wu Luli! Is that you!"

"Baba!" Wu Luli shouted.

They embraced for a long time and wailed.

"I've missed you so much," she sobbed.

He took a step back to look at her whole image, "You've grown into a beautiful young lady. I'm so sorry I missed all those years."

Moved by his words, she laughed and cried simultaneously and faced the General, "You promised we could speak privately, outside."

"Follow me."

The General led them into a garden found in the facility's center. Before sending them out, he gave her a large umbrella and held the door open; they walked to the gazebo, set in the garden's center.

"Has he treated you well?" she asked, speaking loudly over the storm.

"Considering the alternative, quite well."

"I didn't know he was holding you here. I can't tell you how many times I've been in this building. He told me you were free, living somewhere in China. I stupidly believed him."

"I figured as much, but don't blame yourself. None of this is your fault."

"For now, I'm just glad you're alive and well," Wu Luli answered. It had been so many years that all she wanted was to sit with him and hold him. Gently, she touched his neck, kissed his cheek, hugged him, and carefully whispered in his ear, "I just placed a tracking device on your neck. It will blend in with your skin, so keep it on. If you must take it off, hide it somewhere so they won't find it."

He listened to her plan, frowned, inconspicuously removed the device, threw it away, and whispered back, "I want you to listen to me very carefully. Don't try to rescue me. Leave here and never come back."

"He'll kill you," her voice shook, but she kept it at a whisper.

"Then, that is my fate."

"I can't do that, baba. The only thing that has kept me going is the thought of freeing you one day."

"Listen to me," he responded forcefully, "he will never let me go if you continue to work for him. He will use me to control you, dead or alive, so you must take that power away from him."

"You're asking me to do the impossible."

He saw two guards approaching over her shoulder, "Our time is almost over, but I must tell you one more thing before you leave. Your mother is still alive."

"What?" Her eyes widened in surprise.

"She escaped to the Regime. You must find her and tell her I still love her."

The guards arrived, ending their meeting. They embraced each other one last time until the sentries escorted him away. Emotionally drained, she collapsed onto a seat in the gazebo.

Never in her life had she cried so hard than at that moment. The pouring rain only emulated her sadness. A few minutes later, she regained her composure and walked back inside.

"How was your visit?" General Ming-tun Fu inquired.

She glared at him and wanted to kill him with every fiber of her being.

"Not what you expected, I see," he observed. "Let's go back to my office," he turned and signaled his bodyguards to stand about ten feet back.

"Why is he here? You said he was living free."

"I couldn't take the chance that you would find him, just remember, I haven't mistreated him yet."

She grabbed his lapel with her left hand, pushed him against the wall, and growled through gritted teeth, "If you harm him, I promise, you'll regret the day we ever met."

The guards sprang to his aid, but he held up his hand for them to stand down, "I think now you see the hopelessness of the situation. I have your baba, and I've treated him quite well, so if you try to free him or double-cross me…."

He left the threat hanging.

"If you kill him, I swear," she started to say, but he interrupted.

"My dear, you know better than I that some things are worse than death. I can move him at any time, and you would never know where I put him; perhaps a dark cell, deep within the ground, where he will never see daylight again."

She let him go with a shove, and they continued their journey back to his office, where he faced her, "Will you be joining me?"

Reluctantly, she walked in.

"Now, as I was saying, we need to get Chu Lian back into the Regime."

"A transfer will take weeks."

"You are correct; we do not have much time because I want you there within twenty-four hours, which is why I've already told your boss, the Chinese ambassador to the Regime, he will transfer you."

"How am I supposed to do that?"

"I've just been informed that a terrorist group has captured a Regime agent in Frankfurt, Germany. If you help him escape, I'm sure the Regime would be grateful and give you a speedy transfer."

"Why would I be in Frankfurt, and how am I, posing as Chu Lian, going to rescue a Regime agent and maintain my cover?"

"Simple. The ambassador is giving you one last assignment before reviewing your transfer. You'll be the liaison for the Orient Hotel Management Company. Your cover is in Frankfurt to negotiate a contract to build a new hotel there; you will be there on the ambassador's behalf. Ask around and check if anyone has seen this man," he handed her Jared's picture.

She recognized him as Michael's brother, "I know him."

"Yes. He's the dupe's brother. From what I've learned, he was there undercover, looking for Diederich Schmidt, a man who blew up one of their International Transportation Stations."

"If this intel is correct, they will kill me when they capture me," Wu Luli surmised.

"No, they won't. Once they capture you, they'll discover that you work for the Orient Hotel Management Company, which has an insurance policy on all its employees, so I'm confident they'll hold you for ransom."

"I'm not an Orient Hotel employee," she interrupted.

"Since you are negotiating on its behalf, the policy would cover you as a temporary employee. The coverage is public information, so they will investigate and see that you are worth something. If they see a potential profit, they must inform Diederich Schmidt, which means they'll take you to him."

"Which is where Jared will be."

"Correct."

"I'll need one item before I leave."

"Write it down," he handed her paper and a pencil. "I will have it delivered to you on the way. You must leave now before it is too late. There is a helicopter waiting for you outside. I instructed the pilot to leave once you are on board. I know the weather is bad, but I must take that chance. He will land on the mainland on top of a building near an International Transportation Station so you can take a portal to Frankfurt. We have employed a double agent to get you the rest of the way there. I will be expecting to hear from you the moment you are in."

He took the paper from her, "Is that all?"

"Yes."

"Very well, leave and catch your ride."

He walked to the window to watch her leave; through the rain and wind, he saw the helicopter take off and disappear into the night. As the sound faded, he called a guard.

"Yes, Sir," the sentry saluted.

"Check our guest thoroughly. I want to ensure she did not tag him in any way. I do not want any mistakes."

Chapter 82

Akil
Argi City
The 22,276[th] Terrestrial Rotation of the Second Summer

Thea shopped to distract her mind from recent events for most of the work cycle. Considering what she had been through, it only made sense to set aside a little time for herself. She strolled along the avenue with several assistants carrying bags of assorted clothing as she went from store to store on the tenth-level elite plaza shopping strip. It was her favorite place because only nobles could afford to buy the items from the aristocratic shops.

Also, if someone recognized her, they showed her the respect that she rightly deserved, a courtesy she did not get from Gecheana, the other Skeans, or Jadell, so it was the only place she felt appreciated. She saw an empty table on a deck a few paces ahead, protruding away from the promenade. The table sat near a transparent barrier, where she had a "Gau's eye view" of the city. Her assistants stood nearby, waiting for her. She ordered a warm beverage and gazed out over the city, taking in its beauty.

Eating their lunch together on the next level below, a family of four caught her attention. The female stopped what she was doing and dealt with her little ones, wiping their hands and faces. *They are sloppy little eaters.* She got up from her seat to retrieve more food and drink for her family. *That is why we employ servants.* Having been noble for so long, Thea could not imagine doing anything subservient to Zorion or her brood because it was beneath her.

She continued her assessment of the family, realized they dressed poorly, and shook her head with disapproval. *He is obviously a subpar provider. How could anyone be happy in such dire circumstances?* Thea unexpectedly saw the woman lean over and gently kiss her partner on the cheek. She sat, looked at her family, and smiled with pride. Thea looked on with amazement. *How can she be so content?*

Her happiness irritated Thea. There was no reason for her fulfillment, yet her expression showed it. She could not recall having a pleasant meal with Gecheana and the others because, during their gatherings, Gecheana always reviewed strategy, the path of accumulation or reprimanded Nayrah for failing at some tasks. Never did Gecheana recognize what Nayrah and the others amassed.

Thea discovered a hidden void within. Even though the thought of Zorion repulsed her, she decided to try and emulate what the other female did. Thea wanted to see what it felt like to be happy for once in her life. She dropped a few Sovereign Cubes on the table and motioned for her aides to follow her. Along the way, Thea planned an elaborate dinner for Zorion, Otsoa, Yetta, and Va'ron. Her pace quickened now that she had a goal.

I might even set the table myself. She chuckled because it conflicted with everything Gecheana taught her. *Why do I feel this longing?* She surrendered all her bags for inspection on the Sovereign's level at the security station. It was an inconvenience she tolerated but ensured it was uncomfortable for those performing the search. Often, she would quibble with them as they inspected each item.

"If you have already confirmed my identity, there is no need to go through every package," Thea insisted.

"I am afraid we must. We have been on a level one alert ever since the attack. Protocol dictates," the Screener tried to explain.

Thea interrupted her, "I am tired of hearing about protocol. I am Thea! Now let my things through so I can go home!"

"I am sorry, but I cannot honor that request."

Frustrated, Thea ordered her aides to bring the packages once they cleared. The Screener rolled her eyes, and the guards nodded their agreement. Thea arrived at the front of her home and saw several aides pushing carts, loaded with luggage, away from the living quarter's entrance.

Curious about their contents, she stopped one of the aides, "Whose bags are these?"

The aide hesitated to answer.

"Are you deaf? I asked you a question!" Thea demanded.

Reluctantly, the aide replied, "I am not sure. They have been bringing bags to the front door for about four thousand heartbeats."

"Who are *they*?"

"Other aides."

"Whose aides?"

"Zorion's."

"Zorion's?"

Grinning, she thought. *He must be going on another tour of the five cities. Well, it will not dampen my dinner plans. I will have supper with my offspring, and it will be better without him.* Inside, she passed Broll along the way to Zorion's dressing room but found no one there until hearing Zorion's voice down the hall. She realized what was happening and ran to her dressing room, where several aides packed clothes, *her* clothes.

"What is the meaning of this?"

The aides froze until Zorion walked out of one of her many closets and nodded toward them, "Continue."

He faced her, "They are following my orders."

"Exactly; what is that?"

"I am packing your vast wardrobe."

"I hope you plan on replacing them."

"Do not worry. I am not throwing your clothes away."

Thea sighed in relief.

"I am moving them to an apartment on level five hundred," Zorion added.

"It is true, I need more room for my clothes, but you did not have to buy an apartment. You could have just had another room dug out of the rock right here," she pointed to an undeveloped wall.

"I did not buy the apartment just for your clothes. The apartment is for you, too."

"Are you kicking me out?"

"Yes."

"What have I done to deserve such a harsh punishment?"

"I think it is obvious, but if you need an explanation."

She interrupted him, "Stop this, Zorion! You know I - you know I - love you."

"You hesitated and frowned when you said it."

"So?"

"So, I have been with you long enough to know when you lie."

"Do not do this to me, Zorion! I will be humiliated!"

"There is no reason for you to be embarrassed."

"If this is about our argument over Otsoa fighting."

"It is not. I think we know this has been a long time coming."

His aides finished packing the last of her clothes and took the bags outside. Now that they were alone, she called on her powers to persuade him to change his mind.

"You want me to stay."

As her will washed over him, he blinked as if falling into a trance, but it faded, "No, that is the last thing I want. That is why I had your things removed from my home."

Stunned, Thea did not know what to say. Somehow, he resisted her. *Impossible.* Panic took over, and she fell to her knees, begging.

"Please, I will do anything you ask, just do not do this."

It was the first time she bowed to him, but it was too late.

"I am sorry, Thea, I have made up my mind."

"Who will take care of me?"

Ah, yes, there are her true feelings. It is all about Thea. "Do not worry. I will still provide for you, but I *will* be reducing your stipend."

"No! Not the Sovereign Cubes too!" She started crying.

Zorion felt happy and sad. Removing Thea from his life made him feel better. It was as if a weight lifted from him, especially after seeing that her genuine affection was for his Sovereign Cubes and not for him. However, she was the mother of his offspring, so no matter how badly she had treated him, he still did not want to hurt her but had to send her away. He extended a tender hand to help her to her feet.

"Come on; I will take you there myself."

It took a few heartbeats before she could regain her composure, and seeing he would not give in to her weeping, she wiped her face with a cloth, took his hand, and stood. They walked out together. She tightly held onto his arm along the way, so everyone would know he was still her possession and was mindful to keep her chin up to remind them of her status. Zorion escorted her onto his private hover vehicle and ordered the driver to take them to the apartment. His other aides followed in a second vehicle, which carried all her belongings. His aides moved the bags into her new abode and returned to their vehicle once they finished.

"I cannot unpack all this myself."

"Do not worry. I will instruct the aides to return later to help you, but you will only have your attendant for help in the future."

"Only one servant?"

"First, you know I do not like that word. She is not a servant. She is an employee of the city. Second, you should be grateful you have her. I could have left you with no help at all."

Sadness turned to anger. If there were no witnesses on the avenue, Thea would have managed this situation a little differently. *Your time will come.* The thought only gave her a little gratification.

She gently took his hand to stop him as he left, "Perhaps you would join me for dinner tonight?"

If he agreed, she would slip a slow-acting poison into his food. As a result, he would suffer many Terrestrial Rotations.

"Thea, as of this moment, our houses are divided, so there is no point in us wasting time together anymore."

"I hoped there might be a chance."

"Chance? Since you obviously cannot understand what I am telling you, let me be as clear as possible. There is no chance at all for us to reunite. I have already sanctioned a decree for our disunion. You should receive your copy of the proclamation and your first week's allowance tomorrow, so I suggest you spend the Sovereign Cubes wisely. Once you have received the notice, you can be with whomever you choose."

"Is this really the end? We have been together for many yellow harvests, and I have given you three offspring, but you will not give me a second chance?"

"We left second chances several yellow harvests ago. It *is* over. I cannot be any clearer than that."

"What of our offspring? Our disunion will remove them as heirs."

"Only if I start another family with someone else," Zorion replied.

"Ah, that is the reason you are getting rid of me. You *have* found someone! Tell me her name! You owe me that!"

Jealously filled her voice. She would hunt down and destroy the *putok* when he spoke her name.

"There is no one else, Thea. You must understand! I do not love you anymore, and I guess you have never loved me, so at least do me the courtesy of allowing us to part cordially. You *do* owe me that much!"

"I will never let you go, Zorion. You are mine!" Thea screamed.

Her words frightened him. Now, he understood how she viewed their relationship. They were not partners. He was her subject.

He spoke defiantly to her, "You do not have a choice in the matter. I am not yours, and I never will be."

There was an air of challenge in his voice. Thea tried to reverse the situation but stood defeated, unable to change his mind.

"Goodbye, Thea. Try to have a good life," he turned, boarded his private vehicle, and headed home.

The farther away he got from her, the more relieved he felt; starting this new chapter in his life made him feel excited and nervous.

Chapter 83

Earth
Germany - Frankfurt
May 12, 2452

The walk from outside the city limits to downtown took a couple of hours; it was long and daunting. Jared checked into a hotel room right away but did not stop to refresh himself, which turned out to be a big mistake. Instead, Jared strolled Frankfurt's busy streets and approached everyone in his path, showing them the photograph General Green gave him, asking if they knew him. He had been roaming the streets for more than four hours and was tired, hungry, and in desperate need of a shower.

He approached a nearby restaurant and smelled food cooking. Obeying his stomach, he ate a large bowl of Bratkartoffeln and Apfelkuchen for dessert. Having satisfied his stomach, he headed toward his room but stopped to window shop along the way. The reflection showed that someone was following him. *So far, the plan is working.* Careful not to lose them, he strolled back to his room, where he took the opportunity to check in with General Green.

"Home base, this is Jared; come in, over."

"Home base here. How's it going?" General Green asked.

"They've found me. I'll contact you upon my arrival."

"Roger that. We'll hear from you then. Home base out."

Since the Revolutionaries would arrive soon, he resolved to take a quick shower. There was no need to go on any longer in his current state. Four men carefully picked the lock to his room and opened the door. They could hear water running, so two stayed outside to guard the exit, and the other two positioned themselves against the wall beside the bathroom door. Jared came out; one of the men attacked him, and they struggled.

The first assailant fought with Jared; the other came from behind and struck him on the head, knocking him unconscious. Standing in the hallway, the two men came in and gathered all his belongings, and carried him away. An hour later, he woke on a dirty bed with the urge to vomit. He sat, felt dizzy, checked the back of his head with his right hand, and found a bump where the assailant had struck him.

At least he knew why his head hurt. Above his bed, through a small window, he saw sunlight. Using the bed as a step, he reached the windowsill and chinned himself to look outside. They had brought him to some remote area just as he thought, and his captures talked in the adjoining room. *No doubt they're going through my things.* He lowered himself to the floor and sat on the edge of the bed. *Bugs be damned.* As he tried to clear his head, the door swung open, and one of the men walked in.

"I see you're awake."

"Who are you, and where am I? I want to know why you've kidnapped me," Jared demanded.

The man shook his head, "Stop pretending you're innocent. You've been trying to find Diederich Schmidt."

"He's responsible for my brother's death."

The man laughed, "You think you can fool us? You think we are so stupid that we can't identify a Regime agent?"

Extending his arm, he showed Jared the small device used to confirm his identity, which the Regime buried deep within the data chip he carried with him to make it look authentic.

"I found it, but I must say, I don't know how your country became so powerful, making mistakes like this. I planned to kill you; now that I know you're an agent, you're worth much more to me alive. I might even get a promotion."

"I won't tell you anything."

"We will see," he left, locking the door behind him.

Been there; done that. A few minutes later, the men returned, put a cover over his face, and escorted him outside to a vehicle. They put him in the front seat and bound him to it with industrial duct tape. Once he was secure, they drove for several hours. During the entire trip, no one spoke. *Whoever makes the first sound is the loser in this game.* Jared listened carefully. The men did not talk to each other, but their body language spoke loudly. He could tell they were nervous.

For example, the man in the back kept shifting his position, and the driver chain-smoked. He could hear him taking one cigarette after another from a pack in his shirt and lighting the next one off the one he had just finished. *He's throwing them out the window, leaving me an easy trail to follow.* He also listened to the vehicle's song. It sounded like a Jeep's engine. At first, the engine pitch was high and steady. They were traveling over flat land, and the RPMs were constant.

The pitch changed as the Jeep entered the hilly country. The motor whined when the RPMs revved as it went up and down the hills. *More up than down.* There was the sound of the engine bouncing off canyon walls as they headed into the mountains. He pictured Frankfurt's map and surrounding areas in his mind's eye and knew their location. The Jeep skidded and stopped. The men got out, came around to his side, and opened his door.

He heard a knife sliding out of a sheath and felt the blade descend on the tape, holding him to the seat. They pulled him out of the vehicle and across some stony ground. He faked a stumble, forcing his captors to hold on to him more firmly, giving him an excuse to drag his feet to get a better feel for the kind of ground they were covering. It changed from stones to dirt, with many limbs and twigs.

Even with a thick black hood covering his eyes, he could tell they were in the Black Forest. The smell of the trees and the sound of wind rustling the leaves was a dead giveaway until there was no wind. He walked for several minutes and finally realized they had taken him into a cave. Moving deeper into the mountain, he counted his steps to estimate how far down they were taking him. The deeper they went into the mountain, the smoother the ground became.

They thrust him forward, and he heard a metal door slam behind him. Now that his hands were free, he removed the hood. He was in a cell as expected. There were no windows, only bars, so he returned to the door and looked out. His cell was one of several in an underground carved-out prison. *Ok, so far, so good.* Satisfied his mission was going as planned, he moved to the next phase and tried to contact the Regime.

Moving to the corner of his cell, he whispered, "Home base, come in, over."

There was no reply. *Not good. The mountain is blocking my transmission, or they are jamming me somehow.* As time passed, he started getting fidgety until hearing footsteps, so he braced himself for the inevitable, but they did not stop at his cell. Instead, they hauled a woman past his door and put her in the room beside him. As they went by, she stared at the ground, and some of her long black hair nearly touched the floor, making it impossible for him to see her face; they slammed the door and left without saying a word.

Jared whispered, "Are you all right?"

"Yes, thank you," the woman replied.

Great, on top of everything else on my list, now I must rescue someone. "Don't worry. I'll have us out of here soon enough," he offered.

Wu Luli smiled. *I know you will, with my help.* "What's your name?"

"Jared, what's yours?"

"I'm Chu Lian."

"Chu Lian, the Regime software analyst?"

"Yes, why?"

"If you're the same Chu Lian, I knew; you dated my brother, Michael."

For the first time in a year, she finally had the chance to find out how he was doing and ran to the door to get close to him, "How is he?"

"He's been better. After you left him, he withdrew from everyone. Mom said all he does is work. I saw him today for the first time in a year."

She struggled against the tears forming in her eyes, "All I can say is I've missed him terribly."

"How did you end up in Frankfurt?"

"The Chinese ambassador sent me here as a liaison for the Orient Hotel Management Company. It was my last assignment before my transfer to the Regime, but I left my room to eat; four men abducted me, and I ended up here."

"I've met some of them already. They must be the local welcoming committee. I'm curious; why do they want you?"

"The company has a policy that covers ransoms. Even though I work for the Chinese ambassador, the hotel listed me as a temporary employee in Germany. I hope the insurance company will pay them in a day or two, and they'll set me free."

"I see. How did you end up working for the Chinese ambassador?"

"I was first transferred to be a staffer for the Regime ambassador to China. He said my skills would be of significant use to him. That was why I had to leave the Regime in the first place."

"Since you're under contract, you had to go."

"Right. I want to be clear about this. I really, really didn't want to leave, but I had no choice. Anyway, a few months later, the Chinese ambassador took a liking to me, so as a favor, the Regime ambassador lent me to him to improve relations between them. After that, the opportunity arose, so I told the Chinese ambassador that I wanted to return to Fort McNair. He took pity on me and appealed to the Regime ambassador on my behalf. It would have been my last assignment under his supervision."

"I don't understand why you completely cut Michael out of your life. You could have still met with him."

"It's complicated, but I have nine years left on my contract. I couldn't let Michael live like that. To have a long-distance relationship for that long would be cruel to him."

"I think he would have preferred it over what you did."

"How will you get us out of here?" she asked, hoping to change the subject.

"Don't worry. An opportunity will present itself. It always does."

"That's your plan?"

"Don't worry about how. Just be ready to go when I tell you."

"Ok, whatever you say."

Returning to the corner of his cell, Jared whispered, "Home base, come in, over."

He tried for several minutes but received no response, so he gave up.

Chapter 84

Akil
Drard City
The 22,276th Terrestrial Rotation of the Second Summer

As Gecheana entered the training room, the talking among the forty-four acolytes that High Priest Elazar sent to fight in her militia died down. They moved aside to let her pass. She was displeased because some were older than she hoped, and there were not enough of them, but they would have to do for now.

At least High Priest Elazar only sent singles, so there would not be an investigation if one or more died. *The less attention paid to this endeavor, the better.* Gecheana motioned for an assistant to distribute a standard sword to each fighter. Domeka, Udara, and Tesol completed six Skean swords each, and Gecheana was anxious to see which soldiers deserved the honor of wielding them first. With a nod from Gecheana, swords clashed, and the sound of metal clanging filled her with excitement.

She had them practice for four thousand heartbeats and set up a tournament to single out the best fighters. Once it was over, two middle-aged believers made it to the top of the list. *They must be of good stock.* All six winners stood in a line before her, and she walked by each one to scrutinize them. They were not as tall or strong as soldiers, but they would fight better with her help. Gecheana motioned for Domeka to bring her the Skean swords, so she returned with a large box and set it down near her. Gecheana opened it, removed one of the swords, and faced the winners.

"What do you see in my hands?"

She held the weapon out in front of her.

One of the older acolytes answered, "A sword."

"This is not just any sword. Do you remember High Priest Elazar's teaching about Gau?"

"Yes," one of the acolytes replied. "He was the first Skean, who wielded a sword given to him by the Night Lord."

"Excellent. Every Skean who followed him created their sword in its likeness. The blade is razor-sharp, and it will never dull because I made it from the most rigid material on the planet. No furnace is hot enough to melt it, so only a Skean can create it. Each one of you will use one of them.”

“High Priest Elazar revealed your identity. We know you are a Skean and that you prefer to keep yourself hidden, so it is an honor and a privilege to meet you,” another believer remarked.

“It is true. We would not have revealed ourselves if it were not for the pending attack.”

“High Priest Elazar told us that you believe a Saiph is coming to Akil, so we will do whatever you tell us to help you kill him or her,” another follower commented.

“Thank you. I appreciate your loyalty. My goal is to increase our power and numbers through you, so we will be ready to fight.”

“How can we wield those swords when we do not have the Night Lord’s power?” another acolyte inquired.

“I will direct the Night Lord’s power to and through you. Our minds will link together and work as one. Now, I want the six winners to come forward.”

Gecheana handed them a sword and told them to face each other in the middle of the room. She took a deep breath to gather her power, and it filled the room with its physical presence, making the air cold enough for their breath to produce steam. The Night Lord’s energy weaved itself into their minds, and their thoughts joined as one, allowing Gecheana to send the dark power necessary to ignite the swords through them. Six blades, glowing red, appeared at once.

Now it was time for Gecheana to practice using her new militia. She gathered more energy and channeled it toward the fighters. With their minds already linked, the power passed between them. Their limbs moved at her command as if she were a great puppet master. She controlled each soldier through her mind’s eye as if he were an appendage. The six fought for a few hundred heartbeats until Gecheana tired, so she willed them to stop fighting, and the swords lost their crimson glow.

“How long?” she spoke to Domeka.

“534 heartbeats.”

Gecheana sighed. Although it was not long enough, she would increase the time with more practice, but now she needed rest.

“Our practice is over. Be here at the same time on the following Terrestrial Revolution,” Gecheana ordered.

Domeka collected the swords.

"We do not get to keep them?" puzzled one of the believers.

"Of course not. You will only have them if I need you to fight. If you keep the sword with you, someone may discover it. That would defeat the whole purpose."

The six bowed to her, returned their weapons, and left. Gecheana rested and felt Nayrah and Jadell approaching; they entered the training room moments later.

"You summoned us," Nayrah bowed slightly.

"Yes, Domeka told me about your betrayal."

"I do not understand."

"You interfered with Yanamai and Garbi's fight. Garbi would have killed Zorion and Yanamai, but you obstructed my plans because of your stubbornness. Had you allowed the scene to play out, Otsoa would be sovereign, and Tadra would have already searched within the correct sector. Now, Zorion is aware of Tadra's benefactor and has given Thixi the honor of replacing Yanamai in case of death. Your interference has made things even worse than before!" Gecheana yelled.

"I wanted to prove that I could do it myself," Nayrah replied.

"Stop lying to me! At our last meeting, you became territorial, saying that Argi was yours!"

"It is! Zorion and Yanamai are my responsibility!"

"Not anymore. I have learned that Zorion has cast you out of his home like some beggar. Also, he plans to separate your houses, so your failure is complete. Not only have you betrayed me, but you cannot control Zorion any longer, which you would not have to worry about had you allowed Garbi to kill him!"

"I can fix everything. Just give me a little more time."

"No. At this very moment, I am giving Argi to Jadell."

Jadell heard the news and her eyes widened with excitement.

"What? You cannot do that!" Nayrah exclaimed.

"I can and I will," Gecheana answered firmly.

"She is too young. She is not ready."

"I am willing to give her a chance."

"You cannot disgrace me like this! Argi is mine!"

"No, Argi is mine! I will give it to whomever I choose."

"I am ready," Jadell added.

"Silence, I did not permit you to speak," Nayrah snapped.

"She does not need your permission; you need hers," Gecheana glared at Nayrah as a warning.

Jadell stood quietly, trying to hide her smirk.

"My offspring will not rule me!" Nayrah exclaimed.

"You will obey her, or I will destroy you."

Although Nayrah was angry enough to kill Gecheana, doubt crept in again as she moved her hand toward her sword. *Every time I think of fighting her, the veil prevents me.* A few heartbeats later, she abruptly turned and left. Jadell started to follow, but Gecheana stopped her.

"Wait. Let her leave." The door slammed shut, and she continued, "Watch her closely. I do not trust her anymore. She has betrayed us. If you think she is working against us at any time, you must kill her."

"Am I strong enough?"

"Yes, but only if you choose your timing right. By putting a sleep potion in Nayrah's moss, you can wait until she becomes lethargic and slay her at will."

"Until then, what would you have her do?"

"Tell her to assist High Priest Elazar with his interviews for my militia. That should keep her occupied."

"As you wish," Jadell bowed and left.

Chapter 85

Earth
The United States - Texas – Houston - Western Farmland - Burke Home
May 12, 2452

Larkin was away on recon, so Sarah decided to take Dr. Grant's advice to fill a glass with water as a focal point for her nightmares. Sarah entered her bedroom, but Sable was in the bathroom, brushing her teeth, so Sarah searched the room for anything that might give her a clue about her nightmares. Before Sable was born, Larkin painted three walls with unicorns, flowers, butterflies, and bunnies with an ocean scene on the fourth wall displaying dolphins, fish, and whales jumping out of the water. Also, Sarah stenciled different colored flowers into her bed covers.

She thoroughly examined the room and did not find anything that would cause her daughter's nightmares. The bathroom door opened. Sable walked over to the side of the bed and kneeled to say her prayers. Sarah knelt beside her, carefully listening, hoping she would say something to shed some light on her dilemma. Sable finished and had not said anything on the subject, so Sarah pulled the covers down. Sable hopped into bed and pulled the covers up to her chin. To Sarah, she seemed nervous. She could not blame her. The dreams always woke her in terror. Sarah stroked Sable's hair away from her forehead.

"Mommy, will you stay here until I fall asleep?"

Sarah nodded, "Do you see the glass of water I placed on your nightstand?"

"Ya-huh."

"It's a magical glass of water."

Sable looked at her quizzically, "Magic?"

"Yep. Your daddy got it from one of the streams where the unicorns live."

"But daddy said unicorns aren't real!"

"I know, which is why it's magical. During daddy's patrol last night, he came upon a white unicorn, drinking from a stream."

Sable perked up, "Daddy saw a real, live unicorn?"

"Yes, and this unicorn could talk."

"What did he say, mommy?"

"He told daddy that one of the butterflies in your room let him know you were having nightmares. Also, he told daddy to fill his canteen with the water from the stream and that it would keep you from having them ever again."

Sable gasped, "Can I drink some?"

"Sure, but just a little. You must leave enough out on the nightstand to ward off the bad dream."

Sarah held the glass, and Sable sipped from it. Sarah put the glass back on the table and helped her settle back in the bed.

She took out a book from her drawer, "Mommy's going to read to you until you fall asleep."

"Oh, read the one about Cinderella, mommy!"

"I thought tonight I would read the Story of Unicorns. Would you like that?

Sable nodded excitedly.

"Ok," Sarah opened the book and began to read.

"Once upon a time, there was an extraordinary kind of horse."

Fifteen minutes later, Sable was asleep. Sarah closed the book, gently kissed Sable on her forehead, turned off the lamp, and sat on the small sofa near the window. It was something Larkin insisted on having for his daughter. Sarah did not mind and was happy to see his enthusiasm for preparing Sable's room. She pulled the covers up to her chin and faced her daughter. *Sweet dreams Sable.*

Chapter 86

Earth
The United States - Texas - Houston - Western Suburbs - Border of
Gang Territory
May 12, 2452

Larkin, Murphy, and Nelson arrived at the Southampton Psychiatric Center at dawn. They had walked through the forest, along Route 59, for several miles. Murphy and Nelson used their NVGs to keep up with Larkin during the night until reaching Greenbrier Street at about 6 AM, where they followed the road from a distance. To keep hidden, they walked through yards of old abandoned houses, climbed fences, cut through the homes, and stayed out of sight as much as possible.

By 7 AM, Larkin spotted the Psych Center. He signaled Murphy and Nelson, and they headed for the apartment complex across the street, where they searched the fifth floor to ensure no one was there. Larkin took the first floor, and Nelson and Murphy took the third floor, where he pushed open the door to apartment 3A. The door hinges creaked as it moved. *You can't sneak up on anyone with that kind of noise.* Inside, old, torn furniture and garbage lay scattered about everywhere.

Murphy stifled a gag because the stench was overwhelming. The only light came from broken windows. He pushed open the door to a bathroom near the kitchen. Hearing a noise coming from the bedroom on the opposite side of the apartment, he froze. As he walked to the bedroom door, his heart raced and took a position to its right. He turned the handle, cracked opened the door, and heard gunshots.

They stopped, so Murphy kicked the door open and turned into the doorway in a crouched position. Inside, someone pointed a gun in his direction, so he fired two shots, hitting the gunman's chest. Murphy searched the room for others, keeping an eye on the squatter, and walked to the shooter with his weapon trained on him. Blood soaked his shirt. He put his fingers on the man's neck, but there was no pulse, so he walked to the living room and peeked outside to see if the noise attracted unwanted attention. The streets were empty. Hearing footsteps, he spun around.

"I heard the shots. Are you all right?" Larkin asked.

Murphy lowered his weapon, "Yeah, I'm fine. He's in there." He pointed toward the bedroom. Nelson came running.

"Did anyone else hear the noise?" questioned Larkin.

"No, I didn't see anyone outside," Nelson answered.

Larkin checked the body, "He's dead."

"Yeah, I guess he thought I was another squatter, trying to steal his stuff."

"Or trying to move in," Nelson added.

"Let's finish clearing this place because we need to start watching the Center," Larkin remarked.

"Roger that."

The rest of the building was vacant, so Larkin's team sat in a room overlooking the Center's entrance.

"I'll take the first shift; you two get some rest," Larkin commented.

Murphy and Nelson found a spot and settled down for some sleep.

Chapter 87

Earth
The United States - Texas - Houston - Western Suburbs - Gang
Territory
May 12, 2452

When Sable's disembodied voice called out to him, Larkin pushed his body beyond its limits to get home. There was something wrong. *I'm on my way, Darlin.' Don't worry, daddy's comin'.* He tried to teleport himself forward, but the ability had abandoned him, and he did not know why. It felt like he was moving in slow motion until he found a car on the side of the road, jumped in, and started it.

He brought the vehicle to its top speed with his foot pressed firmly against the pedal. The urge to protect his family overwhelmed him. Precious minutes passed until he finally reached the farm. He jumped out of the car and ran to the front door. Sarah stepped outside with someone holding a knife to her throat. He did not recognize the man.

Anger grew within him, and he shouted, "You're a dead man!"

The man just laughed.

"Where's Sable?" Larkin asked Sarah.

Sarah started crying, "She's gone, Larkin. You're too late."

Anger boiled into a rage, "What did you do with my daughter?"

The ground shook beneath him as power flowed through his body. Passion made him strong. However, the man responded only with a smile.

Larkin started to approach him, but Sarah called out, "Stop, Larkin!"

Still, Larkin kept going.

She called out again, "Stop, Larkin!"

Her voice changed to that of a man's, "Come on, Larkin, stop!"

He woke, struggling against Murphy and Nelson.

"Come on, Larkin, stop. Someone will hear you!"

Having woken from his nightmare, Larkin stopped struggling, so Murphy and Nelson released him.

"What the hell was that?" Murphy inquired.

Larkin shook his head, "I don't know. I had a bad dream, and damn, it felt real!"

"You kept shouting for Sarah and Sable."

"They were in danger."

He paused to sense them but felt nothing.

"Do you want to radio in and talk to General Bailey?" Murphy queried.

"No, I don't want to jeopardize the mission more than I already have. By the way, did I attract any unwanted attention?"

"No, there's not much going on here. Tucker must be at one of the other locations," Murphy replied.

Larkin saw it was dark, "We better get movin.' We've got about five miles of populated territory to navigate through."

"Yeah, we've already heard the crack of gunfire a few times," Nelson noted.

"Looks like the natives are getting restless," Murphy added.

"They're always restless," Larkin smiled.

They gathered their things and left from the rear of the apartment building. Now that it was dark, Murphy and Nelson put on their NVGs to maneuver through the urban landscape. People walked the streets, so they avoided them, which hindered their progress.

"We're never gonna get there by morning," Nelson warned.

Larkin looked over the hedge and saw five men lounging around a vehicle near a fire that burned in an old, rusted barrel.

He faced Murphy and Nelson, smiling, "I've got an idea. You two stay here."

He walked to the end of the hedge and peaked around. The night kept him hidden from their view, but he could see everything. All the doors were open on the vehicle. One man sat in the driver's seat, another in the back on the passenger side. Two men lay on the hood, resting on the windshield. Five feet from the driver's side front fender, a man stood, warming his hands by the fire. The two in the vehicle were smoking something. Larkin sniffed the air. *Marijuana.* The two on the hood were sharing liquor from the same bottle, and the man standing near the fire held a beer bottle in his hand. He shook his head with disapproval.

I'll never understand why they drink and smoke in this environment. It makes them weak and vulnerable. He retrieved his

Bowie knife and approached the vehicle from the rear passenger side in a crouched position. Upon reaching the door, he could see the man in the driver's seat fast asleep. *Drugs will do that to you, buddy*. The man closest to him brought a cigarette to his lips, letting Larkin know he was awake.

Larkin was close enough to hear him inhale the smoke and hold his breath. The man set his arm down to his side, and Larkin instinctively moved toward him. It was as if something unseen controlled him, guiding his knife exactly where it needed to go. The blade's tip entered the front of the man's throat, moving through his trachea, vocal cords, and esophagus. It kept going until it severed his spine. The man's body quivered for a few moments until it went limp.

Carefully, Larkin pulled his body from the vehicle and set it down on the ground. *See what I mean? You're vulnerable*. Larkin climbed inside the car, making a special effort not to bounce. He slid behind the driver, put his left hand over his mouth, and plunged his Bowie through the back of the seat and into the man's heart. It happened so fast; the man died before waking up.

He discreetly slid out the passenger side of the vehicle, crept to the front fender, and stood to his full height. The two men had less than a second to notice him, and their eyes widened in fear, but there was no time to react. Larkin pinned the nearest man to the windshield by placing his left forearm over his throat. At the same time, he slashed his Bowie knife across the other man's neck.

Blood squirted from his wound, spraying the other man standing at the barrel. He saw his friend's dead body and reached for his gun. Larkin grabbed the man with brute force (the one he pinned by the throat against the windshield), lifted him in front of him, and used his body as a shield. The other man fired several times. The eyes of the man Larkin held grew wide with pain until he died from his injuries.

Using the man as protection, Larkin moved toward the shooter, who dropped the empty clip and started to reload. Larkin threw the dead man at him, knocking the killer to the ground. Before the other could get up, Larkin took the gun from his hand, tossed it aside, grabbed the man by the throat, and lifted him off the ground. The urge to kill overwhelmed him, and with little effort, he snapped his neck, like a twig, and threw him aside. The other landed on the hood, dead, and slid off. Once it was safe, Larkin signaled Murphy and Nelson.

"You were a little bit noisy, Sarge," Murphy quipped, trying to lighten the mood.

His voice was audible, just above a whisper.

Larkin smiled at him, "Maybe you can take down the vagrants next time."

"No, thanks." Murphy scanned the area for onlookers, "It's a good thing gunfire is normal."

Larkin gave Murphy a playful mean look.

"I was just sayin' is all," Murphy smirked.

"Will you two please stop arguing? The way you bicker, it's like you're married," Nelson joked.

They all laughed.

"All right, knock it off and help me hide these bodies," Larkin ordered.

They dragged them into the brush, covered them, got into the vehicle, and Larkin drove to the warehouse. He parked the car off-road, hoping no one would find it. They started to leave, but Murphy stopped them. Turning around, he went back, opened the hood, removed a couple of fuses, closed it, and put them in his pocket.

"Now, no one can steal it."

Larkin laughed, "I could have used you a few years back; I can't tell you how many cars I stole and had stolen from me."

They got within a hundred yards of the building and stopped. There were cars parked everywhere. They could hear music playing from inside.

"Sounds like someone is having a party," Nelson commented.

"Yep, Tucker likes to entertain," Larkin added.

"You should call him Hollywood instead of Tucker," Murphy joked.

"Yeah, maybe," Larkin spoke distractedly, looking through his binoculars. "Wait, I see him. He's standing at the door."

Murphy and Nelson brought their binoculars up to see.

"Where's he going?" Nelson asked.

"He's taking that lady with him around back," Murphy observed.

"That's no lady," Larkin did not comment further. "You two stay here and watch the front door. I'll go to the back. Signal me if you see him go in."

"He's here; shouldn't we call HQ?" questioned Murphy.

"We have to make sure he's in the building. I know Tucker, and sometimes he goes through the rear entrance for privacy, and with her on his arm, I think he might want it right about now. Once he's in the building, I know he'll be there for a while," Larkin ran off into the woods.

Larkin kept disappearing, making it difficult for Nelson to track him; a few minutes later, he spotted him, "Man, that guy can move fast."

"I know. I'm glad he's on our side," Murphy remarked.

"Yeah, but there's one just like him who isn't. Speaking of which, has Tucker come back around yet?"

"No, I haven't seen him."

Nelson saw Larkin signal that he lost sight of him, too.

"Oh, crap. Keep your eyes open. Larkin doesn't see 'em anymore."

"He hasn't shown up in front yet."

Larkin sat in the brush, gazing through his binoculars, looking for his brother, but felt the hairs on his neck stand up. *Tucker? How did he get the drop on me?* Spinning around, he saw Tucker and a taser hit him. Larkin shook as if having an epileptic seizure because fifty-thousand volts of electricity pulsed through his body. Tucker had no mercy. He kept it on until Larkin blacked out.

"Oh, crap!" Murphy yelled in a whisper.

"What's wrong?" Nelson inquired.

"Tucker's got Larkin. A couple of goons are carrying him into the warehouse's front door."

"The mission's over."

"Agreed."

Chapter 88

Akil
Argi City
The 22,276th Terrestrial Rotation of the Second Summer

Now that Zorion declared Olan a traitor, Dolas assumed the Chief Administrator of Argi's Intelligence Department position. Sadly, the promotion did not come the way he had hoped. As Olan's second in command, he noticed that fate had little to do with anything. Premeditation and planning were their gods, and this Terrestrial Revolution was no different. Dolas sat in his mentor's chair and reviewed several Terrestrial Rotations of the prison's logs and schedules, searching for someone to impersonate.

The ledger said that a guard on Olan's level would not report for duty for a quarter of a work cycle. *That is cutting it close, but what choice do I have?* Dolas walked over to Olan's cabinet of concoctions. They used to joke about it. Within it, Olan kept vials of illegal drugs, selected two, and slipped them into his pocket. One was a deadly poison. Once administered, it was irreversible. Not even their regenerative powers could combat it.

Distilled from a fungus, it was the only thing besides decapitation that could kill them. Only three or four Akilians on the planet even knew of its existence. The other vial had knockout drops. The liquid short-circuited their regenerative powers for a few thousand heartbeats; it was like having a mini seizure. The victim would wake up exhausted from the ordeal.

He loaded one dart with the sleeping serum and changed his likeness into his favorite old Akilian alter ego. *No one pays any attention to the elderly. They are harmless. Crowds leave them alone and let them go about their business.* Using a secret side entrance, he left his new office and merged into the flow of Argians on the avenue. He made his way toward the guard's residence, slipped the dart with the sleeping potion into his right hand, and knocked.

The guard opened the door, dressed for work, "Can I help you?"

"My name is Muss, and I live directly above you. I am having trouble with my waste evacuation system and wondered if you did too?" Dolas inquired, with some trill in his voice.

"No. Everything is fine down here. Would you like me to call a maintenance inspector for you?"

"Would you be so kind?"

"No problem."

The guard turned around, and Dolas hit him in the neck with the dart. The sentry dropped to the floor and shook as the drug coursed through his veins.

"Sorry about this," Dolas paused and continued, "But I need your face."

In a matter of a few heartbeats, Dolas transformed into his likeness, stripped him, changed into his uniform, and made his way to the prison. He approached the entrance and saw several visitors at the security station. The engineers built the threshold to be intimidating and secure.

There were two gates. The outer gate was twenty paces wide and equally high. The inner gate was another forty paces inward; it led to a narrow corridor wide enough for only one Akilian to pass through at a time. The rock between the two gates domed downward like a half funnel to the entrance. It was the only way in or out, plus there were four guards and one Screener on duty. *It is all in the planning.*

During his time in Intelligence, Dolas became familiar with the guards' routines, knowing it would come in handy if he ever needed to break out. Ironically, he used that information to break in. Two guards stood on either side of the outer gate. They did not move from their position. The other two sentries stood near the inner gate, at the entrance near the security station. It was their job to search everyone entering the prison before allowing them to see the Screener.

Dolas walked past the outer gates. The acoustics of the foyer made it so that he could hear his footsteps echoing around him. Engineers designed it to make it easy for the guards at the outer gate to hear what was going on behind them. Several paces from the inner gate guards, he politely smiled.

"Greetings, friend."

The guard nodded and waved him on as expected, but during earlier visits, he noticed that the guards allowed other sentries inside without checking for weapons or identity whenever there were visitors.

"You are early," the guard noticed.

"Desk work," Dolas replied.

The other guard laughed. Once through the entrance, Dolas walked down the narrow corridor to the main lobby of the prison, where he had to choose from ten doorways, each having a symbol categorizing the criminals housed behind them. Each led to a hallway spiraling downward thousands of paces into Akil's crust. Since Dolas put Olan in prison, he knew precisely where to find his cell, deep within Akil's bowels, isolated from the other prisoners.

Although having met some Argians along the way, he was not worried. In his disguise, he was just another guard making his rounds. It took him a little over a thousand heartbeats to reach Olan's cell, deep in solitary confinement. He filled the second dart with the poison and loaded it into a small, air-compressed firing mechanism. It could accurately hit a target up to eight paces, but it would be more than enough in the small confines of the solitary cells. Standing in front of Olan's cell, he opened the viewing port; the window was two arm lengths wide and allowed him to see the cell's interior. Olan was lying on a small bunk on the left side of the cell.

"Get up," Dolas whispered, pointing his weapon at him.

Hearing the stranger's command, Olan stirred, opened his eyes, and scrambled to stand. Inwardly, Dolas ached to see the bruises from the earlier interrogation. *I hated to be the one to interrogate you, but it is my job.* Olan was silent, studying his would-be executioner.

"I have been waiting for you. What took you so long, Dolas?"

"How did you know it was me?"

"I am the one who trained you. Remember?"

"Then you know why I am here."

"I assume you loaded the dart with something from my cabinet."

"Correct," Dolas replied with a grimace.

The thought of killing his mentor did not make him happy.

"Why are you waiting? Shoot!" Olan exclaimed.

"Before I do, I wanted to speak to you one more time," he paused and continued, "For your sake, I hope you tell me the truth."

"My story has not changed. I did not betray him. Someone coerced me."

"Tell me who has the power to force someone like you to betray his sovereign."

Olan frowned, "I have been seeing someone."

"You were having an affair?"

"To my knowledge, she is single."

"Why did you not join houses with her?"

"She has not made the offer."

"This did not make you suspicious?"

"At first, but for reasons unknown to me, those suspicions disappeared, overshadowed by my intense feelings for her."

"This female somehow suppressed your intuition and forced you to attack Zorion?"

"I know how it sounds, yet it is the only thing that makes sense because I have been working frantically, trying to put the pieces together."

"And this is your answer? A female forced you to kill Zorion?"

"I reviewed everything that happened and remembered feeling jealous of Zorion as if somehow he would steal her from me."

Dolas gave Olan a skeptical look.

"I clearly remember her handing me the dagger I used to stab him," Olan explained.

"I came here for the truth, but you only babble about some fable you want me to believe."

"Listen to me!" Olan growled, pointing his finger upward, "If she has the power to compel me to attack Zorion, there can be no doubt she is out there committing other heinous acts! For all we know, she could be plotting to take over the city or, worse, hand it over to someone like Elzer!"

Dolas felt dread creep into his thoughts. Not just because of what Olan told him, but because of the fear he saw in Olan's eyes. *He believes that what he is saying is true.* If this female exists, it is his duty, as the new Chief Administrator of Argi's Intelligence

Department, to find and stop her. The only problem is that Olan is the only one who knows her identity.

"If she does have mystical powers, how do you intend to stop her?"

"I am not sure, but I know we can figure out a plan." Olan saw Dolas waiver and continued, "Look, we have known each other for many yellow harvests. You must agree that none of this makes any sense."

Dolas raised his weapon and pointed the dart at Olan, who raised his arms, holding them out from his body, giving Dolas an easy target.

"It is all based on trust. If you believe me, let me go. If you do not, release the dart."

Olan closed his eyes, waiting for Dolas's decision. Dolas struggled within himself. *Do I believe him?*

For Olan, time slowed to a standstill. He held his breath, waiting for the inevitable. Olan knew the poison within the dart was a fungus. It was the one he would have chosen. Having used it before and seeing it work on other Akilians, Olan cringed, imagining the last few agonizing moments of his life. He heard the metallic click of a lock, opened his eyes, and saw Dolas transform back into himself, standing in the open doorway.

"Thank you, my friend. You will not regret it," Olan remarked.

"For your sake, I hope you are right."

Chapter 89

Earth
The United States - Texas - Houston - Southwestern Suburbs - Gang
Territory
May 13, 2452

Larkin heard murmuring, sat, and found himself on sandy ground, which clung to his arms. He brushed it off and noticed something tacky underneath. Whatever it was, his body already absorbed it. He moved to stand, heard chains rattling, and found thick, metal bands connected to chains on his wrists, running from it to the wall behind him. There were also more bound to his ankles. A quick scan of the area revealed that he was in the Pit, a fighting arena he built years ago as the gang leader.

"Ah, I see you're finally awake," Tucker approached him.

"Do you think these chains are goin' to hold me?"

Tucker smiled, "Try to get out of them."

Larkin focused on teleporting, hoping to dematerialize from the restraints; it did not work, "What did you do to me?"

"Don't worry. It's not permanent. About a year ago, I rubbed some aloe on a wound to accelerate the healing process. I discovered that I had lost my ability to teleport. I thought it was permanent until it left my system, and my ability returned."

"That's what's on my skin, aloe?"

"Yep. I'm not sure how it blocks our powers; it just does."

"What about the attack on my platoon yesterday?"

"It was a ruse to get you to look for me. I say it worked," Tucker smiled wryly.

"Why? I've never bothered you."

"You did kill El Diablo, and his brother Marco wants an opportunity for revenge."

"I didn't kill him."

"You got credit for it anyway."

"I thought they weren't part of your group."

"Marco made me an offer I couldn't pass up. He wants to fight you. In exchange, they join our merry band."

"I can't believe you would betray me like this!"

"You betrayed me when you left! Did you know I didn't find out until a month after you deserted that you were still alive? Do you know how many people I killed interrogating them for information as to your whereabouts?"

"I tried to get a message to you. I wanted you to come with me, but I had to stay when I agreed to join General Bailey's army."

"Thanks for nothing, brother."

A woman came up behind Tucker with a tray of food.

"Set it on the ground," Tucker pointed to an area in front of Larkin.

"You better eat up, brother. You fight Marco in half an hour." Tucker started to leave but stopped, "Oh, by the way, it's to the death, in case you've forgotten."

Chapter 90

Earth
The Regime - Washington, D.C. - Capitol Building
May 13, 2452

Supreme Commander Porter stood in his office, examining his four new androids. He bought them from *Integrated Robotics*, a company with thirty years of experience building and supporting guardians. The Regime had bought the malfunctioning androids from *Latest Innovations*, a company in existence for more than a hundred years, and had a four-year government contract that would expire soon.

They won the deal by underbidding *Integrated Robotics* by several million Regime Talons. They could easily absorb the lost money on the bid because they were a large corporation. He guessed that *Latest Innovations* hoped to put *Integrated Robotics* out of business. Jay disapproved of the tactic personally but could not object since the mandate allowed competition, especially since it regularly saved the Regime millions of Talons.

He fidgeted with the remote control and wondered how the former androids malfunctioned, especially with multiple safeguards. *Was it even a malfunction?* He was always wary of assassination attempts from those outside the Regime, but it seemed almost unimaginable that someone on the inside would want to do him harm. Therefore, the same day the sentries tried to kill him, he ordered the RBI to investigate both companies to find the culprit.

In case it was an assassination attempt, he had Stan order a dozen new sentries under a phony company to hide his identity. His technicians removed the wireless transceivers that came with the androids and replaced them with a closed-circuit receiver, set to recognize only one obscure frequency emitted by his remote control. The clicker gave only one command: shut down at once. The technicians also connected the receiver directly to the power supply so that no software command could override it.

He pointed the zapper at the sentries for several minutes, turning them on and off. During his test, he gave them commands. As they executed them, he pressed the button on the remote, turning them off. They froze in mid-task, but the attack still left him feeling uneasy.

"Are you satisfied, Sir?" Stan Hill queried, patiently waiting in his office.

Completely engrossed by the androids, Supreme Commander Porter did not respond.

Stan cleared his throat and spoke louder, "Supreme Commander!"

"What?" Porter questioned distractedly.

"I asked if you were satisfied with the new sentries."

"They haven't tried to kill me yet, so it's a good start," Porter quipped.

"Excellent, Sir. If there's nothing else."

Stan tried to leave before he changed his mind.

"Yes. That'll be all, Stan. Thank you."

Moments after Stan left, Brandy Miller, Mrs. Bradshaw's temporary replacement, opened the door.

"RBI Special Agent Reed is waiting to see you."

"Send him in," Porter returned his attention to the androids. "Sentries, take your positions."

They walked to their assigned posts and stood at attention. He stared at their motionless, metal bodies, knowing that even though they looked like statues, their sensors and artificial brains were active underneath their façade. As Special Agent Reed entered the room, Porter took a seat behind his desk. Reed wore a dark suit, white shirt, and black tie. Per regulation, he kept his hair cropped, close to his scalp. Porter could tell he had a lot on his mind by his facial expression and movements. Porter nodded; Reed sat across from him and opened a black briefcase.

"What do you have." Porter began to say, but Reed interrupted him.

"Supreme Commander, I would like to formally protest that you've forced me to report all my findings. With all due respect, Sir. It's not your place."

You've got some nerve; I'll give you that. Good, you will need it. "I understand your objection, but someone tried to kill me, and I plan to be close to this investigation, so as I was about to ask, what do you have to tell me?" Porter queried.

Reed sighed, "My preliminary findings indicate a money transaction connecting *Sanya Electronix* and the Comptroller."

Reed handed Porter a folder marked classified.

"*Sanya Electronix*? That name sounds familiar," Porter browsed the file.

"It should because they're a subsidiary of *Latest Innovations,* which supplied the defective sentries."

"Ah, yes. I remember Jake telling me about the acquisition a couple of years ago."

"Jake?"

"Jake is the *Latest Innovations'* CEO; he's a good friend of mine."

Reed stared intently at the Supreme Commander for a moment.

"I can see the concern on your face, Reed. You needn't worry. I will not interfere with your investigation; I only want you to keep me informed of your progress," Porter insisted.

"The fact that he's a friend of yours means there's a conflict of interest."

"It would be if I were telling you how to run your investigation," Porter paused and frowned. "There are several people on the council who review my actions daily. If I do something outside the Regime's mandate, they will be sure to let me know. I understand your hesitation, but I expect you to cooperate with me, or you'll be seeking employment elsewhere. Before you make any hasty decisions, remember that I do have that power, Reed."

Reed swallowed hard, "I'm sorry, Supreme Commander. I didn't mean to offend you."

"You didn't. I'm glad you're questioning my involvement. It means you're a good investigator, but I can assure you that I won't interfere. You have my word."

Reed nodded.

"Good. Now let's proceed."

"You'll notice in the file that someone transferred half a million Regime Talons to an offshore account in the comptroller's name. We've already seized that money."

"What do half a million Regime Talons buy these days?"

"The government contract is up for bid again this year, and I believe that *Latest Innovations* was trying to secure it with a bribe."

"If that's true."

"It's possible that your friend is behind the assassination of the Comptroller and possibly the attempt on you."

Porter felt a knot in his stomach. He didn't want to believe his friend was capable of such treachery. *Does anyone truly know a person?*

"I expect solid evidence, Reed. If Jake is involved, I want to be damn sure of it before dragging his name through the mud."

"Of course. My first step is to speak with the head of *Sanya Electronix* to find out who ordered the payment."

"Sounds like a good place to start."

Reed started to stand and paused.

"Did you forget something?" Porter inquired.

"A warrant from your office would expedite my effort to uncover the truth."

Porter raised an eyebrow, "Normally, I would disapprove of it, but considering the circumstances, I agree. Although the warrant has no limitation, I expect you to use restraint. If I learn that you destroyed someone's reputation or business using it, you'll be wearing a pair of gravity boots."

"I have no intention of doing something that will put me on the moon."

"Very well," Porter typed on his computer and hit the send button loudly with his index finger, "There, you have it."

Reed typed into his tablet and nodded when the warrant appeared.

"Remember, I want you to keep a low profile. I don't want the news media getting wind of this before we know what's going on."

Reed stood, preparing to leave, but Porter stopped him and handed him a small card.

"That's my private line. I want to know as soon as you find out anything important. That's day or night, Reed."

Reed nodded, took the card, and left to conduct his investigation. Porter walked to the window and sighed, looking out over the inner circle. From his office, Jay could almost see the edge of the city. He knew that corruption is part of any human endeavor and wanted to believe that the Inner Circle was impervious to it. Jay conceded to the notion that even a good friend could be dishonest, but it was a hard pill to swallow. As he contemplated Jake's fate, Ms. Miller knocked before entering his office.

"Danny is here to see you," she waited for his response.

Porter paused briefly, "Send him in."

Danny walked in to find Porter standing at the window. Danny could see a solemn look on his face as he stared out the window. He held his arms folded behind his back and stood straight, with his feet spaced shoulder-width apart. Danny took a few steps, stopped, and waited. He could see the sun as it began to set over the Regime horizon from his current position. The Supreme Commander's shadow extended more than halfway across the office floor. Danny hated sunsets because it was a daily reminder of the end. *Is that what the Supreme Commander is contemplating? If so, the end of what?*

"Have a seat, Danny," Porter gestured.

"Thank you, Sir."

Sheepishly, Danny made his way to a chair. Porter finally tore himself away from the view, sat behind his desk, and with some effort, smiled.

"How are you progressing with the disc?"

"Slowly, Sir."

More bad news. I need to know what's on that disc! "What's the problem?"

"We just figured out how to unlock it."

Porter looked at him quizzically, "Explain."

"Whoever put the information on the disc did not use standard formatting, so my team and I had to create an application to access it."

"Interesting, it seems he or she was cautious."

"Yes, Sir."

"Now that you have access, it should be downhill from here. Right?"

"No. The formatting was just the first step because he or she encrypted everything on the disc. Currently, my team is working on software to break the code."

"Now that you finally have access to the data, you can't read any of it?" Porter asked, fighting to hide his frustration.

"Not without the key."

"Do you have an estimate of how long it will take?"

"At this point, no. We should have the software ready tonight, so I'll start deciphering it."

"Do you have *any* good news for me?"

"Actually, yes. We made a few copies just in case it self-destructs when we attempt to unlock it."

"I just reached a new level of respect for your job, Danny. I never realized how difficult it could be."

"Thank you for understanding, Sir; I didn't think you would take the news this well."

Porter smiled politely, "Nonsense, I know you're doing everything to get me the information." He paused to lean forward in his seat, "But the sooner, the better."

Danny nervously replied, "I'll get back to work right away."

"Let me know the moment you have something."

"Yes, Sir."

Danny walked away. Porter sat back in his chair, rubbing his chin. *What are you up to, Santiago?* As he contemplated, the red light flashed on his communicator. He reached over and tapped the screen. Assistant of Defense Neil Long's image appeared.

"Yes, Neil."

"Sir, I'm sorry to report that we've lost communication with Jared."

Damn it! When it rains, it pours. "What's the next course of action?"

"General Green tried to open a small portal at the cave opening to send in a rescue team, but it failed."

"They have a vortex disrupter?" he frowned.

"It makes sense. Diederich was a Portal Technician."

"Do we know how far the barrier extends?"

"Our satellites have confirmed a one-mile circular perimeter around the cave."

"A mile? Doesn't that take a great deal of power to maintain?"

"Yes, it does. General Green believes this is their main base."

"Can we send in troops?"

"Negative. Jared is deep inside the mountain. He would most likely be dead by the time we reach him."

"Even with his protective armor?"

"His armor can protect him from many things, but there are weaknesses. Also, he's been in their custody for some time now. The chemical that gives him the armor lasts for a half-hour, and he only has enough of the chemical for three uses."

Porter rubbed his forehead, feeling a headache coming on, "What are our options?"

"Currently, we have none."

"Someone better figure out something, Neil! I refuse to lose one of my best agents to these Revolutionaries!"

Porter forcefully shut his communicator off. *Let's see if that lights a fire under his ass.*

Chapter 91

Tormented by the same nightmare for the last two weeks, Kraeth tossed and turned in his bed. Guards chased him down a hallway in the dream, so he opened a portal and ran to it. Behind him, a weapon discharged just as he crossed the event horizon. He felt extreme heat engulf his body, and after exiting the vortex, he realized his destination had changed.

Also, the portal was several body lengths above the ground. Kraeth landed off-balance and broke his right arm. With his skin burning and his arm throbbing, pain overloaded his brain. He saw a blinding white light, and everything went black; he sat up in bed. Fear made him sweat, making his clothes stick to his skin. Adrenaline made him take fast deep breaths; he searched the area and remembered it was not a dream.

He climbed out of bed, changed his clothes, and sat in a small chair his gracious and eerily familiar host provided. Julie was the one who called him by name and re-awakened him after the large animal tossed him in the air. *It is impossible. How could she be the same humanoid?* He tenderly rubbed his left shoulder. Except for the deeper burns, all his wounds recovered several Terrestrial Rotations ago. He touched his shoulder and remembered waking up to an assistant leaning over his body and tending to his injuries.

At first, his surroundings made him think he was in a Recovery Station, but he could not sense life in the assistant, which frightened him because it acted sentient, yet it was not. Later, he learned that it was an android, a machine that only looked Akilian. Never in his life did he imagine anything like it. He felt defenseless in its presence because he could neither sense it by scent nor by his powers, which made it only three-dimensional, like a lifeless table or chair.

Yet, there it was, bending over him, spreading ointments and bandages onto his wounds. As it moved, it made rhythmic noises, making him think it was trying to communicate with him. Although he spoke to it, this thing Julie called Ratchet did not respond. Finally, realizing it did not understand his language, he pointed to various objects, giving Ratchet the Akilian name for them.

To his amazement, Ratchet repeated the Akilian word correctly and followed it up with a strange, almost guttural sound. It only took him a moment to realize that Ratchet gave him the equivalent word in his language. Trying to learn the words, he repeated what the android said. Ratchet treated his wounds, left, and returned with a small, flat screen-like object. It lit up, and Ratchet's mechanical finger pulled up a picture of an object.

From somewhere within the screen, another mechanical voice named the object. He repeated Ratchet's movements and touched the symbols on the screen; each showed a different picture. He pressed another, and it spoke different words. *It is teaching me how to speak their language.* Realizing what Ratchet gave him, he grabbed at the screen like a starving Akilian would grab handfuls of moss. He eagerly hovered over it, touching the symbols and getting his mouth around the strange-sounding words.

On the following Terrestrial Revolution, he studied and practiced, and as he grew to understand the new language, the application continued to add more words to his vocabulary, challenging him. Also, a voice recognition application taught him to pronounce each word and sentence correctly. Within two weeks, he had learned a lot. *Two weeks.* The way Earthians measured time baffled him until he deduced that they based it on their planet's rotation.

They broke everything down: seconds, minutes, hours, days, weeks, months, and years. It amazed him. *I have been here for two weeks. Everyone on Akil must think I have failed the mission. I wonder if they have sent someone else.* Outside, chirping caught his attention. From farther away, he heard the rhythmic errr, errr, errk-a-roo of another animal. Having listened to it every morning, he knew it meant it was sunrise. Moving to the window, he looked out.

On the horizon, the darkness of the night was fading, and the sky morphed from black to blue. Before leaving his home planet, the only time he saw an Akilian sky was the projection on the Argian ceiling, but it was different, seeing it with his own eyes. As the sun crept above the horizon, the light made him squint. Never had he felt as weak as in the presence of the yellow Earthian sun. He wished to appreciate the non-lethal star, except the light and those who embraced it were natural enemies of the Night Lord and, therefore, his adversaries.

As the sun moved higher in the sky, it grew brighter, so he closed the window blinds. He retreated into the darkness of his room, returned to his chair, picked up the electronic device, and continued his studies. A little later, the door opened, and Ratchet entered with a food tray. Kraeth's mouth began to water. With all his moss confiscated, he could only eat the local cuisine. This new experience gave his taste buds sensory overload. At times, it made it hard to concentrate on the mission. There were many new things, smells, tastes, and sensations in which had to fight against their distraction.

"Good morning," Julie entered the room a couple of steps behind Ratchet.

"Good morning," Kraeth replied.

"Ratchet has your breakfast, but I want to look at your shoulder before eating."

"Of course," Kraeth removed his robe.

Seeing his injury, she could not hide her amazement, "I've never seen anyone recover so fast from such serious wounds, and you don't have any scars."

"How long does something like this usually take to heal?"

"Weeks, sometimes months. How does your arm feel?"

"Fine."

"A broken arm usually takes six weeks to recover; yours mended in a day. I'm impressed; you're definitely one for the record books."

"How good for me."

"Ratchet, what do you think?"

"He has recovered from his injuries, so the patient can return to normal activity," Ratchet advised.

"I should leave now. You have been more than gracious," Kraeth replied.

"You don't have to leave right away," Julie offered.

"Thank you. I would appreciate a few more days if you do not mind."

"Sure, you're welcome to stay, but I would like to know how you got here."

"Through a portal."

Julie chuckled, "No, silly, I know you came through a vortex; what I don't know is why it opened in my parents' barn."

"Oh, I see. Well, it seems that as I was walking through the event horizon, an energy surge hit the apparatus and changed my destination."

"Where were you headed?"

The question caught him off guard; he paused a moment, thinking of a good response. He fled from the guard without a destination because he had to escape from that prison, but he had an idea.

"I honestly cannot remember where I was going. Home; maybe?"

"Hmm, it sounds like you have amnesia. Do you remember where home is?"

Kraeth shook his head.

"How about your last name?"

Again, Kraeth shook his head.

Julie sighed, "At least your external wounds have healed, but until you can remember your last name, I can't look you up on the global database, so I guess you can stay here until your memory comes back."

She started to leave.

"Thank you, Julie. You have been accommodating."

She smiled, "You're welcome. Would you like to walk around the farm before lunch?"

"Yes. I would."

Chapter 92

Earth
The United States - Texas - Houston - Southwestern Suburbs - Gang Territory
May 13, 2452

Before Larkin finished his meal, hundreds of spectators filled bleacher-style seats around the Pit. It was where they settled major disputes between gang members or anyone stupid enough to challenge Tucker for his position. Larkin's earlier fights as a young gang leader left the walls stained with blood, warning anyone thinking of taking Larkin's position from him.

He ate, tossed the tray aside, and tested one of his chains as his eyes followed it to the anchor. Tucker had fastened a one-inch steel plate to the wall and bolted the anchors to it. Evaluating its strength, he pulled on the chain with all his might but gave up and exhaled loudly. *I ain't gettin' out of this.* The shackles were about five feet in length. In the past, Larkin kept the lighting dim during fights because, for reasons unknown to him, he fought best in the darkness, so it was not a surprise Tucker turned the lights up to their brightest setting.

Across the Pit, he saw a man walk onto the sand, holding a Bowie knife. *That must be Marco.* Tucker walked out into the center of the Pit and raised his fists in the air. The crowd cheered with screams that rattled Larkin's eardrums. A few minutes later, Tucker motioned for the group to settle down, and since there were no microphones, Tucker had to yell.

"You all remember my brother!"

The crowd booed and hissed.

"The Judas has returned to face judgment. Recently, I created a new alliance with Marco, the leader of the El Diablos. He has pledged his loyalty to us for a small price; revenge!"

The crowd cheered loudly. Tucker waved Marco over to Larkin's position and stood between them.

"Aren't you going to unchain me?" Larkin asked.

Tucker smiled, "No. It has to be a fair fight, brother."

"Don't I get a weapon?"

Tucker's smile widened, "No, because, like I said, fair."

"It doesn't seem fair to me. What if I win?"

"Your fate will be up to Rico, his second in command."

Tucker faced Marco, "Here he is, as promised. Remember our agreement."

"I haven't forgotten. If something happens to me, Rico will honor our contract."

Tucker smiled and motioned with his right hand toward Larkin, "Have fun."

Marco held the blade high and walked toward Larkin, who retreated to about a foot from the wall. Marco threw a few fake swings to assess Larkin's reflexes. Larkin did not flinch, so Marco swung down hard. Larkin brought his arm up high, using the metal wrist bands and chain to block Marco's attack. He tried to grab Marco with his other hand, but Marco backed away out of his reach just in time. His eyes were wide with fear. The crowd laughed.

"They don't think you're going to win, Marco, and neither do I," Larkin threatened, with a gritty voice, trying to intimidate him.

Marco snarled and swung the Bowie knife wildly at Larkin; some got past his blocks, cutting his arms and hands. *If it were dark, I wouldn't have this problem.* Marco lunged, but Larkin grabbed the blade between his hands, stopping it. Marco could not pull it away from his unyielding grip until Larkin let it go. Larkin moved to the side, evading Marco's attack. Marco's momentum brought him close to Larkin, who grabbed him.

Marco could not break free from Larkin's grip. He wrapped one of the chains around Marco's neck and tightened it. The crowd went silent, watching the life drain from Marco's body until he went limp. Larkin tossed him out to the center of the Pit. Rico, who watched the fight from a seat near the ring, stood and clapped. He walked into the Pit, stepped over Marco's corpse, and stood before Larkin, who raised himself to his full height, towering over Rico.

"You want some of this?" Larkin yelled.

Rico laughed, "I'm not as stupid as my cousin, Marco. I have something else in mind for you. A punishment, you can't stop."

He took out a radio, spoke softly into it, smiled, and stood silent in front of Larkin.

"So, where are they? Where are your fighters?" Larkin demanded.

"I didn't call fighters. I called soldiers. They're out in the field, on their way to your farm as we speak."

Larkin knew his intention. *The dream I had earlier was a warning. Damn! I should have left for home right away!* Anger swelled within him, and he released an animal-like roar that shook the walls, pulling against his chains.

"You better call them back, or I swear, there'll be nothing left of you or your gang!"

Rico looked at his watch and shook his head, "It's too late. I gave them instructions to go radio silent after receiving their orders."

Chapter 93

Earth
The United States - Texas - Houston - Southwestern Suburbs - Gang Territory
May 13, 2452

Murphy and Nelson stayed hidden in the vicinity all day just in case Tucker looked for them. An immediate evacuation was too risky because Tucker had men searching every exit. They hoped Tucker and his men had given up or at least expanded their search, making their escape a little bit easier. It was getting dark, so they made their way to the vehicle. They approached the car and saw a young teenage boy under the hood. Murphy started to move, but Nelson stopped him.

"I'll get this. You're the medic. Remember?"

Murphy nodded, and Nelson removed a knife from his belt. He crept up behind the teen, but his timing was terrible because the teen had just finished his work and came out from underneath the hood. Seeing Nelson, the teen pulled a knife of his own, and they fought for a few minutes until the teen stuck him in the left bicep. Nelson grabbed his arm, and the teen fled. Murphy ran after him. The wound would not stop bleeding even though Nelson applied pressure to it. Meanwhile, Murphy caught up to the teen, tackled him, cut his throat with one smooth motion, and ran back to help Nelson.

"How bad is it?"

"It's bad; it won't stop bleeding."

Murphy looked at his injury, "He cut the brachial artery; I'm gonna have to put a tourniquet on it."

"Damn it," Nelson swore under his breath.

"We've got to get you back soon. You don't have much time."

Murphy put the tourniquet on him, and Nelson hopped in the passenger seat. Murphy turned the key, and the engine came to life.

"At least one thing has gone right for us."

He pressed the gas pedal and took off.

Chapter 94

Earth
The Regime - Maryland - Farming District - Stewart Farm
May 10, 2452 (<u>3 Days Ago</u>)

On her way home from eating lunch at the Union Station, Julie decided to confront Kraeth. She believed he was running from someone, which made her hesitate to call Immigration. Although Kraeth insisted a power surge struck the portal, she could not understand why it opened inside her barn. Technicians were there to ensure these things did not happen. Since Alex's profession was portal technology, she even considered the possibility that he was pranking her.

Kraeth's injuries should have ended it right away if it was a joke. *No, it isn't Alex. He wouldn't let it go this far.* Kraeth's fascination with the animals made her wonder because most city folks never get close to livestock, so their attraction is typical seeing them for the first time. Even so, Kraeth's wonderment went beyond ordinary appeal. He knew the animals' names: rooster, horse, goat, and the like, but did not know their nature. As they stood near Tank, their parents' prize bull, their conversation made her realize this about him.

*****

"That is a bull. Right?" Kraeth asked, pointing to Tank.
"Right," she replied.
"Is it dangerous?"
"Yes. Bulls are very territorial. You should never go into his field."
"Why?"
"Why? Haven't you seen bullfighting?"
"No."
"What planet have you been living on?"

*****

He often changed the subject if she became quizzical, but she would not let him get away with it this time. She exited her vehicle and

478

headed toward the house. Along the way, she heard hooves pummeling the ground. Tank bellowed, so she ran around to the back of the barn and saw Kraeth sprinting down the nearest hill with Tank right on his tail.

"Kraeth! What are you doing there? Get out now!" she yelled. He looked at her as if it were the first time until he returned his focus to running and headed toward the fence. It was clear that Kraeth was not the better sprinter.

"Run faster! Faster!" she yelled.

Tank hit him, catching Kraeth just behind his knees. Tank flipped Kraeth into the air using brute strength, throwing him clear over the fence. Before he landed, Julie raced to help him. Lying on his back, Kraeth did not breathe. The impact left him stunned. As he blankly stared at the sky, Julie gently smacked his cheeks, trying to revive him.

"Come on, Kraeth, breathe, damn it!"

Seconds before she called Ratchet, he gasped and started breathing again.

Julie was happy he was alive yet still yelled at him, "I told you Tank was territorial! He could have killed you! Also, you're wearing a red shirt! Are you out of your ever-loving mind?"

Again, Kraeth looked at her as if it were the first time.

"Are you all right?" Julie inquired.

Kraeth just stared at her quizzically.

"What's wrong with you? Why won't you talk to me?"

He stood and checked his arms, legs, and torso and looked for something.

"Why don't you come inside and lie down?"

Spotting his backpack, he jogged over, picked it up, and ran away.

"Where are you going?" Julie yelled, but Kraeth just ran faster.

He disappeared over the nearest hill and headed toward town. She shook her head in disbelief, walked to the edge of the fence, and looked at her parents' prize bull. Tank looked at the hill, where Kraeth ran and blew air out his snout.

"Damn it, Tank!" she yelled and headed toward the house.

Kraeth walked out the side door as she opened it.

"I heard you calling me. How can I help?"

Julie's mouth opened in shock, "I just watched you run over the hill. How in the hell did you get back inside the house so fast and with different clothes?"

"What was I wearing?"

"You had on a red shirt and…" she started to say, but he interrupted her.

"A red shirt? Was Tank chasing me?"

"Yeah, why?" puzzled Julie.

Kraeth realized what had happened. Although it was hard for him to believe, time travel was a reality. Elzer built a machine that could do it, which Gecheana planned to use until he destroyed it. It meant that the energy from the blaster sent him back in time twenty-eight Earth days.

"Are you going to say something?" she urged.

Revealing the truth to Julie would be a disaster, but he could not think of any explanation that would make sense. Putting her into a deep sleep seemed like the only solution.

"Please, come inside, and I will explain," he replied.

Out of the sun's light, his connection to his powers increased. Using them, he focused on her mind, "Sleep."

Julie's eyelids became heavy, so she closed them and started to fall. Kraeth caught her and carried her upstairs to her bed. Staring down at her, he saw the blue aura Gecheana spoke about during his training. He had considered killing her, but since she helped him recover and aided him in saving Akil, he decided against it. With the computer Ratchet gave him, he had all the information needed to complete his mission. Besides, killing her could complicate things between Akil and Earth if someone discovered his involvement.

Now that he could speak the Earthian language fluently, it would be easy to create a translation application on Akil. His lips turned upward as he imagined how the sovereigns and, most importantly, Gecheana would honor him for his work. What he learned would put her plans hundreds of Terrestrial Rotations ahead of schedule.

Chapter 95

Earth

The United States - Texas - Houston - Southwestern Suburbs - Gang Territory

May 13, 2452

Murphy turned onto Route 59, or what used to be Route 59. The road was full of potholes and broken asphalt. The car jerked and bounced as Murphy sped and dodged around them.

At one point, he faced Nelson, "How you feelin'?"

"Not good. My arm is numb, and I'm feeling light-headed."

"Just hang on. Here, take the radio and call HQ. Let them know we're on our way."

Nelson took the radio and sluggishly held it to his mouth, "HQ, come in, over."

A hail of gunfire erupted behind them. Nelson turned to look, and Murphy gazed in the rear-view mirror.

"This is HQ."

"HQ, this is Nelson, ID number alpha, two, six, nine, five."

"Go ahead, Nelson."

"We're on Route 59, headed for checkpoint twenty-one."

Someone threw a Molotov cocktail onto the vehicle, setting the roof and trunk on fire.

"Roger that, Nelson, I'll inform the checkpoint of your arrival."

"Tell 'em we're not alone. We're coming in hot, literally. We'll be driving the vehicle that's on fire. Tell 'em to get the 240 bravos' up and ready; some idiot is shooting at us with a .50 caliber machine gun mounted to the back of a pickup."

The road was so bumpy that the gunner in the pursuing pickup could not get a clean shot at their vehicle but kept firing, hoping to hit them by chance. They were close to the checkpoint, and Murphy kept swerving, making them a more challenging target. As they crested the last hill, one of the bullets went through the back window and hit Nelson from behind. It exited his chest, spraying blood and flesh throughout the front seat and dash of the vehicle.

Nelson slumped over. Murphy shook him, trying to get a response. After putting two fingers on his throat, he could not get a pulse. With no rear window, the gas from the Molotov cocktail dripped down onto the back of the seat. Now the car was burning from the inside too. The pickup was close behind him. More shots rang out. As Murphy came down the other side of the hill, his car gained speed. Reaching the bottom, he drove up the grade leading to the road that made up the border and went airborne.

The car landed and bounced on the other side. Murphy lost control, and it rolled end over end. The pursuing vehicle stopped on the roadway. The driver watched the flaming vehicle tumble with pleasure, but two gunners ended his joy because they shot their 240 bravos from the woods. The driver and the gunner were dead within seconds. Murphy's car stopped upside down.

At the checkpoint, Sergeant Jones ordered his men to extinguish the fire; they pushed the vehicle upright and pulled both soldiers from the car. The medic from Sergeant Jones' platoon examined them.

"This one's dead. Bullet shredded his heart."

He hurried to Murphy and examined him.

"He's still breathin', but it's shallow, and his pulse is weak. Get 'em on the stretcher. We've got to get 'em back to HQ now!"

Chapter 96

Earth
Germany - Frankfurt
May 13, 2452

Sitting against the cold wall, waiting to meet his captor, Jared heard footsteps, so he rushed to his feet, went to the bars, and saw two guards dragging Chu Lian by her shoulders to the adjacent cell. As they walked past, her head, which hung down, bounced with their movement, clearly indicating that they had beat her unconscious. Also, her arms and abdomen had cuts and bruises, which he saw through the holes in her shirt. Moving beyond his cell, they opened the door, threw her in, locked it, and stood in front of Jared's bars.

"Get down on your knees and put your hands on your head."

Reluctantly, Jared did what they asked. One of the guards walked in and bound his hands behind him. He yanked Jared up by his wrists, grabbed him by his left shoulder, and guided him down the tunnel. Jared released the chemical inside of his body, making his skin impenetrable. It was the first of three uses, but he had to live long enough to meet Diederich. Jared turned a corner and saw a room with an oversized metal chair, resembling one a dentist would use except much more intimidating. There were also four more guards waiting for him, and standing just to the side of the sentries, he saw Diederich.

"I hear you're looking for me."

"Are you Diederich Schmidt?"

"At your service."

Jared sized him up and estimated the man to be equal to his height and weight. Diederich had lived in the Regime, so he did not have an accent but wore army fatigues. *I wonder how much combat training he's had.*

"Yes, I am."

"I'm afraid you won't carry out your plans, whatever they were. My men tell me you work for the Regime and that the story you gave about avenging your brother's death for the bombing of the Transportation Station in Frankfurt is a ruse."

"Nope, that's my story, and I'm sticking to it."

Diederich laughed, "We will see."

He nodded to the men standing beside Jared and walked away. Jared's guards untied his hands and forced him into the intimidating chair. Jared knew this would be his only opportunity and fought back by breaking the man's grip on his right and elbowing him in the face, smashing his nose. The man instinctively moved his hands to his face, opening his midsection to Jared's vicious sidekick.

Gunfire rang out. Bullets ricocheted off Jared. They stung like hell, but Jared just gritted his teeth, absorbed the pain, and pulled the man on his left into the fire line. Bullets thudded into his hapless victim, and some passed through the man's body, covering Jared in gore. Jared ignored the blood, grabbed at the man's weapon, and returned fire, killing the four guards shooting at him.

Within seconds, the fight was over. Jared turned his attention to Diederich, cowering in the far corner of the room, using a metal pan as a shield against the ricocheting bullets.

Diederich warned him with a shaky voice, "You can't escape. I know my men heard the shots and have already blocked your exit."

Jared looked around the room. There was only one door, the big metal one he entered through.

He smiled, "I'll just bet this room is also soundproof. You wouldn't want your men to hear the screams of your victims. Prolonged agony can be demoralizing."

Diederich stood and faced Jared, "Why don't you join us? We could use someone like you to help stop the destructive force of technology."

"Is that all you've got? You just killed hundreds of innocent people."

"It was an accident. We set the bomb to go off during non-work hours."

"Yet, you claimed credit for it anyway."

"I take responsibility for my actions. That's more than you can say for the Regime."

"We don't kill innocent people."

"Of course, you do. The technology you create has killed tens of thousands of people. You don't hear about it because they hide their mistakes."

"You mean like what happened to your wife?" quizzed Jared.

"Yes. She was a victim. Technology killed her, but you don't have to die walking through an event horizon for tech to kill you. How many people have died in hospitals after a cyber-attack holds their information for ransom? How many vehicles have killed their owners once the application becomes degraded? How many androids have killed humans during a malfunction?"

"I don't know, Diederich."

"I do. Thousands, just this year."

"That's no excuse for what you've done."

"I'm fighting to free us from this electronic drug that has everyone hooked! You can't even eat dinner without everyone burying their faces in their phones! How is that helping us?"

Jared punched Diederich in the throat, breaking his trachea; the attack was sudden, which took Diederich by surprise. His eyes widened as he struggled to breathe.

"I didn't come to argue. I came to kill you," Jared replied.

Diederich collapsed to the floor. Jared watched until Diederich stopped struggling a couple of minutes later and checked for a pulse. There was none. Jared had completed his mission but could not leave Chu Lian behind. He borrowed some clothes from the guards, hoping that anyone who spotted him would mistake the blood for dirt and let him pass. Before leaving the torture room, he grabbed the keys off a dead guard and closed the metal door. There was not much time. In a few minutes, the Revolutionaries would look for Diederich. When they found him, they would demand blood, Jared's blood.

They kept the tunnel poorly lit, causing him to stumble from time to time over rocks and hidden crevices. Upon reaching Chu Lian's cell, he fumbled through the keys until one unlocked the door. Inside, he found her lying unconscious. *That's not a good sign.* He knelt, gently cradled her in his arms, and tried to contact the Regime.

"Home base, are you there? Come in, home base. Back to Oz! Back to OZ!"

Chapter 97

Earth
The United States - Texas - Houston - Southwestern Suburbs - Gang
Territory
May 13, 2452

Knowing his family was in danger put Larkin's mind on the brink of insane rage. All that mattered was freeing himself so he could race home. Although he tried, the chains would not give. It made him feel helpless. Larkin panicked, remembering the dream where he was too late to save his daughter. Again, he pulled on the chains repeatedly until his wrists bled, but it was no use. Frustrated, tears welled up in his eyes. Tucker saw them, laughed, and told the crowd, who joined in with his mocking. Larkin fell to his knees.

It was the first time Tucker beat him, and at the worst moment. Even if he offered himself in their place, Rico could not stop his men from carrying out their orders. His family was in jeopardy, and Larkin needed an answer. To search, he closed his eyes, hoping to find one. Tucker had lit up the auditorium, yet there were always dark places.

The fight caused Larkin to sweat, which meant the aloe started leaving his system. He could see the shadows within the arena in his mind's eye. The darkness gave him power, except he needed more of it. Larkin used what little strength was available to him and destroyed the lights above him. The auditorium went dark, and the crowd panicked. People pushed their way out of the bleachers, trampling each other, fleeing the stadium.

Tucker sensed the power moving through Larkin, stopped laughing, and ran to him, hoping to calm him before Larkin destroyed the arena. The lights continued to shatter, but Tucker's eyes adjusted to the darkness, enabling him to see Larkin stand, take a deep breath, and yell a beastly cry that shook the stadium.

Tucker stopped his approach because Larkin pulled on his restraints. This time, Larkin tugged his chains, and it shook the solid concrete wall behind him. He repeatedly yanked at them until the steel anchors broke free, pulling a section of wall with them. Tucker would never admit that Larkin was the stronger of the two, especially if something enraged him. Tucker ran the other way, stepping on and over people, fleeing the Pit.

Larkin was free of the wall, but the chains stayed on his wrists and ankles. That did not matter to him now. All he could think about was getting home as soon as possible, so he sprinted for the door and brutishly bulled his way through the crowd. Outside, his power blew out the lights, darkening the parking lot. He dragged the chains and large chunks of concrete from the wall behind him at his fastest pace and found a man sitting in his car in the parking lot, trying to leave.

Larkin opened the door as the car moved, reached inside to pull him from the seat, and leaped into the vehicle. A woman in the passenger's seat screamed. Larkin reached over, pushed her out without stopping, pulled the chains and concrete onto the passenger seat, and closed the door. Larkin slammed the accelerator to the floor. He looked at the dash and saw the car's speedometer was flush against its highest reading. He was moving fast, but everything around him seemed to be going slow. The thought of someone hurting his family made him anxious. *I've got to get home!*

Chapter 98

Earth
The Regime - Maryland - Farming District - Stewart Farm
May 13, 2452 (<u>Present Day</u>)

Kraeth ate his last Earthian dinner and gathered the information to take back to Akil. The computer held heaps of data, making his job easier. Its memory held an encyclopedia, which included Earthian history going back thousands of years, including the Regime's emergence from within the United States. Also, it carried a dictionary and a thesaurus. Upon returning to Akil, he would transfer all this information onto his own memory devices, and following protocol, he would give one copy to Zorion, one to Gecheana, and keep one. *You never know who else would pay for this kind of information.*

Kraeth summoned Ratchet, "How is Julie?"

"She is upstairs, sleeping. I tried to wake her, but she would not budge. I took her temperature; she does not have a fever. If she does not wake in thirty minutes, I plan to contact the hospital," Ratchet replied.

That is more than enough time. Kraeth stopped in the kitchen, retrieved a sharp, paring knife, and walked out the back door toward the barn with the blade in one hand and the computer in the other. Julie often took him for walks, and he noticed that the corridor between the horses' stalls was wide enough for a portal to open and was not visible to anyone from the house or the outside, making it the perfect place to leave.

Inside the barn, Kraeth carefully used the paring knife to remove the device needed to contact Yanamai or her replacement to return home. He grimaced, cutting an opening in his arm, large enough to remove the transmitter; he watched as the wound closed, and as it did, the pain diminished, so he took the transmitter out of its protective container, assembled the miniature antenna, and pointed the device toward the probe Yanamai set in synchronous orbit around the planet. Now all he needed to do was wait.

*****

Inside the house, Julie groggily woke from her sleep. Hearing servos, she sat up and regretted it because the room started spinning. Ratchet entered with a food tray, and her stomach growled. Without saying a word, she swiftly ate what he brought.

"It's good to see you awake again, Julie," Ratchet commented.

"How long was I out?"

"Three days."

"What? How?"

"I'm not sure. Kraeth told me you fainted and carried you to bed. I've been monitoring your vital signs. Besides a sound sleep, I could not find anything wrong with you. Since this was the third day, I told Kraeth I planned to contact the hospital."

"Where is he?" Julie asked in between bites.

"I believe he walked out to the barn."

Julie finished eating the last bit of her food, drank the water, and walked to the window, where she heard the horses neighing, which meant something was bothering them. Julie put on her running shoes, went downstairs, and crossed from the house to the stable to see what was wrong. She turned the corner and saw Kraeth standing in front of a vortex, holding the computer Ratchet gave him under his arm.

The portal was more extensive than those used by the Regime, making her curious. She took a closer look and saw people on the other side. Before she could say a word, Kraeth stepped through the event horizon. It made her angry that he not only left without saying goodbye but took her parents' laptop with him. He still had not explained why he ran away from her after Tank knocked him over the fence. There were many unanswered questions, including Kraeth stealing their equipment, so without thinking, Julie sprinted across the barn floor and jumped through the portal moments before it closed.